B L A C K   S E A

N
W
E
S

WITHDRAWN
UTSA LIBRARIES

Nicaea

ke of Iznik
(Nicaea)

Inegöl

Bilejik

Söghüt

Sakarya (Sangarius) River

Ankara

R   K   E   Y

Inönü

Porsuk River

Eskishehir
(Dorylaeum)

Tavshanli

Beylik
Bridge

Polatli

Kütahya

Alayunt

Seyit
Gazi

Sivrihisar

PLATEAU
OF
RENJIK

Gediz

Dumlupinar

Banaz

Afyon

Ushak

**AREA OF THE GREEK CAMPAIGN
IN TURKEY**

1919-1922

Phocaea

Gediz River

Manisa
(Magnesia)

Gulf of Smyrna

(Karshikyka)
Cordelio

Bornova

Nif

Smyrna
(Izmir)

Nymph
Dagh

Buja

Vourla
(Clazomenae)

0   5   10 MILES

0   10   20   30   40   50

SCALE OF MILES

Harry Scott

The Ashes of Smyrna

The Ashes of Smyrna

A NOVEL OF THE NEAR EAST BY

RICHARD REINHARDT

HARPER & ROW, PUBLISHERS

NEW YORK AND EVANSTON

For Joan—
at last, at last

The quotation that appears on page v is from *Faust*, by Wolfgang
von Goethe, translation by Charles E. Passage copyright © 1965 by
the Bobbs-Merrill Company, Inc.; reprinted by permission of the
publisher.

FIRST EDITION

LIBRARY OF CONGRESS CATALOG CARD NUMBER: 69-15284

A Citizen:

There's nothing better or Sunday or a holiday
Than talk about war and war's alarms,
When off in Turkey people up in arms
Are battling in a far-off fray.
You sip your glass, stand by the window side,
And down the river watch the painted vessels glide,
Then come home in the evening all at ease,
Blessing peace and the times of peace.

Another:

Yes, neighbor, that's the way I like it too:
Let them beat out each other's brains,
Turn everything up wrong-end to,
So long as here at home our good old way remains.

—Goethe's *Faust*, Part I

Poor Turks, poor Greeks, poor world.

—Halidé-Edib Adivar–1921

The author gratefully acknowledges the generous financial assistance of the Foreign Area Fellowships Program of the Ford Foundation, which made possible the historical research for this novel.

The Ashes of Smyrna

SMYRNA
MAY 14, 1919

*I*t was sundown when the two brothers took the lift from Karatina and started across the ridge. From time to time, Kenan stopped to rest, leaning on his cane and breathing heavily; and once he had to go behind a bathhouse, because the shrapnel in his side had weakened him.

Abdullah, glad of any delay, waited under a fig tree on the terrace. Throwing down a packet of handbills, he kneaded his shoulders with his hands, wiped the sweatband of his tarboosh and squatted to clean his slippers with a handful of grass. On the dome of the bathhouse, bubbles of glass were glowing like rubies under the red evening sky; and out in the gulf, around the English battleships, the water was streaked with wavering tendrils of bronze and silver. From the streets of the Moslem neighborhood below the hill, there rose a steady drumbeat, the skirling of a reed horn and a hoarse voice crying: "Let all men who love their country gather at the Hebrew Cemetery!"

This is a terrible mistake, Abdullah told himself: an invitation to the most reactionary elements. Left alone, he would have washed his hands and feet and thrown the handbills down a well. But his brother came limping back around the corner, beckoning him to follow.

"God knows, it won't be a congress of European intellectuals," Kenan said, as if he had been reading his brother's

1

thoughts. "But the meeting will show we are alive. Nobody nurses a baby that doesn't cry." And he led the way across a pasture splashed with poppies that were closing for the night.

A stream of sparks was rising to the west, where the sky still gleamed beyond the headlands. Climbing the last slope, Abdullah could smell the wood smoke and hear the voices of small boys who were dragging up branches to throw on the fires.

The cemetery was on a hillside, like a Moslem burying ground, with an unobstructed view from earth to Heaven; but it had been abandoned years ago. Most of the headstones had been hauled away as building blocks. Only a few flat slabs of granite remained, embedded as deep as meteorites in the dry clay, and patches of dark green nettles grew among the stones. Dervishes in monastic robes were resolutely marching to and fro among these obstacles, holding up long black banners and howling: "Ah, God! Ah, Merciful One!" Imams dressed in clean white turbans and long gowns the color of wine had arrived with holy relics wrapped in emerald satin; shepherds in felt cloaks blazoned with talismans against the Evil Eye had descended from the fields of Buja with armloads of prophetic yellow mutton bones. There were furious lycée students in uniforms of blue serge, indignant soldiers in tattered khaki and tearful old men, in skullcaps and baggy Macedonian breeches, who rested on the headstones, drooping their heads in weary piety. As Abdullah had expected, the handbills confounded all of them.

"Principles of Wilson? What's that?"

"Only listen to the speeches, Papa Haj," Kenan said, and they pushed through the murky twilight to the center of the field.

A stately lawyer in a fez and cutaway had clambered onto a gravestone to harangue the crowd. He discoursed on the

Fourteen Points, the Turkish claims and the ethnic composition of the Vilayet of Smyrna, and proved with unassailable logic that the Turks deserved to be treated by the Western nations with as much respect, as much compassion, as any of the other subject races of the Sultan. No one understood a word he was saying; but as he spoke, a deep muttering began among some Turks who had been driven from their farms in Macedonia by the Greeks. Each time the enemy was mentioned, these simple Moslems would pound their walking sticks on the ground, until finally the learned lawyer shrugged his shoulders and descended from his perch. And then the Mufti, Rahmetullah Efendi, appearing at the door flap of a goat-hair tent, cried out, "Ey, Moslems! Ey, Believers!" and delivered himself of a meaningless sermon, replete with lofty Arabic phrases that made the mouths of the men fall open in admiration.

Abdullah looked around at the dust, the whirling sparks and the shadowy faces and fought back a sense of suffocation. A mood of unspeakable grievance, of unutterable misery hung over this dark, slow-moving crowd. Bump a man's shoulder and he would wheel on you with a snarl; bump him twice and he might find a path to your liver with the blade of a knife; yet, in the way of Turks, he would swallow the words that might release the solitary anguish of his soul.

Abdullah stood face to face with a pale old man who was bowing again and again without a sound, touching first his chest and then his forehead with his palsied hand. At last, with great effort, he stammered: "You are the son of Hilmi Pasha!" He brushed past Abdullah, stretching out his arms to embrace Kenan.

Kenan's face tightened, but he did not draw away. Quietly, like a horse in the hands of an insistent groom, he allowed the old man to touch his sacred wounds: the stump of his arm, the empty socket of his eye and the deep white scar that ran from mouth to ear, forming a permanent, sardonic smile on one side of his mirthless face.

"Ah, your father, God rest his soul!" the old man whispered, tugging at the remnants of Kenan's lost arm. "Your father belonged to a race of kings!" And he gazed in rapture at Kenan's disfigured face, as if he saw there an incarnation of all the heroic Turks of decades past: sea admirals who had stormed the shores of Rhodes and Malta, generals who had fallen in Moldavia, martyrs of the faith who had carried horsetail banners from the Danube to the Persian Gulf. "He should be addressing us. Your father would know how to win the war."

Kenan grunted in agreement, although it was not clear what war the old man meant. "We have a new sort of leader now," Kenan said, and he drew Abdullah forward. "This is my brother. He went to school in Germany."

The old man glanced over, vacant and distracted. For an instant his eyes flicked down at Abdullah's patent-leather shoes and his neatly creased trousers, which were drab with dust; but he did not seem to apprehend that this, too, was a son of the redoubtable Hilmi Pasha, and every inch a Turkish gentleman. Abdullah, to his own profound regret, was not the sort of man who makes a favorable impression on strangers. His jaw was too plump, his nose too flat and flaring, to look patrician; yet his features lacked the rustic vigor of the common herd. Although he affected the costume of a Cabinet Minister, he was smaller, softer and rounder than an adolescent boy; and his face, reflecting his awareness of these deficiencies, expressed a sulky disappointment that other men mistook for nonchalance.

The old Turk, apparently disvaluing Abdullah, quickly turned away. All his attention was focused on Kenan. In a moment, he lured his hero to the head of a procession of ragged dervishes that swept him to the pulpit stone.

Abdullah could hear Kenan's voice, strained and uncertain at first, then growing in resonance, railing against the puppet government, "those pawns of France and England, who have drained away the blood of Turkey." Look how the army had declined! Less than four thousand men in the XVII Corps, and only forty or a hundred to defend the Smyrna barracks. How could these poppy seeds protect the Fatherland? To make it worse, the commander hid behind a curtain, sniveling into his coffee cup, while the governor sat in the Konak going *"kem"* and *"küm"* in the back of his throat and making sheep's eyes when anybody asked him a question!

The holy dervishes, appalled by this seditious criticism, inhaled with an audible gasp; but the infuriated students cheered, the vengeful Macedonians pounded their walking sticks; and Kenan went on.

Abdullah sat on a gravestone, pondering the ironies of primogeniture and physical appearance that put the uneducated older brother on the speaker's platform while the younger rotted in the background. For it was he, and not Kenan, who was an educated man, not only in the pious, legalistic, old-fashioned learning of the Islamic schools, but also in the skeptical scientific pantology of Europe. Abdullah's knowledge ranged from vertebrate anatomy to Central Asiatic folklore. He could discourse on thermodynamics, politics or sociology; and his encyclopedic grasp of classic Turkish poetry had dazzled visitors from Göttingen and Leyden. He could recite odes, apostrophes and evocations of the rose and nightingale; lyrics, epigrams and lamentations to the Angel Gabriel; and he was by no means ignorant of the poetry of Goethe, Schiller, Lessing and Shakespeare.

In Europe, such a man would have been invited to address an assembly on the intellectual implications of the instant crisis. Here in Turkey, the dead heartland of a dying empire, he was accorded only a curt bow and a vaguely disapproving

5

clothing inspection. To these ignorant and superstitious Turks, it meant nothing that he had written paeans in the manner of the Mevlevi, had taken courses in historical dialectics and had conversed with Gökalp Zia Bey about the trans-Altaic roots of Turkish culture. The only culture they understood was that implacable Turkish sense of discipline that gave them courage to endure excruciating pain and intolerable hardship in defense of a benighted religion and an oppressive, military aristocracy.

An Allied patrol boat, cruising below the palisades, pointed its searchlight into the billowing smoke. Turbans and skullcaps fluttered like dusty white moths in the moving beam. A rumor passed around that the English were landing to prevent a massacre; but the patrol boat only drifted up and down the coast, flicking its beam along the shore.

In the intermittent light, Kenan resembled an excited boy. His hideous scars were smoothed away, and the eye patch looked like a decoration for a masquerade. Abdullah, staring up at him, felt a rush of pity. Kenan's hair was turning white, although he was not much older than Abdullah; his forehead was etched with pale blue lines, like the veins of a baby's tender skull; and his neck was thin and vulnerable. But it was difficult to sympathize with a man so harsh and bellicose. War had crippled him, cheated him, almost devoured him; yet war had become his consuming passion. In the presence of these fanatics, he was inflamed with ancient battle cries. He called down the sword of God, the sword that was the key to Heaven and Hell. Had not the Prophet said, "A drop of blood shed in the cause of God, a night spent in arms, is of more avail than two months of fasting and prayer"? Had not the Prophet said, "Whosoever falls in battle, his sins shall be forgiven at the Day of Judgment, his wounds shall be resplendent as vermilion and fragrant as musk, and the wings of cherubim and angels shall supplant his lost limbs"?

The fires were dying. Darkness swallowed the hill, and the long yellow nightstick of the patrol boat stroked the shore; but Kenan raved on. Rivulets of perspiration trickled down his cheeks.

"It is the darkest night of Turkish history," he cried. "After fighting for four years, we have lost almost everything a people can lose. Our capital is occupied by foreign soldiers. The leaders of our government have fled. Our enemies are cutting apart our empire, limb by limb. They have taken away Arabia and Syria. They are taking Baghdad and Basra and the Valley of Mesopotamia. They are taking the pasture lands of Thrace, the holy shrines of Palestine and the mountain of Lebanon. And they will take the highlands of Armenia and Kurdistan, the plains of Cilicia and the coasts of Pontus—all these rich territories that have been part of our Ottoman Empire for hundreds of years.

"Our land will be chained in treaties, charters, mandates and concessions and handed over in everlasting slavery to the colonial powers of Europe. This, honorable gentlemen, is the fruit of all our suffering, our freezing, our starvation and our death."

He paused and let his singular, blazing eye rove over the faces of the men. In the bitterness of his passion, his voice diminished to a rasping whisper, as if he were recounting news that was too horrible to be breathed aloud.

"And now, my brothers, the worst blow of all! The Allied fleet is bringing an army of Greeks across the Aegean Sea. This is the compensation to those admirable people for their self-serving decision to join the victorious side in the final months of the war. Tomorrow, the Greeks will land in Smyrna. They will help themselves to as much of our country as they can hold."

A shuddering moan, like the expiration of a dying animal, passed through the crowd: "Ay, God! . . . Are you sure? . . .

7

Must it be tomorrow?" But Kenan ignored their questions.

"Are the Greeks more numerous here than the Turks?" he whispered. "Not yet, my brothers in Islam. Not yet . . . That is why we have gathered tonight in Bahri Baba. To show the world our overwhelming majority. And they have seen us." He pointed to the searchlight. "But bonfires and speeches are not enough."

Reaching into his tunic, Kenan drew out a rectangular object. He turned it over and handed it to one of the men.

"Do you feel that deep intaglio? That is a silver carrying case, worked at Bursa. It holds a copy of the Sacred Book that lay on my father's breast, against his heart, when he pressed his leg against the other in the final agony."

At last Kenan allowed his voice to rise, high-pitched in exhortation.

"My brothers! I beg you to press your hands upon the Book and swear with me that you will never give up our Fatherland while the breath of life is in your lungs, while the blood of life is in your heart!"

And the men pushed forward, groping in the light of the dying fires to touch the Blessed Koran of the saintly Hilmi Pasha, muttering, "So be it!" and "I swear!" One by one, they yielded themselves to a sublime hysteria, a rhythmic paroxysm of emotion that would in time dissolve their chronic anger, leaving them inert and glum. The dervishes were falling to their knees. You could hear the rustle of their shoddy rust-colored robes and the rumble of their voices, reciting the Fatiha, the Beginning of the Scripture, commencing, "In the name of God, the Bounteous, the Merciful: Praise be to God, Lord of the Worlds . . ."

Abdullah sat without moving, regretting that he had not turned down the hill at sunset. He had foreseen the danger of fanaticism, but he had not imagined that Kenan would entice his listeners into holy suicide. He dropped the remaining handbills behind the stone. Without waiting to speak to Kenan, he started walking. When he felt the ground slope downward, he quickened his steps, searching for a path that would lead to the Karatina Road. The chanting of the dervishes rose and fell behind him. They had come to the Surah that describes the disaster of damnation; and their voices grew coarse with frenzy as they evoked the scene of mankind flocking as thick as quivering moths to the Final Judgment.

"Abdullah?" his brother called. "Where are you? Have you pressed a hand on the Book?"

Abdullah hesitated. Looking back, he could see only a handful of men: ex-soldiers, workmen and riffraff from the bazaar. The only one he recognized was Crazy Ishmael, a huge, slope-shouldered moron who ran a dirty flophouse near the Konak Square. Others were plunging past him in the darkness, whispering about the prison and the powder magazine.

"Abdullah? Are you there?"

He turned and continued down the hill. To set his hand against his brother's hand had never been his wish. But Abdullah did not believe in God; he did not believe in the Fatherland; and he was in love with a Greek.

Her name was Eleni Trigonis, and she was the only daughter of a raisin shipper named Christos Trigonis, who had made a fortune buying sultanas from farmers in the Meander Valley and selling them to bakers and distillers in London and Copenhagen. They lived in a three-story house on the Upper Quay, one of those haughty fawn-colored mansions built in the reign of Sultan Abdul Hamit in imitation of a townhouse in Belgravia. Although Abdullah had never penetrated deeper than the foyer, he knew from that room alone that the Villa Trigonis was the most imposing residence in the city.

9

As for Eleni, Abdullah had known her, so to speak, for most of the years of his life. He had watched her growing up, had admired the freedom and vivacity of her European manners and had coveted her soft black hair. He had planned his courtship with the confidence of an intelligent man who knew that his own refinement, education and good intentions ultimately would overcome all barriers of religious prejudice.

Eleni, on the other hand, had no idea that Abdullah existed. Or, to be more accurate, she knew him only as an unimportant visitor to the house—a Turkish dandy whose family in Alashehir sold raisins to her father. Far from realizing that the educated younger son of Hilmi Pasha thought of her constantly and regarded her as his future wife, she had a distinct impression that she was not engaged to *anyone,* and that if some person were going to remedy this depressing situation, it probably would be a certain Athenian army officer named Dimitris Kalapothakis, with whom her father had been corresponding for several months.

The fact that Eleni did not know Mr. Kalapothakis, either, did not trouble her at all. She could take Mr. Kalapothakis or leave him, exactly as she wished; and that was just one of several advantages of being the only daughter of an indulgent and worldly man who was old enough to be her grandfather.

Another advantage was the southeast bedroom, which had a window with a little seat from which one could look across the tops of loquat trees into the center of the garden. Often, when Eleni came into the room after dark, she would fold back the shutters before lighting the lamp; and, standing by the window, she would hear nightingales serenading their lovers.

On the night of the Turkish meeting at Bahri Baba, the garden was filled with harsher sounds. There were hollow echoes from the bay. Freighters moaned. Warships blew their

10

sirens. Down on the Quay, men were calling back and forth in strained voices. Eleni wondered whether she might already be hearing the voice of Dimitris Kalapothakis, supervising the landing of his regiment.

Obviously, this Mr. Kalapothakis was a poor sheep looking for a rich dowry. Why else had he asked for her? What could he know about her? Nothing but her name, her age and the wealth of her father. Why not ask for some other Smyrna girl? Why not Maria Papadopoulos? Hadn't anyone told him that Maria Papadopoulos was as beautiful as St. Marini and as gentle as a cherub? Hadn't they told him that old women always kissed Maria Papadopoulos on the cheek and said, "You'll marry well"? No one ever told Eleni she would marry well; they told her she would *never* marry. The reasons were obvious. She had a plain face, a blunt manner and an orderly, masculine mind. Whatever value these qualities might have in a boy, they did not create a desirable young woman; and if Eleni regretted her nature, she also accepted it with the cool realism that was her habit.

She never had lacked admirers; but they had a way of falling out of grace or out of orbit. A tiresome old professor of mathematics, twice her age, had begun negotiations with her father and then abruptly died. A boy in Bornova, who smelled of peppermint, wanted to squeeze her hand and indecently asked to see her underclothes, and she ordered him out of the house; and a dark, agitated Alexandrian, brought home by her brother, was continually absorbed in new business ventures—a newspaper, a cigarette factory, a cotton gin—up to the day he was taken off to jail for embezzling from his employer's accounts.

After losing several suitors to such hazards, Eleni had decided to become a teacher. She had spoken sensibly to Papa about enrolling at the American College for Women in Constantinople. Later, she could take a respectable position teaching children to read. But Mama had interceded, saying it would *ruin* a girl to go to an American college where they let girls neglect the lubrication of their skins, the cultivation of their French and the pursuit of their piano lessons, in order to cut up dead frogs. In the end, her father had agreed that he could not endure the shame of having his daughter cut up frogs and neglect her skin. While Eleni drooped and sighed, appalled by the bleakness of her future, Mama had said consolingly that life, after all, is made up of two things: What you don't expect, and what surprises you.

Lieutenant Kalapothakis was one of the surprises. He had sent his letter through a friend of Papa's, an important member of the Parliament in Athens. Eleni had refused at first to take the offer seriously. It was too absurd to think of a young man she had never seen writing from an army camp in Larissa, "for the hand of your exquisite daughter...."

None of them had heard of him before, not even Papa. But Papa was impressed by the testimonial of the eminent deputy. He decided Eleni should at least look at Mr. Kalapothakis and judge him for herself, as an English girl would do.

"After all," Papa said, without much logic, "he used to be a Cabinet Minister."

Eleni put down Dimitris Kalapothakis as an atrocious Cretan boy with rotting teeth and mustache like the horns of a water buffalo. Probably a hashish smoker, too. Belly like a sack of figs and skin that smelled of asafetida!

Mama naturally visualized him as a god, a latter-day Apollo or an approximate reincarnation of Lord Byron, dressed in the uniform of a Hellenic revolutionary, with a scarf at his throat and his cap set back to show the noble configuration of his brow. Daydreaming over photographs of bridal parties in the *Illustrated London News*, she sewed yards of brocade on velvet bodices and knitted dozens of pairs of bedroom slippers for Eleni's cedar chest; and, one afternoon, she con-

12

trived a séance with Polixeni in the cook's little room under the kitchen stairs.

Polixeni could read the future. In particular, she could foretell disasters, which were invariably the result of sexual misconduct. She could detect the precursive signs of tragedy in coffee sludge, tea leaves, colored beans, melted lead, cracked mirrors and poached eggs in water. In Eleni's coffee cup, Polixeni found a stranger, a baby and a marriage.

"Not in that order, I hope!" Eleni said.

But the cook was offended by the laughter and refused to go on.

In fact, the whole family was annoyed by Eleni's lack of enthusiasm, as though she had scoffed at a gift they were offering. But that was the sort of girl she was, and no one knew it better than she: a girl who could not lie to herself and would not try, who refused to magnify a lemon seed into a pearl or make a mouse into a monster, who could not bear to be treated with condescension and who was not frightened, folding back the shutters of her bedroom, to see a Turk standing in the garden.

Another girl—Maria Papadopoulos, for instance—would have collapsed with stomach cramps, shrieking for mercy. Or Polixeni! She would have panicked even if the man were someone she *knew*.

But Eleni, holding her breath, stepped back from the window and waited. The man could not be planning a crime or he would not have stood there with his hands along his trouser seams and his little fez neatly on his head, wearing that confused expression of disbelief and apprehension.

From the style of his coat (Edwardian) and the shape of his head (canine), she knew he was a Turk; but that was scarcely grounds for a general alarm. Turks were always coming to the house: fig peddlers, customs brokers, petty officials amenable to bribes. This one evidently considered himself at home in

13

their garden, among the oleander bushes and under the loquat trees; and his impertinence delighted her.

"Are you grazing your goats?" she called.

The Turk stood there gaping at her, moving his lips without a sound, and finally stammered: "Is it the house of Christos Trigonis?"

"Do you think I would be here if it weren't?"

"And is Mr. Trigonis receiving visitors?"

"At this hour? Do you think he is an astronomer?"

The Turk muttered something about important business.

"He's in bed," Eleni said. "Why don't you talk to me instead?"

She could see that her boldness horrified him. The Turks were such sober, slow-thinking, punctilious people! Half the fun in life was playing tricks on them, and women seldom got an opportunity. She leaned on the windowsill to get a better look at him.

"Did you come to ask for my hand in marriage?"

That struck him like a blow. He squirmed around so bashfully that she wondered what had come over him. For a moment he seemed too embarrassed to speak. Then he said in a hoarse whisper: "Do you recognize me? I am Abdullah, the son of Hilmi Pasha."

A siren began to moan across the bay. Rising and rising, the tense, insistent monotone resounded on the Quay and echoed up and down the harbor, from Cordelio to the Black Fatimas.

"Listen!" Eleni said. "That's the signal!"

Then, to tease the Turk: "I suppose you won't like it, having the Greeks in charge?" Abdullah, the son of Hilmi Pasha, said it made no difference to him. One government was as bad as another. The important thing was social progress. International boundaries would tumble. Didn't she agree? But Eleni was getting tired of him.

14

"I'm sorry, it means that our romance is over," she said. The Turk opened his mouth and began to say something; but Eleni added: "Anyway, I am engaged." And she closed the shutters on him and drew the blind.

Someone had left several dresses on the bed. She picked them up one by one, wavering between the ivory satin and the emerald taffeta. She saw herself playing the piano, serving rose-petal jam and talking to Mr. Kalapothakis. He would not hold still, would not remain an ugly Cretan with a snuffling mustache, but kept changing into the very image of Lord Byron. Eleni pranced between the mirror and the chiffonier, holding the dresses to her breast, piling up her hair in fanciful arrangements and succumbing to irrational, inexplicable anticipation.

The sirens woke Christos Trigonis at his desk. He had been asleep for hours, face down and driveling gently on the fourth stanza of a panegyric he had composed to celebrate the rebirth of Ionia. His face was resting on a pen or pencil —some object that had left a welt along his cheekbone. He fingered the indentation thoughtfully while wondering where he was. Then, with an anguished cry, he leaped up and rushed into the drawing room. Daylight was seeping through the shutters.

"Go wake up my son!"

The maid dashed past him, barefoot and uncombed. Groaning with impatience, Christos thrust his shoulder against the window casement and threw back the iron shutters, which crashed against the walls with the sound of a cannonade.

A Greek man-of-war was creeping through the haze beyond the outer harbor, wavering and gleaming like a fish in melting silver gelatin. The mist obscured it, then revealed it, as lustrous as a pearl. The brassy piping of a military band drifted up the Quay. Bells were tolling from St. John's and Bella Vista, then from St. Dimitris' and St. Katherine's and St. Photini's, the metropolitan cathedral. The Armenian cathedral rang a fierce, demonic elegy; and even the Italian Catholics at St. Polycarp's sounded the chimes of their schismatic chapel in a halfhearted clang. Only the mosques were silent, as if the muezzins had been strangled on their balconies.

Christos took off his spectacles and wiped his eyes. His heart seemed to be swelling, and he struggled to draw his breath. Christ is risen! It was the Easter of the dispossessed, the Resurrection of the Golden Age.

The buildings all around were hung with draperies of blue and white, celebrating the philhellenic statesmen who had authorized this expedition. Woodrow Wilson floated in a wilderness of palm leaves; Lloyd George wallowed in the Union Jack; Clemenceau peeked through a framework of tricolor bunting. As for the Greek Prime Minister, Eleftherios Venizelos, his enormous likeness, painted by seven artists on a field of canvas sailcloth ten yards wide, covered the entire façade of the Villa Trigonis, from the pediment above the door to the crenelations on the roof. Christos himself had stood over the painters, directing their brushwork and dictating the apothegm at the top: "Smyrna Today—Constantinople Tomorrow!"

Watching the words take shape, Christos had marveled at how recently these hopes had seemed unattainable. For centuries, the Great Idea of the Greek revival had lain like a seed in winter, waiting for the touch of spring; and now, in a few months, it had sprung into glittering reality. It was not unlike his own life, which had had so many fallow years of exile and discontent before Sophia warmed his bed, George and Eleni filled his heart and Venizelos inflamed his mind. Christos was amazed that the germ of life could survive so many decades of sterility. He had been over forty when he was at last married and sired his children, and past fifty when Venizelos squeezed inside his soul. Yet here he was, at sixty, witnessing the fulfillment of the ancient dream, with a strong son to carry along the glory.

George personified the new life. While he was forming in Sophia's womb, she had experienced a vision of St. George of Cappadocia, lifting his sword to kill the dragon. From this omen they knew that the baby would be a boy, and that he would grow up to be a soldier.

Now George was almost seventeen, a future hero. He towered over Christos. His hair was darker and thicker, his voice was deeper and his arms and legs were longer, than his father's ever had been.

Still, everyone said the son was like his father: vigorous, militant, aggressive. It was not that Christos was belligerent; it was only that he had a unique intensity, the result of a sublime inspiration. Unlike most men, Christos could see the vast design of history taking shape like a mosaic from a multitude of scattered fragments. To Christos, the landing of a few soldiers on the Quay at Smyrna was not a trivial event but the retribution of an ancient wrong, the incarnation of a five-hundred-year-old dream. The Moslem conqueror had fallen at last; the Christian Greek would rule again.

If George was blind to this, it could only be that Christos had failed to open his eyes; for there was nothing inconspicuous about the dream. The fleet advanced like angels gliding through a pearly fog; the music rang like an angelic choir; and the water shimmered like the floor of Heaven.

"Oh, where the devil is my son?" Christos shouted, pounding his fist on the windowsill. "He should be seeing this! Is George awake?"

And he strode to the foot of the stairway to listen for George's voice.

The boy was not lazy, but like all adolescents he preferred

17

to do his sleeping in the daytime. Christos remembered a time several years ago, just before the war, when George had overslept. That time, they had planned to go shooting early at Halkipinar. In the cool gray-green solitude of the kitchen, waiting for George to come downstairs, Christos had wrapped up two packets of white cheese and olives, boiled some coffee and cut some bread. Then he had noticed the slow-breathing silence of the house. Upstairs, he had found the boy, rosy and warm as a young bullock under the covers. George had looked up in a daze and said: "Papa, I don't like hunting." Christos had poked him gently and told him to stop that nonsense; but George had sat up, his eyes brimming with tears, and shouted: "I mean it. I hate guns. I really hate them!" At that, Christos had lost his head and lashed out his hand. The boy had stared at him in a twisted, opaque blur and then tumbled backward, yowling. Sophia woke up. Eleni began to cry. Maids ran up and down the hall, screeching like dervishes. Later, George had come down, damp and red-eyed and smelling of soap, and said he was sorry. Christos had held out his arms. "I understand," he said magnanimously. "A boy will say anything to stay asleep." It turned out to be their best day of shooting. George learned to squeeze the trigger slowly, like a widow's tit, and they came home with three redheads and a teal. For several days George had hung around him; and they remained as close as doves until the pain of their emotions faded. Remembering this—the boy's reluctance and his own dismay—Christos hesitated this morning by the stairs. But George's voice came down to him reassuringly, and Christos went back to the drawing room.

The gulf was turning pink. Transport ships crystallized from the mist and slowly steamed toward shore, past Allied battleships that stood by like hulking side boys. Cannon salutes rolled over the Aegean. Horse trams rang their bells, and a kettledrum began to thunder from the rooftop of the house next door. That ought to bring George downstairs in a hurry!

Rehearsing for his son's arrival, Christos began an instructive monologue on the components of the Allied fleet: British, French and, of course, Greek: the *Leon,* the *Patris,* the *Av*—Suddenly sucking in his breath, Christos dashed back to his desk to get the binoculars. In a moment he had found the old-fashioned tripod masts of the *Averoff,* standing up like a familiar landmark against the lavender sky. His eyes began to water, squinting at the sea, and his hands trembled so violently that he could scarcely hold the glasses. He sat down on the arm of a mohair settee.

"You see, George," he continued, still in rehearsal, "you are witnessing the very moment of rebirth. The Metropolitan will bless the troops. The squadron will march across the city—" Then, in a muffled growl: "Ah, shut up, you old horn! How can the boy learn anything if his old man never stops talking?"

But he supposed this must be the way of all men who have come to their great convictions, their great achievements and their great loves late in life. They spoke out of compulsion, breathlessly, with the zeal of converts who saw that their time was short. In any case, who was better qualified than he to instruct the boy? Who was more devoted? And who had given deeper thought to the new Greek Empire?

He fell into a reverie in which he lectured George as they strolled through groves and colonnades and duckponds, with shotguns under their elbows and olives in their pockets. Subject: the new Greek Empire. A golden chalice resting on a tripod of immortal cities. Athens, of course, would be its capital of culture: Athens, the legatee of Pericles and Solon, and the first prize won in the national revolution a century ago. Constantinople, naturally, would remain the spiritual capital, the patriarchal throne. The Moslem minarets would be torn down, and the Patriarch would enter the Cathedral

19

of Holy Wisdom at the head of a glittering convocation. They would resume the Holy Liturgy exactly at the point at which the Mass was interrupted when the Turks broke down the city walls in 1453.

As for Smyrna, it would be the commercial capital. It was more populous than Athens and almost as Greek, and it commanded a more fertile hinterland. Its rails and roads ran deep into Asia Minor, through the valleys of the wandering Meander, the little Meander and the Caicus, which circled leisurely around the crag of Pergamos.

How easily Smyrna could become the broker, shipper and grocer of the eastern Mediterranean—the New York of the Orient! The greatest dreams are always simple.

His wife and daughter came in, clinging together like thieves; but they only glanced out the window and went on talking. Christos waved his hand for silence. Wasn't that typical of women, permitting their domestic chatter to intrude on a solemn occasion of the state? Eleni was puckering the corners of her mouth in a patient schoolteacher smile. "Mama, you know they'd never let Mr. Kalapothakis off today!" And Sophia, clutching the girl's elbow, whispered insistently: "Why not?"

Eleni's face was locked in that insipid, patient mask. She was bracing herself, even now, for disappointment. With her mind absorbed in her own unhappiness, she stared blindly toward the harbor, as if the magnificent procession streaming up the bay was nothing more than a string of sponge boats coming in from Samos. Christos observed her with a frown; but his heart was opening in tenderness. A girl of that age was so pathetic in her vulnerable, feminine concerns. How could she be expected to understand the politics of empire and the rising flood of history? He led her gently to the window, and they watched the Metropolitan Chrysostomos ride past in gold and yellow silk. The troops were landing far to the south, beyond the line of palm trees on the Passport Quay, and a secondary column was disembarking at the north end of the waterfront, near the Point of Alsanjak. Christos was explaining the strategy when George came in at last and hesitated by the door.

"Come on, come on!" Christos exploded. "I suppose you'd rather stay in bed?"

But George, wringing his big stiff-jointed hands, said in an uncertain voice that he reckoned the expedition was moving along as scheduled.

"I suppose they're ashore by now. Did you hear the rifle fire a few minutes ago?"

"Why not?" Christos said. "Who ever heard of a Greek celebration without some shooting?" Leaving Eleni, he went to inspect George's appearance. "That's the way we Greeks always have been, all through our history. This exuberance, this love of pandemonium." George had dressed in a good suit, European cut, and had combed his hair. Christos was pleased to see that. So often George went around in sloppy Turkish clothes: indoor slippers, pajamas and soft, silk robes; and sometimes he looked bleary, as if he had been reading too much. He had his mother's wide, translucent eyes, which were unpredictable in color—brownish, greenish, gray—but always moist and pale. Set below that broad, high-colored forehead, under those strong, black brows, they looked strangely timid, like the eyes of a small boy peeking under the visor of a helmet.

"You should eat some breakfast," Christos told him. "You look peaked."

"Oh, I'll have an orange or something. I've got to go out."

Eleni asked for *café au lait* and Sophia wanted *thé complet* with English marmalade and sweet butter, a combination that she associated with Paris, where her cousin was ambassador. But Christos ordered George a primitive Greek breakfast of black olives and white cheese—simple, Socratic and neoclassical. It was the sort of breakfast Christos liked, because it was inherently wholesome and Greek; but he was too agitated to eat.

While they were waiting, a dark squall blew in from the sea and drops of rain came through the window. Suddenly, there were footsteps on the cobblestones outside. George bounded toward the window, stopped halfway and turned back with a startled smile.

"It's our own soldiers. Greek soldiers."

Christos felt tears spring into his eyes. He told Eleni to get the flag and bring it to the window.

The soldiers were in a single column, moving at a jog. You could see them coming down the alley, single file because the pavement was slippery and narrow. When they came to the Quay, they raised their eyes and spread ranks, thrusting their arms straight out to space themselves. Eleni leaned out with the flag in her hands. A soldier turned his head and smiled. He had a gap between his two front teeth.

Christos called: "Is Lieutenant Kalapothakis with you?"

"Oh, *Papa!*" Eleni said, flushed with embarrassment. "Why don't you stop?" She tried to break away, but Christos wrapped his arm around her waist and dropped his other hand on George's shoulder, which seemed to quiver under his touch like the tense body of a closely bridled horse. The thunder of a naval battery broke over them, rolling against the buildings with the roar of Doomsday.

"I suppose that's just a salute," George said, in a voice that sounded peculiarly tight, and Christos, looking up, saw that the boy's lips were colorless.

"Why, of course it is," Christos said. He stared at those colorless lips and an intolerable doubt raced through his mind. He crushed out the thought by digging his fingers into the boy's shoulder. George pulled away with a cry of surprise.

"Cross yourself!" Christos said sternly. "They are exposing the holy ikons."

The echo of the naval guns grumbled over the city like the earth taking leave of the earth. Under cover of the artillery and the gusty rain, Kenan lifted the butt of his rifle and smashed out the garret window of the Anatolian Soldiers' Rooming House. He rested the barrel on the sill and sighted on a storehouse across the street. Then, drawing in the rifle, he glanced at Crazy Ishmael. "Are you ready?" Ishmael dipped his eyelids.

Two hundred yards away, where the Konak Square opened out to the sea, the banner of a Christian saint was rounding the corner, swaying like the mainmast of a sailboat in a storm. The crowd began to mutter in anticipation. There were commercial clerks with sprigs of gentian in the bands of their straw hats, stevedores in open shirts and adolescent boys who held up painted signs that trembled like disks in a religious procession. They pressed forward, elbowing each other and stretching their necks to catch a glimpse of the soldiers.

Kenan sat on the floor with his legs folded under him, tailor fashion. By tucking the stock of the rifle under the stump of his left arm, he could work the breech bolt with his right hand; but he would not be able to reload while lying down. In any case, there probably would not be time to fire a second round. He looked regretfully at all the weapons Crazy Ishmael had stolen from the powder magazine—three Martini rifles, a heavy old Lagant revolver, two cartridge belts and a hand grenade. It was too much for a half-wit and a cripple. And the garret was a mediocre salient. Through the broken window you could see only the front of Giraud's Warehouse and the clump of pepper trees around the Clock Tower; the entrance to the Ottoman barracks and the government Konak were blocked from view by a row of open cooking stalls on the corner. Of all the pillboxes Kenan had occupied from the borders of Bulgaria to the hills of Palestine, this would have been his last choice for the fortress of the Turkish race. But Crazy Ishmael owned it, and he regarded it with holy awe. Entering the building, he had pulled off his black rubber overshoes as though he were ascending to the Hisar Mosque on the highest holy day. To a man of Kenan's temperament, this endorsement from a blessed idiot was as good an omen as could be imagined for a doomed endeavor. Bending to touch his forehead to the floor, Kenan had commended himself to the mercy of God, the Forgiving, the Compassionate, reflecting that death would be the best of several alternatives that might befall him.

As Kenan was bringing his rifle into position again, the first Greek soldiers came into view, following the holy banner. They were carrying rifles with fixed bayonets at right-shoulder arms and singing a foolish song. Little flags hovered like butterflies above their heads. The first column forced a passage toward the Konak; but the soldiers were soon engulfed in the crowd, which flowed together like a muddled current. Then a second column turned the corner, and the Greeks began to lose their senses.

Men at the edges of the crowd were pushed against the walls and lost their hats, and their faces stiffened suddenly in panic. Late arrivals rushed out of the alleys and hurled themselves like pouncing animals against the backs of others who were straining to see through hats and flags and painted signs; and the roar of excitement rose to a shrill note of hysteria.

Kenan drew in his breath and stretched himself out like a dog. Somewhere to the right of him there was a crash of glass. He took sight on the Christian banner, counted slowly to three and fired. As Crazy Ishmael was handing him a second rifle, half a dozen shots resounded across the Square.

Out in the center of the crowd, a ring of space appeared like an eddy circle on the surface of a pond. At the edge of the ring, the holy banner tottered and lurched sideways. A convulsion rippled through the crowd. First a clot formed around the banner. Then the clot swirled sideways and burst apart like a cluster of marbles struck by a shooting agate. Stevedores tumbled into the sea; soldiers scrambled into the pepper trees around the Clock Tower; clerks disappeared into doorways. Almost instantly the Square was empty. Raindrops splattered on the cobblestones. Out in the middle of the empty Square, a man in Cretan pantaloons and a blue-and-white striped jacket was lying face down. A soldier was dragging himself on hands and knees in the direction of the pepper trees. Kenan aimed carefully and squeezed the trigger. The soldier's face disappeared in a little burst of red liquid.

"Kenan Bey!" Crazy Ishmael whispered, as if the room were filled with eavesdroppers. "Why do you spend your bullets on ordinary soldiers? Why don't you shoot the general?"

"When you see the general, point him out to me," Kenan said. And he put another bullet into the soldier's twitching body. Somewhere beyond the row of cookshops, there was steady rifle fire and the tap-tap-tapping of a machine gun. Puffs of grayish plaster erupted from the walls of Giraud's Warehouse across the street. It was impossible to see what the Greeks were doing to the barracks and the Konak.

"How do we get out of here?" Kenan said.

"Out?" said Crazy Ishmael. "Why, the same way you got in. Down the stairs and out the door and into the street."

"Imbecile. No other door?"

Crazy Ishmael pleated together his black eyebrows. His

eyes shifted sideways in fear of Kenan's displeasure. Finally he hunched up his shoulders and clicked his tongue. Kenan clenched his fist and ground the knuckles on the stone floor. "Go barricade the door," he said.

Crazy Ishmael wiped his nose on his thumb and muttered something about the pleasure of serving the Fatherland. His great shoulders scraped the sides of the doorway, and his naked feet slapped the stones like two flounders. He closed the door behind him.

The tapping of the machine gun stopped, leaving a ringing in the ears. For several moments there was silence, and then the Greeks began to cheer. Six or eight soldiers, bent over like dwarfs, darted out of the clump of pepper trees and scurried behind the cookshops. The rain stopped. Shreds of gray and pinkish cloud, like the feathers of a dead bird, were blowing overhead, chased inland by the storm.

Kenan put down his rifle. The garret was plainer than a gypsy's hut, without a closet or a stick of furniture, and the door was as thin as parchment. In fact, the building was nothing but an empty husk, a shell of cubicles around a court-yard, like a caravan hotel in central Anatolia. Rivulets of dirty water trickled along the corridors, and the stairway was as dark as Hell. One flight down, there was an inside balcony that overlooked the courtyard. You could see some withered plants in white oil cans and a pair of underdrawers dripping on a line. The only way out was the door to the street, which was wide enough to pass an oxcart.

Kenan threw the rifles and the cartridge belts one by one into the courtyard. He stuck the Lagant revolver inside his belly sash and put the hand grenade in the pocket of his tunic. When he got back to the window, a strange procession was coming across the Square from the direction of the Otto-man barracks. At the front was a Turkish colonel with a white handkerchief tied to his wrist. His hands were clasped to-gether on top of his head and the handkerchief flapped against his face, which looked rigid and putty-colored in the watery gray light. The officers and common soldiers followed him, single file, holding their hands on their heads. They did not look at the Greeks who were standing with glittering eyes in the doorways and the alleys.

The first to break out of hiding was a red-haired man, one of those northern Greeks with more than a drop of Slavic blood in his arteries. He had a heavy, lumpy body and thick, bare arms, sunburned to the shoulders, and he was holding a wooden café chair lightly in one hand, as if it were made of paper. Kenan could hear his high-pitched voice, haranguing the others. All at once, they rushed out, carrying broken bottles and the legs of chairs. At the edge of the Square, they overturned a wagon and swarmed over it, picking up splintered panels, metal bars and broken pieces of the yoke. The red-haired Greek ran straight to the Turkish colonel, who was ambling along like a sleepwalker, with the handkerchief flapping against his face. With a triumphant cry, the Greek raised his naked arms and brought down the wooden chair like a sledge. The Turkish colonel pitched forward, and the Greeks fell over him. The prisoners began to run, bobbing awkwardly. Greeks were striking at their heads and shoulders with broken bottles, legs of chairs and pieces of the wagon. At the end of the line, two privates of the Ottoman garrison picked up the unconscious body of the colonel, who had a glistening purple indentation in his forehead.

Slowly the public buildings emptied. Clerks in suits of gray Vienna worsted came out of the Konak and stared with damp, twitching faces at the throng of Christians, silently swaying forward on the toes of their light felt boots. Old *hajis* and *hojas* from the Konak Mosque cupped their hands above their eyes to ward off rotten fruit. Schoolboys from the Sultan's Academy, goaded along by soldiers with bayonets, ran with their arms up, hugging their heads.

Kenan lay on the stones by the window and closed his eyes.

He had walked the retreat from Luleburgas and had lived in Sultan Ahmet's Mosque, where half the men had died of sepsis and starvation. He had been at Suez and Anafarta and in Syria with the Yildirim; and he could sleep in a sandstorm or standing up or lying in a pool of freezing mud. The Greeks gave him three minutes of sleep before they struck the street door with a clap of thunder. The building shook; the corridor resounded with a deep *"grüm-grüm-grüm"*; and the house burst open with a roar like the sound of gases rushing up a chimney.

Kenan looked down and watched the Greeks taking Crazy Ishmael. Two men were holding him under the arms. His bare feet were bouncing loosely on the ground. His turban had been torn off, and his head was streaming blood. As the men were dragging him out, his cotton trousers dropped around his ankles like an old skin shucked off by a lizard. Kenan could see his eyeballs rolling wildly, as white as pebbles.

"Say it!" the Greeks were shouting. "Say, *Zito Venizelos!*"

"Dead?" somebody said. "Oh, the devil he is!"

But the crowd reached out for Crazy Ishmael, and they lifted his long, pale, naked legs higher than his head and pulled at his arms until his body was attenuated as a fleece. Ishmael reared up in panic, and the veins stood out along his neck; but the men who were holding him spread his legs apart, muttering softly, almost caressingly: "Ey, *Is'mael! De-lis'mael!*"

Ishmael thrashed from side to side. A man darted out of the crowd and lashed at his head with a piece of chain. The Greeks were giving each other orders: "Make him say 'Shit on the Koran!' . . . Make him shit on the Koran! . . . Hold his arms!" They carried him like a trophy, round and round, while men on either side clawed his face.

Then a big soldier, with his cap off and his purple face convulsed with madness, rushed forward, scattering the crowd, and lunged on his victim. Ishmael jerked upward with a scream of agony and quivered like a scarecrow on a pole. For an instant, he seemed to hang in the air. Then his shoulders slumped, his mouth opened and he fell backward. The soldier withdrew his arm, stained with blood to the elbow, and the crowd turned away in disgust.

A moment later, men began pushing into the house again. Kenan ran into the corridor, fused the hand grenade and threw it down the stairs. Without waiting for a report, he kicked out a rear window and jumped down fifteen feet into the embrace of a Greek officer who was crouching in the garden.

The Greek rolled back and stared at him in horror. They were lying in damp weeds, with the rain falling in their faces. Both of them, for an instant, were too stunned to move. Then Kenan wheeled and sprang to his feet. Before he took three steps, the Greek was firing and shouting in a hoarse, panicky voice. Kenan stopped. The Greek came up behind him, breathing noisily.

"Raise your hands. Your hands." Kenan, although he understood, did not obey. He slowly turned and faced a young lieutenant who was waving a pistol up and down, pointing it first at Kenan's head and then at his ankles. "Your *hands*, I said! Ah, you only have one hand? Then put up one hand." The lieutenant danced on one foot and then the other. His face was tight with anxiety. The point of his pistol wobbled with the nervous trembling of his arm. "Keep your distance! I'll send you to Paradise. Throw down your weapons. . . . *No!* Stop! Keep your arm up!"

Beside himself with agitation, the lieutenant darted forward, twitching and grimacing, and snatched the old Lagant revolver from Kenan's sash as if it were on fire. Kenan watched in a stupor. He wondered whether the grenade had gone off. If he had kept it, pressed to his heart, he could have pulled the fulminating pin even as this Greek was disarming him. He reached out, smiling at the thought of carrying this frightened Greek across the threshold of eternity. But the lieutenant recoiled, shrieking. Faces came to the window above their heads, asking who was there.

"I have him," the lieutenant called out, raising his voice in sudden bravado. "Nothing to worry about."

He took Kenan to the far side of the garden, where a shed roof gave shelter from the rain, and faced him to the wall. Kenan could hear him fumbling with his tobacco box, lighting a cigarette and exhaling with a wavering sigh.

"You almost killed me, Mehmet," the lieutenant muttered. "My heart came into my mouth." He struck Kenan a stinging blow on the back of the head. "I ought to peel you like an onion, you sodomitic, masturbating, pig-shit Moslem. . . . Don't look at me, pig shit! I'll put out your other eye!" And he stamped around, snarling at Kenan's back, pausing now and then to draw a deep, shuddering breath of air. The very idea that his life had been in danger seemed to bring him to a boiling rage. Kenan waited for another blow to fall.

But the lieutenant's fury ebbed away. He quieted down, made himself another cigarette and appeared to be waiting for something to happen. When Kenan dared to turn his head again, he saw the young officer leaning against a woodpile, cupping the pistol between his two hands.

They stayed a long time in the yard. The rain stopped and the sounds of riot died away. Finally, the lieutenant roused himself and herded Kenan through a passage between the buildings to the Konak Square. The gulf was glowing like a pewter plate. Across the bay, the tumbled peaks were masked by mist, and spray was splashing on the empty esplanade. As they were crossing the street, an officer with a gray mustache drove up in a touring car and scowled at them.

"Kalapothaki! What the devil are you doing here?"

The lieutenant poked Kenan with his pistol. "I've got this prisoner, Colonel."

"Jesus and Mary! *Everybody's* got a prisoner. Where are your men?"

"My company? They're searching the neighborhood for snipers."

"Devil they are," the colonel said. "I found some of them halfway down the Quay to Photi's Candy Shop. If it weren't for your father, I'd court-martial you. Get back to the landing platform and collect your men."

With a gasp, almost a whimper, of indignation, the lieutenant trotted over to the running board of the colonel's car, leaving Kenan behind. "Colonel, I ask you! What should I do with my prisoner?"

"Turn him loose," the colonel said. "Can't you see he's a cripple?"

"Sir, he's a bad one. Look at his face."

But the colonel repeated, "Turn him loose," and told his driver to get going.

When the automobile was out of sight, the lieutenant turned around. "All right, Mehmet. Take off." Kenan hesitated. The lieutenant waved his pistol. "Go on. Run."

But as Kenan ran, the lieutenant fired. The first shot missed. The second bit into his right leg, somewhere below the knee. Pounding the muddy cobblestones, his foot came apart, splintered red screaming pulp on the hard, slippery cobblestones. He fell down, scrambled up and fell down again. And, with the wings of Gabriel beating against his shoulders and the breath of God scorching his skull, he pulled himself up and ran again.

At dusk a maid came upstairs to wake George. The guests were beginning to arrive. Below the stairs there was a clatter

31

of crockery and silverware, the creaking of cupboard doors and Polixeni's irritable voice: "I should think on a night like this, with guns going off and people lying dead in the streets . . ."

George lay with his eyes closed, thinking about the immutable, inescapable Thursday-night *soirées* that his mother had imposed upon the Greeks of Smyrna with the sublime rigidity of a holy calendar. If Doomsday should fall on a Thursday, it would have to be postponed until after midnight, because Thursday evenings belonged eternally to Sophia Trigonis. The landing of an expeditionary army, a gunfight at Konak Square and the imprisonment of several hundred rioters were only preliminaries to another festive gathering *chez Sophia*. All her friends would be there—the Baltazzis, the Photiadis, the Pestimazioglous—glowing with the excitement of the new adventure, slapping George on the back and shouting, "Hey, I bet you're ready to take a crack at the old Turks!" And George would respond, as usual, "Oh, sure . . ." He would bob his head respectfully, swallowing his soul, muting his heart and mouthing that pusillanimous, choked-up murmur of agreement, "Oh, sure. . . ."

It was one of the disadvantages of being large and sturdy that everyone expected you to have the emotions of a gladiator. If a boy was small, he was allowed to daydream and bounce a ball in the garden. But a strapping boy was expected to own a fighting camel, hunt wild boars and wrestle Turkish-style. He was expected to enjoy such volumes as *A Pictorial Account of the Macedonian Tangle, by a Neutral Observer,* which George's father had bought on the assumption that case histories of atrocities and photographs of corpses would give any large boy a patriotic zest for battle. A large boy was expected to yearn for dangerous adventures and primitive violence. George, who was not only large but also dutiful, did his best to live up to expectations.

A footstep on the stairs aroused him. He swung his feet off the bed and sat up. If his father were to come in and find him lying on the bed with his eyes closed, there would be the devil's scene: elaborate surprise, mock scolding and, finally, a series of aggrieved questions, insinuating that George was trying, for some vaguely discreditable reason, to avoid the invigorating masculine companionship that awaited him downstairs. And perhaps it was true. Certainly George had been trying all day to avoid the invigorating masculine companionship of his father. Early in the afternoon, he had slipped out and walked all the way to Mount Pagus, keeping to back streets and taking the Buja Road to skirt the Moslem neighborhoods. On the way, he had counted five shops and a warehouse that had been broken open and looted. When he reached the stone revetments of the citadel, which the Turks call Kadife Kalesi, the Velvet Castle, he had seen a platoon of soldiers lolling by the empty cisterns. An infantry patrol came in. Somebody shouted, "Paleologos," which seemed to be a password; and a man who was lying near the cistern, eating bread and cheese, glanced up and answered, yawning, "Constantinople!" And the soldiers rolled on the grass like puppies.

George had concluded that the occupation was making a bad start. While he was sitting on the edge of his bed, however, his father came in and told him the occupation had made a superb start; and George knew it would be another of those evenings of back-slapping and hypocrisy. As he went downstairs, with his new collar scraping his neck and his hands in white gloves, he could hear the self-assured rumbling of new arrivals: "Christ is risen!" "Truly risen!" "The old Turk has been knocked on his heels."

George waited on the landing until the men had gone into the reception room. Then he went slowly down to the foyer and peeked between the velvet drapes into the drawing

33

room, where some women were practicing the tango. In the music room, the familiar widows in their weeds were nodding on a row of walnut chairs. A girl in yellow organdy—one of the Baltazzis?—was playing "Für Elise." The younger children were chasing a kitten around the room.

A few years ago, George had considered the amusements of women and children absurdly trivial: parlor games, fortune-telling, gramophone disks from Europe, piano recitals, plates of chocolates and honey pastries—an endless waste of time. He had regretted all his boyhood years among those effeminate pleasures, which formed a fragile outer shell around the real, adult society of men. An eternity of boredom passed before he was old enough to be admitted to his father's reception room, where men smoked the narghile and lay like Bedouin on camel-skin pillows. But what had he discovered there? The very matrix of boredom. An inexhaustible laboratory of dull and meaningless conversations, punctuated by huge puffs of nauseating tobacco smoke and bursts of heavy laughter. False heartiness, feigned curiosity, superficial robustness of manner and tongues that babbled what their ears wanted to hear.

From outside the reception room, he could hear two melon farmers from Akhisar, old friends of his father, boasting about their adventures killing wolves. Professor Paleologos was tediously describing the maneuvers of Themistocles; and someone else was raving about the quality of Karaburun sultanas. All of them whipped their heads around joyfully to welcome a new diversion.

"Ah, George! Are you ready now to take a crack at the old Turks?"

And George, feeling a surge of hot blood burning in his temples, wondered if anyone knew how often his father had challenged him with those words. Did they know what came next: the detailed criticism of his poor marksmanship, his lack

34

of interest in firearms, his sluggish Asiatic tastes? George bobbed his head, swallowed his soul, muted his heart and said: "Oh, sure . . ."

"Why, of course!" his father cried. "Every Greek is ready to serve his country." Christos stretched out his hand and took an olive. "Everyone knows we'll have to control the inland valleys to protect the city. It may require a few months of martial law in certain places."

The olives went around. Knuckles drummed punctuation marks on the scalloped edges of the coffee tray. Statesmen of the raisin bourse expatiated on grand designs of military strategy. Under the curtains seeped the pounding of the gramophone; and George could hear his mother calling out directions for the tango. His father began a disquisition on the economic history of Asia Minor, going back to the time of the Amazons and mentioning the Lydians, the Seljuk Turks and the Knights of St. John of Jerusalem. The burden of it was that Asia Minor was a single state, an economic unit. In accepting a mandate to govern the city of Smyrna, the Greeks had taken clear title to the agricultural hinterland, despite the large number of Turks now living there.

George stirred with uneasiness. To him it was obvious that the Turks would resist. Yet the Greek troops appeared to regard the occupation as a holiday. What good were those soldiers loafing around the cisterns on Mount Pagus? How could they secure the New Ionia, picnicking on a mountainside? He was at the point of raising the question when his father put up one hand and solemnly uttered the words "Smyrna Legion!"

Ah, yes. That was it. Everyone rocked back and slapped his thigh. They themselves, the Greeks of Asia Minor, must form a holy army of liberation! A brilliant proposition. Christos acknowledged modestly that it was not his idea alone; Chrysostomos, the Metropolitan of Smyrna, also endorsed the pro-

35

ject. No one would be too old or too young to join the saintly band. To wear its uniform would be the crowning achievement of his own life. And as for his son—

But the recruitment of volunteers was interrupted by the arrival at the outer door of Lieutenant Dimitris Kalapothakis, the Athenian officer who had come to see Eleni. Papa went to meet him, and their voices echoed in the foyer: "Rioting . . . Curfew . . . Thankful to be alive."

Then the lieutenant came into the reception room and shook hands all around, in the manner of the English. The old men stared at him in dumb admiration—they who had once been young and virile, too—and young boys from the children's party crowded the doorway, pink-cheeked with excitement. It was not merely that Dimitris Kalapothakis was handsome, but that he also had the unmistakable aura of a hero. He looked crisp and golden, as though he had been baked like a loaf of bread in a clean, new oven. George took in the silky mustache, the gleaming eye, the curl of black hair, the row of shining teeth, and turned away, stabbed with envy. This was the sort of man he should have been himself: the *real* incarnation of St. George. In the moment of recognition, George worshiped and hated Dimitris, not for his looks but for his ease, his confidence and the uncomplicated courage of his bearing.

Everybody wanted to hear about the landing; but Dimitris said there was nothing more to worry about. He had been on the scene himself. The army was in full control. A battalion was holding Basmahane Station. Another had sequestered the Cathedral of St. Photini; a third the Evangelical School; and a fourth the Shevket barracks. Guards were posted now in every neighborhood—Kokarli Yali, Karatina, Alsanjak. (This last Dimitris called "La Punta," in the fashion of the Catholic Levantines, but no one corrected him.) Advance patrols had gone out to secure St. Kyriaki, Tria Pighadhia,

Cordelio, Göz Tepe and the road to Bornova. Soldiers were quartered everywhere: in the Giorgiadis Warehouse, in the churches, even in the sheds of the Tobacco Régie along the Aydin railway tracks.

"So we really surprised the old Turks," Papa said with satisfaction. "Thank God for fine soldiers like this!" He lifted his glass to Dimitris, who looked down smiling. Someone had brought in a flask of raki, and Dimitris was dribbling water into his glass, rotating the stem between his fingers as the liquor turned white.

"We ran into a little trouble at the Konak," he said. George got the idea that "we" meant "I," but Dimitris was self-effacing. "Some Turkish hotheads got together last night and broke into the powder magazine, and they more or less attacked us from ambush." He touched the glass of raki to his lips, breathed the fumes and then swallowed the liquor at a gulp. "My men were absolutely magnificent. I've never seen Greek soldiers so calm." Leaning back, radiant in his self-assurance, he watched Christos refill the glass. "We had to deploy, you see? To search the hotels around the Square. It required what you might call independent initiative to spread out that way, because the staff officers hadn't foreseen this situation. But the commanding officer agreed that it was a devil of a good thing we scattered. We caught one old Turk who was packing an arsenal."

George moved closer. "What did you do to him? I mean the Turk."

Dimitris laughed. "Well, that's one Turk who won't be picking on any more Greeks."

"You killed him?" George said. He noticed his father squirming restlessly.

"Never mind," Christos muttered, for he had always resisted talk of bloodshed in his home. Reaching over, he gently slapped George on the shoulders, like a hunting dog brought

37

out for display. "Well, now!" he said. "What do you think of this big fellow?"

Dimitris cocked his head. "How old are you?" he said.

Again, George felt a rush of blood throbbing in his face.

"I'm almost seventeen."

"Old enough to get in and help us," Dimitris said. "You know, there's nothing to keep you from enlisting in the army, now that you're out from under the Turkish rule?"

"Why, that's right," George said. "I certainly would like to do that." He stared back without blinking. But from the mocking glitter in the lieutenant's eyes, he recognized an acute and cynical critic. Although George might fool his father and a handful of melon farmers from Akhisar, Dimitris obviously knew that he was lying.

This insight, although it amused Dimitris, did not lessen his generally favorable impression of the Trigonis family and their style of life. The entire party was invited to sit down to a French supper after midnight, sixteen at a table, in the dining room and drawing room. After an instant of portentous silence, during which all the raisin brokers and their ugly wives, with their eyes protruding greedily, hovered like gulls above the cold buffet, everyone pounced on the food with glad little cries, gasps and squeals and elbow nudges, handing dishes around and passing back empty platters to the maids, who ran up and down with long strands of hair flying loose at their temples.

There were slabs of dried beef spiced with garlic, lumps of pickled roe in wax, hard cheeses spread with olive oil and soft cheeses sprinkled with red pepper, minced-meat tarts, black olives, cucumbers and melons, plates of dried bonito, sliced hams, vegetables in oil and vine leaves stuffed with rice and currants. The French element consisted of a huge

38

crock of liver paste with truffles, which most of the company considered an abomination.

Tear-stained children gobbled pilaf in the music room, old women gummed shreds of slobbery pink mutton in the pantry. There were even some tables in the foyer, where a group of good-tempered cousins who had come all the way from the farm at Vourla sat gleefully among the hunting trophies and the family portraits, wolfing down great platters of tomatoes, cold boiled shrimp and mussels stuffed with rice.

As for Dimitris, he was placed at the host's table, next to old man Trigonis, surrounded by clouds of sweet-smelling tobacco smoke, mounds of coral-colored shellfish and jugs of purple claret.

The old man seemed to take to him. He poured glass after glass of wine, offered cigarettes and tore off pieces of the loaf, which he shoved insistently across the tablecloth, blinking through his lavender glasses. The mother, a bubble-head with maroon hair, seemed delighted to find a soldier from Old Greece who would listen to her endless catalogue of remarkable similarities between Smyrna and Paris; and that great, hulking George, who always looked as if he were about to burst into tears, obviously was dazzled by the sight of a uniform. Dimitris loved all of them, right down to the last drachma.

In fact, the only one he would have changed was the girl. She was unalterably, undeniably plain, although it was fairly difficult to appraise her in that barbaric disguise. She had darkened her eyelids with kohl, piled up her hair in an ebony knot and put on long garnet earrings, which lashed at her throat when she moved her head; and her face was spread with talcum powder. Just below her eye, she had made a tiny mark of beauty with a pip of antimony paste, and then rubbed in a crimson spot of cochineal. It was not a vision to set your guts aflame; and to make it worse, under that layer of talcum powder, speckled with tincture of gallarium, she was as haughty as the whore of Corinth.

Every time Dimitris tried to catch her eye, she would give her attention to a fat, excitable old man who was disclaiming on the perils of the Greek position while stuffing himself like a python.

"Our government depends entirely too much on the good will of England." And the old man paused, pink-eyed and panting, to salt a plate of cucumbers. "It's a grave mistake. The Turks, on the other hand,"—he raised a dish to smell the pickled aubergines—"have no friends at all. None. None in Europe. None in Asia. None in America. As a result"—he helped himself to garlic sauce—"they are free to play their old diplomatic game of setting foreign powers against one another. The Turks can dangle themselves, so to speak, before the French, the Italians, the Russian Bolsheviks—in other words, any nation that is not completely satisfied with the rewards of the war. And one or all of these great Christian nations may be only too happy to help the poor old Turk slip off the English hook"—and he nipped off the tail of a prawn with a snap of his yellow incisors—"in return for concessions that rightfully should go to *us.*"

Dimitris leaned forward to command the old man's attention. In competition with the shellfish, the smoke and the crossfire of loud conversation, he had to repeat "Sir?" several times. He noticed that it was the girl who turned and looked at him, long before the old man raised his pink-rimmed eyes.

"Sir, do you think it would have been any better if we had stayed neutral, as the King wanted?" Dimitris was pleased at the sound of his voice, which was as strong and clear as a peddler's horn. After the scare the Turk had given him that morning, he was afraid he might never be able to speak again without quavering like a goat. The old man peered at him shrewdly, anticipating the argument that lay behind the question. "Of course not, as things turned out, who can argue with a winning number?"

"Then you agree Venizelos was right to bring us into the war on the side of England?" Dimitris said. "To win us a seat at the peace conference?"

"I am only saying that it's foolish to tie all your donkeys on one piece of rope. This is a hazardous adventure, reaching out to reclaim an empire, and we are relying too much on the support of England. What if the English change their minds?"

But Dimitris, having attracted Eleni's attention, was no longer interested in pursuing the conversation. "If that happens, we'll just have to take care of the Turks all by ourselves," he said. "The way we did today." Turning, he creased his mouth into a polite smile. "Did you watch the landing, Miss Trigonis? It was magnificent. Truly, the Resurrection! My company was on the *Patris*, with the regiment of evzone guards. And when we came to that little platform with the palm fronds—in front of the Kraemer Hotel?—the commander jumped ashore and the Metropolitan embraced him like a son. He knelt on the pavement and kissed the soil of Asia Minor. Then the priests began to sing. 'The universe regains its liberty. The men submerged in darkness become the sons of light. . . . The host of nations, yesterday in misery, sings today the hymns of grace. . . .' "

"I didn't see it," Eleni said.

"Oh, of course you did!" old man Trigonis cried. "It was inspiring, inspiring." He pressed his hand on his heart. "It stirred me so deeply—I've composed the most impressive speech of my career. I felt like an amanuensis for the very *soul* of Greece." In the course of the day, it appeared, he had written a Pindaric ode in the ancient language, a French *ïambe* in the manner of André Chénier and a panegyric in English, beginning, "Venizelos, what a thrill! Thy name rhap-

41

sodic'ly we trill!" Freshets of poetic language had boiled from his chest; an inflammation, like the heat of a divine afflatus, had seared him, consumed him—Homeric!

"What an un*us*ual rain!" the mother interrupted, twisting her fingers in her burgundy curls. "I never *saw* such a heavy rain this time of year. Do you think it's a good omen?" And she plied Dimitris with garlic sauce. "Tell me, Lieutenant? What do you think of Smyrna? Does it surprise you?" Dimitris said yes, it surprised him. "And doesn't it surprise you to find us so cosmopolitan? The Dutch, the French, the English? Some of these foreign families have lived here for a century or two. Have you seen the Agora?"

"Oh, Mama! Of course not," Eleni said. "How long do you think he has been here?"

The mother giggled stupidly. Suddenly inspired, she snatched up a dish of sugary brown globules and thrust it under Dimitris' nose. "Why don't you eat any of these *marrons glacés?* They're from Lyons—*bien choisis.* I've never tasted anything so delicate, *jamais rien!*" The poor woman was relentlessly *gallicée*—one of those fresh-water Franks who never leave the East but like to scatter copies of the *Messager d'Athènes* and the *Revue des Deux Mondes* around the drawing room and force their guests to drink vermouth —and she was determined her daughter should behave like a heroine in Maupassant. "Eleni? Why don't you play for us? *Un soupçon de Saint-Saëns.* That piece about the swan— *C'est tellement mignon!*"

But Eleni had withdrawn her attention again. She sat close to the table, scowling, with her fingers knotted together in her lap. Her mother tapped her on the wrist. *"Attention, chérie!* Play something for the lieutenant."

"Oh, anything," Dimitris said. "Something lively. Do you know any marches?"

"I only play waltzes and mazurkas," Eleni said. But her mother hustled her out of the room. With eyes straight ahead, she led Dimitris across the foyer, past a nude statue of Hermes and a ludicrous portrait of old man Trigonis dressed up as a bandit. The empty music room was strewn with greasy plates and crumpled napkins and blazing with the light of a dozen gas jets in amber lotus cups. The gas made a gentle hissing sound and filled the room with heat. A fortune in silver tobacco boxes, wedding crowns and pewter raki bottles glittered on the blue glass shelves of the knick-knack; an arsenal of yataghans and powder horns dangled on the walls; and the carpets sank underfoot like meadow grass.

Eleni spread her skirts on the piano bench and struck a resounding chord. "Do you know this one, Mr. Kalapothaki?" Her tone was that of a teacher catechizing a pupil.

Dimitris did not know it. It sounded to him like something that might have been made up by a shepherd to entertain a goat. He went and stood behind her, resting his knee on the bench, in the folds of her skirt, and reached over her shoulder to poke at the keys with one finger, singing:

> "Oh, the Greeks who go to Russia
> To chase the ruddy Bolsies,
> The girls run out to meet them,
> And shower them with posies."

He put his jaw near her cheek, so that she would be able to feel the warmth of his breath on her skin; but Eleni seemed oblivious to this endearment. She picked out the tune once, slowly, then played it through with a firm military beat.

> "And ask them where they're going
> On the road that lies before them,
> Since they seem so young and reckless—
> Snows and guns do not confound them.
> And the soldiers answer bravely,
> Their hearts with courage burning,
> ' The road we take from Russia
> Leads our footsteps straight to Smyrna!' "

43

"I don't see what Russia has to do with it," Eleni said.

"It's a song we made up in our regiment when they sent us to help General Wrangel's army."

Eleni studied him with her strange, almost masculine directness. "Did you help them?"

"With a few more like us, we could have saved the Petrograd government," Dimitris said. "But Wrangel's troops were unreliable." He noticed that the door had swung shut. This intimate situation obviously had been contrived with the complicity of the girl's own mother. For an instant, his mind was afire with fantasies of sexuality, the famous voluptuousness of Asiatic women. Then he remembered what a romantic, provincial matron Mrs. Trigonis was. Imagining herself "broad-minded," "modern" and "Continental," she was exactly the sort of mother who would close the door and hide behind the velvet draperies to protect her daughter's hymen from the Army of Occupation. Furthermore, there was nothing sensuous about the girl. She looked at him squarely and said: "I read your letter to my father, in which you asked permission to court me."

Dimitris tightened the corners of his mouth to suppress a smile. He gazed back at her, trying to give his eyes a shy, respectful quality. In fact, he could not think of anything to say. But Eleni was waiting, so he asked: "Have you decided to allow it?"

She gave her head a little tilt—more of a Turkish nod than anything else. Her ridiculous garnet earrings flailed around, glittering like drops of blood.

"I am delighted," Dimitris said, feeling a great bubble of laughter struggling around in his chest. "When shall I begin?"

"I think it would be sensible for you to call on me several times so we can get acquainted. Will you be stationed in Smyrna?"

"God willing."

"My father will see to it that you are stationed in Smyrna."

Dimitris had the impression that he was now expected to bow out of the room. In a flash of mischievous inspiration, he seized Eleni's hand and pressed it to his forehead, Turkish fashion. She permitted him to hold her fingers longer than he had expected. He stroked their soft warmth with the edge of his thumb and rubbed them gently across his forehead. To keep from laughing, he inhaled long, quivering breaths through his nostrils. Eleni quickly withdrew her hand.

"You don't need to think you've won me just by writing a letter." And she went out, brooches and earrings flashing and hips swaying, while Dimitris grinned at the back of her head. Jesus and Mary, what a puffed-up little partridge! The thought of stripping off her feathers made his mouth fill with water.

He went out into the moist, brooding night with his chest so bubbly it almost tipped him upside down. He kicked the spokes of carriages as he went past and pissed against a wrought-iron gate a few doors down the Quay.

The last to leave, to no one's surprise, was Professor Paleologos, puffy-eyed and red in the face from gorging prawns and shouting down the other guests. He loitered in the foyer, fussing with his coat and complaining about English imperialism, American idealism and French duplicity. Christos finally edged him to the door and down the marble steps.

It was long past midnight. Christos was longing for privacy to talk with his wife and children. He had sensed in George tonight a kindling of the patriotic fire that Christos had been trying for more than a decade to ignite; and he did not want it to flicker out for lack of encouragement. From Eleni, he hoped to receive an endorsement of young Kalapothakis,

45

who struck him as the most promising marital candidate ever to enter the house.

By the time Christos had gotten rid of the professor, however, Eleni had gone upstairs, complaining of a headache; Sophia was asleep; and George, as usual, had made himself scarce. Christos prowled through the dining room, eating olives and spitting the pits into his fist. In search of companionship, he went out to talk with the Cretan guard, who stood at the garden gate dressed in a turban, bandoleers and coal-black breeches.

Like Christos, the doorman was reluctant to relax until he had extracted every advantage from this triumphant night. He gladly took Christos around to inspect the cast-iron shutters, the fence and the back wall, which was topped with bits of broken glass. After they had assured themselves that no looters could invade the house, they stood together on the front step, breathing the moist air from the Aegean. The signal lights of a Greek destroyer were winking across the greasy tide pool; a filigree of water lay among the cobblestones, reflecting the misty stars; and frogs were groaning in the garden. On such a night, sleep was superfluous, if not impossible. It was the night for which they had prayed in fear and expectation; and it should not be wasted.

Christos reminded the doorman of the importance of the occasion; and the doorman, whose island breed was never skilled at flattery, said gravely: "I suppose it is thanks to men like yourself?"

Christos was willing to accept this as a compliment, because he knew a compliment was deserved. Once every week throughout the war, he had put on a frock coat and fez, swallowed his leaping heart and paid a call on the Turkish vali. As an Elder of the Greek community of Smyrna, he had a duty to present petitions from his people to the local governor; but it was not a pleasant occupation. The Turkish government considered the Greeks only slightly less traitorous than the Armenians, and Constantinople was constantly projecting schemes to relocate Greek villages, incarcerate Greek leaders and expropriate Greek properties.

And, once every week, in spite of vigorous measures of security, Christos would leave the Konak with a stolen list of Christians impressed into work battalions, coastal villages transplanted inland, rapes and robberies attributed to Moslems. Each month, he would multiply the current total by ten to allow for oversights and by ten again to allow for foreign skepticism and would dispatch the adjusted statistics to the Metropolitan of Smyrna, who would multiply again by ten to allow for Turkish perfidy.

From this degraded espionage to the moment of victory had taken only a few months' time. During the transition, many new patriots had appeared among the Greeks of Smyrna. Christos regarded them with the contempt of a pioneer for a late convert. After all, he had given the best years of his life to his nation. Not *all* the years of his life, admittedly; but who can guide his own destiny?

In truth, the entire Greek nation, diffused, submerged and unenlightened, had muddled for a century among diversions and false paths, unable to perceive the Greek Idea of national rejuvenation. The confusion was understandable. Even Christos himself had once imagined that there could be no future for the Greek people except as a dispersed internation, like the Jews.

That had been long ago, of course, when he was only an awkward boy. He lived in those days in an old, unpainted mansion on a hillside in Psamatia, which overlooks the Sea of Marmara. Like many other Christian youngsters of Constantinople, he was training for the civil service. He used to get up very early, while the sea was as gray as marble, and walk to the Greek commercial school through alleys that were ringing to the round brass cups of milkmen and the cries of servants throwing back the shutters and flinging quilts across the windowsills.

He always wore a well-brushed fez, a necktie and a clean collar; and, as he walked, he clasped his hands behind his back and thumbed an amber rosary. Halfway to school, he would stop and buy a sesame ring from a blinded Turk, who held out a long stick with circles of bread hung along it like bracelets on an emaciated arm.

In that city, in that time (it was late in the '70s of the nineteenth century), Christos could not have imagined any sort of life other than a sprightly rivalry of races. The streets were jammed with frenzied little Jews who carried panniers of animal droppings on their shoulders, Greek boys with trays of unbaked yeast rolls on their heads, adolescent Turks in circumcision crowns and Kurdish porters with pianos on their backs. It was unthinkable to dream about a world without such manifest diversity or an empire without the gloomy, bumbling Moslems in command. Political freedom was an unknown concept. Christos lived without it as happily as he lived without such nonexisting luxuries as an automobile. As a Greek, he was proud to be more scrupulous than an Armenian, more polished than a Kurd, more diligent than an Albanian, more stable than an Arab, smarter than a Bosnian and cleaner, *far* cleaner, than a Bulgarian; but he left the deeper yearnings of national culture to the parish priest.

He might have lived out his life at peace with this medieval Oriental polity, which had endured so long and which accorded so well with the nature of the Ottoman dominions, had he not fallen in love. It happened to him on a Sunday afternoon when he was almost seventeen—just George's age —in the seaside village of San Stefano. He was walking along an avenue of plane trees, when suddenly a white pigeon fluttered out and settled at his feet. He heard a cry, turned and saw a young girl peering through a wrought-iron fence. She was unveiled, bareheaded and dressed in a spotless white chemise that stood out from her body like the plumage of a swan.

Christos easily caught the pigeon. But when he put it through the metal bars, the girl deliberately let it go. She fixed him with a look of such intensity that he began to tremble in a confusion of apprehension and modesty. He dared to ask her name: her name was Mignonette.

Mignonette! A lovely flower! He detected the fragrance of her skin—a soft, waxy emanation, like the scent of lemon blossoms. Inhaling deeply, he pressed himself against the iron bars. The girl drew closer. Their bodies were together, and his nostrils touched her hair. To his astonishment, she let him put his arm around her waist. His hands slipped down her hips; his mouth was pressed against her forehead; and she began to rub herself against him, slowly, deliberately, with an incredible lubricity: catlike, up and down, until a spasm of delight began to paralyze his legs. With every movement of her body, it constricted more deliciously around his loins until it rose seething, bursting, pulsing through his veins like seltzer water. He fell to one side, gasping against her temple, clutching at the bars that separated them; and Mignonette broke away and disappeared among the laurel bushes, laughing at him. Christos went home slowly, past Seven Towers and through the mustard fields, burning with excitement and humiliation.

Nothing had prepared him for this terrible eruption of desire. At the grammar school of the Phanar, sin had been denounced in general. Students were expected to fill in details by watching animals as farm boys do, or from the usual carnal intimacies of schoolboys. His father, who was often away in Europe, had been too busy to instruct him.

Night after night, Christos suffered excruciating dreams in

which the girl became an animal, a giant pigeon, smothering him in her feathers, hungrily engulfing, moistening, attenuating, hardening the aching pivot of his groin; and he would wake up, damp and swollen, shuddering with rapturous pulsations like electric shocks. He imagined that the winter wind from Africa was causing these pollutions. He took cold baths and lighted candles to the Virgin.

It would be impossible, of course, to meet the girl again without her parents' invitation. In those days, women of every race kept to their homes in imitation of the Turkish Moslem women, who never ventured out unless completely hooded, veiled and wrapped in colored sheets. He consulted a famous matchmaker named Granny Black; but the old woman laughed when she heard the conditions. That was worse than sending a gypsy to buy yeast! So Christos wrote a letter himself, in barbaric French, addressing it to "The Honorable Parent of Miss Mignonette." Within a day, a messenger brought him an answer. The girl in question was not half so rich as certain people imagined. It would be necessary to discuss important questions of religious nationality and property.

Christos took the letter to his father, whose neck turned red with fury.

"You might as well have asked to marry a Turk!" his father said. He threw the letter on the floor. "You know we don't marry such people! Have you no perception what it means to be a Greek?"

Mignonette, it seemed, was a Gregorian Armenian, the ward of a banker named Bogosian, whose children she was tutoring. Her guardian was rich and probably would dower her adequately. But for a Greek to marry her? Unthinkable.

Christos stood kneading his hands and watching his father pace back and forth. Darkness was falling, and a bluish mist stood at the windowpanes. A can of charcoal had been lighted in the brazier. Its sour, carbonic odor filled the room. There were accusations and denials. His father called him an ungrateful libertine. Christos shouted back recklessly. What difference did it make that he was a Greek? That was an accident of birth. What did it mean to him—this Greek community, this Greek religion, this Greek language? He would give up all of it to marry Mignonette.

Suddenly his father calmed, put out his hands and said that he would not oppose the marriage if the girl became a Christian—that is, Greek Orthodox. They wrote a letter to Bogosian. For three weeks there was no reply. Then came a note. Without explanation, Bogosian ended the negotiations.

Christos galloped to San Stefano; but the iron gate was locked. For the price of a glass of mastic, the gardener put down his trowel and said with a rough laugh: "Well, you won't be seeing *her* again."

Bogosian had decided to give her to a Turk, the son of a pasha who was in favor with Sultan Abdul Hamit. It was considered a cunning match. The Turk had pledged himself to take no other wives, and a vulnerable priest had promised that the girl would be allowed the sacraments of her religion. Under the Moslem law, her marriage portion was to be inalienable.

The next day, Christos heard that the *bedel,* the special head tax that non-Moslems paid instead of giving military service, was to be increased. Greeks were being squeezed inexorably from the civil service. It was impossible to buy the meanest position in a clerical department for less than two hundred pounds.

Christos stopped going to school. A single resolution dominated his mind: to leave the Empire. He borrowed money from his sister, pestered the clerks of foreign chancelleries, begged help from total strangers in the offices of banks and shipping lines. In his haste, he snatched at the first commission work he heard of, peddling English yarn along the Black Sea littoral. As his steamer left the Bosphorus, he looked back and spat in the direction of the Giant's Mountain.

In Eupatoria he bathed among the Jews in tubs of boiling mud. He drank with Russian sailors in the pot shops of Sevastopol. He sailed to Bessarabia and Bulgaria and down the craggy coast of Georgia, filling his purse with double-eagle shillings, imperial rubles and Venetian sequins dug from pouches in the folds of feather mattresses. Housewives in Odessa bought his spools of boilfast cotton; whores in Varna knew his sudden moods of scalding passion; and tavern keepers in Constantsa sold him cherry brandy to soothe his lonely tears.

Often, as Christos traveled down the coasts from Scythia to Aden, he would meet a look of recognition and a smile of brotherhood, and someone would speak to him in Greek. In this way he learned that he was following the highroads of a vast, submerged Hellenic empire, with frontiers in Kiev, Batum and Port Said. He came to know all the provinces and circumstances of this Diaspora: the boisterous Greeks of the Dobruja, the sophisticated Greeks of Bucharest, the Russified Greeks of the Volga, the Italianate Greeks of the Dodecanese, the grasping Greeks of Syria, the bland, disdainful Greeks of Alexandria, with faces like halvah.

They really did not have much in common, the scattered Greeks of this sequestered realm. They did not preserve the tongue of Homer; they spoke Italian, Russian, French or Arabic—whatever language happened to be used in trade. They did not profess a secret allegiance to the King of Greece and his weak, erratic little state at the bottom of the Balkans; they tried to escape his agents and evade his taxes. They did not gather in European spas, Armenian fashion, to brood and shout and pass inflammatory resolutions demanding national independence; they carried multiple passports and specialized in changing currency.

If there was any common property within the Greek Diaspora, it was the memory of the purloined cathedral, the Basilica of Holy Wisdom, known to the world as St. Sophia, which the Emperor Justinian had built at the crown of the unforgettable city to dazzle the detractors of Byzantium: such a church as had not been since Adam and would never be again. That memory they shared, along with a universal impulse to make money. If there was any sense of nationality in the Diaspora, it was seen primarily as a tool of trade. Fraternity, clan spirit and religious fanaticism were credit balances in a sturdy, international bank. A clever Greek could draw upon them as he moved around the world, transported by a wave of fellowship along a chain of cousins.

Traveling the Diaspora, Christos would hold his head cocked to detect the lisping rattle of Greek speech. His nostrils flared to catch the incense of Greek churches. As he entered an unfamiliar city, he could tell immediately whether Greeks were living there. He could identify a fellow Greek in a fur greatcoat, a guardsman's vest or a burnoose at the public bath. Although the man might be carrying a British passport he had picked up in Cyprus, and Christos professed to be a subject of the Tsar, they both would cross themselves conspicuously, swear on the Virgin of Tenos and sell their goods at discount to the subjects of the hidden empire.

"Your race is like a master key," a shopkeeper once said to Christos. "Use it to get inside the door; there are few enough openings in the world."

Christos had no complaints. Many times a year he sold the total daily output of the mills of Lancaster. His commission list stretched from the Fish to the Moon. He was richer than Prince Ypsilanti. His belly grew and his hair did not; but he enjoyed the brotherhood of the Diaspora; and the sisterhood

53

of the barbarian world, which he sampled like little plates of spiced hors d'oeuvres. There was a Jewish girl, immense and blonder than a Swede, in Odessa; a Rumanian of Jassy, with the soft, strong, soapy-smelling fingers of a bathhouse operator; and a little Coptic dwarf, as hairy as an ape, whose father owned a swath of Cairo from the Nile to the Mokattam Hills. Unwed, Christos passed his thirty-seventh birthday impaling a twitching Arabian bawd in Latakia. His thirty-eighth birthday differed only circumstantially: the woman was Maltese.

Only once did he feel the centrifugal magnetism of the heartland. That was in 1897, when Greece went to war against the Turkish Empire. Ethnic societies formed in the cities of the Greek Dispersal. In Bucharest, a horde of weeping clerks and grocers gathered in a church and pledged themselves to fight in Thessaly among the legions of philhellene volunteers who were gathering with volumes of Byron and Thucydides in the pockets of their velvet jackets. Rash, romantic English boys came on holiday from Oxford. Redcoats of the Neapolitan Risorgimento, drugged with memories of Garibaldi, arrived in dusty caps and rusty boots. There were Greek bootblacks from New York, Greek cooks from Boston and Greek diamond thieves from Amsterdam.

The war lasted only thirty days. The terrified Hellenes scattered like flights of crows before the Turkish cavalry. The Bucharest brigade dissolved on the shore at Phaleron, and Christos was left in Athens, disheartened and unimpressed *pro patria.*

The city itself, this half-cooked Athens of the latter days, was perhaps his greatest disappointment. It had very little but its ancient reputation to commend it: a country town of plaster pediments and dusty pepper trees and roosters in the courtyards; an unimportant place, with an embarrassing light-opera quality about its uniforms and ministries, royal palaces and torchlight parades. Fifty or sixty years ago, it had

54

been nothing but a village of Albanian hovels and a provincial Turkish garrison among the pillars of the Parthenon; now it was a cardboard Munich, perennially short of water, that called itself the capital of Greece, the epicenter of the human mind and heart.

For Christos, the only entertainment was a nightly call at one of those pretentious mansions in the neighborhood of Kolonaki Square which trace their architectural ancestry to the topless towers of Ilium by way of Heinrich Schliemann's house on Panepistimiou Street. The Maison Villaras had Trojan spires and Persian windows, Doric columns and Gothic doors, and it was guarded by two hyperpygidial marble sphinxes with ruby eyes. You entered through a courtyard, paved with tile mosaics in the style of Delos; crossed a vestibule in which were mounted several neoclassic bronzes illustrating celebrated acts of rape by gods in the guise of animals; and waited for a servant to announce you in the drawing room of Mrs. Villara, who had been born a Mavrogordato, and whose sister Mrs. Sarrou was a widow with large, moist eyes and a sulky mouth, which she covered negligently, *à la Turque,* with the corner of her scarf.

From the instant of their meeting, Christos had recognized in Mrs. Sarrou one of those accommodating widows whose insatiable and perfumed secrecies are recommended in mature societies for the instruction of inquisitive young men. This discovery blurred his vision and stiffened his nostrils. Pressing Mrs. Sarrou's hand against his lips, he seemed to drown in clouds of musk and Burdur roses. The black lace of her kerchief cast a shadow on her cheek. She had a dainty little mole, a tiny olive tucked among the creases of her chin, and her hair, through some delightful artifice, appeared to be the color of sweet mavrodaphne wine.

Her hands were small and dimpled; the jet-black taffeta of her sleeves made them look as pale as ivory. Squeezing her fingertips, Christos let his mustache hover over her silky wrist; and, when he raised his head, he saw that she was studying his face with interest.

A voluptuous desire inflamed him. While he regaled the hostess with a flow of gossip from the coffeehouses, Christos tried to mesmerize her sister with erotic glances. But Mrs. Sarrou gave her attention to a Persian kitten on her lap. Christos could draw her notice only now and then, with a prolonged and languid glance, or with a gift of *babas au rhum*, nougat, candied almonds, colored marzipan. She had a prodigious appetite for European sweets.

He launched a cautious courtship, moderated by his long experience and by the eccentricity of Mrs. Sarrou's manners, which were alternately prudish and licentious. Sometimes, she would greet him with enthusiasm, smiling moistly, offering her exquisite hand. At other times, she stared at him remotely, without a sign of recognition. He was afraid that in her Olympian mood she would refuse him; and he was panic-stricken that in her torrid phase she might take on some panting, pubescent little satyr from the boys' lycée. Tormented by impatient longing, he would arrive each evening determined to impose himself upon her; but he would go no further than to kiss her hand, present his box of candy and rivet her from time to time with an imploring glare. No one ever had moved him to such adoration as did Mrs. Sarrou: not the tall, albino Jewess of Odessa, the stunted Copt of Cairo, the soapy Rumanian of Jassy; not even Mignonette, floating like a dove among the laurel bushes in San Stefano. Yet he could not bring himself to tell her this.

For one thing, Mrs. Villara was always present, gloating over stacks of English biscuits and Lenox teacups. And there were others—lawyers, archaeologists, English ladies with villas in Ekali and, on rare occasions, Mr. Villaras, who sold currants in Brussels and kept a Flemish mistress.

But it was not these witnesses that intimidated him; it was the long solitude and selfishness of his bachelorhood. His heart had slowly withered in detachment; he had almost lost the need of love; and he was terrified that love would destroy his freedom. He might have stewed indefinitely in this dilemma if Mrs. Sarrou had not turned to him one night in the midst of a general conversation about shellfish and whispered: "Let's get out of here."

They stopped in the loggia, face to face, next to "Zeus and Europa," and Christos, inhaling the delicate evanescence of her perfume, fumbled for Mrs. Sarrou's hand. It turned out, however, that Mrs. Sarrou wanted to get out of not only the drawing room, but also of Kolonaki, Athens, Attica, the Balkan Peninsula.

"You'll take me away with you?" And she gazed appreciatively at his shoulders, his mustache and his ears. Christos, pinned against the bronze bovine rump of Zeus, promised that he would.

Three days after the wedding they left for Egypt, and their first child, a girl, was born on St. Helen's Day in Alexandria. But the desert winds irritated Sophia's skin, the cotton trade was slow and Eleni was sickly; so they moved to Beirut to prepare for the boy, whose birth was heralded by such powerful and prophetic dreams. Later, they set up residence in Larnaca and Port Said, in Tripolis and Valetta; and Christos began for the first time to feel the weariness of exile. He daydreamed of settling down in Athens or even in Constantinople. Somehow, his longing was connected with his son: How could George, lacking a country, become a hero-saint?

It was on a return trip to Cyprus that Christos first heard the name of Venizelos, on the lips of a boatman rowing in to Famagusta. Surely everyone had heard of Eleftherios Venizelos? The leader of the revolt against the Turks in Crete? The boatman compared him to a salesman with the devil's charm:

he would take Greece as he had taken Crete, by forcing the kitchen door. "Then he mops the good woman's tears, makes her a cup of coffee, drinks it himself and gets into bed with her. A few moments later, she's moaning, 'Oh, my God! You're wonderful!' That's Venizelos!"

A week later, the Military League seized power in Athens and Venizelos got into bed. Five years after, when Christos stopped again in Athens, Venizelos had reorganized the Parliament, won two wars and doubled the extent of the kingdom. He had become the Balkan Bismarck, celebrated in the chancelleries of the European powers; and Christos knew him, as did all the Greeks of the Diaspora, as "the Cretan," the man you went to see in Athens to enhance your own prestige.

Europe had begun to shudder with precognition of the fatal war. The Greeks of the Diaspora, like derelicts rushing to the town square at a moment of excitement, were crowding to the Motherland; and the Prime Minister held massive daily audiences, as well attended as the levees of the Patriarch. Venizelos sat there in a corner of the office, which was congested with perspiring demarchs, nomarchs and ministers extraordinary, and stared serenely at some dust motes swirling through a beam of light. The shutters had been closed against the glare of sun and whitewash, but a resinous, dusty wind blew through the slats. Petitioners approached the desk, made jokes, smoked cigarettes and drained their coffee cups, while Venizelos, pondering secret thoughts, was gazing at the sparks of dust.

It was a scene, one might have said, from any tacky Balkan capital. Venizelos might as easily have been a Magyar count, a Turkish governor or a Phanariot hospodar. He seemed to lack the candor one expected of a mountain rebel. Far worse, he also lacked the grandeur of a European statesman. He had a peasant's features, warty and harsh, like the face of Lincoln.

Indoors, with a black skullcap covering his naked crown, he looked like a preoccupied, scholastic rabbi, peeking across the tops of steel-rimmed spectacles. His white beard trembled.

Christos looked around and regretted coming to this provincial court. It was demeaning to a man of his importance, who dealt with all the capitals of Europe. When Venizelos spoke, in a benign, pedantic voice, Christos could scarcely bear to listen. Venizelos droned on about the future of the country; Christos interrupted to boast about the eminence of Greeks *throughout the world.*

"The future of the Greeks, Your Honor, is to spread a network of Hellenic skills and culture into many lands."

"Do you really believe this?" Venizelos asked. Christos closed his mouth abruptly. For years he had believed, or had pretended to believe, in the evangelistic mission of the Greek Diaspora.

Suddenly, he knew his suppositions could not endure scrutiny. He heard himself saying: "Well, no . . . As a matter of fact—I don't." And then, with a swelling in his heart: "I actually have believed for many years that the destiny of Greece is to rebuild Byzantium."

He stared at Venizelos like a conspirator. The Prime Minister stared back with intense and concentrated interest. Christos felt a curious assault on his emotions. It was as if he, Christos, were a hypnotist, and Venizelos his victim. Christos knew that he had said nothing remarkable; yet Venizelos had made him feel unique—inflammatory, passionate, aglow with almost inexpressible ideals. At last he understood the secret of the Cretan's power, and he submitted to it with a sense of relief that was close to ecstasy.

"Why do we do this to ourselves?" Christos went on in a husky voice. "I haven't set foot in my city since I was a boy. I've traveled up and down the Straits, consuming myself with

59

jealousy and hatred for the Turks. But I have always turned my back on Constantinople, pretending I can live without the Red Apple that my soul is crying for."

His eyes began to water. The room dissolved. The crowd of demarchs, nomarchs and ministers extraordinary quietly disintegrated, and Christos entered the aloof, portentous zones of dreams where Venizelos lived. Venizelos smiled: an intimate communion.

"My friend, could you go back to Turkey now?"

"Under Turkish rule? Life for a Greek is unbearable."

"We must have more Greeks in Turkey."

"Why? To be massacred?"

But Venizelos gestured as if to brush away a fly. His mind was on the coming war, which would destroy the old, medieval empires and raise up martyr nations to subsume the ancient territories. The claims of Greece in Turkey would rest upon the number of Christian captives in a Moslem land.

"Soldiers are killed in wars," Venizelos said. He put out his hand to touch Christos on the arm. "You will be the plinth of our national shrine."

So Christos had come back to Smyrna, to begin a new life filled with joy. His duties to the Greek community proliferated like a coral. He translated passages from Byron to inspire the Christian spirit and made secret speeches on the Hellenic heritage to shivering schoolboys in the lecture halls of Greek gymnasia. He dashed off epic poetry, inspected hospitals, gave money for a gold-embroidered flag to be flown over the Turkish barracks on Liberation Day. The Greeks called him a Solon; the Turks detested him. He had achieved the ripeness of his life.

For several years, the actions of the government in Athens were a disappointment. King Constantine, professing neutrality, leaned to the German side. He refused to enter the war as an ally of France and England. Venizelos quarreled with the King, left office, was re-elected, resigned again and finally disappeared. Months after the event, the Greeks of Smyrna learned that he had gone north into Macedonia, to the city of Salonika, to organize a revolution. With the help of the French ambassador, he was successful. King Constantine fled. Greece joined the Grand Alliance.

By these uncertain steps, Christos and his country had arrived at this transcendent night, this ripple in the flood of time that marked the end and the beginning of their hopes, their fears.

CONSTANTINOPLE
JUNE, 1919

*O*n the first night of Sugar Bayram, the festival that ends the fast of Ramazan, Abdullah, the son of Hilmi Pasha, was wandering the alleys of Shehzade-bashi, searching for his youth.

Here in this pensive, untidy, thoroughly Turkish neighborhood, he had passed the swift years of his adolescence, insulated from the European affectations of the Christian quarter, yet stimulated by the flow of secular ideas from the university; and he loved these dark, old-fashioned houses and quiet, twisted streets with the passion of an exile for his childhood home. Shehzade-bashi was his Heidelberg, his Saint-Germain-des-Prés, the only place on earth in which he could regain his self-esteem.

The Turks of Shehzade-bashi had a sentimental fondness for display. In celebration of the holiday, the gardens gleamed with lanterns and the streets were lighted up with flares. Green banners, decorated with verses from the Holy Koran spelled out in brilliants, hung among the minarets. Smoke rose from hundreds of braziers where lamb kebabs were slowly turning, and hawkers wandered past, twirling strings of walnuts candied in grape juice. Doors stood open; windows were raised; and women leaned out like harlots on the sills, scarcely bothering to draw the corners of their scarves across their mouths.

The coffeehouses smelled of vaseline pomade, rose water and Samsun tobacco; and all the chairs were occupied by freshly shaved men, abstracted and reposeful, running their fingers thoughtfully around the neckbands of their shirts and frowning at the ground.

On nights like this during his student years, strolling from pharmacy to university, Abdullah would have stopped to take a slice of halvah and a glass of cool water with three or five other young scholars from the Aegean provinces, who always listened with respect to his opinions. Whispering like conspirators, they would lean their heads together while the table trembled under the pressure of their elbows. From time to time, Abdullah would look up and snap his fingers for another double-sweet, some mineral or a saucer of pistachios. Then, turning back, he would resume his exposition of Turanian prehistory or continue his analysis of Durkheim's treatise on the origins of primitive religion.

Fresh from the vineyards of Alashehir, he had all the intellectual arrogance of the young and guiltless. He lapped up ideas like cherry syrup—lectures at Hamdullah Subhi's Turkish Hearth, debates behind the bookstalls near the Mosque of Beyazit—and spewed them back, flavored with the saucy confidence of a pasha's younger son who had been assigned to reconstruct the world. He had opinions on horses, wrestlers, philosophy—everything. Surrounded by his coterie— Fuad, Rauf, Refet, Arif, God rest them!—he made boat trips on the Bosphorus, out to the Sweet Waters of Asia, arguing the nature of organic evolution. Together, they took long, contemplative walks through the cypress groves above Eyüp Sultan, where everyone would sit on fallen gravestones and discuss the moral implications of the Fox Trot. Their minds were afire with social progress, constitutional reform, Comte and Rousseau; and they gave their hearts to Enver Pasha and the Ittihat ve Tarrakki, which Europeans called the "Young

Turk" movement. Abdullah wore a white fez to show the Austrians (who made red fezzes) that they would never be allowed to impose their rule on the Sanjak of Novi-Bazar. His favorite words were "constitutional" and "national sovereignty" and "representative institutions."

The center of that abundant life, so rich in hope and inspiration, had been a certain coffeehouse on the ridge behind the mosque. It occupied a corner where the street was squeezed between the pillars of a Roman aqueduct. Strands of ivy wilted over the decaying stones, and the coffeehouse was draped in foliage. Approaching that unpainted wooden shed, nestled among the ruins of Byzantium, Abdullah felt his heart float upward on a flood of memories—moist tabletops and drafty corridors, thin soup, stale bread and the smell of coal-oil lamps on winter nights. Was it possible that students still gathered there, with their hair uncombed, their fingers frozen and their eyelids hot with anger? Did they still imagine they could save their nation with their dreams?

In his eagerness, he brushed past the Bayram carnival, oblivious to the squeal of horns, the thud of drums, the blur of sweating faces thronged around the platforms of the belly dancers. Young girls, old enough to be veiled, skipped past him on the cobblestones; dusty nurses trailed behind them, stuffing themselves with fig paste, nougat waffles and kittens made of scarlet fudge. Abdullah passed them blindly, with the rigid face of a fanatic.

Just as he reached the coffeehouse, a crowd of beggars swarmed out and surrounded him. They had deduced from his collar and his boutonniere that he was a "bey efendi," privileged by God's will to live in a kiosk of colored glass above the Bosphorus and obligated by God's law to give alms to the eternally poor. Plucking at his sleeves, they called him "my little pasha" and "my lord." Abdullah longed to explain to them that he was not some bloodsucking aristocrat but that

64

rarity of rarities, an educated Turk, a man whose mind and heart were turned to the cause of the common people. But the sight of them elbowing each other in their greed constricted his throat. He threw out a few four-para coins, then twisted away from the groping hands and slipped through the door.

It was unchanged: wood rot, damp gravel and the musty scent of ivy leaves. Even the newsboy at the entrance was the same half-witted wretch whose head was blotched from ear to ear with favus.

Naked light bulbs floated in the winding yellow smoke. The only sound was the click of backgammon chips on a wooden playing board. A Persian with a hennaed beard was sitting by the open window, quietly chalking up accounts in the old-fashioned way, on a slab of pine wood. He kept a pot of basil at his elbow to ward off flies and a lithograph of the Kaaba above his head to emphasize his piety. Seeing Abdullah, he sprang up, touching his fingers lightly to his chest.

"Come in, Professor! A pleasant holiday ..." And he led the way to a table in the middle of the room. The patrons, glassy-eyed with reverie, slowly turned their heads. A professor entering the coffeehouse? Well, perhaps not exactly a *professor,* but an educated man. They studied his waxy fingernails, his shiny mustache and his patent-leather boots.

There was no way of telling whether or not the Persian remembered him, and Abdullah did not want to ask. He spread out a copy of *Tefkidi-Efkiar,* smoothed the creases and bent his head to read. The men around him screwed their eyeballs silently into the back of his neck. There was no one Abdullah knew. His heart contracted. Not a soul.

Behind him, muffled voices: "You know, the English and Minglish have taken the harem sections out of the street-cars?"

65

"No more separate seating? Have they lost all respect for the rights of women?"

"Did they have any respect to lose? They put a little woman, just like my mother, right out in public with the men!"

A rumble of indignation shook the floor. Abdullah glanced around the room. It was a Moslem coffeehouse, a Moslem neighborhood; but there was no place on earth where a Turk could speak so openly against the Allied administration.

"Then along came one of those civilian cops—a Greek with a face like a turbot—calling for passes. And he stepped right up, as boldly as a dog in rut, and started fumbling this poor little woman with his hands. A woman like my mother!"

Abdullah clapped for the coffee boy, who ran among the tables, pushing back his long, limp hair with his hand and clutching a wet towel under his arm.

"Spring water," Abdullah said. "Lemons. Sugar. And some mountain snow." And, as the boy was turning away: "Do the students still come here?"

"University students?" the boy said. "They do and they don't, Your Honor. Are you looking for someone?"

"No. Well, not exactly. It doesn't matter."

He turned back to the newspaper. Half a page of type had been deleted by the censor. A Turk simply had to learn to hold his tongue. But the voice at the adjoining table grew louder.

"He was touching her on purpose! I swear to God he was, and every hair on my body stood up like a thistle. Oh, I really blew my top. I grabbed that so-called cop by the collar, took hold of his uniform and slapped his face!"

"You really slapped him? Beautiful!"

"I slapped his face. I slapped his ear."

The boy came back. Alas, there was no mountain snow in

all of Constantinople. It had been eaten by the English soldiers with their whisky. Abdullah shrugged his shoulders. He drained a glass of water, lit a cigarette and pressed a slice of lemon to his teeth, trying to ignore the conversation. The hero of the streetcar almost shouted in excitement.

"God willing, I broke his cheek, and then the crowd split open, and I flew off that streetcar like a bird, just as we passed Top Hane. All the people in the car were shouting, 'Run, darling! Run! God bless you!' And I ran until my soul was coming out my mouth."

Abdullah turned around with his hand against his heart. Tilting his head back to give dignity to his face, he pointed in silence to a sign that read: "DO NOT SPEAK IN A LOUD VOICE."

The slapper of the gendarme clamped a toothpick in his mouth and glared at Abdullah with eyes like a pair of bloody butcher's basins. He was a large, coarse, heavy man with a dirty sash around his belly and stains on his shirt—probably one of those thugs who hang around the sheds along the Golden Horn, weighing stevedores with loads of firewood on their backs. His face was Balkan Slavic, brown as paper, with red-rimmed eyes, a mustache the color of burlap and a lower lip like a wet plum. The other two were strange, furtive men in cast-off army uniforms without insignia. One looked as though he had been torn in half and badly put together: his head was wrapped in filthy rags, and a scar as pale as silver glistened through the stubble of his beard. As for the third— what a gaunt, tormented face! He seemed to be paralyzed by inexpressible rage. His hands were clasped together in a bony knot, and drops of sweat were running down the bluish creases of his cheeks. Something in his resentful gaze reminded Abdullah of faces from the past. It crowded back on him like an inarticulate reproach.

"I am speaking as a friend," Abdullah whispered, with his

hand against his heart again. "This is not the place for agitation, in front of every Ali and Eli in the coffeehouse."

But the plum-lipped thug reached out and tapped Abdullah's table with a thick black fingernail.

"How can you read that stuff? *Alemdar* and *Tefkidi-Efkiar?* How can you stomach that camel dough?"

"All newspapers are full of falsehoods," Abdullah said. "You have to read between the lines."

"Oh? Is that the secret?" said the hero of the streetcar. He squinted his bloodshot eyes and twisted his mouth in a peculiar smile. "I suppose it's different when you're rich."

Abdullah's face turned hot.

"It has nothing to do with being rich. Or poor. If you talk this way in public, you'll wind up in the Arabian Khan."

"Yah, God!" the streetcar hero bellowed suddenly, thrusting out his glittering lower lip. Abdullah jumped back in surprise. "Arrests! Yah, God, God, God!" The corners of his mouth twitched in a bitter spasm. His shirt fell open on his bushy chest, glistening with sweat. His legs spread apart, and he began to rock back and forth like a holy madman, grinding his teeth and beating his fists on his knees. "Yah, God! What we've suffered! They're grinding us like grist between the stones!"

"I don't like injustice, either," Abdullah went on hopelessly. But the streetcar hero rocked back and forth, with his ripe-plum lip gleaming and his thick brown knuckles pounding on his knees; and Abdullah stood up and folded his newspapers. "I know what it's all about," he whispered. "I was in Smyrna when they came."

At the name of the sequestered city, the gendarme-slapper left off his hysterical rocking. Every man in the coffeehouse seemed to be drawing in his breath. The men at the table stared at Abdullah. At last the strange, infuriated one, as blue and bloodless as a corpse, unwove his bony hands and stretched them out, palms upward, like two pale, glossy shells from the bottom of the sea.

"How can anyone who was at Smyrna tell us to be silent?"

And Abdullah, with his face throbbing, turned away and went out into the garden to escape the bitter and accusatory atmosphere that contrasted so unkindly with the sweetness, the vivacity, the joy he had remembered. Even the garden, which once had sparkled with ideas, was gloomy and deserted. A star and crescent, cut out of silver paper, dangled from a crumbled arch. A scent of roasted pumpkin seeds suffused the air, and a slender moon was dancing in the branches of a jujube. These symbols of the holiday oppressed his heart. He walked the gravel paths in mournful retrospection.

From the edge of the terrace there was a view across the Golden Horn, the murky glimmer of the water and the lights beyond it on the slope of Kiasim Pasha. Abdullah stood with his head bowed and his hands behind him, tangled in his rosary.

The noises of the city rose. He could discern the soft "gr-gr-gr" of small boats carrying passengers up the Golden Horn to holiday dinners in the suffocating sandstone villas of Balat; and heard, or thought he heard, the bells and automobile horns along the Grande Rue de Pera, which would be crowded at this hour with Greeks in shirtsleeves, making the homeward promenade with packages dangling on loops of twine around their fingers.

Under the clamor of the festival, Constantinople seemed to be crying out to him with its expiring breath: the precious city, ancient, dark and shimmering; the felicitous city, crowned with domes and bristling with minarets; the shadowy city, mossy and resounding like the cistern of a thousand and one columns; the odorous city, redolent of seaweed and stagnant water, fish nets and horse dung, wood smoke and melon rinds; the dying city, trembling like a galaxy collapsing into dust. This Constantinople had enthralled an empire longer-lived than Rome and stranger than Cathay; but even that had passed away at last, as all things must do except God's face. An English general ruled the Eastern Empire from an office at the head of the funicular in Galata. The Infidel held the Red Apple in his hand; he had apportioned the city among his armies as he would now apportion the world.

The French, so free in matters of the mind, so ruthlessly arbitrary in administration, commanded the old Turkish quarter, which they called Stamboul. The Italians, with their easy grace, had accepted the shores of Asia across the Straits —the cemeteries, the plague hospital and the railhead to the east. The English, of course, had taken everything else—the banks and whorehouses of Galata, the embassies and hotels of Beyoglu, the football field at Taxim, the Findikli Palace, where the Ottoman Parliament gathered to ogle the azure water, the Yildiz Palace, where the Sultan pouted in his rococo pavilion under the shadow of the deodars.

Every morning, the Greeks sent up their sassy flag above the Grande Rue; and every night, Allied policemen collected intransigent Turks and shipped them off to Malta. Senegalese mercenaries were roasting and eating Turkish babies in the Seven Towers; thieves hid in the ashes of burned houses; and a Turk could be arrested in the street for carrying a chicken by its feet or lighting someone's cigarette.

All hope had expired. This was the end of all those dreams of progress and prosperity that he had cherished as a boy; and he was a fool to chase after memories, hoping to console his spirit with the self-assurance of the past. The world had forgotten the Sanjak of Novi-Bazar. Who but Abdullah could remember those young patriots, burning with sublime devotion, who would go to bed in their unheated rooms, dressed

in white fezzes and long black shawls, to dream of brotherhood and love? Nothing remained of that ardent spirit. It had
seeped away in Libya, in Yemen, in the Balkans. One by one,
like pawns swept from a chessboard, all the fine young men,
with their pretensions and their histrionics and their hopes,
had disappeared.

Fuad had been the first to go, and he was blown to pieces
by a mortar shell at Edirne. Then Rauf, Refet, Arif, with their
illusions fresh and uncorrupted as a wreath of laurel leaves.
Their aspirations were immune to change, and they had
never left the university.

Muttering to himself, Abdullah wandered to the window of
the coffeehouse. The three brave Turks, now sunk in gloom,
were sitting where he had left them. It was a table he had
often occupied himself.

As he was going in, a spirit nudged him gently. A wild hope
stirred in his empty heart. He went to the table, tore off a
corner of poor, clawless little *Tefkidi-Efkiar* and wrote on it:
"Turan Chemists, Emin Önü."

"Come tomorrow night," he said. "I will tell you something
important. I am not the man you think I am." And, slipping
the paper underneath a glass, he left the coffeehouse.

For two days, Abdullah hung around the pharmacy, waiting for the three men to appear. Afternoons, he pounded
senna leaves; evenings, he locked the door and climbed up
to the loft, which was hot and smelled of rue. In the center
of the floor there was a trap door with a ladder that led down
to the laboratory, and on the wall above Abdullah's cot hung
a plaque of black glass, decorated with a calligraph in gold
leaf, like a quotation from the Holy Book:

A Turk am I, my race and faith are great;
My breast, my soul are filled with fire.

Abdullah paced back and forth, under his glass plaque, with his clasped hands resting on his buttocks and his face set in a reposeful smile. He was sketching in his mind a series of lectures to instruct the men in the technical language of sociology and the Marxian dialectic. As an introduction, they would analyze the class structure and its relationship to the problem of poverty in the industrial proletariat. Then they would study economic exploitation as a cause of war and would consider methods whereby the current struggle against foreign oppression could be channeled into a workers' and peasants' rebellion. Finally, they would constitute themselves a revolutionary cell, a secret committee to seize power on behalf of the international revolution.

From the dingy little window, Abdullah could look down on Emin Önü and the waterside of the Valide Mosque. Carriages and wagons clogged the square. Beyond the paving stones, the viscid water of the Golden Horn crept under the Bridge of Galata and slowly wheeled like syrup as it met the currents of the Bosphorus. Golden snakes of light, reflected from the minarets, writhed in the oily stream. The domes of the mosques were lighted for the holiday. They shone like pearls on the hills of Asia, and streaks of summer lightning broke above the hills as Abdullah paced back and forth like a man wrestling with a fearful conscience.

On the third night, just as he was about to give up waiting, he heard someone speaking to the clerk downstairs, and footsteps came up the ladder. A gaunt bluish face, a mangled face and a plum-lipped face rose out of the floor like the mugs of three shadow puppets in the Karagöz.

Abdullah found them cushions, sent out for coffee, apologized for the stink of rue. Might he know their names? Jafer (the blue ghost), Remzi (the human wreck), Faik (the plum-lip cop-slapper). Would they like to begin by talking about money? Their eyes glittered. But his next question astounded them. Did any of them really understand what money is?

The three men laughed richly. *Everybody* knew what money is! Money is precious metal, pressed into pieces small enough to be swallowed if you are ambushed by bandits. Money is the seal of the Sultan, God bless him. Money is the weight that drags a rich man down to Hell.

Jafer, the blue one, proved himself to be a veritable genius. He waited until the others had blurted out their answers and then suggested, bellowing in triumph, that money is—a sesame seed! By itself, it would not feed you, clothe you or slake your thirst; but if it were planted in a fertile field and tended year by year, it would eventually make a harvest that could sustain an army.

Abdullah decided to postpone until later his explanation of the labor theory of value.

He did no better illuminating pan-Turanism. The men were neither pleased nor surprised to learn that there were brother Turks all across Central Asia, and that the Turkish tongue was spoken clear to the borders of China. They already knew that Turks lived everywhere, and that Turkish was the dominant language on earth. However, the notion that their brother Turks might be liberated from foreign oppression stirred their imagination: they would be honored to join an immediate campaign to destroy Russia.

The subject of pan-Asiatic war brought them naturally to the problem of the Greeks. How could they best be exterminated?

"Don't worry about the Greeks," Abdullah said. "The occupation is only the symbol of a dying economic system. Overthrow the system, and the Greeks will disappear."

Crafty Jafer was not to be put off.

"That may be true, Your Honor. But those symbols have gobbled up our country in forty days. They've taken Aydin and Ödemish and Manisa."

"What do you propose to do about it?" Abdullah snapped. "Our army is prostrate. Do you think you can accomplish anything by slapping policemen on the streetcar?"

"I thought you had a specific proposal," Jafer said. "After all, Your Honor, cannons don't eat honey."

In all, it was a bad beginning. The men were as dull as rose-water pudding. Three ciphers on the left side of the column. Why should a man like him, a scholar of Karl Marx and Auguste Comte, a disciple of Bergson and Rousseau, a poet of cultural renaissance and social revolution, spend his time in a stinking loft instructing three clods as dense as ever rolled in from Merzifon? It would be better to devote his energies to writing, to reach the minds of the Asian proletariat directly—although that task admittedly was not easy in the face of almost universal illiteracy.

But the three men returned, and Abdullah's heart was touched by their fidelity. In a burst of enthusiasm, he lectured above their heads, bombarding them with grandiose concepts of the Asiatic interworld. Then, suddenly remembering their ignorance, he changed his tactics and spoke in simple parables, using the language of a village hoja.

Day by day, Abdullah's spirits rose. He seemed to be reaching his target at last. Faik seldom fell asleep during their discussions of materialist determinism. Remzi brooded less on gun plots and assassinations. Jafer stopped slipping away to mass meetings in the courtyard of the mosque at Kadiköy. Abdullah's soul expanded.

He was rediscovering the meaning of his own life: not the dead life of his student days in Shehzade-bashi, for that was irretrievably lost; but a thread of life that connected him to a great future filled with work and ideas and achievement. He seldom thought of Eleni any more; and when he did so, it was without resentment for her childish cruelty. His wounds were healing; he was forgetting her. When he thought of Kenan, it was without the guilt that had followed the futile meeting in the Hebrew Cemetery. At last, Abdullah was doing something that his brother would have admired, yet it was broader and richer than Kenan's narrow patriotism.

One morning, however, the men did not appear. Shrugging his shoulders, Abdullah decided to devote the day to journalism. He stayed in his pajamas, inhaling the breeze from the tiny window. But when he got out his writing paper, a headache and a vertigo attacked him. It was the fault of the *lodos,* which blew from the south, out of Africa and over the Aegean. He called down to the shop for pastilles and a box of factory-made cigarettes. For hours he melted analgesic troches on his tongue and blew smoke from his nostrils while pondering the publication of a pamphlet versus the establishment of a clandestine newspaper. Finally, he took out a piece of paper, dipped a pen in ink and wrote, "Eleni Trigonis." He copied it again and again, a thousand and one times, adorning it with arabesques and furbelows until his senses grew numb and the name became as meaningless as a cuneiform. When he saw what he had done, tears came to his eyes.

Night fell and the lamps were hoisted on the minarets. A wave of despair came over him. A whole day gone, and he had lost his men! He blamed himself, his conceit, his over-confidence. He was too stout, too soft, too headachy, too entranced with books and poetry to command the devotion of other men, as Kenan could do. It was the same flaw of character that had cost him the girl. Now, by his arrogance, he had failed the revolution, the heritage of his father and his own aspirations. It was the typical failure of an intellectual who had tried to become a man of action.

The thought almost choked him. He clenched his fists and shouted down the ladder for a carriage.

He found Jafer, Faik and Remzi huddled over a cluster of empty tea glasses. It seemed that they had gotten tired of

Abdullah's lofty talk, which was leading nowhere. Jafer had found an army telegrapher who was going to teach him to speak to the villages of Anatolia with electric writing; Faik was building a shot tower in the ruins of the city wall; and Remzi—well, he would find a means to defy the Allied authorities, if only by carrying chickens in the streets.

"Ah, yes," Abdullah said at last. "I know you're the sort of men who want action instead of words, isn't it so?" He did not remind them that when he had found them a week before, they were moaning in despair. "So I have started a new plan."

Studying their simple faces, he felt a renewed surge of power. He took his time, letting mouths hang open and lips turn dry while he ran thoughtfully through his beads. When he was certain of everyone's attention, he stretched out his finger, dipped up a drop of tea and drew on the table a picture of a rifle. He let them take a good look at it. Then, with his heart flying up, Abdullah wrote under the rifles: "5,000."

This time, when he left the coffeehouse, his men followed.

But Abdullah had stretched the truth. He had not actually begun negotiations to obtain five thousand rifles, or even five rifles, but had merely contemplated such negotiations; and the contemplation had taken place only a minute or two before the plan was announced. Now, in one splendid burst of energy and zeal, he must throw himself into the international traffic in illegal weapons, about which he knew absolutely nothing save the name of an elusive jack-of-all-trades who was said to hold the key to every warehouse from Rome to Baghdad.

He composed the opening letter with meticulous attention to the traditions of Ottoman petition-writing. The text was penned in India ink on vellum, dusted afterward with *ponce* and sent by messenger's hand to each of the known addresses of the Honorable Addressee. The humble writer, Pharmacist Abdullah of Emin Önü, obediently kissed from the eyes of Monsieur Pefko, Efendi; asked God's peace and blessing on him; and begged the honor of meeting him to discuss an affair of profit and significance.

After a day or two, Abdullah received an unsigned note, written in French on a flimsy sheet from a tobacco counter, and bearing a date (according to the Julian, Gregorian, Moslem and modified Ottoman calendars); an hour (according to the European and Moslem clocks); the name of a lane in the neighborhood of Shishli; and the Roman numeral four. Abdullah took it for an answer, never considering that it might have come from a policeman, a terrorist or an *agent provocateur*. There seemed to be no question that its author was none other than Monsieur Pefko, Efendi. And there was no point in asking, "Who, pray God, is Pefko, Efendi?" because everyone—and no one—knew who Pefko was.

The name was a mask, of course—a Greek word meaning pine tree. Its artificiality stirred a general curiosity that thrived, like an appetite for hashish, on a lack of satisfaction. None of the usual indexes of Ottoman society—domestic language, faith or occupation—precisely applied to Pefko. Pefko had no face, no home, no family—nothing but a *nom de guerre* and a shifting and opaque environment. According to report, he was a Hindu prince, a South Sea islander, a Moldavian, a Croatian, a Maltese or an Egyptian. He worshiped among the Jews, the Catholics, the Protestant Armenians and the Druzes; he was related to the Hohenzollerns, the Romanoffs and the Rothschilds; he was an agent of the German Embassy, the French Army and the Pope.

But if Pefko was not exactly human, he was unquestionably the living embodiment of a historical tradition, an eternal Byzantine personality recurring through the centuries. There had been a prototype Pefko to warn the Emperor Justinian that the Blues and Greens were planning a riot in the Hippodrome. Pefko's lineal progenitors had revealed the weak spots of the outer walls to the besieging Persians and disclosed the hiding places of the holy ikons to the fanatical ikon-smashers. A gelded Pefko snooped through the royal harem, carrying rumors of disloyalty directly to the ear of Suleyman the Magnificent; a catamitic Pefko warned the grand vizier of new conspiracies among the janissaries; and hundreds of fanciful, prolific Pefkos carried morsels of intelligence to nourish the paranoid imagination of Sultan Abdul Hamit and to stuff the diplomatic pouches of the American ambassador, Henry Morgenthau.

In short, Pefko was a mercenary spy, an essential messenger in a governance of secrecy. Abdullah sought him out as one consults an expert in technology. When dusk fell on the appointed day and the carriage sounded its klaxon at the door, Abdullah strutted out, infused with confidence that he was about to place his dangerous problems in the hands of a skilled adviser. This mood sustained him across the bridge and up the hill, past the guarded doors of the British and Italian banks, out of the familiar Turkish city and into the hostile territory of capitulations, forged passports, plural citizenships, diplomatic immunities and the cult of Jesus Christ in all its menacing peculiarities.

Throngs of Greeks were strolling the Grande Rue, with their boots polished and their hands loosely clasped on their behinds. Their bellies were stuffed; their dark eyes shifted lazily; and their moist chops glistened with lamb grease and reeked of oregano. It was not a becoming hour—not even a safe hour—for a Turk to drive through Beyoglu. But Abdullah rolled on, buoyed up by the excitement of his mission and armored with his majestic, careless Turkish contempt for the fidgety, cosmopolitan Christian herd, with their walled cathedrals, their pork butcheries, their crimes of vengeance and their endless plottings to resuscitate forgotten kingdoms.

This was Pefko's world: the embassy compounds, the Pera Palace Hotel, and the gardens of the Petits Champs des Morts, where a Negro orchestra was playing the turkey trot under a string of Chinese lanterns. To deal with Pefko, one needed only the fortitude to meet him on his own grounds, be it a Russian nightclub called the Golden Bear, a pastry shop where prostitutes came in at noon to gorge on petits fours or the dome of Holy Trinity. Undismayed, Abdullah passed beyond the playing field of Taxim, the tenements of Pancaldi and the blank apartment blocks of Shishli, their windows sealed with newspapers to advertise that the occupants had gone to Europe for the summer.

All at once the carriage left the built-up city and was wallowing through dusty groves of mulberries. At the end of a deeply rutted lane, the driver reined his horse. Abdullah said incredulously: "Is this it?"

It was a solitary place beside a pasture. In front was a dry garden, strewn with broken chairs; in back, at the end of a graveled path, an ancient konak, three or four stories high, of dark, unpainted boards, patched here and there with flattened oil cans. Stovepipes wormed out of every window, climbed the wall and poked through the immense, projecting eaves, which stood out like the cornices of an Alpine chalet.

As Abdullah pushed the gate, the crickets suddenly were quiet, like children when a stranger passes. Abdullah stopped and listened. It struck him that the correspondence leading to this appointment had been hazy and irregular. He wondered why he had neglected to tell anyone where he was going. Backing away, he let the gate swing shut and walked a few yards down the road. But the carriage had gone, leaving a long white roll of dust disintegrating in the moonlight.

The konak consisted of several apartments. On one of the doors a Roman numeral four had been drawn in chalk. Inside, presumably, was Pefko. Unless, of course, it was a policeman, a terrorist or an *agent provocateur*. Abdullah raised the knocker, dropped it heavily and waited. The crickets whispered: "English spy."

A bald man, unshaven and poorly dressed, came to the door and admitted Abdullah to a teeming little room that smelled of candle wax. The walls were crowded with photographs of brides and babies, interspersed with views of the Alps and holy lithographs of Jesus, Mary and the various saints of the Orthodox hagiocracy, embossed with nimbuses of shiny gilt. A circular table almost filled the room. Two children in underclothes were picking at some bread and cucumbers spread on a newspaper; a man in a hat was talking; and a kinky-haired Christian woman, wrapped in a crimson dressing gown, was smoking a cigarette. "My sister," the bald man said offhandedly.

The woman nodded them into the house, then turned away to resume a conversation in Greek with the man in a hat. Abdullah squeezed past a dresser covered with piles of plates and a display of drooping purple coleus in moldy pots. His face stared at him, round and white and solemn, from a mirror that hung on a long cord with tassels. He entered a glass porch occupied by cats. The man pointed out a stool where he could sit down.

"An honor," said Abdullah, taking out his beads. "Is Monseiur Pefko, Efendi, here?"

"I'm Pefko."

"Ah." Abdullah stared straight ahead. He felt as if he had been cheated. "I thought—"

"Yes?" Pefko's hands were small and strained. His fingertips were the color of bark, and the nails were dirty. He was offering a single cigarette, holding it out between his thumb and forefinger like a tidbit for an animal. "Yes, please? What did you think?"

"I thought you might send a representative."

"Do accept a cigarette!" Pefko swept a cat aside and groped for matches on the coffee tray. "Why should I use an intermediary? I want to *meet* you, my dear friend. I *want* to answer your questions. . . . What are your questions?"

"I thought you might have a secret place. Because of the risks."

"Risks, misks," said Pefko. "Come, what do you want to ask? Ask me anything." And, clasping a hand to his breast, he hurled himself onto the sofa. Cats and dust flew out of the bolsters. "Is it an article? My answer is yes! All the newspapers know me." He hoisted up his legs and tucked his heels under his rump. The grimy hand that had been pressed against his heart slid down and burrowed in his crotch. "How about a Montagu? You know what I mean by that? An article about Lady Mary Wortley Montagu and her love for Turkey. Restores an atmosphere of mutual respect."

Abdullah closed his eyes. A sudden dizziness overcame him.

"Ask me!" Pefko cried. "Lord Stratford de Redcliffe? There's an authentic pro-Turk. Material for three—five articles."

The pockets of Pefko's jacket bulged with folded papers. He pulled them out, riffled them, whacked them on the edge of the tray and dealt them around like cards—essays on the mineral springs of Yalova, the fat-tailed sheep of Ankara, the Blue Mosque, the Baghdad Railroad and the world position of the Islamic Caliphate. Every hack in Beyoglu sold articles to lazy foreign journalists who prowled around the embassies searching for rumors and lunch.

"No. Not articles," Abdullah said. He stared at Pefko, who was digging into his groin while a cat crawled over his shoulder switching its tail against his face. "I want . . . not articles."

"Listen," Pefko said, clawing relentlessly, "You are my

dear, *dear* friend. My dear, *good* friend. May I tell you something? The trouble with you Turks"—he raised his hand to block off protest—"is, you have no idea what the world thinks of you. Do you know what they call you in Europe?"

"Yes."

"The Unspeakable."

"I know."

"No missionaries to plead your cause. No philhellene clubs. No Armenian Protection Leagues— Please! Allow me to finish, my friend. I sympathize. I have in mind a pamphlet. *Smyrna Is Turkish.* A gory figure on the cover, holding up a tattered Turkish flag. In the background flames. A black-veiled woman, weeping. Enormous eyes above her modest yashmak. Tears of blood. Corpses of children. Ten thousand copies, French and English editions. I write both languages. Also many others, you understand?"

"No, not a pamphlet."

Pefko exhaled explosively through his nostrils. "Look. You're a Turk, my friend. Do you think there's a Save the Turks Society in Manchester, England? Pamphlets are the best you can do, my dear friend. What would you say to *I Was at Smyrna, an Anonymous Firsthand Report?* French and English. Pages of statistics. Atrocity photographs."

"Not pamphlets," Abdullah repeated, feeling helpless and stupid.

Pefko, sighing, thrashed his body to and fro. With a groan he raised himself, releasing another eruption of cats and dust, made a final assault on his ballocks and then took hold of the doorknob. For a moment he stood as if listening to sounds from the other room. At last, turning his head: "Permit me to ask directly, my dear friend, what is it you want?"

Abdullah's tongue felt as stiff as a knot of wood. "I need . . . materials. I want to buy something."

Nothing had gone as he had expected: not Pefko, not the

scene, not even his own words. He had preconceived a long and subtle colloquy, leading by insinuation to the subject of his visit. It was to have been Pefko who would mention dangers, money, influential friends, and Abdullah, cunning and elusive, who would set terms, turn corners and make abrupt demands. At the end, they would bargain. Pefko would cry out for mercy. Abdullah, smiling, would play with his beads. Each of them would profess to doubt the other's sanity. Pefko would try to unload a boat, a farmhouse in the Dobruja, some German helmets, moldy wheat. Abdullah would demand nitroglycerine and an airplane. It would go on for hours.

Instead, the opportunity was flashing past as quickly as the Sultan's carriage at the Friday mosque. In desperation, Abdullah cried out: "It's *guns* I want."

But Pefko opened the door and went out.

Abdullah covered his face with his hands. What a fool to blurt out your objective! Pefko had dandled him like a child; and the fatal words could no more be recalled than spit restored to the mouth. Certainly Kenan would have never allowed himself to be panicked into moving too fast.

A cat leaped up, clawing at Abdullah's thigh. He gasped and flailed his arms. The house was too quiet. He got up and pressed his ear against the door. Should he jump out the window? But Pefko came back, followed by his sister, who was carrying a wooden tray with some coffee cups, tumblers of iced water and a small zinc coffee pan with a long, straight handle that trembled like the tail of an abominable cat.

The coffee reassured him. Not even Pefko would betray a guest to whom his sister was serving coffee. Abdullah crouched on the stool again and gazed in gratitude at the folds of the woman's crimson dressing gown. She filled two cups. Bending forward, she whispered something to Pefko. Abdullah thought he heard the word "police." Pefko did not answer. He studied the cups and pushed forward the one with more froth. That, too, was reassuring. Even Pefko would not be hospitable to a guest he was betraying.

The woman stood back, watching them, with her hands on her hips. Raising his face, Abdullah tried to smile. "It is excellent coffee."

"She doesn't understand Turkish," Pefko said. "Never learned it, never will." There was a note of satisfaction in his voice, as if he were bragging about the success of some cunning plot. Abdullah forced himself to go on smiling; but he felt anger boiling up in his chest. "Turkish is required, isn't it?" he said. "Every subject has to study it in school."

"We are not subjects of the Sultan," Pefko said. Turning, he translated his remark. His sister laughed. She said something in Greek.

"Is that so bad? Abdullah interrupted. His voice began to tremble. "Don't you think a Turkish subject ought to study the language of the country? *You* speak it."

"My dear friend, I speak everything."

"No, it's really intolerable. In every country the children learn the language. Here, if you try to teach Turkish to Arabs or Greeks or Armenians they call it persecution."

"This is not a normal country."

"No, that's right," Abdullah shouted. "And we're sick of it! For centuries, we've sheltered every nation in the Holy Book while the French were driving out the Huguenots, and the Spaniards were driving out the Jews, and the Germans and Slavs were burning each other alive. No, every tongue in the Empire imagines it's a martyred nation. I say they should speak Turkish!"

"I speak everything," Pefko said, shrugging. His sister sang a scrap of song that, from the tone of it, was scurrilous, and whisked the coffee cups away. In the silence, Pefko said: "Is it rifles you want?"

Abdullah felt his anger draining away. A vast calm engulfed his spirit. He stared at Pefko and saw a pasty, vulnerable clerk in a cheap worsted suit, a man without nationality, friends, culture or personal honor, who was offering himself for sale. By comparison, Abdullah's own humiliations, his contemptible self-abasement in the garden of that slut in Smyrna, his degrading escape, his ludicrous efforts to educate the *Lumpenproletariat*—all of them were patrician adventures. A smile tweaked the corners of his mouth.

"Yes, it's rifles," he said calmly. "Five thousand rifles."

His throat swelled as he felt himself passing over the impassable barrier that separates the man of intellect from the man of action. Like certain of the Bolsheviks, he had stepped directly from the library into the town square, with a club in his hand and a rock in his pocket. At the moment, it seemed to be a matter of no consequence to look from side to side, to examine his circumstances with a wary eye, to try to avoid a disastrous mistake.

*T*o Kenan, the journey home was like passing through a foreign country. The vines were green, the apricots were ripe and young oxen waded in the streams—yet everything under the sun looked withered and pale, as if a powdery mildew had blighted every leaf. The railroad cars were filled with fidgety Greeks, popping up and down and peeling oranges with their pocketknives. At noon they spread handkerchiefs across their laps and squabbled over loaves of bread and jugs of water.

At the station in Manisa, some Turkish prisoners were taking down signs that marked the names of the streets in French and Turkish, and putting up new signs in Greek. The Greek passengers leaned out and jeered at them.

After four days by train and oxcart, Kenan reached Alashehir. His foot was puffed up like a camel's hoof, jet-black and mushy. His mother came to the door and clutched his shoulders. His sisters cried and kissed his hands.

"Are you going to bleed me or wrap me in a gravecloth?" Kenan said.

Several hours later, the barber came around, perspiring in new clothes and a clean collar, followed by two flunkies who carried an immense display of swabs and lancets in a wooden chest with griffins carved inside the lid. After honing each of the knives and feeling it with his thumb, the barber incised

86

the foot and drained the foul-smelling hematin, emptying the basin twice. Yildiz, the older sister, rolled a cigarette and placed it tenderly between Kenan's numb lips; but he could not hold his jaws together. The cigarette fell to the floor, and he closed his eyes.

For a week or two, they kept him in the kitchen. His mother wiped the cold sweat from his forehead with a sponge soaked in vinegar; his sister Gulnar spooned syrup of quinces into his mouth; and Yildiz made innumerable cigarettes. At last, his uncle Mahmut Zia, who exercised undisputed authority in this household of spinsters and widows, said it was time for Kenan to be moved to the selamlik. The windows were opened to the fragrance of the vineyards. Servant girls came in unveiled, with feather dusters under their arms, offered him nectarines in bowls of water and skated to and fro with rags around their feet.

Mornings, he sat in the garden kiosk with Yildiz. He wore silk pajamas and one leather slipper. Lattices of scrollwork dimmed the light. An old wisteria bent nearly to the path; and as the heat increased, the garden smelled of stagnant water and iodoform.

Yildiz liked to wait on him. Blushing and bowing, she would snatch the tray from a servant's hands to offer him cucumbers and yogurt. She could sit for hours in perfect silence, slowly picking little pebbles from a bowl of dried lentils. It was the only sort of work she ever had mastered. Even trimming the tops of vegetables was beyond her ability: she always cut her fingers, like Potiphar's wife distracted by the beauty of Joseph.

Kenan endured her ministry as long as he could. Then, one morning when she tried to lift him from his chair, he pushed her away with the stump of his arm. Yildiz jumped as if she had been burned. For a long time, Kenan sat with his head down, staring at his knee that would not bend, his truncated

87

arm and his foot that would not bear his weight. He touched the tips of his fingers to his eye patch and to the deep scar that creased his chin. He thought he was crying; but when he felt his eye, there was no moisture in it.

That day he dressed himself for the first time. Leaning on his cane, he went upstairs to see the women of the house— his mother, his sister Gulnar, his grandmother and his Aunt Emine—who seldom left the harem section.

Aunt Emine, the wife of Mahmut Zia, was as stupid as a stone, and so old-fashioned that she thought herself compromised if male eyes met her own. For days she had pretended that she did not know Kenan was in the house. Then she greeted him by sending down a box of rose loukoum. When he came upstairs, she hid in a wardrobe.

As for Grandmother, she was asleep, sitting upright on a cushion with her cheek against the jig-saw screen that had concealed her from the rudeness of the world for more than eighty years. Her lips were sunken; her face was like a pink rose that has withered and turned brown. Kenan woke her by touching his forehead to her hand, which trembled like a dying moth. At last, with an anguished effort in the wattles of her throat, and spewing up a smell of vomit, the old woman woke and said: "I *know!* I *know!*" After asking him for a cigarette, she fell asleep again.

The harem, being on the upper floor, was always warm and stuffy. Syrian hassocks were strewn across the carpets. The cabinets were filled with yellowed damask cloths, tarnished silver coffee trays and overshoes with shriveled, curling toes. On the marble console were bottles of astringent lotion for the skin, pots of kohl for the eyelids, flasks of liquid kermes for the fingernails and jars of copper sulphate for removing hair. This mess belonged to Gulnar, who usually wore a beaten egg yolk on her face and an unfinished dress across her arm, with the pattern of tissue paper clinging to it like a shadow. Her hairbrushes, skin bleaches, almond milk and tinctures of gall were scattered on all the little gilded chairs, which no one ever sat on.

Gulnar begged Kenan to talk about the modes of Smyrna. She had been told that Greek girls walked outside unveiled, as bold as men, and she wondered whether it was true that men and women danced together, face to face. Her cheeks began to redden as if she had been running. Kenan said the girls of Smyrna were dull and homely and the men were savage. Gulnar smiled in disbelief, pressing the back of her hand against her flaming cheek.

"But isn't it true that the girls wear white?"

"No."

"Not even the Greek girls?"

"No."

"And they don't go walking outside?"

"I've told you."

Gulnar stared down at the sewing on her lap. Then she asked to be excused. A few moments later, Kenan heard the treadle of her sewing machine begin to pound with a steady rhythm. Gulnar worked in the sewing room every day. She had filled a camphor chest with bed sheets, tablecloths and napkins.

But it was his mother who irritated him most of all. She was a strong, intelligent woman whose interest ran to vineyards, stables, furniture and houses. After a few days of furtive weeping, she put on the bland face of a houri and set about jollying him with farm news. She could talk with precision about the price of figs and the quality of raisins. In her opinion, the Alashehir sultanas would be as clear this autumn as the best from Karaburun, if the weather held. . . . The barn at Chakirjali was in need of thatch. . . . Did he think it was time to shoe the horses? Then, suddenly, gazing at him with a fierce intensity:

"Oh, son! What can we do to help you, son?"

Kenan stared at the wall. What was he supposed to say? That he was tired of dying one limb at a time and would prefer to die all at once?

To escape from the house, he ordered Hassan, the stableboy, to get out the gig and drive him to the Chakirjali farm. Passing through the town, he felt as he had on the train from Smyrna. There were tiny Greek shops with tins of English peppermints and piles of nougat in the windows, Turkish butcher stalls with wasps devouring strips of darkened meat, Persian coffeehouses and Circassian liveries. All of these had once been familiar and even precious to him. He had counted it a pleasure to walk along these quiet streets, under these locusts that were white with dust; and he had known the names of all the shops and their proprietors. But they interested him no longer, and he urged the stableboy to lay a whip across the gelding's back.

They took an upper road that hugged the flank of the three little hills above the town—Doghren Tepe, with gravestones leaning from its crest like rows of spears; Düz Tepe, which bore a crop of sallow grass; and Top Tepe, surmounted by a cannon that was fired to signal dawn and sunset during the fasting month of Ramazan. From the road they could see the valley and the yellow vineyards throbbing in the heat. Peasants stood up and touched their foreheads as the carriage passed. At the farmhouse, Kenan got down and stood in the yard, holding on to his cane. Cold sweat trickled down his neck. He drank a glass of water and got back into the gig.

At sunset the fields were empty. Wagons creaked along the road, and the valley filled with haze. Kenan leaned back with his eyes closed and his jaws clamped in agony.

That summer there was an "incident." A basketmaker found a rotting body in a thicket of osiers by the river. No one could identify the man, or even determine his religion. The

90

corpse was naked, and that part by which a Moslem might be distinguished from a Greek had been slashed away.

But the Turks were convinced that the body was that of a Moslem, mutilated by the Christians. Hadn't the Greeks for years reported spurious atrocities to arouse the sympathies of Europe? This one would be used as an excuse for Greece to take Alashehir.

In confirmation of these fears, a Greek manifesto, written by a bishop of the Christian church and published in Constaninople, circulated through the Turkish coffeehouses. It dealt with the redemption of Holy Places, a subject that always stirred profound emotion in the missionary societies of England and North America. One of the Holiest of Places, it now appeared, was this drowsy town of Alashehir, which had been the ancient city of Philadelphia. From Philadelphia, the Hellenes had colonized Asia Minor; later, the city had been a stronghold of the apostolic church of Jesus. In the Book of Revelation, St. John had praised the church of Philadelphia for its courage in the face of Roman persecution. Centuries afterward, Christian Philadelphia was the last Greek city on the mainland to withstand the Ottoman Turks, enduring like the final star that glimmers in a clouded sky.

It should now be known (the bishop wrote) that the Christians of Philadelphia were again in frightful danger. The Turks were threatening to murder them and build their violated corpses into a gate of bones, just like a terrible memento left by Sultan Beyazit, whose masonry could still be seen in a portion of the city wall. So wrote the Christian bishop, *ex cathedra,* from Constantinople.

Kenan took a copy of the pamphlet and went into town with the help of the stableboy to call on his uncle. Mahmut Zia, as a man of property, held a privy council daily in his office. The door was guarded by a thug in pantaloons. From dawn until the call for midday prayer, there were petitioners around the desk, along the hall, even lying in the spittle on the stairway: army officers and village clerks, coppersmiths and weavers, some enjoying coffee, others of lower rank enjoying cigarettes and some enjoying neither, but all demanding, pleading, supplicating, in the full assurance that a man like Mahmut Zia Bey, on the evidence of his wealth, enjoyed the special favor of the Almighty. And Mahmut Zia, shifting his weight from side to side to cool his buttocks, would lower his eyelids sleepily, dispense advice, suggest palliatives, promise due consideration and counsel faith in God.

He brought Kenan into the office and showed him around like a trophy.

"It's my nephew, come from Smyrna. He saw them taking Smyrna, isn't it so?" And he insisted that Kenan drink a glass of sour cherry syrup for his blood. While they waited, Mahmut Zia braided his fingers and talked about Gulnar. It was difficult to find a husband for her: she had been spoiled by knowledge. That was her father's own fault. He'd hired an Armenian woman, who called herself Mademoiselle Helène, to give the girl lessons in piano playing, freehand drawing and science. These so-called lessons had been terminated after the woman made a grossly irreligious remark about the ocean rising and falling as a result of pressures from the moon; but the damage had been done. Now Gulnar could think of nothing but the fashions of Smyrna. . . .

Kenan threw down the Greek pamphlet.

"Ah, yes," Mahmut Zia said vaguely. "I've seen that. The Greeks have been making claims like that for years. But, you know, there are only a few thousand Greeks here. Not a sixth of the population. Nobody takes them seriously."

"That is why they are in Smyrna," Kenan said, and he left.

Halfway to the house, he made Hassan stop the gig. There was a steady drumbeat from the side street and the wavering

92

voice of an old crier, shouting the ancient formula: "Don't say, 'We've heard, we haven't heard . . .' "

Hassan, who was as hunchbacked as a frog, looked at Kenan in bulging, conspiratorial excitement. "They're calling out the men!"

It was a column of fifteen or twenty, led by a flute and drum and followed by a ragged officer who sat like a peasant on the shoulders of a barebacked, spavined horse. The officer wore a handkerchief tied as a sweatband around his head. His tunic was unbuttoned. The men were dressed in coats and trousers sewn from gunny cloth. As they marched, they threw back their dark-blue closely-shaven heads and widened their nostrils like animals responding to a call. These drumbeats had called the Turk to war before his history began, when he was a restless tribesman in a felt tent, wandering around the desiccated plains of Central Asia, beyond the River Oxus and the Altai Range. Hearing the summons of the drum, each man imagined he was marching under a horsetail banner, toward the Danube, the Euphrates or the Volga.

> "Smyrna! If you go, we die;
> Without you life can't be.
> Your sorrow, like a knife,
> Has stabbed our souls with agony.
> Welcome, soldiers of the nation!
> Blest be your holy cause!
> Long life and strength to Turkish youth!
> Blest be your holy cause. . . ."

The stableboy swayed with rapture. "Brothers!" he called out. "God bless you, brothers! But you haven't got a rifle among you."

Two of them lifted rusty flintlock muskets, and the officer waved his sword.

"Will you take me too?" Hassan cried. "Will you take a man with a hump on his back?"

93

"God willing, we'll take any man who loves his country."

But Kenan seized hold of the boy's arm with his good right hand and dug his fingers to the bone.

"I need you," Kenan said. *"I* need you."

And the column marched off, with the officer quivering on the withers of his wretched horse and shouting: "Unsheath your swords! We'll march to Baghdad!"

The Moslem volunteers met in a deserted college of theology at the Mosque of Sultan Beyazit, the Lightning Bolt. There were blacksmiths, peddlers and fanatical women who tore off their veils and howled the names of their martyred sons. Heavy Mausers, taken from the army sheds, were stacked in the embrasures of the walls. Cartridges were heaped on tables. As each man pledged his service to the Fatherland, he took a cartridge belt, a rifle and a band of scarlet ribbon for his arm.

Later, these bashi-bazouks assembled in groups of sixty at Greengrocer Ali Vehbi's place and streamed from the town by any trail they thought would lead them to the Greeks. Some of them took a cart track through the vineyards to Salihli. They fired their rifles into the air and harangued a congregation in the courtyard of a mosque. Others galloped along the flanks of Boz Dagh to the ruins of Sardis, where they camped for a fortnight, feeding on unripe pears and bickering over trinkets stripped from the corpses of travelers. One company of zealots, waving emerald flags, descended the valley in procession, led by a woman named Ruhiye, who wore a belt of rifle shells around her waist, carried a revolver on her hip and straddled a huge white horse with widely rolling eyes. As Ruhiye rode through the pastures, farmers would run out crying, "God! Great God!" and lifting their upturned palms in a gesture of piety.

These patriotic cadres thrilled the coffeehouses of Alashehir. Practitioners of the canon law consecrated them as fighters of Holy War. They quartered themselves in public baths and ruined towers, harassing Greek outposts at night and punishing halfhearted Turks with pebbles in the nostrils.

But the Greeks killed the youngest and best of the Turkish irregulars; and the bands that did not fall apart came under the leadership of Sari Efe, "the Yellow Chief," or Ethem the Circassian, who had been renowned before the Great War for kidnaping the son of the Governor of Smyrna.

Kenan told the stableboy what had happened.

"When I go to war again," Kenan said, "it will not be to lose."

The Greeks took the valleys of the Meander, the Little Meander and the Gediz; and the countryside around Alashehir was quiet.

*O*n the morning of St. Dimitris' Day, which is October 12, Lieutenant Kalapothakis invited George Trigonis to spend the evening at the Army Club. George tried to make up an excuse that would not offend his future brother-in-law; but every alternative sounded weak and evasive. In truth, the prospect of chumming around with Dimitris terrified him. Dimitris always seemed to be peeking inside his skull, turning up discreditable and ludicrous thoughts and storing away the evidence, to be exposed at some future scene of public humiliation. What pleasure or advantage could Dimitris gain by entertaining a young man he appeared to despise? It was impossible to fathom. In the end, George's Greek curiosity overcame his caution, and he accepted the invitation.

The Army Club, reflecting a current French influence in Hellenic military affairs, was known officially as the Cercle Militaire de Smyrne. It was on Frank Street, where a man's club ought to be, and was furnished like an authentic London establishment, with armchairs of golden oak, leather cushions, antlers, boars' heads and trestle tables piled with copies of *Chronos* and *Thetis*. In every room, one met the penetrating eyes of Eleftherios Venizelos, glaring from a life-size photograph. Dimitris pointed out the dominance of Liberal Party newspapers on the racks.

"We're strictly Venizelist," he said. "Solid as the Anchor." And he gave George a probing glance that seemed to imply the boy was somewhat unreliable in this regard. "I suppose we might let a Royalist in, as long as he kept his mouth shut. But none of this swaggering around, clanking swords and singing German beer-hall songs. . . . Here, take these to the kitchen." And he seized hold of a doddering old servant and handed him two brace of woodcocks, strung together at the beaks, which George's father had rather wistfully contributed to the occasion. Dimitris should have invited *him* instead of George: Christos would have been delighted, and there was no doubt of *his* political loyalties.

The cardroom had been built as a salon. Its lofty ceiling, wreathed in golden serpents, magnified the sound of voices to a roar. The setting sun reflected from a row of blazing windowpanes across the street; awnings flapped in the wind; and cigarette smoke curled around the crystal tulips of the chandelier. Along the walls, the frozen faces of dozens of high-ranking army officers stared down on the newer generation of military strategists.

"Venizelist, all of them," Dimitris said, leading George like a diplomat reviewing troops along the row of sepia photographs. George pretended to be fascinated by the fleshy Cretan nose of General Zimbrakakis and the rounded Bavarian cheeks of General Nider. As a result of his father's tireless instruction, he knew their names and correctly identified them as leaders of the Balkan Wars and of Venizelos' National Defense Movement in 1917.

Dimitris drew his attention to the French and American medals worn by General Paraskevopoulos. Then, abruptly, under a portrait of General Smolenski at Velestino: "Look, I accept the fact that she needs time to make up her mind. But it's been almost five months. She treats me like a stranger."

"Eleni?" George said. "No. I think she likes you."

He knew, as a matter of fact, that Eleni, for all her whims, was entranced by Dimitris. In a situation involving family honor, however, it was better to remain cool. "She's very shy."

"No," Dimitris said. "It's getting me down. I've about decided to give up."

An officer with a purple nose, a reddish mustache and a row of medals on his chest rushed up and grasped Dimitris by the back of the neck. "Well, here he is! The deflowerer of Ionia!"

Dimitris pushed George forward. "This is the brother of my fiancée."

The officer roared with glee. "Her *brother?*" He rubbed his enormous nose, which was as dark and shiny as an eggplant. "Oh, you horn! Are you trying to horn every member of the family?"

"This Kostas!" Dimitris said. "I love him like my own flesh." Nudging George, he pointed to a half-filled table in the corner. "Three empty chairs. We'll join."

It seemed dishonorable to sit down while a point of family pride was unresolved; but George could not think of anything else to do. In loyalty to his sister, he thought he should demand an apology from Dimitris. At the same time, he was not sure that any offense had been committed. Chewing his lower lip, he leaned against the back of a chair while Dimitris introduced the men around the table: two lieutenants from the Archipelago Division (both Athenians, but slow), and a country captain from Levadhia, who said he was the commander of an incredible, magnificent, invincible mountain gun attached to the 13th Infantry Division at a location he was not allowed to name.

Dimitris called for raki. Impatiently, he slapped the seat of the chair that George was leaning on. "Sit down, sit down! Don't you even know how to play Russian Bank?"

"Maybe I could arrange a meeting with my papa," George said. But Dimitris frowned.

"I'm afraid it's just no use."

In half an hour, George lost thirty Turkish pounds, twelve drachmas and a guinea, sterling. Dimitris offered him a glass of raki but George preferred a second lemonade. The sun went down. The waiters lit the chandelier and drew the shades. Dimitris ordered olives, hazelnuts and another bottle; Kostas wanted a hubble-bubble pipe. George paid the waiter and then lost another hand.

"You're a nice kid," Kostas said, pouring raki all around. "We could use a big, intelligent, nice kid like you in the First Division. But listen—don't wait around for somebody to invite you to get in. You Smyrna Greeks all say you hate the Turks—but where's this famous volunteer brigade you're supposed to be forming?"

George tried to smile. He turned to Dimitris.

"What if you wrote another letter to my papa?"

Dimitris let his eyelids droop. He slowly fanned out his cards.

"The trouble is," he said, "Your father won't talk about the dowry until *she* agrees. Frankly, I don't know whether it's worth pursuing."

George opened his mouth, but Kostas poked his arm.

"Listen, no one had to invite your old friend Dimitris to get in," Kostas said. "No one had to invite *me.*" Clamping the blackened mouthpiece of the water pipe between his lips, he took a long, gurgling breath and expelled a cloud of smoke from his vast nostrils. Old friend Dimitris, gazing across the table with a warm and bleary smile, served himself another glass of raki.

"You know, this Kostas was my classmate at the Academy," he said, "I was a horn, but this Kostas! He was the devil's stocking."

"I was the devil himself," said Kostas, tapping the pipe-stem on that great, prune-colored nose. "The day we got our uniforms, we went right down to Piraeus and climbed aboard a little blue caïque and held a pistol to the captain's head. I says to him, 'All right, old man. You're going to take us to Salonika to join Mr. Venizelos.' That's how *we* got invited to join the National Defense!"

"Three years ago," Dimitris said. "Like yesterday. That was the way to get to be a second lieutenant overnight." He scrutinized George. "How old were you then? Thirteen? Fourteen? Still wearing short pants and drawing dirty pictures in your schoolbooks."

George licked his lips, writhing under Dimitris' probing stare. The conversation made his head whirl. Names he barely knew, or did not know at all, bounced back and forth: General Panayotis Danglis, Admiral Koundouriotes, Colonel Negropontis, General Zimbrakakis. Kostas talked about Lake Dorian and Macedonia and the Bulgarians; and George remembered photographs of men with sunken eyes and arms like sticks: "Fresh Evidence . . . Caitiff Bulgaria."

A captain came over to the table, helped himself to a handful of hazelnuts and said: "You've got a new recruit." The captain was pale and jaundiced. He had oily hair, a row of little moles along his jawbone and a tiny black mustache, so thin and neatly trimmed that it resembled an eyebrow painted on with a stick of gall wood. Dimitris eyed him without answering; but the captain went on scooping up hazelnuts. "I suppose you're training him as a Venizelist? You've seated him under General Danglis."

"He could do worse," Dimitris said. "We're using Schneider-Danglis guns all over Asia Minor."

"Have you seen them?" the captain said. "I thought you never left Smyrna."

"I've been in and out," Dimitris said, stretching his arm to show a band of tape around his wrist. "Got this up near Bergama. Where have you been, Captain?"

"Cheshme."

"The resort? I envy you."

"Sultry," the captain said.

Dimitris turned to George. "This is Captain Loukas Mavropetros. From Athens." Under his breath, he added: "Shitty Royalist."

"Technically, Danglis was a deserter," the captain said. "No matter how much you admire his politics, you have to admit he broke the fundamental rule of military conduct. He could have been executed."

"He wasn't," Dimitris said.

"He was lucky," the captain said.

"In any case, there were others to take his place," Dimitris said. "This room is filled with them. Ten, twenty years from now, you'll see the faces of these youngsters on the wall."

"Or lined up against the wall," the captain said.

Dimitris laughed and reached out for the raki bottle.

"Take a drink, Captain. This is my name day."

"Not now."

"What's the matter, Captain? Are you sorry we joined the war on the winning side?"

"No."

"Are you sorry we're here in Smyrna?"

"No." The captain wiped his little mustache with the tip of his finger. "Not necessarily." He took a box of tobacco from the pocket of his tunic. "Only, why do you tell this kid to imitate an officer who helped overthrow the government?"

"This kid is old enough to think for himself," Dimitris said. "As for me, I say an army officer has got a duty to the nation. If the future of the country requires him to oppose the government, he should oppose the government. Does he stop being a citizen when he puts on a uniform?"

"That's not the point," the captain said. He put his finger-tips on the table and leaned forward. His pallid face was glittering with moisture. "The point is, it weakened us. Politicians playing soldiers. Officers becoming Cabinet Ministers."

"Oh, the devil!" said Dimitris, suddenly stiffening. "You Royalists are all alike. You think the King's politics are the national interest and everybody else's politics are treason."

The captain's white jaw throbbed.

"Lieutenant," he said, "you should apologize."

Dimitris waved his hand from side to side. "Oh, what the hell, Captain. I apologize." Then he added in Turkish: "Go away smiling, Captain."

But George, in an impulse of conciliation, put his hand on the captain's arm.

"Captain, I agree with you," he said. "I think the civil war hurt all of us. But how could it have been avoided?"

Ignoring him, the captain stared at Dimitris. "Whenever I think of people like Colonel John Metaxas, that brilliant man, the man they call 'the Little Moltke,' rotting in Sardinia as a political exile—"

"Oh, skewer Metaxas!" Dimitris shouted. "If Metaxas had his way, we would never have sent this expeditionary force to Asia Minor. The German General Staff corrupted Metaxas. Let him rot."

The captain gazed back silently, and the muscles of his throat moved as he swallowed.

"Never mind," he said at last. Straightening his back, he turned to George. "I'm glad to meet this brave young man. He has a mind of his own. We agree."

"Do you agree, brave young man?" Dimitris said.

"Of course he does," the captain said, putting his arm around George's shoulders.

"A great historical event," Dimitris said. "Two Greeks agree."

George began to laugh. It was almost the only remark he had completely understood since entering the room, and he thought it not only witty but gracious. He looked at Dimitris in gratitude. What a good guy he really was! How could Eleni hesitate? Did she think men like this were a drachma a dozen?

The waiter brought a plate of fried sardines; but Dimitris, whose anger had cooled, waved them away.

"Bring those woodcocks," he said. "I've had enough of these blotters." He stood up, stretched himself and crossed the room to speak to some musicians who had come in and were tuning the strings of their *bouzoukia*. George saw him bend over to press a coin in the wrist of the leader, a tall, bony corporal, blond like the Walachians of Mount Pindus.

The captain, still pale, sat down at George's elbow and began complaining about the average man in Athens, who read his *Kathimerini* and had *no idea,* not the slightest; while Kostas leaned on George's other side snarling in his ear: "Men like Danglis didn't wait to be invited, boy. If Dimitris and I had waited until the King was ready to do something, you Anatolians would have been under the Turkish yoke for another five hundred years."

Dimitris came back and said: "Why don't you leave it where it is?"

Kostas looked up and laughed. "You're right, Taki. It can go to hell." The captain did not answer.

"This is my name day," Dimitris said. "I offer."

"You're right," Kostas said, "Let's drink some champagne. I want to drink and get drunk. All right, Captain? Let's all of us shut up."

But the captain went on deploring the benighted citizens at home in Athens, who thought that Asia Minor could be handed to Greece like a pasha's favor.

"They think the job's accomplished when the Prime Minister signs a document in Paris. But it's not easy. It's an enormous country, and the Turks are dug in like pebbles in the roots."

"Waiter?" Dimitris said. "Bring champagne."

"If only Athens would judge a military officer by his ability instead of his politics," the captain said. "Reunited, we could handle anything the Turks gave us."

While the waiter was setting a bucket on the table, the blond musician came over, struck a chord and began to sing. The captain glanced up, then closed his mouth and stared at the floor. Dimitris waved his fork like a baton and sang: "Venizelos . . . only you . . . know the road . . . to St. Sophia."

Other voices around the room joined in the Venizelist march. The Walachian musician, solemnly and fondly peering at his fingers on the struts, played the melody a second time. The captain did not raise his eyes. George could hear his heavy breathing. Then Dimitris sprang up and proposed a toast to the Prime Minister.

"Wait," said the captain, sitting back. "First to the King."

For a moment no one said anything. Dimitris put down his glass.

"Captain, you're trying to make trouble. I offer you a toast to Eleftherios Venizelos."

"Now, wait," said the captain. There was a nervous ticking at the corner of his mouth. "I offer you King *Alexander.*"

"Alexander?" Dimitris said. After a moment, he began to laugh. "Why not? Where is your glass, Captain?"

"Well, I have no wine," the captain said.

"I offer," Dimitris said. "My name day." And he walked around and poured some champagne into the captain's water tumbler. Everyone drank to young King Alexander, whom the Venizelists had put on the throne after they had exiled his father, Constantine. The toast to Venizelos, coming second, sounded awkward.

Then it was Kostas who demanded music, throwing down his winnings from the game and calling for a Butcher's Dance. With his lighted cigarette behind his ear and his tremendous purple nostrils flaring like the muzzle of a buffalo, he wheeled and hopped among the tables while the officers bombarded him with coins. Dimitris looked at Captain Mavropetros.

"You know his worst mistake?"

"Whose?" said the captain.

"King Constantine's."

The captain clamped his fingers on the edge of the table. "No. Let's hear you tell it."

"Listen," George said, "why don't we go along now? I think I can arrange a meeting with my father."

"His worst mistake," Dimitris said, "was trying to keep us neutral when all our interest was with France and England."

"So they destroyed him," the captain said in a heavy tone. "They cooked up a civil war and brought back Venizelos and imposed him on us like a vampire from the dead."

"Venizelos *united* us," Dimitris said. "He gave us pride. He gave us courage."

"Courage?" the captain said. He clenched his fists on the table and the small black lines of his mustache quivered like the legs of a cricket. "What do you know about courage? All you do is talk. When the fighting starts, you disappear."

With a sigh of forbearance, Dimitris shrugged his shoulders and closed his eyes. But Captain Mavropetros, whose face was drenched with milky perspiration, drew in a rasping breath. "If this army weren't so screwed up with politics, you'd have been busted to corporal for what you did on landing day. Is that what you call courage?"

Dimitris, tapping one finger gently on his bandaged wrist, answered calmly: "Look, Captain. You know I'd hack my rump off for a chance to get back to the Front—"

The captain snorted contemptuously. "Front? You'd fly like a sparrow if you took one look at the Front."

"—but until they can fix this arm up—"

"You don't even know where the Front is."

"—I'm confined to Smyrna."

George was choking with indignation. Was no one going to step in and defend Dimitris? Doubling his fists, he leaned toward the captain. "Why don't you take off, Mister? Nobody asked you to sit here."

Captain Mavropetros turned with a look of astonishment. Just then Kostas, in a torrent of sweat, rushed up, demanding to know what was wrong.

"I want him to dance with me," the captain said.

Dimitris said in a stifled voice: "I don't know your kind of steps."

"That's enough," Kostas said. "Everybody have a drink."

But the captain got up and swayed above them, pressing the tips of his fingers on the table. Some reddish blotches appeared along his cheekbones. His lips were the color of ashes. "I want him to stand up and dance with me."

The gunnery captain from Levadhia, blinking stupidly, chimed in: *"He* only dances to 'The Son of Mount Ida.'"

Dimitris looked from one face to the other. "Are all of you trying to insult me?"

"Only I am," said Captain Mavropetros. "I hate a coward."

Dimitris rose with a strangled cry. His chair fell back and overturned. He lunged against the captain, and the impact of his body threw them both against the wall. The room erupted with a panic roar; and George, lurching in with his shoulder to deflect the silver glitter, flailing his arms and awkwardly falling, came between them. The captain gave a sudden shriek. Dimitris sprang back, howling like a madman, with his wrist clasped tightly to his chest. With a look of horror, the captain touched his fingers to his thigh. He brought them up wet with blood.

Kostas whipped his head around and said to George: "In the name of God, get out of here. You cut the captain."

"But I didn't," George said helplessly. "I only tried to get in his way." And the captain cried: "Look at this! My God, just look!" And he held his sticky crimson fingers stiffly outstretched.

Dimitris turned and ran whimpering across the cardroom. George found him in the lobby with his head resting against the rack of Venizelist periodicals. His shoulders were convulsed by frightful sobs, his face was as white as yogurt and his arm was pressed to his body like a broken wing.

"Why didn't you tell us you were hurt?" George said. Not reproachfully, but in a warm torrent of compassion, of affection for this brother who was so much like himself: "Why didn't you let us know?"

"Would anyone have cared?" Dimitris asked.

As they were going out, they passed the waiter, who was bringing in the woodcocks cooked in wine.

Early that evening Eleni had gone downstairs to consult Polixeni—not as a soothsayer, but as a minister of moral counsel.

In soliciting the cook's advice, one had to bear in mind that she was virtually a saint. She had the natural spiritual vigor of women born on Amorgos; and, to her further unction, she had lived for several years on Naxos, where the presence of numerous Latin Catholics inspires the Greeks with competitive piety. Polixeni went to church with amazing diligence: Mass every Sunday, Vespers in the chapel, special liturgies on holy days, extraordinary fasts and strenuous confessions, longer and more frequent than her exemplary life could possibly have warranted. Her own sanctity naturally gave her a certain prudery toward normal human functions, and in matters of sexual morality she was particularly severe, having survived a prolonged personal struggle with Satan.

As she remembered it, her entire childhood on the stony islands, swept around by winding seas, had been a lonely, unremitting battle to preserve her chastity against the machinations of a horde of men and boys who wanted to proselyte her to the cult of Priapus. They had used every imaginable device to conquer her: gymnastic games, ecstatic dances, assaults from ambush, corrupted foods, erotic drinks and every sort of aphrodisiac. It filled her glowing eyes with tears to talk about her struggle with temptation. The devil had sought to invade her by every orifice, with an arsenal of weapons unbelievably diverse in shape, size, color and tumidity, most of which she could remember and describe in full detail. As a result, she understood the cause and remedy for every moral crisis, including the excessive voluptuousness aroused by the south wind, the palpitations caused by horseback riding and the debility produced by Solitary Vice.

Eleni had none of these complaints. It was simply that she had begun to dream about Lieutenant Dimitris Kalapothakis. Sometimes she would see him standing in the garden below her window, where she had once surprised a Turk. Without asking permission, he would try to climb inside. Leaning a heavy wooden ladder against the wall, he would begin to climb right up, while Eleni screamed silently and tried to fend him off with quilts and bolsters. His grinning brick-red face came up relentlessly; he opened the shutters, parted the lace curtains and tumbled panting over the window seat. Sometimes he only teased her, throwing loquats through the open window; but even these encounters terrified her.

It was becoming difficult for her to talk with him. He had a way of misinterpreting her most innocuous remarks. If she should ask, for instance, whether he liked the way she wore her hair, he would answer, with a suggestive leer, that he would prefer to part her hair in the middle, a remark that seemed vaguely improper. If she commented that the day was warm or moist, he would smile as though she had disclosed the most intimate information. Each time they met, he grew more impertinent.

So Eleni had excused herself from the drawing room, where her mother and father were playing baccarat, and gone back to the little servant bedroom under the kitchen stairs.

She envied the idiosyncrasy of Polixeni's room. It was furnished with only a marble-topped commode, a wooden stool and a sagging camp bed that almost completely filled the narrow space between the walls; yet it had enshrined the comprehensive mysteries of Polixeni's life for twenty years. Above the dresser was her altar: an ikon of the Virgin as the Font of Life; a stalk of dried fennel, filled with pith, in which to carry home a spark from the church candles to light the ikons of the house at the Resurrection; a lithograph of Our Lord in benediction, printed in Constantinople and purchased at the entrance to the Patriarchal Palace in the neighborhood of the Phanar; and a string of turquoise beads to ward off the Evil Eye. The room smelled of incense from the clothes Polixeni wore to church, which hung on a row of wooden pegs next to a picture of her late brother, Panayotis, framed in a wreath of ebony roses; and every level space was crowded with the things poor people save: pyramids of cast-off candy boxes, rows of empty perfume flasks and baskets of discarded spools, abandoned buttons, broken pencils and bits of twine.

But Polixeni reserved her room for her possessions and herself. She took Eleni to the kitchen to hear confession.

Unfortunately, this was not an easy problem to explain. Aside from the dreams, there was the paradox of her emotions. If Dimitris had meant nothing to her and had cared nothing for her, like that Turk in the garden, she would have experienced no difficulty in treating him courteously. But as soon as he had begun to show interest, she felt an irresistible desire to tease him, thwart him and find fault with him. She scarcely could speak to him in civil language; and she took every opportunity to remind him that they were not engaged.

Polixeni, putting a kettle of water on the stove, said criticism never hurt a man. As for the danger that he might lose interest—that simply did not exist.

"They thrive on denial," Polixeni said with authority. "They store up their fluids, and it nourishes them."

Eleni found this idea entrancing. Accepting a cup of tea, she promised to insult Mr. Kalapothakis incessantly so that he could store up his fluids, whatever they might be. The thought of nourishing him delighted her.

A few moments later, George brought Dimitris into the kitchen with blood on his tunic, and Eleni's kind intentions vanished. The lieutenant leaned like a bride on George's arm. They stumbled. Eleni had to help them through the door. Dimitris was as pale as paper. He refused to sit down, lie down or lean against the wall. He stood there, clinging to George, with a look of horror on his face.

"It's his arm," George said. "I think they smashed it."

Eleni noticed with surprise that George, who could be counted on to fall flat at the sight of pain, was unusually calm. Left to himself, he might have ministered competently to forty broken arms. But Polixeni, eager to take over, rushed away in flapping bedroom slippers to the cabinet where she kept her herbs and tinctures.

"Now, George? Go tell your father." That would get rid of him! "Eleni? Bring some cotton batting from my room."

"We ought to call a doctor," George said, while Dimitris

moaned and clutched his arm against his side. Polixeni prescribed a poultice and a splint. Rooting into bins of cardamon and wintergreen, she came up with a handful of dried herbs that filled the room with pungent fumes.

Eleni helped her brother put Dimitris on the kitchen table. He stretched out, quivering like a woman in travail. George fumbled, thick-fingered, with the buttons at Dimitris' throat.

"Let me," Eleni said, forgetting how quickly Mr. Kalapothakis could take advantage of an exposed position. But Polixeni called again for cotton; and Eleni ran. Trembling with haste, she threw aside the candy boxes and the empty perfume flasks and spilled a precious silver box, shaped like the pyx that holds the Eucharist reserved for Passion Week. It overflowed with damp, metallic fuller's earth from a holy mine in Cappadocia.

"Where do you keep it?"

Polixeni, having crossed herself three times, was instructing George in the application of a forearm bandage.

"Why three? Everything goes by threes among us Christians. Three candles at the feet of the dead—three splints to bind an arm. You only have to think about the Holy Trinity itself. How many kinds of wood in the Cross of Our Saviour? Three. How many days from the Entombment to the Resurrection? Three. What hour of the day did Our Saviour die? Why, three! How many hours upon the Cross—"

"The cotton!" Eleni called. "Where do you keep it?"

It was under the bed in an empty cigarette box, labeled "Régie Turque."

They had Dimitris sitting up. His back was toward her. She could see the black hair on his shoulder blades, in two thick patches, and the top of his white underdrawers above his pants. His back was whiter than his neck. There was a line of sunburn at the collar. Lowering her eyes, Eleni stepped forward and put the cotton wool on the table.

111

"I can't lift it," Dimitris was saying, in a sobbing wail. Polixeni dipped a linen cloth in boiling vinegar, called for a handful of eucalyptus leaves and made the sign of the Cross in the air above the table. As she threw the poultice against his wrist, Dimitris howled and beat his knees together.

"Whoever did this to you should be damned to Hell," Polixeni said, with the finality of the Last Judgment.

Wrapping the splints in cotton wool, she tied three strips of cloth around the brace, knotted each strip three times and sprinkled the outer covering with three drops of vinegar. Dimitris closed his eyes. The vinegar was dripping onto his pants. Eleni watched it trickling from the poultice, forming a dark stain across his thigh. She did not want to lift her eyes for fear she would be staring at his naked chest. Was it as hairy as his back? The thought of touching it aroused her to a strange excitement.

All at once, Dimitris swung his legs off the table and asked for a cigarette. George said: "Thank God! I was afraid you'd broken it." Then he turned pale and suddenly sat down. He had discovered a deep cut on the back of his hand, which was oozing blood.

"God in Heaven, another one," said Polixeni. Crossing herself, she put the vinegar to boil again. As she bent to wash George's hand, she muttered: "I ought to physic you, too. You stink of raki."

Eleni frowned at her brother until he raised his eyes and blinked self-consciously. It was so characteristic of him to have cut himself just when Dimitris needed help!

"What happened?" she asked. "Did you get drunk?"

George glanced over quickly; but Dimitris smiled and said everybody had a right to get a little tipsy now and then. As for the fight, that really had not been George's fault: the other man had brought it on himself.

"I was only trying to stop him," George said, looking from

one face to another, with his forehead wrinkled in apology. Eleni glared at him. Often she sympathized with George: he was oversized and uncertain, burdened with the expectations of a demanding father. But to have gotten drunk and started a fight! Mama would be furious. And all of it seemed to strike him as a huge surprise. His mouth fell open when Dimitris talked about his cool, courageous stance.

Dimitris was lashing his free arm to and fro. Muscles leaped like stallions under the smooth white skin of his shoulder. In the heat of the kitchen, his color returned. His throat swelled, his eyes flashed. Polixeni, scratching her hennaed scalp, stared at him.

"He's good-looking, all right," she muttered. Then she turned on Eleni. "Why don't you join your mama now? Remember what I told you."

But Eleni said to the lieutenant: "I hope you won't think George is bad-tempered. He is usually a gentleman."

Dimitris smiled. The hair on his body was crisp and black, like the hair above his temples. It formed a cross. The stave ran down from his collarbone to his navel and disappeared below his belt; the bar was on his breast. His nipples were as flat and dark as coins, and he wore a golden medal on a golden necklace chain.

"Good-looking, all right," Polixeni repeated. "The women like those white teeth, don't they? They like to kiss a nice, young mouth like that, eh?" And she seized Dimitris roughly by the neck and ran her knobby fingers through his hair, stroking his jaw, his ears and his naked back. Eleni, with a shiver, turned her head away. But Polixeni smacked her lips and laughed.

"By God, our Greek men are the handsomest on earth! The Blessed Loukas was so beautiful he had to pray to God to give him the face of a dog, so he could learn humility."

Dimitris went on smiling, breathing gently, with his lips

113

half open and his eyes on Polixeni's face. Now and then, he moved his moist gaze over to Eleni; but the cook went on lingeringly patting his shoulder.

"You like all this attention, huh? You'd like to be the only ram in the pasture, wouldn't you?"

Dimitris threw back his head, and his eyes gleamed. Polixeni tugged at his hair. Gently, she slapped his cheek.

"You think you've got some *special* thing that's so *particular*, so *wonderful*—"

She stopped abruptly, glancing at Eleni. Removing her hand from Dimitris' head, she said stiffly: "You better put your blouse on, Mr. Kalapothaki. It isn't decent for you to prance around here like a statue, in front of this girl."

Every time Eleni raised her face, she found Dimitris staring at her. There was no place she could rest her eyes. She looked at the ceiling, the window, the puddle of vinegar on the floor. But when her eyes went back to Dimitris, she met his impudent stare again. Her blood rose and tingled in her cheeks. Dimitris held out his shirt.

"You help me."

But Polixeni took the shirt and threw it rudely over his shoulders. It hung open on his chest; and the golden medal, coruscating with the rhythm of his breath, held Eleni in hypnosis. She gazed at the smooth blue line of his chin. Her mouth went dry. She scarcely could hear what the cook was saying: Mama wanted them to bring Dimitris to the drawing room; she was dying to embrace him, to console him. Later, she would serve a cold buffet in the Parisian style.

Dimitris stood up with his shirttails hanging out and offered Eleni his bandaged arm. But she drew away, made a formal European curtsy and said good night. A moment after Dimitris left, she moved to follow him, shaking her head in bewilderment.

George touched her arm.

"You are driving him away."

"He's disrespectful," Eleni said. "I can't bear his attitude." Then, regretting her earlier harshness, she added: "I'm sorry your evening turned out so badly."

"We had a fine evening," George said. "We played cards, drank champagne, danced. Dimitris introduced me to his army friends. This Kostas—he's the devil's stocking!"

Eleni knew that George detested men's clubs, military organizations, card games and dancing, and she suspected that the fight had terrified him; but for obscure reasons of his own, he never would acknowledge certain dislikes that to her seemed completely sensible.

"I'm very impressed with Dimitris," he said.

"Last week you said he was a braggart."

"I never said any such thing."

They went to the drawing room without speaking.

"Juicy as geese," Dimitris was saying. "You really should have been there." And Papa, looking surprised, said, "Yes, I would have liked that."

When Dimitris began to describe the fight again, Eleni felt her strength drain out like water whirling down a sink. She asked for a sip of brandy. As Dimitris handed her the glass, she rested her fingers lightly on his wrist. The smoothness of his flesh reminded her of a piece of polished oakwood warmed by the sun. She raised her eyes and met and held his gaze. Another wave of dizziness swept over her. Dimitris found a chair and drew it up beside her place. His knee pressed against her leg. She fumbled with a piece of cheese, but her fingers were too weak to lift it to her mouth.

Her father stood up to read his latest piece of verse, a saga of the Hellenes since the glorious recapture of Salonika on this date, the feastday of the city's patron saint, in 1912. It was called "The Seven Years of Sunlight," and was dedicated, "in danger of presumption," to Lieutenant D. Kalapo-

115

thakis on his name day, at the threshold of another seven years of sunlight.

Dimitris put his hand against Eleni's leg, as if by accident, and left it there. She could hear his breathing, and she wondered whether anyone else would notice it; but Papa was trumpeting like a drayman. The moment he was finished, Dimitris asked to hear over again the part beginning, "For 'tis better to die in freedom—"

"—Than to live forty years as a slave!" said Papa in a ringing voice.

"That's it," said Dimitris, with his fingers sliding down Eleni's thigh. "I like that. Don't you like that?"

Eleni gasped, licking her dry lips.

"It reminds me of a line of Rhigas," Dimitris went on, running his cupped hand to and fro. *"Better one hour of freedom than forty years of slavery."*

And Papa, turning scarlet, said he was glad someone had observed the similarity.

"Better to die in freedom!" Dimitris repeated. "Isn't that wonderful?"

Eleni, panting, echoed: "Wonderful!"

Her mother was eying them.

"You look feverish," she said, and she came and touched Eleni's forehead with the back of her wrist. "I'll ring for some sage tea."

"Yes, I'm exhausted," Eleni said. She struggled to stand up. "I have to go upstairs." In the hall, she passed the cook, who was grumbling about the incessant ringing of the servants' bell.

"Take the back stairway, Miss. Don't wait."

But, as Eleni passed the bins of fragrant herbs, she paused in a confusion of desire and indecision. She could feel Dimitris close behind her, breathing against her hair; and the aroma of the vinegar, the eucalyptus leaves, the perfume of

116

his skin, the musk of Polixeni's little shrine, the metal fumes of fuller's earth rose in her nostrils like a cloud of incense. Dimitris caught her from behind and drew her back against his chest.

His hand was clasped around her breast. He pressed his wet mouth on the back of her neck, like an animal biting the nape of its bitch. She turned, and somehow he had lost his shirt again. Her hands were lost in the down of his naked chest, touching little pips of flesh as small and hard as copper coins. Her mouth went up against his mouth in a moist saltiness of lips and perfumed hair and the soft, warm trembling of their indrawn breath.

She twisted free, dashed up the stairs and locked her door before she dared to look around.

Next morning, while Dimitris was drinking *café au lait* in the officers' mess, George Trigonis came in, wringing his big, heavy-knuckled hands. He was having what he called a "crisis of conscience" in regard to Captain Mavropetros. Last night there had been too much raki, too much talk, and everyone had picked on the captain, forcing him into a fight. George wanted to go to him, clasp his hand and apologize.

Dimitris rolled his eyes upward. The kid was so naïve he could scarcely believe it!

"Look," he said, "this Mavropetros isn't the type of man you want to make friends with, believe me. Theban. Descended from some Mavropetros who was assassinated years ago. More monarchist than the King. Hates Venizelos. He ought to be in exile."

"Well, I don't see why I can't apologize."

Dimitris groaned. That kind of sanctimonious cheek-turning always rubbed him the wrong way. You could be sure Captain Mavropetros wasn't thinking of making an apology! He had probably spent the morning precisely as Dimitris had, pondering his chances of winning or losing a court-martial conducted by a Venizelist officer.

"If I were you," Dimitris said, "I'd get busy and file an affidavit against Mavropetros before he can bring charges against you."

"Against *me?*" George said, and his childish face went limp. "But I only jumped in to warn you. I don't even own a knife." He shook his head. "You know, if you're big, everybody thinks you're Herakles."

Dimitris sipped his coffee.

"Let me tell you something I learned at the College of the Evelpides," he said. "A cartload of dung always rolls downhill, and a wise man jumps out of the way before it reaches him. Do you understand?"

"But why should it roll over *me?*"

"Because Kostas and I are Venizelist officers and Mavropetros is a captain. You're only a civilian."

George stared at his feet. He wiped a line of perspiration from his upper lip.

"Should I talk to his commanding officer?"

"Jesus and Mary, don't you know anything about the army? As far as the army's concerned, an incident like this is poison. It makes people think we're a bunch of roughnecks. Go talk to the High Commissioner. Or talk to the Metropolitan. You heard those things Mavropetros said about exiling people and shooting officers against the wall? The guy is dangerous. He wants to overthrow the government."

And, to assure himself that George did not lose heart, Dimitris drained his cup, laid the palm of his hand between the boy's muscular shoulder blades and firmly pushed him toward the Cathedral of St. Photini, the office of the Metropolitan Chrysostomos, the highest religious authority of the Greek community.

As they were passing through the arch, a midday bell be-

118

gan to ring, and pigeons burst like puffs of gun smoke from the fenestellas of the tower. The paving had been freshly swept and sprinkled; it glittered like a golden paten. Bougainvillaea vines hung over the walls, and the smell of incense drifted from the sanctuary.

Near the door to the chapel, a rosy, dark-eyed girl looked at them with interest. Dimitris stopped and crossed himself three times, wondering whether he should follow her inside on the chance that she might let him feel her up. But the girl took hold of her old mother's arm and scuttled away, casting back a glance that made his stomach seethe with longing.

The Palace of the Metropolitan adjoined the courtyard. Supplicants entered through a musty gallery hung with etchings of the national revolution. There were drawings of the maids of Souli, flinging themselves from a parapet above the Adriatic, and of the wives of Missolonghi, clasping infants to their bosoms as they fled across the pestilential marshes. In the anteroom were the Patriarch, King Alexander and Venizelos; a triptych of Golgotha, flanked on the left by the Acropolis of Athens and on the right by the Basilica of Haghia Sophia, stripped of the four Islamic minarets that the Turks had built around its sacred dome; and, on the opposite wall, the Sacred Battalion of Prince Ypsilanti, white-faced and solemn in doublets of Byronic velvet, marching to their death through swirling Danube fog.

George stood with his mouth half open, contemplating the agony of Athanasios the Deacon, who was turning like a skewered lamb above an open fire, while a platoon of Turkish soldiers warmed themselves around the pyre.

"It's not exactly an inspiration to love your enemies," he said.

"Nobody ever won his freedom by loving his enemies," Dimitris said.

"I know," George said, "but I don't like cruelty. It seems to me most wars are just an excuse to murder someone who has something you want."

Dimitris snorted. Even for an Anatolian, the kid was a cream puff—always pretending he was itching for a fight, but scared to death of losing his own sweet butt.

"Is that why you'd like to forgive that shit-bespangled Royalist who tried to murder me?"

George did not answer. He went and sat down on a wooden bench, next to a woman in black who crossed herself at every sound. He made some notes on a piece of paper. An hour passed before the door swung open on the office of a *locum tenens,* Deacon Gabriel, as deaf as a judge.

"Come in! Ah, yes, this picture interests you? It's Saint Polycarp, of course, Bishop of Smyrna, martyred in the year 155 After Christ."

"I know," George said. "When may we see the Metropolitan?"

"The Metropolitan holds Saint Polycarp in high regard," said Deacon Gabriel, "although the Latins act as if they'd invented him." Jerking his head in the direction of the Roman Catholic church, he made a face. "It was a dreadful persecution of our ancestors! So many Christians taken! Some of them were scourged and others burned. One man broke loose just as the Roman guards were bringing him before the populace, and he ran across the stadium and clasped a snarling beast against his naked body! That very night, in a dream, the Bishop saw his pillow in flames. He said to his friends, 'Now I understand. I must be burned alive.' "

The deacon gazed in satisfaction at the immolation of St. Polycarp. At last, he turned and waved Dimitris to a chair and offered him a box of cigarettes.

"I suppose this boy has come to enter the Smyrna Legion?"

Dimitris laughed. "Does this boy look as if he came to enter the Smyrna Legion?" In fact, George looked as if he were about to desert his skin.

"Well, he could do much worse, you know." The deacon fastened a pince-nez between his bushy white eyebrows and studied George's face. "You're a Smyrniot, aren't you? Don't I know your father?"

George shouted his name three times and finally wrote it on a piece of paper. The deacon looked and gave a cry of pleasure.

"Why, of course! Your father is a splendid patriot. He understands the glory and the burden of our patriotism."

And the old man got up and paced around the room, raving in a loud, toneless voice about the birthright of the Greeks. A Greek of Asia Minor had to win his country for himself. It was the resurrection of his soul, his recompense for centuries of slavery, his opportunity to claim the legacy of hope that he had tasted in his mouth incessantly, like a coin placed under the tongue of the dead to be spent in Paradise.

Then, while George was staring at him in horrified silence, he flopped into his chair, pulled out a ledger and carefully transcribed the name onto a clean page.

"It's a list we're making of the patriotic young men who can be counted on to volunteer."

Dimitris looked at George and showed his teeth.

"Hey, boy! Now you'll be able to attain the glorious martyrdom of Saint Polycarp!"

"Saint Polycarp?" the deacon said. "What an inspiration to the Christian spirit! Just look how the artist has depicted the flames, the crowd! It was Saturday, you see?—the Hebrew Sabbath—and the Roman games were over for the day. They dragged the Bishop before the Proconsul—his name was Statius Quadratus—for a sort of trial. 'Polycarp?' they said, 'do you swear by Caesar's fortune?' And, over again: 'I ask you, Polycarp—do you swear by Caesar's fortune?' But Polycarp repeatedly answered—"

"Listen," George said, in a tense, uncertain voice, "how long do we have to wait to see the Metropolitan?"

"Metropolitan Chrysostomos? Oh, he isn't here today. . . . See how he has painted all these people carrying armloads of faggots from the public baths? Look here—this one is laughing!"

"He isn't here?" George said.

"No, no," said Deacon Gabriel. "Over *here.*" And he went and tapped his finger on the martyry. "You see? They stripped him and they bound him to the stake. But, as you see, the flames arched over his body and whirled around him. There was a beautiful fragrance, like a fresh loaf from the oven. Like gold and silver melted in a crucible. The pagans were terrified. They sent a butcher in to stab him with a dagger, and the torrent of blood put out the flames. And at the last—a dove flew out of his body!"

"Tomorrow?" George shouted, almost sobbing. "Will he be here tomorrow?"

"Metropolitan Chrysostomos? Oh, yes," the deacon said. Piously, he added: "God willing." He used the Moslem term, *inshallah.* "You *are* an eager volunteer, aren't you?" And he laughed and patted George paternally. "Well, my dear boy, you can't have your rifle and your kit today. I'm only the *locum tenens,* you see. In any case, it can't be done with pumpkin seeds. There are documents to sign, authorizations, records. . . ."

"Oh, God in Heaven . . ." George murmured. Rolling his eyes, he looked over at Dimitris, who saluted cheerfully.

On the way out, George unfolded the notes he had made, anathematizing Mavropetros.

"It's no use," he said. "He'll probably have me arrested."

"Oh, give it here," Dimitris said. "I'll see to it that Chrysostomos gets your deposition."

They stopped in the shadow of the arch, under a marble pediment engraved with a delicate relief of Jesus at the well of Sychar, talking to the prostitute who was enlightened by His Grace: "Whosoever drinketh of the water that I shall give him shall never thirst. . . ."

George ventured an opinion that it did not matter whether or not they wrote your name in a book.

"Oh, it matters, it *does* matter," Dimitris said, and he gave George's arm a malicious squeeze. "Won't Papa be proud of you?"

CONSTANTINOPLE

MARCH, 1920

*T*hat winter the Allied police patrolled the capital in search of certain obscure and sinister Turkish agitators whom foreign correspondents called "Kemalists," after General Mustapha Kemal, the hero of Gallipoli, who had escaped the city and was organizing an army to resist partition. The "Kemalists" themselves did not adopt the name. They called each other "Vatandash"—Compatriot—or sometimes, like the Russian Bolsheviks, "Comrade." But the newspapers of Europe and America needed a distinctive term for these intractable revisionists, the villains of the Turkish insurrection; and, as a result, every Moslem criminal in the capital became, in name at least, an agent of Mustapha Kemal.

For Abdullah, it was a winter of interminable waiting. Sometimes he waited for Plum-Lip Faik, who had established himself in a hut by the city wall and was keeping a record, with a stylus on a pat of clay, of every French and English vehicle that passed along the road to Thrace. Every Friday, God willing, Faik would bring his kiln-baked hieroglyphs to the courtyard of the Fethi Mosque, whence they could be peddled to an agent in the service, surprisingly, of the Italians. Often, Abdullah would stand there for an hour or more, watching the swaying canvas curtain at the door, and then would leave with nothing to report except the unreliability of Plum-Lip Faik.

Sometimes he waited for Jafer the Blue, who had become a telegrapher at the Red Crescent organization. In a single day, Jafer could dispatch a message to Mustapha Kemal, eight hundred miles inland, receive the answer and decode it without drawing the attention of the Allied censors. His intelligence reports were delivered in a stall at Sirkeji, where shish kebab was broiling over a charcoal fire. Jafer would traffic only in benign and optimistic rumors. He joyfully reported that Mustapha Kemal had moved his headquarters to some delightful little city on the Baghdad Railway line, or that a group of plucky villagers in Bolu had seized a telegraph. If there was a disheartening message to convey, Jafer stayed at home.

Too often, Abdullah waited for the infamous and dilatory Pefko. Far from the shelter of his drugstore, he would lurk for hours on some remote and windswept corner, cowering under the projecting bay of some decayed old house. At last, a figure in a dripping cloak would dart around the corner, pass him a note embedded in a cigarette and disappear: "No news."

And then, consumed with fury and despair, Abdullah would stamp his numb feet in the freezing mud and trudge back down the hill to Emin Önü, where the Turan Pharmacy provided a damp and rueful sanctuary for the flame of revolution. The tedium weighed on him. He yearned for noisy meetings, demonstrations, secret missions. He was tired, tired, tired of waiting.

But never had he waited so patiently, so willingly as he was waiting for Namik. Namik was a patriot and an intellectual, a teleologist of Turkish lore and Western science; he was a propagandist and a purifier of the Turkish spirit; and, furthermore, he was the richest man in Turkey. If anyone could supply the money to buy five thousand rifles, it would be Namik.

Unfortunately, Namik's resistance was immense. He was eating rosebud conserve, with his eyelids closed and his tongue against his spoon.

"Who is this Pefko? Do I know him?" And, belching through his nose, he dipped his sticky teaspoon into a glass of water. He had been eating, silently and greedily, for half an hour: first, citron peels and greengage plums; then apricots and melon rinds, and, finally, an almost unbelievable number of sugared roses, from which a crimson syrup trickled down his hairless chin.

Enthroned on a velvet cushion in a window bay above the blackness of the sea, Abdullah watched in sick amazement. His reply was slow and carefully composed.

"Pefko is—well, the *proper* man for this. *À-propos,* as the French would say."

"My dear Abdullah, what do I care about the French? We're Turks, not Europeans."

"Ah, God knows that's the truth," Abdullah murmured. No matter how asinine his host's remarks, he would try to keep a short tongue in his head: Namik liked to do the talking.

How well Abdullah understood this breed! Born in Paris, ripened in Berlin, polished in London, frequently (and gratefully) mistaken for a Spaniard, a Neapolitan or a Serb, Namik was exactly the sort of Turk one met in every spa in Europe. His parents owned a factory in Egypt, a villa on the Côte d'Azur. They spent their summers by a lake in Switzerland. Their rugs were stored in Boston and their bank deposits in Geneva.

In Europe, Namik had developed a curious, synthetic sense of nationality. For entertainment, he had joined a Turkish literary club in Bern. The members, who had lived for decades in sight of the Alps, called each other "Brother Turk," while wallowing on thick Bokhara carpets and drinking fermented mare's milk. They tried to purge their speech of Arabic and Persian phrases, raved about the cult of the Red Apple, *Volkskultur* and the social status of Turkish women at the time of Genghis Khan.

Namik had been entranced and then engulfed by their deceitful chauvinism. He began to dream of Ottoman revival. The success of the Young Turk coup d'etat unhinged his mind: he sold his flat in Bern and bought a ticket on the Orient Express. When the war trapped him in Constantinople, he understood why other members of the Turkish literary club had remained in Switzerland; but it was then too late. Namik was established in Sokullu Mehmet Pasha, the oldest and most dignified quarter in the city; and his house had become a shrine of Turkism. Students gathered to wallow on the thick Bokhara rugs and call each other "Brother Turk"; and Namik became the keeper of a flame.

In times past, Abdullah might have joined these young Turanians, drinking *kümiss* and talking nonsense. But now that he had more important things to do, Namik's affectations amused him. While Namik was arguing about the use of French, he, Abdullah, was immersed in the dangerous realities of revolution.

"Of course, he *isn't* Turkish," Abdullah ventured, wondering where all of this was leading. "He may even be a double agent. But he *does* have the materials we need."

Namik closed his eyelids and his nostrils flared and whitened with a stifled yawn. "You'll smoke?"

The servant had brought in a water pipe and a glowing coal between a pair of tongs. Namik, the paragon of Oriental manners, was occupied for several minutes inspecting the meerschaum bowl. When the pipe was filled, he looked up.

"What are they?"

"Your Honor?" Abdullah said.

"These materials you need."

Abdullah took a breath, leaned forward and whispered: "Five thousand rifles."

Namik, pipe in hand, began to laugh.

"Rifles? Oh, my dear Abdullah Bey! How priceless!"

"Is that so funny?" Abdullah said. "Cannons don't eat honey."

"Ah, you are right!" Namik cried, still smiling. "Are you a Kemalist, then?"

"After a fashion."

"And you want to buy some guns for Mustapha Kemal?"

Abdullah hesitated for an instant. Then he tipped his head affirmatively.

Namik laughed again. "For a moment, I thought you actually wanted guns for *yourself,* and the idea struck me so marvelously funny—the idea of *you*—the idea of *us,* poets and intellectuals, taking up arms!" He wiped his eyes.

"Poets have toppled thrones," Abdullah said, swallowing his anger in an obsequious smile.

"Why, of course they have, my dear. But not with the *sword*. Why, I do all sorts of poetic throne-toppling myself!"

Shifting on his enormous hams, he murmured something to the servant, who drew back with an expression of disapproval.

"Never mind," Namik said. "Do as I say." Then, to Abdullah: "I have something for you."

The servant brought in a flat metal box and put it on his master's lap. Abdullah strained forward eagerly; but Namik brought out a ledger bound in marbled boards and took from it some sheets of writing paper that were tucked among the pages of accounts.

"As you know, Abdullah Bey, one need only to live in Europe to understand the true meaning of his country," he said, putting on his spectacles. "Now, this is a public letter to Lloyd George. I've sent copies of it to the Manchester *Guardian* and the *Petit-Parisien*. You know those European liberals"—and he gave Abdullah a confidential smile—"they look upon themselves as great humanitarians, but they're the ones who hate us Turks so vindictively. Think of Gladstone! Any sort of vengeance is justified—as long as it's directed against the Turks." He laughed again; but Abdullah could not force a smile.

"Here's what I wrote. 'The treaty now proposed between the Allies and the Ottoman government is cruel and unjust. It is a vestige of medievalism—a new crusade against the Moslems.' What do you think of that? Good, isn't it? 'But the Turks are going to show you something new. They are going to show you a new nation, rising out of the dust of the old Empire.' Do you like it?"

And, with many pauses, chuckles and elaborations, Namik read to the very end a three-page letter to the Prime Minister of Great Britain.

"You see? I see my role—and yours, dear friend—in the field of intellectual leadership. Not buying rifles." He smiled at Abdullah who sat in glum disappointment on his elegant cushion. "Now, if you had come to me with a proposal for presswork—say, a pamphlet like *Smyrna Is Turkish*. Have you seen it? Flames on the cover? But rifles!" He stretched out his open hands. "It's too absurd, my dear." He seemed at the point of breaking off the conversation. Abdullah cast around with a feeling of desperation. He wished now that he had lied about the use of the money as well as its beneficiary. Namik was struggling to stand up. "Besides, I never have reposed much confidence in General Mustapha Kemal, and he is eight hundred miles away, stemless and ropeless. . . ."

But Abdullah, trembling, took hold of the rich man's sleeve and cried: "Listen—I lied to you. I was embarrassed. The rifles *are* for me."

"Ah, Abdullah Bey! Now you *do* surprise me." But this time Namik did not laugh. "For yourself alone?"

"Myself and my men. Faik, Jafer and Remzi."

"No others?"

"Many more, Your Honor."

"Five thousand?"

"There will be hundreds of thousands, Your Honor. All over Asia."

"Ah, I see," Namik said. He sat down again, took up the amber mouthpiece of his water pipe and sucked it thoughtfully. "You are asking me to contribute to an international revolution."

Abdullah did not answer; and Namik went on: "Why should I give money to revolutionists? What will become of me if revolutionists take over?"

Abdullah looked Namik in the eye. "Your Honor, if you do not give money now, out of compassion, the same money will be taken from you later, by force. I think it is wise for a rich man to assure himself of a place in the world of the future."

"You are selling insurance?"

Abdullah bowed.

"This Pefko," Namik said. "He's a Greek, isn't he? They always play the double game. How much is he asking?"

Abdullah glanced around the room, sizing up the old Ladik carpet, the reading stand, the cloisonné: to ask too little would insult the great monographer of Turkish culture.

"Twenty thousand pounds."

"Ridiculous! I'll lend you five at interest."

Abdullah pretended to be shocked: "Do you expect us to carry slingshots and ride on donkeys?"

They came to rest at ten thousand pounds. Namik dug slowly into the metal box.

"It will be a good investment," Abdullah said. "You will not be forgotten."

Namik sighed.

"I should be honored to be ignored," he said. "If Mustapha Kemal comes to power, I will certainly be hanged."

The hour of Abdullah's next appointment, being *à la Franque,* was too early. The air was chilly in the celebrated bistro, where an unauthenticated bastard of the Russian royal house served Black Sea caviar and watered brandy and allowed his customers to pinch an exiled duchess. Half the tables were deserted, the remainder occupied by a dejected Monday-evening clientele—commercial travelers and foreign military officers of minor rank, staring into space. The band was playing "There Are Smiles," while an English sailor pushed a Russian whore around the dance floor with his thighs.

Abdullah chose a table near the wall and sat down cautiously, remembering not to peer around or touch his belly with his hand. A money belt was hanging like a snake around his loins. It held ten thousand Turkish pounds, the seed of the new world.

Abdullah's feet were cold; he was the only person in the house who was wearing a fez; the waiters looked like secret agents; and every time he moved his head, he felt the swift, lascivious attention of an array of mercenary Russian women who were nodding over tinted soda water at the corner table.

Still, he was swept along by the exhilaration of a personal victory. Inflamed ambitions had compelled him to accept this task; and, having set himself to buy an arsenal for the insurrection, he had carried out the wearisome details with the skill of an old campaigner. This was his final master stroke— a meeting with Pefko at the Golden Bear, which was notorious from Berlin to Baghdad as a place of treacherous intrigue. Pefko would have been more circumspect. He had as many meeting places as he had transactions, but most of them were dull and inconspicuous. Abdullah, however, sensed the deep current of history flowing. A cat-infested konak in Shishli might be suitable for planning propaganda pamphlets; but this transaction, which would ignite the Asiatic revolution, required a memorable setting—a public place, depraved but debonaire, that would forever symbolize the dying world.

He ordered whisky, although he was aware that it would make him even more conspicuous. An ounce of whisky cost more than a meal, and it could strike you as blind as a mole. The Russian women nudged each other. The waiter poured a double dose and set the bottle on the table.

"You'll have some ice?"

"What for?" He tasted the liquor and shuddered uncontrollably.

Forty minutes passed before another soul came in. Then the tables suddenly began to fill with questionable, surreptitious folk, the very sort you might expect to find in a White Russian nightclub on a winter night—blond Italian spies, noisy Greek spies, morose Bengali spies, enterprising Spanish-Hebrew spies, who talked in French about commercial ventures in the Danube states. Murky figures drifted past him, staring down through rings of smoke and shafts of yellow light, and all around him voices rumbled in that lifeless calm with which Constantinople masks its passionate, unstable temper. Each time the door was opened, a cold draft swept around the room. The Spanish Jews, addressing one another as *"mon cher"* and *"mon p'tit,"* began a critical analysis of someone named Maurice, who had sold in Bucharest at fifteen francs the oka.

Abdullah swallowed a second glass of whisky. He touched his watch but was afraid to take it out. He called the waiter.

"Listen, have you seen Mr. Pefko?"

Instantly, there was a lull in the conversation, and Abdullah heard somebody say the word "police."

132

"Mr. Pefko, sir? I'll ask the manager."

"No, no. I'll wait. Just take the whisky back and bring some raki."

This, too, he tossed off quickly, hoping it would calm his heart. Instead, it made his ears unbearably acute: "Police. . . . Allied police."

He thrust his index finger quickly through the buttons of his fly to feel the money belt. The Russian women stirred like sleepy hens. Unable to sit still, he stood up, swallowed a glass of raki neat, and walked over to the corner table.

Without a word, the nearest girl stood up. Her face was made of little crescents, black and white: black crescent eyebrows, tiny crescent eyes and high white crescent cheeks. Abdullah grasped her waist. But when he tried to dance, he bumped against a column set with chips of mirrors.

"Pardon, " he said, stopping to wipe his face. "I'm druggist. Did you know that? . . . No, I'm poet, really. There aren't many of us left." They bumped against the column, then against the English sailor. The Spanish Jews were leaning close together. They had forsaken French and were berating one another in Ladino. The band played "There Are Smiles."

Abdullah's partner rearranged the crescents of her face like decorations on a mask. That was a smile. Abdullah squeezed her waist and rubbed himself against her, comforted in his loneliness, yet thinking suddenly: How bitterly Hilmi Pasha would have hated her!

The girl was pushing him around the dance floor, through the miasma of wet wool and muddy overshoes, moving her eyebrows in the rhythm of the music. What in the name of God was everybody celebrating? The decline and fall of Rome? The first of Lent? The ides of March?

In his father's lifetime, it had been possible to say, "I despise these things." Those were the days of Islamic certainty, Hilmi Pasha's days. It was possible to pray five times a day

133

and to be unequivocal and proud. The Turks did not know the cost of pride; they had not yet paid the price of defeat. They simply said, "Hold tight, God knows what's right," and knew that God would save the Empire.

But God cared nothing for Turks or Greeks, Germans or Serbs. The souls of men ran through his hands and fell like grains of sand, the white in Heaven and the black in Hell, and God cared not; and the earth was given to the strong, regardless of prayers or pride.

The music stopped. The girl was cocking back her head. Her hand fell naturally against the fly of Abdullah's trousers, and he shuddered with a spasm of desire.

"Look here," he whispered. "Something I want to know." Then, with a start: "What time is it? . . . Do you speak Turkish?"

"No, baby. What you want?"

Trembling, he drew out his watch. It was half past twelve, European style. The girl allowed her hand to move in an impertinent caress; then she raised her fingertips and covered the face of the watch.

"I'm very nice. You like me?"

Abdullah led her to his table. He poured himself another glass of raki. For several minutes he held the watch cupped in his hand and tried to understand what twelve-thirty meant. The girl plucked at his sleeve.

"Where's whisky-soda?"

"You a Greek girl?" he asked at last.

"Hunh?"

"Are you Greek? . . . French?"

"Not understand," she said, laughing.

"You Greek? *Grecque?*"

"Ah! *Non—Russe.*"

He reached under the table and felt the inside of her leg with his hand.

"Turks hate Russians," he said. "In fact, Turks hate everyone, and everyone hates Turks."

"You want me?" she said, fingering the ringlets of her hair.

"Yes . . . No, I feel sick. I need a little raki with some plain, fresh water. . . . Some sleep."

Mechanically, the girl massaged Abdullah's knee and yawned while he was gazing at her. With difficulty, he could separate her eyes and eyebrows, which had melted together into a single pair of crescents. The curve of her throat intrigued him; he drew her to his side and touched her earlobe with his tongue. A thrill constricted his stomach. Then, suddenly queasy, he pressed his face against her hair.

His mouth was filled with water. He swallowed repeatedly and struggled to draw more air into his lungs. The girl, who was shivering with incessant yawns, leaned heavily on his shoulder. Under the table, her relentless hand was like a rabbit burrowing into a nest. Suddenly, she was quiet. He felt her fingers touching his canvas money belt.

He reared back, pushing her away, and overturned the bottle. Clapping his hands for the waiter, he tried to stand up. The girl clutched at his sleeve; but he broke loose and staggered through the banks of smoke, the blinding bars of light. At the door, he clutched a velvet drapery, and a fountain of scalding raki erupted from his throat.

Pefko. Twelve-thirty. What a fool!

The cobblestones were glittering with moisture, and the street was filled with cold mist and the smell of kerosene. Abdullah leaned against a wall. The boiling fountain burst again, and tears ran down his cheeks. Then he stumbled toward a narrow stairway, darker than a cistern, and sat down, shivering and spitting.

A moment later he reared up and gave a fearful groan. Pefko! Twelve-thirty! He ran all the way to the dance hall in the Petits Champs des Morts; but the janitors were sweeping

135

up. Next, he thought of trying the Hungarian café below the Flower Passage, and then Tokatlian's Hotel on the Grande Rue. The chandeliers were shining dimly on a row of potted palms and empty leather chairs. He visited a German beer hall, a corner coffeehouse, a printer's shop and the padlocked office of a magazine called *Bülbül*, which was published in French by a Greek from Egypt. Finally, he hired a carriage near the gates of Galata Saray and drove to Shishli, to the corrupt old konak beyond the groves of mulberries. Nobody answered his knock, and when he pressed his face against a windowpane, he could see that the rooms were empty.

On the way back, the rain began again. The driver stopped below Taxim to fasten the side curtains and put clogs under the wheels. Three English roadsters passed them, filled with Allied officers and followed by a motor truck with rifles showing below the canvas hood.

"Arresting some poor Turk," the driver said.

They crept down the hill of Beyoglu. The Golden Horn came into view, seething in the mist, with the hills of the old city spread out beyond it like an ash heap scattered with chips of burnished glass. Another turn, and the old, the Moslem city vanished like Byzantium. Raindrops sizzled on the roof. At the bottom of the hill, they stopped again. Abdullah held his breath for a moment, listening. Just as he was about to call to the driver, somebody rocked the carriage, trying to open the side curtain.

"Hand out your pass and then get down."

Abdullah put his eye against a crack and looked down at a young man with a scrubby mustache and a pimply forehead, dressed in an English uniform without insignia. The rain was bouncing on the floorboards of a wagon up ahead. There were six or seven carriages beyond it. It was too dark to see the Galata Bridge; but you could see the tolltakers in their white smocks and the Sikh patrolmen standing guard.

Abdullah handed down his pass. The young policeman put

it on the bottom of a soggy stack of yellow cards.

"Get down, now. You're required to pass inspection." He walked away to meet another carriage coming down from Beyoglu.

A car went past the line and stopped at the tollhouse. An English officer got out and stood in the beam of the head lamps; then a small man in a rubber cloak; and then Pefko.

He had on a thick, wool coat, a scarf and a beret, pulled down to his ears; but his face was clearly visible. Under the lamps, his skin was as white as cheese. He was shaking hands with a guard inside the doorway. The officer was waving toward the bridge. Pefko looked back at the carriages and shaded his eyes with his hand. The policeman with the pimples ran along the line, clutching his stack of soggy cards: "Inspection! The toll bridge is being closed!"

Abdullah waited until Pefko turned his back. Then he got down quietly and walked away. As he reached the flooded gutter at the edge of the street, he heard them calling him. Somebody shouted for a lantern. He lowered his head and ran. The money belt slapped like a kurbash on his genitals. When he came to the steps below the Tower of Galata, he lay down, gasping like a fish. How, how in the name of God, would he get around without a pass?

He picked out his shelter for the night the way a man selects his meeting place with death: after running to the limit of his breath, he found a threshold, shuddered feebly and turned in. It turned out to be a whorehouse called the New Berlin, a verminous pension priced midway between the Yankee House in Beyoglu and the twelve-cent shacks on Peach and Almond Streets.

A woman in purple velvet came downstairs and scrutinized him. She had flecks of mica in her curls, a hairy mole above her mouth and a crucifix around her throat. It was a Christian house, of course (the Moslem places were in Üsküdar and

137

Kadiköy), but she was not a Greek. At best, she was a Latin Catholic, schooled to detest the Greeks and their religious separation; at worst, a European Levantine, with an exile's contempt for every nationality. Quite likely, she was also an informer: the Allies, like all police, gave protection in return for information.

But Abdullah was too tired to run again. He asked for a room.

"A room?"

"All to myself."

"Ah, *well*, my pet . . ." And, hooking her hand beneath his elbow, she led him up the stairs. "I thought you were a stallion." She turned a doorknob. "White and bright. Smells just like musk."

It was a tiny room, as cold as death, with roaches scurrying across the floor. A man was stretched out on the white iron bedstead, covered with a pad of cotton ticking, another on a narrow settee with a horsehair cushion. They were obviously proper Balkan townsmen. Before going to bed, they had stripped off their outer clothes and packed them into cardboard suitcases, which were stacked on top of the garderobe; and they lay there as still as corpses in their muslin underdrawers, with their faces covered by their quilts and their feet protruding.

"Those are some peeled bananas," the women said with a contemptuous laugh. "You'll get along fine."

Abdullah wrapped himself in his cloak and lay down on a pallet in the corner. He listened to the building shudder in the wind. After a while, he got up and tried the bolt. Then he pulled up his shirttails and untied the money belt. It had ten large pockets, each divided into ten small pockets for a single coin. When he moved it gently to and fro, it made a dull, ambiguous thumping sound. He laid it on his chest, turned to the wall and closed his eyes.

A moment later, the limp gray curtains filled with strands of light. Getting up quietly, he shuffled past the Balkan townsmen, drew the bolt and went downstairs.

The foyer was dark, the chain lock on the door. A clock was ticking in the hall. A boy of eight or ten, whose skull had been shaved and dabbed with gentian violet, was standing by the wood stove, rubbing his palms on the seat of his trousers and curling up his naked toes. For a moment, he surveyed Abdullah blandly. Then he plunged his dappled brown-and-purple head into the fuel box and began to root around.

Abdullah sat down on a hassock. In the pocket of his coat, he found some flimsy writing sheets that he had bought at a tobacco counter during his elaborate exchange of notes with Pefko. Pressing his arm against his side to curb the trembling of his hand, he wrote:

"The salesman has betrayed our confidence."

But when he read this over, it appeared to be unnecessarily ambiguous, yet at the same time vaguely indiscreet. He tore it up and wrote instead:

"My Honored Friends: Our business venture has been terminated by the other party. It is essential that I see you. The bearer of this note will lead you back to me."

Then, after wavering between his name and his initial, he folded up the note unsigned and called the boy, who was broadcasting sawdust as energetically as a lumber mill.

"Look, do you know Emin Önü?"

"Everybody knows Emin Önü."

"There is a coin for you over there. But the size of it is shrinking every minute."

"A coin?" the boy repeated, studying his toes. "At Emin-Önü?"

What a saltless idiot! Abdullah gripped him by the arm and drew him down.

"Look here. You're Turkish, aren't you?"

139

"Sir?"

"Are you a Turk?"

"That's exactly what I am. A Turk."

Abdullah cleared his throat and made an effort to speak gently.

"Let me hear you say, 'Squeeze these sixty-five hazelnuts.'"

"Sir?"

"Squeeze these sixty-five hazelnuts."

The boy, picking his nostrils, drew a circle on the floorboards with his toe.

"Sixty-five of them?"

"Oh, take the letter!" What was the point of catechizing such a dummy? In any case, there were some Greeks—even a few Armenians from certain areas—who spoke without an accent. "Wait . . . Is there a stairway to the roof?"

They went up three floors and climbed a ladder. A stiff wind was blowing, and the tiles were dry. Abdullah went directly to the edge and looked down on the empty street. Although it was past the hour of first prayer, the steps that led down to Bank Street were deserted and the candy shops were closed. Screens of heavy wire had been drawn across the windows. The only movement was the rush of water through the gutters. At the bottom of the hill, the harbor shrank away, showing its gray and heaving belly like a dying fish. Abdullah nudged the boy.

"Turn your head in the direction of Valide Mosque. . . . Now, look to the left. Do you see a wooden building with a sign?"

But the boy was staring in the wrong direction. "Hey!" he said. "Is that an English ship?"

Turning to look, Abdullah felt as if someone had laid cold fingers on the scruff of his neck. Far out, beyond the point of the seraglio, there was a blue-gray cruiser, slowly wheeling toward the land. You could see the sailors standing on the decks and the little pennants whipping in the wind.

"What's the matter?" the boy said.

But Abdullah shoved him toward the stairs.

"Go! Don't stand here catching flies."

The English cruiser drifted in toward Cannon Point, where the pale cupolas and chimneys of the Sultan's old seray protruded from a blackened woodland. A signal lamp was blinking on the bridge; the heavy guns were raised.

Abdullah began to shiver. Clasping his hands across his eyes, he swayed back and forth, muttering that he was lost, betrayed, forsaken. Then he got down clumsily on the tiles and tried to pray. But his thoughts raced ahead of the movements of his prayer, straight out of his head: boat tickets, pistols, a headcloth, a veil . . . He sprang up and staggered to the ladder.

Down in the vacant streets, an automobile engine started up, a siren whined.

That night, wrapped in a sheet and blinded by a veil, Abdullah waited on the landing stage at Karaköy, holding the boy's inconstant arm.

"How close? Speak up! They've dropped the chain?"

"Not yet."

"Then why is everybody pushing? Wait—don't speak!"

The dock lurched underfoot. Around them rose the uproar of the ferry, churning the sea below the pilings. An iron gate rolled open with a crash, a whistle shrieked and soot blew through the shed. The boy pressed his mouth against Abdullah's ear.

"English patrol. Checking passes at the gate."

"They'll catch me or they won't," Abdullah said.

That struck him as a rather tragic and poetic phrase. He hoped the boy might keep it in his memory, the single moment of nobility in a degrading masquerade. But the boy was snickering and posing like an actor, drawing the attention of the pass control. Choked by a wave of fury and despair, Abdullah pinched him.

"Mama! You're hurting me!"

Abdullah, groaning, pressed his veil against his mouth. To conceal his height, he had to bend his knees. The money belt hung in his groin like a breechclout of stone. Each time it swayed, it gave him a painful thump in reminder of the manhood he was trying to disguise. His heart was fluttering unevenly; his body quivered with exhaustion and his mouth was dry. When a woman turned around and looked at him, he jumped aside.

The roustabouts along the pier were shouting: "Hey, let's go! Let's go!" A voice was calling, "Üsküdar! Haydar Pasha! Moda!" And a man behind—some clerk or grocer, hungry for his plate of beans and rice—was pressing them.

"Go through, Madame. . . . Go through."

Abdullah staggered forward. The pass card of Afife Hanum, widow of Mahmut of Hasköy, trembled in his outstretched hand, ignored by an English sergeant who was talking to some soldiers.

"Beyoglu . . . celebration in the streets . . . arrested."

The metal gangplank rang like a tocsin underfoot. Abdullah reached for the boy; but he squirmed away and disappeared.

Every passenger—and even the slow-rolling, throbbing boat itself—seemed to conspire to strip away Abdullah's costume, to drive him to extremes of pretense and abasement. By habit, he turned toward the Men's Saloon; a steward rushed over to direct him to the harem. There an enormous woman with a creamy face assailed him with cologne and rose loukoum, addressing him as "Granny," pressing her hand against his rump and blowing her warm, sweet breath, which smelled of cloves, into his muffled face.

"Now, then, my dear. Let's loosen up that heavy veil. This air is terrible."

Abdullah, squealing like a slaughtered sheep, clutched at his draperies.

"You're all excited, Granny. Panting like a dervish."

To get rid of her, he had to feign a violent attack of retching, which frightened away some Greek girls who were sharing out a bag of hot cheese tarts. Reeling along the aisles, Abdullah stumbled over moaning women, rolling their frightened yellow eyes, gnawing their handkerchiefs and puking half-digested oranges on their shoes. He found the water closets locked, the outside doorways stuck, the passages impenetrably clogged with bags of onions, strings of sponges and tethered nanny goats.

At last he reached the open deck and sank down like a peasant on his haunches. For a moment he could not remember what had driven him to this humiliating escapade. Where was he going? Why? He drew up his knees against his chest and recklessly raised his veil.

The ferry was rolling through the treacherous black waves that thunder south from Russia in the month of March. The city was descending in a blue metallic mist. Its amber lights declined and died among the pinnacles and domes. A British picket boat went spuming past.

If a Turk could get to Beykoz, halfway up the Straits, he could enlist a patriotic roughneck called the Orphan's Son to shelter him. There was a chemist named Ferit Bey, who could hide you in his laboratory, and a justice of the peace named Hakki Bey, who had a chestnut mare to carry you across the ridge to Tepeviranköy, where the village elders had a posting station and a telegraph to Mustapha Kemal.

Everyone except Abdullah found the whole thing irresistible, this Turkish game of hide-and-seek, this famous Moslem sport of flight-by-night. It was so charming, so hilarious: the perfect instrument of Oriental politics. In every coffeehouse, the stories went around: how Dr. Nuri Bey had scouted Anatolia, dressed in the kaftan of a Whirling Dervish; how Enver Pasha would dress up as a European diplomat to eavesdrop on his junior officers in cabarets; how Haydar Rüshtü had slipped past the Greek police in Smyrna, cloaked in a widow's weeds. Nobody who respected Moslem ways would lift the yashmak that concealed a bearded face. No one would stop a monk, a nun, a garbage man, a priest.

What a disgusting subterfuge! Staring down at his small, clean hands, Abdullah felt as though he had been stained with filth. He could remember how his proud, reflective father had held him up to see the fading panorama of the city. He had felt a childish pleasure in his own importance. Never had he imagined he would leave Constantinople in disguise. Tears of self-pity trickled down his cheeks and blurred his vision. His head fell backward helplessly against the bulkhead.

It was in this defenseless posture that he heard a hard, metallic click directly overhead. A ticket seller stood there snapping a paper punch and watching as Abdullah struggled to reclaim his veil.

"Look, you were in the cabin, Ma'am. I saw. And now you're trying to give me only four piastres."

Abdullah showed his empty hands. It was the only coin he could find in the widow Afife Hanum's little purse.

"You'll have to pay for a ticket in the cabin, Ma'am," the ticket seller said. Like all the ticket sellers on the boats, he was a Christian of one sort or other; and his speech was like the whining of a gnat. "You got to have a ticket at the pier."

Suddenly, he reached down and thrust his hand inside the veil. With the appraising fingers of a barber, he felt Abdullah's chin.

"They count the tickets, Ma'am," he went on, lowering his voice.

Abdullah pressed his back against the bulkhead. He could see the slope of Asia rising on the water like a tier of dominoes. He dug into the money belt and handed over the first coin his fingers touched.

"Why, Ma*dame!*" said the ticket seller. "Do you think they're playing games?" Abdullah found a second coin.

"The streets are full of police today. There was a gunfight. . . . No, no, Ma*dame!* Do you think I'm a dancing bear?"

Each time the ticket seller pushed away the coin, Abdullah added another. The haste and crudity of the transaction terrified him; but the boat was scraping on the pier. The cries of baggage porters mingled with the heavy thudding of the hull against the piles.

"You'll take my arm?" Abdullah whispered, adding another coin. "Through the lines?"

Struggling to his feet, he clung like a houri to the ticket seller's shoulder as they moved toward the gangway. They passed the inner fence, the outer fence and a row of soldiers yawning over rubber stamp pads.

"You see?" the ticket seller murmured, bracing Abdullah's feeble steps. "Without me, you were lost. Already in a prison cell. And I took a modest fee, no more."

He bent and pressed his greasy forehead to Abdullah's hand.

"God help you, Ma*dame.*" And he left.

The wind was blowing down the slopes, filling the forest with a moaning sound, as if the Moslem spirits in the great necropolis were stirring in anxiety. How fares the Eastern Rome, the bright red apple of our dreams? Rahat Fatiha. Rest in peace.

A few days later, the last Chamber of Deputies of the Ottoman Empire gathered in the Findikli Palace on the shore of the Bosphorus and voted on motion of Dr. Riza Nur Bey, the honorable deputy from Sinop, to protest the Allied violation of its parliamentary immunities; and, immediately afterward, to conclude its sitting *sine die*. Within the week, seventy deputies who had elected to evade arrest through the new Turkish game of masquerade were hurrying east by muleback, horseback, ox and wagon.

Sometimes, the travelers took shelter for the evening in a schoolroom. The headman of the village would sit up and talk until the lamp ran out of oil and heavy sleet began to blow against the paper windowpanes. At dawn, the cavalcade of politicians, publishers and woman suffragists, who had been the intellectual élite of Turkey, would pick up their cups and combs and ride along by oxcart through the storm.

A chilling wind was blowing from the coast, and the road was strewn with shattered blossoms. The travelers climbed through forests of enormous chestnut trees, moaning and hissing in the wind, and descended into silent canyons, filled with dripping beeches, where one could hear the crash of wild pigs in the underbrush. Beyond the ridge, the cart track rolled across a range of heather, leafless oaks and dead brown ferns. The sky was white, and a few light flakes of snow blew over the deserted downs.

At Kushjali, there was a telegraph to Mustapha Kemal. The telegrapher crouched on a wooden stool, his legs apart, his back against a whitewashed wall and his belly undulating placidly as he touched the key. Every message to "Their Esteemed Honors, Our Pasha," began with an invocation of the Fatherland, Freedom and Parliamentary Integrity and ended: "Honored and Esteemed Our Pasha—can you tell us where we are?"

This no man's land between the capital and Mustapha Kemal's insurgent army was like a marsh with shifting pools of quicksand. The path was constantly decaying, disappearing and emerging somewhere else. The neighborhood was thick with English soldiers. There were hostile villages of Armenians and Circassians; and, eastward, bands of brigands in the Forest of the Alemdagh.

The distinguished émigrés, dressed in cavalry jodhpurs, muddy boots and kalpaks of black astrakhan, would crowd around the key to listen for the guiding click.

"Izmit is dangerous. The English have it still. . . . You should go farther north, perhaps by Kandira. Avoid the villages. . . ."

And the travelers, passing the edges of a settlement, would see men with flintlock rifles in their arms and women on the rooftops, gripping heavy sticks.

Army colonels and Islamic lawyers rode in pairs along the snowy ridge above Sapanja Lake. Writers and surgeons trudged through fields of dingy stubble, past rows of naked poplar trees and frozen ditches. No one could say what you might discover just beyond the nearest hill. If you should learn that enemy insurgents had blown up the crossing called Forked Bridges on the road to Hendek, then you must hurry south and cross the flooding river in an ore bucket drawn along a wire. If Mustapha Kemal controlled the station, you would find his soldiers lying in an empty boxcar, with a bonfire on the floor to dry their clothes; if not, you might be greeted by a gang of cutthroats called the Army of the Caliphate, who would strip you like a snake and leave you in the fields to die.

It took a week or two to get to Lefke on the bank of the Sakarya. There was a raft of oily railroad ties, pulled back and forth by cables. On the other side, the track was clear.

Mustapha Kemal sent down a railway car to gather up the refugees. It waited for them in the rain beside the overflowing river. At night, a locomotive, burning logs, came down from Bilejik to haul the carriage up the canyon.

Some of the deputies decided to get off at Eskishehir. They wanted to appraise it as a new location for the Parliament. But when the train went through the town, the locomotive

147

did not cut its speed. Mustapha Kemal Pasha had already chosen the seat of government.

At dusk, they saw his capital, the two-humped citadel of Ankara, dark brown against a flaming sky.

SMYRNA
JUNE, 1920

*I*n Smyrna every summer day is brighter than the one before. There is a scent of iodine and lemons from the sea, a reek of camel stalings on the cobblestones. The luster of the harbor makes one dizzy, and the sky is so resplendent that the earth seems to be powdered with a purple dust.

Eleni and her mother had gone to Bornova to spend the season, leaving George and Christos in a state of bachelor barbarity. For Christos, it was a pleasant change, an opportunity to lunch with the High Commissioner, to talk with visiting philhellenes about establishing a University of Smyrna, to send out a flood of letters asking for political support from Panhellenic clubs in other countries. For George, it was a time of acute anxiety.

Never had George been more intensely conscious of his immaturity, his lack of confidence. Not only did his father lecture him incessantly about the duties of a patriot, Dimitris also treated him to anecdotes about Greek boys no greener than he who had shot themselves, gone mad or died of terror in their first encounter with the Turks. A ceaseless stream of photographs arrived at the house in heavy yellow envelopes: "The Severed Head of a Greek Priest Near Tralles," "The Mutilated Victims of Atrocity at Philadelphia"; and George was invited to enjoy them all before his father sent them on to Alexandria or Manchester or Pittsburgh, Pennsylvania.

149

Just when George had begun to hope that the Paris Conference would smooth away the last uncertainties and end the Turkish threat, he overheard an alarming conversation. It was in one of those cafés along the Quay. Somebody was complaining in a somber voice about the current price of hordas, the low-grade figs they ship from little harbors south of Smyrna; somebody else was ordering a whitefish salad fixed with mayonnaise; and a third voice was analyzing Mustapha Kemal.

"He's been raiding Allied posts. He brags that he can take Constantinople. Fortunately, the English have awakened to the danger. Now they're willing to let our expeditionary force move out of this ridiculous, untenable occupation zone and complete the annexation of Asia Minor."

"You mean a Greek offensive?"

"Any day. In fact, any hour."

George put down his cup untasted. He felt as if a hand had gripped his throat. He could think of nothing except the military levy of the Metropolitan Chrysostomos and the ledger with his name among the list of volunteers. Without waiting to hear any more, he ran to the barracks where Dimitris had a room.

In recent months, Dimitris had become his counselor. There was nobody else in whom George could confide. His father expected him to live with an empyreal perfection; his sister always anticipated failure; his mother kissed and coddled him and made him feel as helpless as a baby. Dimitris, on the other hand, was fraternal, skeptical, enlightened. Meeting George on the street, he might exclaim: "Hey, kid —you're all in a sweat! Don't you know that's bad for your performance in the saddle? In this kind of weather, bathe in the sea and eat a lot of mussels." And George, who was as virginal as snow, would eat prodigious numbers of stuffed mussels and take the Belgian tram to Göz Tepe to soak his loins in brine.

He pounced on every word of advice Dimitris uttered. He agreed with every opinion. If Dimitris should say the day was good, was bad, was orange and green, George invariably admitted that he thought so, too. Merely knowing that he saw eye to eye with a man so confident, so worldly, strengthened George as though he had been taken under the protection of a patron saint.

Their disagreements never lasted long. Once, George had suggested that his father should entertain some Turks in an effort to improve relations; but Dimitris disapproved.

"Why are you people always so hospitable to them? Turks have no place in the city. Basically, they're a nomadic people. They have no aptitude for civilization. Don't encourage them."

George acknowledged that he probably had developed an excessive tolerance from living too long under Moslem rule. He vowed to isolate himself from contact with the Turks.

That morning he found Dimitris lying almost naked on a canvas cot, staring at the ceiling.

"What's the matter?" George said, startled by the lowered blinds and the smell of liniment. "Did you hurt yourself again?" A few months ago, Dimitris had strained his back and was assigned to light duties in the record depot of the quartermaster's corps; but he had appeared to be recovering.

"Matter?" Dimitris said. "They're trying to send me off to Aydin."

"On the Southern Front? That's a relief."

"What's a relief about it? They've chopped my ass off."

"I mean, I thought you wanted to get to the Front."

"Not *that* Front. Your father has got to help me."

"I'll see him tonight."

"Too late. By that time I'll be on my way.... What the devil are you staring at?"

"Nothing."

"The devil! You look as if you're picking chiggers from my navel."

"Your back isn't taped."

"It still hurts, all the same." And Dimitris stroked his belly tenderly with his fingertips. George asked if he might raise the window. "It's raised," Dimitris said. He lit a cigarette and then held out the box. "Go on, take one. These are good Macedonian tobacco, not your Anatolian camel shit."

George reached out quickly and put a cigarette behind his ear. Dimitris had been teaching him to smoke, and he did not want to seem ungrateful. He kept his eyes averted so that Dimitris would not accuse him of staring.

"Why is it so bad?" George said. "Sending you to Aydin?"

"Because I'm disabled, that's why."

"I thought you were feeling better."

"Also, it's a waste of talent. Aydin's nothing but a flank position. A man of my ability should be used in the center, in the General Staff."

George understood at once. He put out his hand; but Dimitris drew away.

"In God's name, be careful of my back!"

"Look, I'll go," George said. "I'll try *Amalthea*. Papa sometimes writes a poem for the correspondence."

"The hell with *Amalthea*. Go to the Club. Walk up and down the Quay. Leave messages. Tell him I've got to see the High Commissioner."

"I'll find him," George said. Then, gazing at the floor, he drew a long breath and added: "I just heard something that bothers me."

"It can wait."

"I mean, have you heard rumors about a summer offensive?"

Dimitris rolled onto his side and stared at George.

"Why else in the dear name of Christ do you think they want to send me to Aydin?"

"Do you think they'll call up the Smyrna Legion?"

"It's about time."

"But I was thinking, I'm really not quite ready to go. I'm only seventeen."

"Jesus and Mary!" Dimitris said. "What do you want to do? Stay home like Papa and write letters to the patriotic clubs of Cappadocia?"

"Well, I was thinking, I have this unmarried sister and my mother to look after, and my father is getting pretty old."

"Jesus and Mary," Dimitris repeated. "No wonder you Anatolians could never get rid of the Turks. What do you want to do, sit around all your life and brag about the glory of Greece, to which you've never contributed anything except the bubbles from your mouth?"

George flushed. There was no secret that could be hidden from Dimitris; and he was bitterly contemptuous of anything that smelled of cowardice.

"I thought we might ask them to delay until we finish negotiations on the dowry."

"Oh, I'll talk to someone. But for Christ's sake, get going!" And, as George turned away: "How is she? Your sister?"

"She's well. It's cool in Bornova."

Dimitris scratched his chest.

"It's cool in Bornova," he echoed in a mocking tone. "I'll *bet* it's cool in Bornova. Holy Virgin, these endless Greek courtships!"

And he thrust his hand inside his dingy cotton underdrawers, rubbed himself voluptuously, gave a couple of frog kicks and sat up with a groan.

"What the devil are you staring at *now?*" he said. "Take off."

To further insure himself against a disagreeable transfer, Dimitris got dressed, perfumed his hair with verbena cologne and walked over to the office of the High Commis-

153

sioner which adjoined the army barracks. His cousin Stephanos, soft and bilious, raised his head and murmured:
"Well, imagine! Look who's here!"

The racket in the office almost drowned Stephanos' feeble
voice. Swarms of peevish clerks with pencils stuck behind
their ears were rushing to and fro, depositing papers on each
other's desks and shouting: "Take care of this at once!"

Stephanos opened a box of cigarettes.

"Imagine—both of us in Smyrna. And now, just as the army
is leaving town—"

"I'm sure you've been busy," Dimitris said.

Stephanos was a first or second cousin and flagrantly degenerate. His eyes were deeply shadowed; his sideburns
were shaved to a line above the ears; and his bluish lips
turned down in an expression of refined contempt. Like a
Chinese aristocrat, he wore the nail of his little finger four
inches long to show that he had been spared the indignity of
working with his hands. Recently, by God knew what inde-
cencies, he had attained a position directly under the Hellenic High Commissioner. He had a wooden barricade
around his desk, two ink pads, seven spindles and a view
across the Konak Square.

Dimitris blew tobacco smoke across the desk and dribbled
ashes on the floor. It was his firm belief that the average man
would rather do a favor for someone who insults him than for
one who feigns admiration. But Stephanos did not respond to
this overt disrespect. With an irritable sigh, he muttered:
"Well, you want something? What is it?"

"Only to welcome you to Smyrna," Dimitris said.

"I've been here six months," Stephanos said. "What do you
want? Just name it." He swept his hand around to indicate
the grandeur of the office. The ceiling was flaking off in
patches; the calendar was out of date; the clock was twenty
minutes slow; and one of the clerks had overturned a cup of

coffee on a record book, which was drying on the counter, surrounded by fresh peaches, chunks of bread and clouds of flies. "An import-export license? Are you dealing in commodities?"

Dimitris blew another puff of smoke across the desk.

"The only problem I have—" he said. "Well, it's beyond your influence."

Stephanos frowned.

"My dear, *dear* cousin! If it's something for *yourself,* some little favor—"

"No, no. I wouldn't think of asking it."

"—it can be done."

A boy brought coffee on a copper dangle tray. Stephanos drew his chaplet out and rolled the beads between his soft white fingers.

"I suppose you're glad we're taking the offensive again?"

They looked at each other silently. Dimitris put his coffee cup aside.

"Cousin Stephano?"

But Stephanos turned to stop a passing clerk, took from his hand a sheaf of documents, read one of them and pecked at it with a rubber stamp. Folding his hands, he turned again to Dimitris.

"Can you imagine what was among those papers? *Very* exciting. General Order No. 1892–3 from General Paraskevopoulos. . . . Now, what were you saying?"

Dimitris felt a numbness creeping through his soul. His cousin, blood of his blood, was playing cat-and-mouse with him! He stared at the floor for several moments, struggling against an impulse to jump up and run away. Finally, abandoning his careless manner, he raised his eyes, gazed at his cousin solemnly and said: "Stephano? I want to offer you an opportunity to serve our country. I have some information that will change the history of Greece." He tapped the pocket of his blouse. "It could court-martial fifty men."

"Oh, military discipline?" said Stephanos. "You're right. That's not our field.

"Political," Dimitris said. "A *plot.*"

"Expose it. You'll get a good promotion."

Dimitris pulled down the corners of his mouth.

"Expose it to whom? A military officer is vulnerable. The Royalist clique . . ."

"Ah, yes," Stephanos said, blocking a yawn. "They're with us like the poor. . . . Well, make sure you pick a loyal officer before you give your proof."

Dimitris chewed his lower lip. The success of his petition depended on its presentation, and there were many possible approaches. He might be bold: "My proof is my word as an officer and patriot!" Or philosophical: "Proof? What *is* proof? The illusions of the fallible eye, transmitted by the faltering tongue." Arch: "If you were an officer who wanted to destroy the government, would you notify the government?" Or passionate: "On my honor as the son and grandson of martyred Greeks!"

He concluded in favor of a grandiose appeal to paranoia, which is endemic in the civil-service class of every nation. Flattening his palms on the top of the desk, he looked Stephanos in the eye and said: "This is a matter that may involve the very life of the Prime Minister. I can tell you only a little. The rest is in the form of intuitions, clues and traces that will take months to unravel. I am the only man in the position to pursue these leads. But the evidence I can reveal to you is so shocking that to ignore it would be treason."

And he handed over the notes that George Trigonis had written seven or eight months earlier in the office of the cathedral.

Stephanos flipped through the pages.

"But this concerns things that were said last October."

156

"Not all of them," Dimitris said. "In any case, the point is not *when* these remarks were made. The point is that the person who made these threats is still at large, plotting against the government."

Stephanos shrugged his shoulders. "If we tried to keep track of every officer—" But Dimitris reached out and clutched his wrist.

"There is more. Much more. I have other proof. Important leads. If only I could stay here and investigate. If only I could stay in Smyrna."

Stephanos leaned back in his chair, lowered his eyelids and smiled.

"So *that* is what you want! Why must you be so evasive, my dear? Do you think you can outwit your own flesh and blood? Let me see what I can do."

And he took up the notes and went to an inner office.

Only after Dimitris was outside in the blazing sunlight did he recall that he had promised to do something about a deferment for George Trigonis.

By one o'clock George had left messages for Christos at every printing press and Christian social club in Smyrna. He had not been able to find his father or to confirm the rumors of a Greek offensive, although Professor Paleologos had detained him for twenty minutes with a disquieting analysis of the "dangerous game" Venizelos was playing. For lack of another destination, George wandered to the Quay and looked in both directions. The trams had stopped; shops were closing for the afternoon; and the waterside cafés were crowded with merchants and their mistresses, drinking lemonade and eating shellfish under the shade of green-and-white awnings.

Near the office of the port, he heard a newsboy crying the word "offensive." He rushed to buy a paper. There were only the familiar cables from London, Paris and Rome, dealing with affairs in Egypt, Ireland and Afghanistan. He looked in vain for datelines from "the front," "the high command" or "the army in the field."

As he stood reading, a shadow fell across the page, and he jumped like a lizard shadowed by a hawk. It was an old woman selling terra-cotta censers to thurify the holy ikons.

"Another procession?" George said. But his chest tightened. The Metropolitan always ordered a procession of the ikons when there were intimations of a military crisis.

To calm himself, he folded the newspaper and walked slowly toward St. Photini's. As he approached the cathedral, the air began to tremble with an excitement like the fluttering of wings. Shopkeepers in white smocks pushed past him, wiping sweat from their necks. Workmen with handkerchiefs around their heads came trotting from the Fruit Bazaar. Bells were throbbing in the tower. There was a constant rumbling from the sanctuary, where the liturgy was under way. Acolytes were peering from the open doors, through which the crystal lusters of the chandeliers were visible as feeble embers muffled in oily fog; and women dressed in black were scurrying inside like beetles plunging down a hole.

Just as George reached the gate, he glimpsed his father among some Elders on the far side of the courtyard. Then the acolytes strode out, dispersing the crowd by thrusting right and left like pikemen with banners of magenta silk. Behind the banners came the disks and crosses, mounted at the ends of gilded staves that swayed from side to side like rows of spears. The silver disks were set with chips of coral, pearls and colored stones; the golden disks were like blinding emanations of the sun; and the crosses seemed to sputter with a phosphorescent flame. The garments of the crucifer exhaled a musty odor of the sacristy, which mingled with the fumes of incense and the perspiration of the crowd.

George was pushed back among some soldiers who were discussing a gunbarrel that had got so hot you couldn't touch it. The block had frozen like a dead man's jaw, and when they called for help, the lieutenant was in the shelter, vomiting.

"What were we supposed to do? Wait until the buggers climbed the hill and then choke 'em with our naked hands?"

"Well, *they* never run away. The commanding officer stands behind them with a pistol."

His father saw him from across the courtyard and began to wave. They came together, jostled by the crowd. Christos spread out his arms. He was smiling strangely, and moisture glittered behind the violet lenses of his spectacles.

"My boy, my boy! They've told me everything!" He threw his arms around his son. "You really are a blazing patriot, aren't you?" Then, with a convulsive sob, he broke away and turned his back. Taking off his glasses, he breathed on the lenses and wiped them carefully. When he showed his face again, he was smiling.

"So you want to cut off some Turkish buttocks, is that it? Well, I ask you! How can you stop a Greek from loving his Fatherland?" And he swung away again, choked by tears.

George felt a numbness engulfing his heart. His lips would not open. He moved his hands up and down in a meaningless gesture. The Metropolitan was passing; his hair hung loosely, like the mane of an enormous, grizzled animal, and his beard was parted on his chest. On his shoulders was a stole of ivory satin, worked in golden vines and ears of wheat. He held an inlaid crozier in his hand; and as he walked, he slowly turned his head from side to side, searching the congregation.

George leaned forward, raising himself on tiptoes, and stretched out his neck as if to take the Holy Eucharist. But there was no communion, no compassion in those gray-blue eyes. Chrysostomos preached the testament of power, rather than persuasion; of ardor, rather than tolerance; of convic-

159

tion, rather than humility; of justice, rather than forgiveness. Compared to his incandescent zeal, the devotion of an ordinary Christian was like a candle burning in the sunshine.

When Chrysostomos lifted his hand to bless his congregation, he was consecrating them as soldiers of the faith. The Holy Virgin rode above them in an ark of polished myrtle wood. Two soldiers held her on their shoulders, and their faces were flushed with exertion. On either side, the censers swung their thuribles. The ikon passed under the arch. A cry of triumph echoed in the street.

George drew a deep breath.

"I've been looking for you, Papa. It's about Dimitris. . . ."

"Yes, yes!" Christos said. "They've just been telling me. What a stroke of luck! He's been reassigned to the civilian section of the High Commissioner's. Some sort of liaison, I understand. Oh, I'm proud of my boys, both of my boys!"

And he edged George toward the sanctuary. The atmosphere inside was dense and turbid. Candles in memory of the dead illuminated every recess. They found the ikon of St. George. Christos genuflected and kissed it noisily.

"Three okas of the finest oil!"

He crossed himself three times and went to look for the sacristan. George put his head between his hands and bent forward on the shrine. At last he raised his eyes. The Blessed St. George of Cappadocia, the Champion of the Cross, looked down on him: beloved St. George, who had slain the dragon on the banks of the Euphrates. His charger reared up in a crackled field of gilt and varnish, encrusted with layers of ochre and silver foil. The horse's hoofs were shod with silver platens; the warrior's sword was tipped with a silver dart; and his nimbus was embossed with silver leaf.

Amulets and offerings festooned his shrine: a flask of olive oil, a censer, innumerable silver hearts, arms, ears, hands, shreds of clothing, locks of hair; for St. George is the patron, above all others, of the Greeks—a simple knight, of dauntless courage, who did not fear of this life or of the second death.

"Help me, Saint George!"

The universe began to open like a cold night sky. The darkness of eternity appeared beyond the great façade, as if a beautiful ikonostasis had been parted to reveal, not the Holy of Holies, but a featureless void. George was confronted by a Turk, a myriad of Turks, who slavered blood and whirled their yataghans in hissing circles overhead. He saw himself running and falling, vomiting, impaled and burned with fire. His last moments passed: he called out to his mother, but she could not hear him; and his tears ran into his dry mouth.

St. George looked down at him without dismay. His oval eyes and tiny mouth expressed conviction rather than compassion. The dragon died eternally beneath his spear. He was the knight of valor, not of discretion; of justice, not of humanity; of commitment, not of temperance. The Roman soldiers pierced him with a lance; they threw him into caustic lime; they made him walk across the points of nails; they cast him into flames; and still he did not perish. It was only when the Lord was ready to call him that his persecutors seemed to triumph. His head was severed from his body. In mortal agony, his soul departed from his flesh and rose into Heaven to claim a martyr's crown.

It was this golden crown, glowing in the mist of precious incense, that descended in splendor through the empty darkness. George bent his head to receive it; he covered his face and wept. When his father returned, he dried his eyes, and they left the church without a word.

That night, with a hundred other volunteers, George took the train to Manisa.

ANKARA

JULY, 1920

*A*t the time of the Greek attack, the center of
Turkish resistance was the town of Ankara, a mean, muddy
little settlement of clay and thatch—crowded, flyblown and
choked by the vapors of a quagmire called the Bloody Lake.
In the middle of the village lay a neglected graveyard; and
on the slope of the citadel was a neighborhood of ruins,
charred by fire. Milky water trickled down the alleys, under
the wooden wheels of oxcarts. Tanners scraped the reeking
hides of buffaloes into the gutters and goats were bedded on
the ground floors of the houses. Day and night, the coffee
shops were thronged with mercenary soldiers wearing black
turbans and heavy cartridge belts.

The national assembly, which had adjourned in Constantinople, had reassembled here on April 23 in an unfinished
clubhouse of the Union and Progress Party. As recently as last
winter, the building had been a barracks for the wives and
children of some Frenchmen in the Army of Occupation. To
complete the roof, the assembly had to confiscate a load of
Marseilles tiles from a schoolhouse; and the meeting room
was furnished with unpainted desks borrowed from a teachers' college. This extraordinary parliament, opened by proclamation of General Mustapha Kemal, was the only effective
government left in a nation that once had ruled from Vienna
to the Persian Gulf.

Among the lesser delegates, in political experience as in seniority, was a crippled, half-blind ex-soldier from Alashehir, who had arrived late and unprepared after a difficult two-week journey by way of Afyon Karahisar. His good name as a son of the late Hilmi Pasha and his admirable record as an officer in the Ottoman Army had guaranteed that the headmen of his district would select him as a representative; but if the village elders had balked, Kenan would have elected himself. For several months he had been following the progress of Mustapha Kemal's resistance movement through gossip in the coffeehouses; and he had concluded it was the only hope of salvation for a dying race. A few days after the Allies invested Constantinople, he went to his uncle Mahmut Zia Bey, gave him a letter for the women of the family and rode out of town with a saddlebag full of bread, a revolver on his hip and some gold coins in his belly sash.

Even to a man of Kenan's submerged and gloomy temperament, however, Ankara was an appalling disappointment. The grievance was not the town itself; for Ankara, after all, was merely a crude offspring of expediency and forlorn hope. Fate had given it a precarious importance: an interior ministry in the agriculture school, a parliament in the clubhouse, councils of war in the boys' lycée. And no one expected much comfort in a provincial town of 20,000 on the steppes of Asia. The water was brackish; the streets were strewn with chaff; the swamp exhaled mosquitoes and miasmas. There were two coffeehouses; one drafty little restaurant called the Anatolia, where the waiters ran to and fro like frightened animals, serving bowls of lukewarm lentil soup; a damp hotel with roaches; and plenty of fine, invigorating vistas from the citadel, which seemed to tremble like a heat mirage above the endless coffee-colored prairie.

The grievance was not the town but the resistance leaders —the three hundred deputies, gathered from mountain crannies on the Persian border and fishing villages on the Uxine Sea, who were wavering unpredictably between bravado and despair, obsessed with their prerogatives, their duties and their liabilities. Some of them were tribal chiefs, as ignorant as savages. Others were bland Constantinople aristocrats, educated out of any native sense. Most of them were thoroughly frightened of being hanged. They knew absolutely nothing about defending the Fatherland. To the majority, the army was a mystery of God—a blood levy by the Sultan, dispatched to die in foreign lands. They would have preferred to discuss the Sacred Traditions of the Prophet and vote restrictions on the distillation of liqueurs.

Night after night, they met in the little granite clubhouse, which looked like a bungalow with an overbearing roof. A barricade of sandbags reached the windows. Along the street there was a line of trenches, backed up by a double run of barbed wire and a squad of somber peasant boys from the coast of Georgia. Even so, the delegates did not feel safe. While they talked, the Western Front was caving inward like a failing dike. Defeat weighed upon them like a chronic illness that releases its victim to sleep but is lying on his chest again at dawn.

It was, above all, Mustapha Kemal Pasha, the President of the assembly, who tormented them, with his exhausting speeches, his imperious disregard for parliamentary prerogatives and his intransigent determination to unify the scattered remnants of the Turkish Army under his own stern, solitary leadership. Mustapha Kemal was a difficult, tedious and monolithic man; and he had as many enemies as admirers. When the Greek attack began, some of his enemies brought forth the names of other commanders—Kiazim Karabekir, Ali Faud, Ethem the Circassian—as tempting substitutes. Other delegates, imagining themselves to be master strategists, grouped into precious little camarillas and began

164

to speak of stringing up the generals and the civil governors along the Western Front.

One night when Kenan came limping down the cart track from the Ministry of War, one of these obscure, self-righteous critics was standing in the twilight at the clubhouse door, recruiting dissidents to his party—an oddly dressed cabal of priests and pilgrims, whose dappled brown robes trailed on the ground and whose turbans bobbed around like onions boiling in a stew. The rebel deputy, who wore a cotton sweatband tied around his head, looked for all the world like a butcher standing in a market stall: eyelids drooping, lips protruding, fingers twined behind his back; and he was, in fact, a butcher from a town in Kastamonu. As a member of the national assembly, however, he suddenly had become an expert advocate of proletarian resistance—"little war," he called it, in the Spanish parlance. Nothing would ever convince him that guerrilla bands were unreliable. Didn't they spring from the people? Didn't they live on air and water, moving as slyly as the shadow of a cloud? A band of irregulars could not be outflanked, besieged or enclosed. In truth, a bashi-bazouk was practically a miracle of God!

"Mustapha Kemal's demands are ridiculous," one of the clique was saying. "You can't expect the leader of a roving band to fill out a requisition every time he needs a chicken for a pot."

"Requisition, reckless mission!" cried the celebrated butcher from Kastamonu, smiling at his own wit. "Let them help themselves to *Greek* cannons! *Those* don't require any requisitions. As for our giving supplies to the guerrillas, what's so bad about that? They'd make better use of a Krupp than these so-called commanders we have."

"That's God's truth, Hikmet Bey."

"These so-called field commanders can't do a thing except retreat. We ought to hang them."

And the butcher nodded pleasantly to Kenan and beckoned him to join the group. Kenan leaned against the wall and stared at them in hatred. The effort of walking from the Ministry had almost killed him; he had to gather his strength even to speak.

But there was a commotion in the street behind him. A black phaeton approached the gate; and Mustapha Kemal Pasha was coming up the steps. His face in the yellow light was as pale as marble.

It was the first time Kenan had seen him out of uniform. The effect was a shock. Mustapha Kemal was wearing a dingy suit of European worsted, cut in the nondescript style of the late Hapsburg Empire. It would have been a respectable outfit for a prefect in Salonika; but worn by Mustapha Kemal, it was a signal of surrender: soldiers in despair throw off their helmets and their boots. Without a uniform, the Pasha was no longer a heroic general who had fled the capital to organize a national rebellion, but merely the President of a rump assembly whose legality was moot and whose members were hardly worth a bag of bile.

Kenan studied the Pasha's face for signs of resignation; but it was impossible to read the features of Mustapha Kemal. His bony cheeks, his narrow mouth, his heavy eyebrows and his pale, elliptic eyes were like instruments manipulated by a virtuoso. They expressed only what the master player wanted to convey. They did not publicize his sentiments or broadcast his political opinions.

Walking into the crowded hall, the Pasha nodded ambiguously to men on either side. The Prime Minister, Fevzi Pasha, strode along at his shoulder like an enormous, gloomy bodyguard. Scowling toward the meeting room, Fevzi whispered into the Pasha's ear. Mustapha Kemal, listening in silence, stroked his chin.

It was after dark when the doors closed on the secret ses-

166

sion. The generator, by the will of God, had failed again; a secretary carried smoking lanterns down to the platform that was used by delegates who wanted to address the forum. Three men had to sit at each school desk designed for two; and although the eight tall windows had been thrown open to the vapors of the swamp, the atmosphere was closer than the comradeship. The deputies were fanning themselves with copies of *Yeni Gün,* which reported minor skirmishes along the Milne Line. Not in words, but in the spaces between them, could one read the tragic news: Salihli had fallen to the Greeks. Alashehir had fallen. The time had come to force a showdown.

The butcher from Kastamonu, with the subtlety of his profession, opened the debate with a two-hour attack on the commanders of the Western Front. If it was not the commanders who were responsible for the loss of territory, who was it? Nobody rose to answer. At the end, a deputy stood up and moved the convocation of a summary court-martial.

Kenan rested his forehead on his hand. The voices in the chamber thundered like muffled drums. Outside, a wagon was slowly climbing the hill; the screeching of its wooden axles shattered the murky night. A man from Lazistan was on his feet, saying for the fortieth time that the commanding officers must be held responsible. What did that Pontic pirate know about responsibility? What did any of them know? Like all Turks, they were fond of making speeches: twenty deputies had indicated a desire to talk. Again and again, the word "responsibility" recurred.

Kenan looked over at the Presidential table. Mustapha Kemal's face was ashen, but his deep-set eyes were blazing under his heavy brows. He alone possessed the fortitude to bring this sorrowful people through their great travail; and he was being strangled by the tongues of imbeciles.

167

In a trance, Kenan rose to ask for the privilege of the floor. Alas, there were other deputies who held priority. Would someone yield to the representative from Alashehir? Men in the front rows turned around and craned their necks. Few of them knew him, although everyone had heard of Hilmi Pasha. Could this bandaged ruin be the great man's son? The speaker who had preceded him, a deputy from Van, had droned on for fifty minutes; and Mustapha Kemal, defending his field officers, had used three hours. Kenan took less than a minute.

"I was in Smyrna when the Greeks came," he said. "My home is in Alashehir. I have lost these and other treasures to the enemies of our country. I do not wish to lose more. But I am less concerned with limbs than I am with hearts. There is only one man to whom I would entrust the heart of our Fatherland, and he is Mustapha Kemal Pasha. I offer him one hand, one ear, one eye, one life."

Some men who were talking in the aisle looked up in surprise. A nervous sibilance, like an embarrassed snicker followed by a sigh, passed through the room. Then the Pasha's men began to applaud.

At dawn the vote was called, but Kenan had left the chamber. Suffocated by the atmosphere, he went to the antechamber, which was crowded with officers and orderlies waiting for the result of the debate. Wisps of smoke were curling and unwinding like fragile scarves around the kerosene lamps. The officers stretched out their legs; the orderlies squatted on their heels; and scores of oily clerks hovered near the door, trading glances implying they were privy to the outcome of the deliberations.

Finally, when it was daylight, Mustapha Kemal came out. He did not smile, but Fevzi Pasha, the Prime Minister, stopped and shook hands with some men around the entrance. At the outer door, Mustapha Kemal turned back, and his pale eyes fell on Kenan. He crossed the hall and scrutinized Kenan's scarred face.

At last he said: "I accept your offer, but I will ask for more. Come to my office today."

And he went out into the street, where a crowd of young men in ragged clothes ran after his car, swallowing clouds of dust.

A message came from the Front that morning. The Greek offensive had resumed in force.

ESKISHEHIR
JULY, 1920

*A*t the same time, reports of the renewed attack reached the town of Eskishehir, a railroad junction midway between the Sultan's palace in Constantinople and Mustapha Kemal's rebel parliament in Ankara.

This brindled, dusty, horizontal town was the third capital of the Turkish realm; and it was as far from Constantinople and Ankara in sentiment as in geography. Day and night, the streets of Eski radiated heat and turmoil. Angry voices resounded in the coffeehouses. Radicals from Cairo and Bokhara published broadsheets heralding the advent of a Green Revolution and Socialism of the soil, and posters on the walls proclaimed the establishment of a Peasants' International. Eski was the refuge of heretics, deserters and renegades; the stronghold of such astute guerrilla leaders as Circassian Ethem; and the birthplace of Abdullah's Army.

To recruit an army of agrarian reformers, one had only to wait at sundown in the garden of a coffeehouse beside a mosque. The wind was always blowing along the valley, and the Porsuk River, which flows through the center of the town, was running swift and milky by the dusty esplanade, passing over dams and sluices and under little wooden bridges. The locust trees were wilting in the twilight; the dogs and birds were silent; and men came down the path to look at the water reflecting the crimson sky.

Abdullah would invite them to his table, startle them with sudden penetrating questions and then begin to talk about the rising East, the force of destiny, the radical traditions of the Turkish tribes. He had discarded his old techniques of argument and ideology: those were devices of a Western culture. These simple Asiatics were not impressed by logic but by mysteries. Abdullah hoped to wake them slowly, like the rays of daybreak on the desert. Little by little, the Orientals would recover their unique ideals: tribal and egalitarian, mystic and absolute.

His first disciple was a man named Hairy Murat, a dim-witted stevedore whose eyes were covered with cataracts like an icy film on the surface of a pond. Hairy Murat had matted hair, a matted beard and tufts of matted fur protruding from his ears and nostrils. Whenever he heard Abdullah speak, he began to scratch as if the voice awoke a colony of dormant vermin nesting in the creases of his body. Hairy Murat could ride and shoot, and he was struck with wonder at the splendor of a coin Abdullah produced from his money belt.

Next, they enrolled a pair of Mehmets—bulky, gentle, stupid, less like men than oxen; a Rauf, who was cautious; a Daddy Mahmut, who was old; and a Midhat, who was young. They were not the best of men: Yellow Faik was sullen, Hakki was careless, Shükrü had a bad aroma and Ertoghrul the Ironsmith was a pederast. But even a goat commands respect in a land where there are no sheep.

By midsummer Abdullah had enlisted fifteen riflemen and had bought them cartridges and horses. They rode along the parched streets, scowling, with their turbans tipped above their eyebrows. Like Abdullah himself, they wore the baggy pantaloons and high felt boots of mountaineers. Bandoleers hung on their shoulders. Their mustaches were greased with mutton fat; their bellybands were filled with knives. They called Abdullah "the Black One." Nobody knew his trade, his education or his father's name; and he did not bother to inform them. If anyone should ask what army they belonged to, Abdullah would answer: "Whose are you?"

Perhaps Abdullah's Army did not understand his ideology, but they understood the coins he handed them. Did the Fatherland ask, before it took your last drop of blood: "Are you a Kemalist? Are you a Marxist?" Abdullah's mind had grown. He had begun to understand the Turkish tragedy.

The moment he heard about the Greek attack, he called his men together and issued them each a ration of cracked wheat, sugar and tobacco tied up in a homespun woolen saddlebag. Single file, they rode out of town along the railroad tracks, climbed a range of hills at Inönü and hurried southward through canyons and across a sloping plain, raising a cloud of dust and grasshoppers along the road to Ushak. The rocks on either side were as black as iron, wavering in the heat like specters, and the cloudless sky was as luminous as a copper bowl.

Crossing this bitter desert, Abdullah's Army was entirely alone. A cloud of dust rolled out behind them like an endless ribbon, and the vacant air hissed past their ears. But when they were farther south, in a red volcanic land, they began to sense the presence of other riders, moving with them night and day.

Hairy Murat, in his blindness, was the first to feel the tremor of their hoofbeats. He came to Abdullah at night, while the other men were sleeping in their blankets.

"Do you hear them? Is it a handful or a horde?"

Abdullah heard a sound like the muffled footsteps of a funeral passing down a quiet street. Hairy Murat whispered into his ear: "I've heard them before, you know? Like an echo . . ." He paused with his face turned up and muttered: "God have mercy."

172

Abdullah climbed a knoll from which the fields of lava tumbled toward a black horizon. The murmur of other riders, slowly winding through the darkness, was as gentle as the breath of cattle in a fold. Perhaps they were villagers, protecting the outer limits of their fields, or another band of irregulars drifting down to Ushak. At worst, they were a Greek patrol, outnumbered, spying on the Turks.

Ordering Hairy Murat to stay awake, Abdullah closed his eyes and gave his thoughts to the development of revolutionary dogma. The sound of the others sank below the level of his senses, like the whining of a gnat, ignored by a man who is devoting his attention to the thunder of a cannon.

He dreamed of his apprenticeship to Haig Essegian et Fils, whose trade was multifarious: part medicine, part magic. Handbills in Hebrew, Turkish and Armenian, posters in Greek, Italian and Ladino, spread the praises of Essegian in every quarter of Constantinople. Essegian was a surgeon and a bleeder, famous for his leeches, which were kept alive in tanks of water from the Terkos Lake and fed at midnight on the tripe of freshly slaughtered goats. His attar of roses, from an alembic in the forests of Bulgaria, lasted a lifetime. His rubefacients, his bleaches, his depilatories, his dyes, his waxes, his kohl for the eyeballs, his musk for the skin—all were compounded on secret formulas passed down from the Empress Theodora. His anthelmintics were distributed from Van to Urmia; his adsorbents and cathartics, carminatives and contraceptives won the adulation of viziers and foreign princes. His potion against the French Disease, bottled in amber glass, went by the case to Kastamonu, where its alcoholic content and the secondary uses of its bottles were extolled in every household. A mongrel clientele assailed his laboratory; but in his dream, Abdullah had forgotten all the recipes. He fumbled with the balance scale, upset the herbs and trampled the order slips, while old Essegian pestered him with consignments to "the patronage of Eros," as he called it—the Pan-Islamic trade in sexual refreshments, which went by camel to his cousins, who had pharmacies in Baghdad, Jaffa and Aleppo. There were philtres of hyena dung, sweet basil, powdered goat horns, Java pepper, rhinoceros snouts and cantharides, dry and liquid; pastes of fish roe; boluses of formic excrement; salep, ground from the little orchis tubers that the Arabs call "fox's testicles"; and dehydrated sea slugs from the Somali coasts. The Arab market was insatiable.

Prescriptions piled up on the bench. The pestle broke. The pills disintegrated and the boxes fell. As in all such dreams of impotence and obligation, there was no terrifying climax, only a monotonous reiteration.

When the column moved at dawn, the sound of the others followed, neither closer nor farther away. One by one the men detected it, lifted their heads and cradled their rifles in their arms. In the heat of the day, when they stopped in the shadow of a holm oak, Abdullah studied the hillsides through a pair of glasses. The soft wind smelled of dried grass. The slopes were empty.

Abdullah led the column at a slow *rahat,* the easeful gait of mountain bandits. Nobody spoke, but each man parted his lips, listening to the stifled footsteps that pursued him as his shadow stretched along the plain.

That night, Abdullah gave a lecture on the meaning of the war. He compared the Turks in their historical beginnings to a flood of clear, refreshing water that had flowed across the arid empire of the Byzantines. In a few decades, every race and custom had dissolved in that fresh Turkish stream. For many centuries, the empire had held them in solution; but, in time, the foreign particles had begun to poison it, like salts. Now that the Turks were turning back to their authentic Asiatic culture, they would precipitate out this foreign matter that had polluted Turkish life. In the end, through this ordeal of heat and distillation, the Turks would be clean and simple once again.

The clean, simple Mehmets looked at each other in disbelief. Hairy Murat scratched and Yellow Faik stared at his boots. When Abdullah stopped, the night was filled with restless sounds, as audible as the twilight squeaking of bats and insects. Abdullah spoke about the coming holiday, Kurban Bayram, the Festival of Sacrifice, which fell at the end of the week. He promised to slaughter the fattest sheep in Anatolia and roast it whole, even if the Greeks were firing on them with a cannon. He spoke with confidence about defending Ushak and Gediz, and even hinted at the possibility of spoils.

Finally, because his men stared at him so stupidly, and the presence of the others was so obvious, he felt he must make some sort of explanation. He began to tell them stories of hallucinations: camel drivers, crossing a wilderness, who had imagined they were followed by invisible assassins; shepherds driven wild by solitude; whole armies maddened by contaminated grain; and pilgrims to the peak of Moses who were deafened by the cries of spirit voices.

Before daybreak, they got up silently and went forward, urging their horses through the dust. This time, Abdullah posted Hairy Murat at the head of the column, because he was known to have an extra eye behind his right ear, and put himself at the rear with one of the Mehmets, who was leading a mule that carried the shaft of the machine gun.

The grass and thistles woke around them. Magpies fluttered in the thickets. As the sun rose, Abdullah looked from one face to another. Each man was moving his eyes from side to side and clasping his rifle.

In the center of a naked plateau, Hairy Murat allowed his horse to falter. He turned around and shook his head, with his milky eyes protruding hideously from his sunburned face.

The wind parted his beard to show the whiteness of his chin.

"They've stopped," he said.

"Go ahead," Abdullah said. "Is this an army or a flock of lambs?"

But his people's army seemed to shrink away, each man betrayed by flaws appearing on his face like spots on a rotting pear, the marks of a corrupted soul—a twitching lip, a squinting eye, a flush of dark blood on the cheekbones. The careless Hakki tightened the bridle of his little pony; the cautious Rauf peered gloomily across the plain.

"Go on!" Abdullah shouted, whipping his horse along. "Move forward!" And he pierced each of them with an unloving glance: You, Shükrü—chrome yellow and mephitic! You, Ertoghrul—barren, surrogate mare! How dare you hesitate?

He had supposed that men so lacking in imagination would be immune to fear. They did not look like timid men. Moreover, they were Turks: they understood the natural order of humanity and the will of God, which rules the hearts and hands of men and sets the pattern for all other human institutions. It was natural that they should obey their leader, unthinkable that they should not. Reluctantly, they moved along.

Hairy Murat was the last to go.

"Abdullah Bey?" he said.

"Be still!" Abdullah said; and he lashed the old man's cheekbone with his leather quirt. "You've already caused enough trouble!" Spurring his horse, he cried out, "*Heydi!* God is great! Let's go!" He left the column behind him like a cast-off snakeskin on the road. Glancing back, he saw the leading horseman, Careless Hakki, pressing a hand above his heart. Abdullah drew a pistol, fired at the sky and drove his animal in reckless bounds across the heaps of rhyolite, the bitter little streams, in purblind chases over wasting slopes, through empty gullies, screaming the name of God.

Just beyond a shallow ridge, he came suddenly upon the other riders. They were Turks, and drawn together like the members of a caravan at rest. Their leader sat a chestnut stallion at the center. He was an immense Circassian, girdled in oxhide, turquoise and buckles of ormolu. His back was as stiff as a marble pier embedded on the pillion. Sunlight glittered on his dagger and the silver pommel of his saddle. When he turned his head, the coins around his turban threw out blazing darts of light; but his boots, his vest and his pantaloons were black, and his face was shadowy and barren.

Abdullah stopped, expecting to hear his men behind him, but only the empty wind sighed in his ears. The Circassian stared at him. He raised his hand, and the line of riders shifted, touching their sabres with their hands. Abdullah faced them mutely. Finally, he tapped his breastbone in a gesture of respect.

The chieftain called out: "Brother Turk?"

It was a deep, demonic growl, a fearful echo of Abdullah's feeble battle cry, which had wasted like the puling of a baby in the expanses of the desert.

"God bless you," Abdullah said. He felt that every word betrayed him as a foolish druggist playing at a game of war.

"In God's name, come ahead, my brother!"

And Abdullah, nodding graciously, descended past the phalanx of the riders and embraced the huge Circassian, who wiped his beard on Abdullah's cheeks and made a catlike rumbling sound.

"God sent you, my friend," the Circassian said. "You're going to join us now."

Abdullah heard his men approaching. They were as numerous as the others, and no worse. He noticed that the Circassian's lips were cracked, his eyes were bloodshot from the dust and one of his knuckles was bleeding. These marks of

177

human vulnerability inspired Abdullah to a burst of arrogance.

"Why should we trust you?" he said. "You've been lurking around us for two days and nights. Why didn't you show yourselves?"

"Show ourselves?" the Circassian said. "We have not moved from this spot."

Abdullah turned around with an ironic smile for Hairy Murat and the other men to see. But they gave him back a rotten, shrinking look, dark with the corruption that he had detected when they halted on the rim of the volcanic plain.

"All right," Abdullah said, as carelessly as possible. "Why shouldn't we ride together?"

Thus, in a single line, they rode together, with their eyes fixed on the jangling turban of the Circassian bandit. Within an hour they reached a village gilded by the sunlight. Forty yellow poplars stood like candles in the haze. At the foot of the knoll there was a splendid pond. Some ducks were lying on the mossy bank. When the Circassian galloped through the pond, bright plumes of silver splashed from his horse's hoofs. A goose stretched out her neck and beat the water with her wings, and the Circassian swung his yataghan and struck off her head.

The Circassian called the people to the pond. He lined the men and boys against a building. It was a rich and stubborn village: a knife would not open their mouths. First, the Circassian cut their pockets off. Then he cut the drawstrings of their pants. One of the boys began to whimper, clutching at his trousers. The fathers frowned until the boy was ashamed and held his breath.

"All right," the Circassian said. "Let the Moslems now step forward and profess their faith."

Nobody moved. One of the elders, who was quivering with palsy, said in a strong voice: "There are no Moslems here."

178

But another bleated like a nanny goat: "Don't listen! All of us are Moslems. The Greeks have run away."

The Circassian said: "These *must* be Greeks, they disagree among themselves so much."

His men began to laugh. The villagers were staring at the ground. They could hear shrieks from the barn where the bandits were slaughtering a heifer.

"All right. If you are Christians, let the Christians show their faith."

No one moved. Daddy Mahmut shouted: "You see? They must be Jews!"

The Circassian turned away, made a face and spat on the ground.

"How can you help a village that has sunk so low?"

And he told his men to search the houses. Abdullah rode forward holding his right hand above his head.

"Remember why we came and why we didn't," he said. "No man of mine will eat from the mouth of a child."

"That's right," said the Circassian, flashing his white teeth. "The Red Cross would not approve."

The men howled and galloped around the village. In a hayloft they found a Greek infantryman, a brown-haired boy whose face was streaked with tears. The Circassian ordered him to take off his boots. The boy lay down and pressed his face in the dirt.

"Kill the spy!" the men cried, slapping their hands on the sheaths of their daggers. Smiling, the Circassian took out his knife. He carefully cut the laces of the Greek boy's boots, pulled off the boots and stripped away the woolen socks, which had been good hand-knitted socks, but were worn out and hanging in loose shreds. The boy began to pray aloud, crying, "God help me! Jesus help me!" and reaching for his socks as if he valued them more than his life.

But the men pushed him down. They brought a pair of

horseshoes from a barn. Midhat grasped the boy by the ankles and raised his bare feet like the hoofs of a colt; and Ertoghrul, who was a blacksmith, drove the nails. They used ordinary shoeing nails and a hammer Ertoghrul had found.

The boy fell back, as limp and green as Jesus in the Christian paintings. Great drops of purple blood oozed from his feet. After the nails were driven through, the Circassian came up and hammered the points to hold the shoes on. Then they turned the soldier loose and let him run in the direction of the Greek lines.

At sundown they set fire to the village. The loot was marvelous. Even Yellow Faik, who lacked a single notion in his brain except the impulse to avoid work, made off with a sack of millet; and all those ideologists of the new Asia carried away huge skins of cheese and bags of grain and crocks of butter. As they galloped off, they heard a piercing scream; and a priest ran from the church with his skirts afire.

The men were singing. Neither devotion to the Fatherland nor aspirations for the human race, neither the hope of ecstasy on earth nor the promise of a tender concubine in Heaven—nothing could warm the soul so well as blazing thatch.

But Abdullah rode with his head bowed. His heart had shriveled in his breast.

*H*is army and the others camped together in a ruined caravanserai beside a grove of poplar trees. In the darkness the trees resembled the decaying pillars of an ancient temple. The roof of the caravanserai had fallen, and the vaults of yellow stone were blackened by the smoke of nomad campfires.

Before the Circassian would go inside, he sent two scouts on foot to search the building. They circled it twice in their soft felt boots, holding their carbines under their arms as they looked through the open doors. Then they waved, and everyone went down the hillside in a boiling cloud—horses, men, guns, cooking pots and pack mules, jingling with rings of brass and strings of turquoise beads.

The Circassian, roaring like a maniac, rode his sweating horse around the inner courtyard. He demanded an enormous fire, in spite of the heat. Even Abdullah's men ran out to gather baskets of sheep dung, bundles of poplar wands and kettles filled with water from the spring.

Abdullah rested on a heap of rubble in a corner of the court. When his men dashed past him, turning their faces away, he would try to catch them by the sleeve.

"Hey, Mehmet! Unsaddle my horse. Have you forgotten? . . . Midhat! Bring me my pipe."

It was impossible to make them listen. Their eyes rolled

sideways whenever the Circassian, on his magnificent and pungent stallion, cantered past. Abdullah was forgotten; he had lost his face and hands. His men combined their wheat and threw it into a common pot; they struck up conversations, friendships, rivalries, erotic courtships with the other men; and they ran obediently to the bandit's call.

As soon as the sky was dark, while the mash was cooking in a copper casserole, Abdullah slid behind the stones and crawled through a fissure in the wall. Smoke was pouring from the broken building, smothering the grove and blotting out the early stars, which seemed to swirl like flecks of mica in a murky lake. The harsh and repetitious groaning of a bullfrog, like the lamentations of an outcast god, pressed on his heart. He heard a clink of metal. The guard at the spring was getting up.

"What do you want?"

"Only a drink of water," Abdullah said.

"There's water in the caravanserai."

"It's stale," Abdullah said.

"Lütfi doesn't want you here."

But Abdullah crawled ahead until he felt the gravel. Then he waited. "Guard? Who are you?"

"I'm Mehmet. The Younger. Please go back, Abdullah Bey. Lütfi Bey gave orders."

"Is that his name? Lütfi Bey?" There was no answer. "You're a good guard," Abdullah went on. "How could you recognize me in this blackness?"

"I recognize your voice, Abdullah Bey."

"You're very acute."

He scraped up some pebbles and threw them forward.

But the Younger Mehmet laughed and said he had a pair of ears, thank God, that knew a pebble from a man.

"Good God!" Abdullah said. "Have you a cat's *eyes,* too?" In a hollow where the soil was damp, he began to dig with his fingers. The Younger Mehmet said: "I know where you are, Abdullah Bey. I'm sitting by the spring, and I don't intend to leave it."

"Obedient to orders."

His irony did not affect the Younger Mehmet. Abdullah loosed his sash. The money belt was like a band of fire around his loins. It had rubbed away his skin. Blisters rose and took on water, broke and festered under its incessant rubbing. Ulcers had formed that were as hot as blood and sticky to the touch; but he had never dared to take it off. It was his magic girdle. In a sense, it was the sinew of the new Turkey, the fiber of the revolution. So long as he wore the belt, his men could not betray him or desert him. Tenderly, he laid it in a crevice of the stones, pressed down the folds and covered it with dirt. Then he thrashed around until the stupid guard sprang up and told him to go back.

"I'll die of thirst," Abdullah said; but he crawled away at once. God willing, he would punish the Younger Mehmet on this earth and in the flesh.

The caravanserai was full of smoke. The men had overturned the cooking vessel and were crouching over mounds of steaming porridge, which they dipped up with their hands in sticky yellow balls. Groaning like cattle, they stuffed their mouths while sweat poured down their faces. Lütfi the Circassian was lying on a carpet. He raised his hand to beckon, but it fell back limply on his naked chest. He had eaten and was breathing placidly.

"I wanted you to eat with me. Where did you go?"

Every man around them looked up like a good dog answering his master's voice. There was not a one who would have scrupled to insert his knife directly into Abdullah's bowels—and that in return for all the training he had given them, the money, the political instructions, the Oriental dogma. Abdullah felt a spasm in his throat. He looked at the faces of his men: Midhat, as black and slimy as a toad, his skin reflecting opal lusters from the fire; and Hairy Murat, glowering beneath a scruffy mat of hair that overhung his forehead like a camel's mane; and Ertoghrul the Ironsmith, wet-eyed, with his fingers twining in the fingers of a panting little hostler, king of the night. The detestable miasma of their breath mingled with the smoke. Their eyes turned restlessly at every sound.

"Eat with you?" Abdullah said. "I eat alone."

"Then you've eaten?"

"Yes. And I have drunk. At the spring."

He glared at Lütfi, whose face was masked by shadows. But the bandit neither moved his head nor spoke. He was lying on his back, his vest thrown open and his damp chest glittering. His muscular body, laced with scars that shone like golden wax, reposed in perfect ease among the lava rocks.

It would have been so easy to dispatch him! Lightly, like a traitor in a sultan's tent. But when Abdullah touched his fingers to the handle of his knife, he felt a quick movement at his back. He lowered his hand. Lütfi, gazing up calmly, said: "Are you a Rumelian?" His tone expressed the low opinion of the Asiatics for the men of European Turkey, with their notorious infusion of Albanian and Slavic blood.

"No," Abdullah said.

The bandit blinked his eyes.

"You're Anatolian?"

"I am."

"Very good," the bandit said without enthusiasm. "Yet you seem to be a city man?"

The men were creeping near. Assuming Abdullah had been deposed, they wanted to enjoy the final baiting. He turned his head to let them know that he had noticed them and would remember. Lütfi eyed him closely.

"How did I deduce you were a druggist?"

"Perhaps you can read tea leaves. It is not a secret."

"Strange profession for a Turk."

"Strange? No."

"I call it strange. In my town, only Jews and Armenians would have it."

"What town was that?"

The bandit waved his hand.

"It doesn't matter. I am its leading citizen." He showed his teeth and the other men laughed. "Well, Mr. Druggist, I suppose you can read?"

Abdullah tipped his head.

"Alas, we have no books to read."

The men laughed again.

"Don't laugh!" the bandit said. "It's a shame there aren't any books. I would like to have you read to me. I like the stories from the *Mevlana* and the *Thousand and One Nights*. If one of my men is martyred tomorrow, I would like you to read above his grave."

"My friend," Abdullah said, "if you should join the martyrs tomorrow, I swear I shall recite the Blessed Koran."

"Who can guess his own hour?" said Lütfi. He rose on his elbow. "When I die, I want my men to bury me the way a Moslem should be buried. With the proper recitations. The poem of the Prophet's birth, so on, so forth. If you go tomorrow, God willing, we'll bury you properly."

"I won't give up tomorrow," Abdullah said.

"God knows," the bandit said, and spat among the stones. A pious rumble shook the men.

"I won't give up my ghost." Abdullah said. "My own men will protect me." He looked around him, but his men stared back in silence. "Then I'll take them back to where I've hid some money. I'll dig it up and make a distribution."

No one spoke.

"Then I can join the martyrs."

And he gave a foolish laugh.

The bandit chief was holding something in his hand—a shiny little pellet pressed between his fingers and his thumb. He showed it like a jewel on his open palm. The gleaming seed of metal drew Abdullah's eyes. There are omens that are sinister, even to a disciple of Auguste Comte.

"I have hidden the money well," Abdullah said. Once more he looked around at all his men.

"Lie down while God permits you to," the bandit said; and Abdullah watched him drop the bullet harmlessly among his savage ornaments and weapons—his buckles of false gold, his silver daggers, his turban wrapped with strings of coins— which lay together in a careless pile a few feet from his elbow.

After the fire had died, Abdullah heard a footstep on the stones. But Lütfi said distinctly: "No. Not now."

They left the caravanserai and rode in darkness toward a territory that had been abandoned to the Greeks. When the sky was turning pale, they stopped in a field of lava, and even the dullest of them sighed and glanced around.

"This is far enough," Abdullah said. "The engineer can't see around the curve."

But the bandit frowned.

"Somebody has to go and break the track. To welcome the Greeks."

Far below them in the canyon was the famous Smyrna line, a thin, suctorial extension of the mouth of Europe, insatiable and parasitic, embedded in the body of the Turkish Empire by the Société Ottomane du Chemin de Fer Smyrne-Cassaba et Prolongement, concession of 1893. Europeans owned the tracks, the cars, the sheds, the docks, the bulking bins, the sacks of acorn cups, the tubs of tallow and the mounds of licorice root; and they had insulated their possessions—*di-*

vide et impera—with a colony of hostile Christian immi-
grants. Wherever the tracks had touched, Greeks had
bloomed like weeds along the right of way. With every station came a station keeper and a little shop; with every shop
a grocer; then the grocer's wife; and next a school, a church,
a priest; and, finally, a European soldier to protect this settlement of Christians from the inhospitable, rapacious Turks. In
effect, the Army of the Hellenes had been marching up the
Smyrna line, invading Asia Minor by the railway route for
generations; and now the vanguard of their infantry had
reached as far as Eshme, riding in a cattle car.

"Somebody has to break the track," Lütfi repeated, rolling
his eyes while his vassals nudged each other. "Abdullah
Bey?"

"Why not?" Abdullah said.

"And someone with him," Lütfi said. "We'll let him choose
his own . . . assistant."

That was an Arabic refinement—letting you choose your
executioner, the least among your enemies. Abdullah scrutinized their faces. He could sense the merciless contempt of
Lütfi's men. Murder Abdullah Bey? Why not! As for his own
agrarian reformers, picked up like donkey droppings from
the streets of Eskishehir, they showed their fangs and snickered. Hairy Murat's cheek still showed the stigma of Abdullah's quirt; Yellow Faik was polishing his dagger on his vest.
Abdullah turned his back on them.

"*You,* Lütfi Bey," he said. "You come along."

Lütfi laughed. He gestured to Shükrü and Hakki. Shükrü,
grinning like a jackal, touched the hilt of his knife; and Hakki
wheeled his horse around.

"No, Lütfi Bey. I've chosen you."

Their eyes met. The bandit laughed again and lifted a
salute. He was heavier and taller than Abdullah, and he
moved with sinewy dynamics that resembled the light,

preliminary swaying of a wrestler. Fighting by rules, Lütfi could have bettered forty druggists softened in the coffee-houses of Shehzade-bashi; and he would not be fighting by rules.

But Abdullah started forward with a curious anticipation, giddy and lighthearted. It was Lütfi who dismounted to cinch up his saddle, who suddenly remembered fulminates and crowbars, who turned back to give his last instructions.

The men were staring at the ground. Without a word, they handed up the sticks of dynamite.

Abdullah led the way. There was no point in trying to force Lütfi to go first. Eventually, he would contrive to get behind Abdullah's back, and then the point of leadership would be decided.

In a quarter of an hour, they reached a dry ravine beside the tracks. It was the moment of impalpable division between night and day when a thread of black can first be distinguished from a thread of white, and, in the month of Rama-zan, the daily fast begins. Abdullah tied the horses in a clump of kermes oaks and carried down the tools and dynamite. Standing on the metal rails, he felt the deep vibration of the locomotive straining up the pass. Before long, they would begin to hear the clatter of the wheels, the pistons rushing back and forth, the clashing of the rifles stacked together in the baggage cars.

Abdullah took out his pouch and offered Lütfi the materials to make a cigarette. The bandit waved him away.

"Look, can't you start digging this with your pick?"

"I haven't tried."

"Well, then—don't stand there counting flies." He forced the handle of a mattock into Abdullah's hands. "Dig under the ties. Scrape out a little trough."

But Abdullah let the mattock slip between his fingers. Lütfi stared at him, astounded. Then he took out his pistol and aimed it at Abdullah's head.

"Don't be such a fool," Lütfi said. "The train is going to come."

Still, Abdullah only blinked his eyes against the growing light. He felt benumbed, as if he had been stunned and tied. It stupefied him to consider that the bandit soon would press the trigger.

"You'll never find my money belt," he said.

"Here is your money belt," Lütfi said through his teeth. He raised his shirt with his left hand to show the canvas girdle, which was darkly crusted with soil. Abdullah stared at it for long time. Finally, he bowed his head.

"Why don't you finish?" he said.

"No, no," Lütfi said. "Fix the tracks."

"Oh, do it quickly!" Abdullah cried. He took a step forward. But the bandit drew back, raised his pistol overhead and fired a shot. The horses whinnied in the scrub oaks as the echo crashed around the gorge.

"The tracks," Lütfi repeated, forcing Abdullah to pick up the mattock and apply it to the tracks, which had begun to hum with an insistent warning. And then: "The dynamite!"

And so Abdullah turned and found the box of dynamite and threw it in Lütfi's face.

They fell and rolled together, hugging one another, while the sticks of dynamite slid down the rails. Then Lütfi reared up and they rolled together down a bank and fell against some thorny branches. Abdullah got his hands around the bandit's throat. He squeezed, and Lütfi quivered violently, rasping, breast to breast. His lips drew back and whitened like the jowls of a slaughtered bullock. A drop of blood began to bubble at the corner of his mouth. He gave a feeble little moan, rolled up his eyes and shuddered; and Abdullah mounted him, panting, tore out his silver dagger, pressed its point against Lütfi's convulsive jaw and cut the great blood vessel of his neck.

Then he lay down in Lütfi's blood and waited for the men

to come, who surely must have heard the pistol and the shrieking of the horses.

That night they had a funeral. None of the bandits could recite the Holy Koran by memory. Abdullah knew some verses, but he pretended that he had forgotten them. At twilight, standing forty paces from the cooling carcass of the late commander, he pronounced the invocation that begins the Holy Scriptures:

"In the name of God, the Merciful, the Compassionate. Praise be to God, Lord of the Worlds, the Merciful, the Compassionate. Owner of the Day of Judgment. Thee we worship . . ."

Then, opening the Book, he read the verse beginning:

"Every soul shall taste of death. . . . The present life is but the goods of vanity."

A brooding silence weighed upon the men. They gazed at Lütfi, their old lord of lords, whose brow had been so dark and terrible, whose tongue had spoken massacre, whose hands had rendered death, whose feet had trampled on the corpses of his enemies and who had been called so swiftly to the Lord of Judgment; and their shoulders rose and fell with heavy sighing as they felt the domination of a stronger and more ruthless master.

The bandit lay surrounded by his weapons on a bed of boughs, with a coal-oil lantern at his feet and a bloody turban on his head. Owls were calling in the branches; moths were spinning through the light; and Lütfi lay upfacing, with his nostrils stagnant and his eyelids closed with two brown pebbles, which seemed to sprout like budding antlers from the sockets of his head. His thick beard, streaked with white and amber, rested on his chest.

The Younger Mehmet, in appreciation of his special loyalty, had been appointed washer of the corpse. But he was languishing among the shadows of a green valonia tree, his nostrils twitching with the morbid sweetness of his master's flesh. Abdullah had to call him to his duty. Even then he hesitated, casting glances at the others. But Ertoghrul brought up a basin filled with turbid water, the others slipped away and the boy was left to carry out the duties to the dead.

He circumambulated seven times before he touched the bandit's flesh. Then with a shudder, glaring at Abdullah, he unwound the belly sash. Using it as a sort of sling, he put in the knives and daggers that were scattered on the ground. In his girdle, Lütfi had carried two gold pounds, some silver mejidiyes and a brownish photograph of two young men—himself, apparently, and someone who resembled him, dressed in decorated vests and riding pants. There were, as well, a burning glass, a box of pills, an envelope of worthless yellow powder for venereal disease and a tobacco box of Tatar silver, worked in arabesques and calligraphs that said: *"Mashallah."*

Impatiently, Abdullah watched the Younger Mehmet fumbling with the buttons of the vest. He was an awkward boy, and obsequious in his superstitious reverence; he kept his eyes away from Lütfi's throat, where flies were working in the clotted blood. When the body was completely stripped, he spread a piece of cloth across the loins and went away to wash himself and pray. Finally, he began to bathe the body, starting on the right and working to the left, as in the ritual ablution before prayer.

"I will perform the tonsuring," Abdullah said.

"What tonsuring?"

"He is to be completely shaved."

The Younger Mehmet looked at him openmouthed.

"You can't do that, Abdullah Bey."

"Why not?"

"It's not the custom. It offends."

"I will start here," Abdullah said, pointing with his fingertips, "and work from right to left, the way the Prophet has prescribed." He took out the knife that he had used to slit the bandit's throat and honed it on a little block of adamantine. "First the beard. Then the hair. From crown to toenail."

"It offends," said the Younger Mehmet.

"I know," Abdullah said. Clenching his fists, he shouted: "It offended me when he robbed me! Tried to kill me! In God's name, it offended me!"

And he drew the knife across the bandit's cold and flaccid cheek. Lütfi's beard reached to the nipples of his chest. The whiskers slipped away without a sound, like threads of mold.

"The custom," said the Younger Mehmet, "is recitation, ablution."

"Be still," said Abdullah, "or I shall bury you in the same grave."

He began to shave the skull. As he ran his blade along the neck and shoulders, skimming downward, to and fro, the metal flashing in the yellow light, Lütfi's body seemed to shrink and soften. Abdullah took the pebbles from his eyelids, and the old lord of war, of vengeance and oppression, gazed up innocently at the mossy branches. It pleased Abdullah to imagine he was seeing the black pit of Hell, infested by such creatures as himself, dead gods and legendary monsters.

They wrapped a clean white sash around his waist and sprinkled him with powdered cinnamon—the only shroud, the only spice they had. Then Abdullah called the men to watch the burial.

But when the others saw the bandit tonsured for the Resurrection, they were stricken with a sort of holy awe. There lay the great and overbearing Lütfi, naked as a snake and beardless as a eunuch. It was as if he had yielded up his manhood with his hair, his beard, his axillary tassels and the plumage of his groin.

Some of the men began to weep. They panted in confused emotion, shook their heads, and ran and touched their fingers to his wounds, the way the Shiites touch the wounds of their beloved Huseyn.

Abdullah read the verse beginning: "We will surely try thee with somewhat of fear and hunger. . . ."

Then he moved the rigid body through the postures of the prayer.

Two days later, learning that the town of Ushak had been captured by the Greeks, Abdullah turned his army northward toward Kütahya, where there were other bands—enough of them, in fact, to dictate to the feeble government at Ankara.

*T*he train from Ankara to Kütahya was slower than a caravan. It burned oak logs and cakes of dung and stopped at frequent intervals to cool the bearings of the wheels, because the Turkish railroads had run out of axle grease. The train stood for an hour outside Polatli, then paused at odd, deserted places where the Porsuk River rushed among the willows and rain beat steadily against the windows of the cars.

Kenan lay back in a corner seat and rubbed his knee with his hand to warm the joint. The cold dampness of the car, the lonely silence of the fields, the whispering of the soldiers lulled him into a trance. He had been sitting almost motionless for hours, with nothing entering his mind except a vague, reptilian sense of light and sound. He knew—or had been told—that this ability to hibernate showed that a man was lacking in vitality: it was a common failing of the Turks, according to such admiring neighbors as the Greeks. But Kenan regarded this deficiency (if it was a deficiency) as one of God's rare blessings. Nervous energy, like a vivid imagination, is an enemy of discipline; and only discipline can sustain the soul when armies fail and cities crumble.

In any case, there was nothing good to think about. First, Ushak and Gediz had fallen. Then the commander of the Western Front had enlisted several thousand undependable guerrillas in a counterattack. The Turkish forces had been routed; the guerrillas had dissolved; and now the Greeks were raiding in retaliation all along the line.

Out in Kütahya, Ethem the Circassian was increasing his control of the irregulars. He acted like a rival prince, ignoring the orders of the General Staff, and sent his brothers to Ankara to negotiate with Mustapha Kemal. The Pasha, in turn, was sending his own proposal directly to the irregulars: a full amnesty for every man who had a record of banditry, in return for accepting authority and merging into the regular army. It was not an offer that was likely to be received with enthusiasm in Kütahya.

The train crept in at nightfall, after the soldiers had put out a fire that was burning in the undercarriage of the baggage car. It had been raining on the mountains, and the ramparts of the town were wrapped in shreds of greenish mist. Kenan leaned from a window. A boy in homespun wool stood next to him, peeling an apple with a silver dagger. The boy said he came from Ushak and could tell you a few things.

The station platform was covered with wet brown leaves. Little girls stood barefoot on the gravel, begging for newspapers. The boy from Ushak said you couldn't trust the papers.

"There were plenty of things in Ushak they wouldn't print," he said. "God willing, it won't turn into a civil war."

"It already has," Kenan said; and he climbed down into a crowd of peasant farmers, dressed in ragged clothes that smelled of garlic.

He rode up to town in a donkey cart that was decorated with mild Batavian landscapes—windmills, sunsets and canals—in lozenges along the sides. The driver cut across the fields to avoid the marshy places in the road. As the cart bounced over the ruts, the women who were squatting on the floorboards slithered to and fro like bags of wool. Their heads were draped with coffee-colored shawls that reached their hips, and they held the selvages together to conceal their mouths.

Kenan leaned forward.

"I suppose you've never heard of Ethem Bey or Tewfik Bey?"

The women turned away, pretending they had not heard him. The driver, after a long silence, answered: "Ethem? Tewfik? Never."

"Have you ever heard of General Mustapha Kemal?"

"No, sir. I don't know anything about those military people. I'm a farmer."

In a little square above the mosque, the driver stopped the cart and waited for Kenan to get down.

"Is this where I'll find them?"

The driver shrugged. Kenan began to laugh.

"Do you think I came here to assassinate the patriots?"

But the driver did not answer.

As the cart pulled away, the women stared back through the peepholes in their shawls, enjoying to the end the curious experience of seeing a foreigner: a strange, outspoken man in knee boots and wool jodhpurs, a plain tunic and a kalpak of gray astrakhan, with a patch on his eye, a tuck in his sleeve and a cane in his hand.

The upper stories of the houses overhung the street on either side. Dampness glittered on the cobblestones. A lamp was shining in the doorway of a potter's shop, which was almost completely filled with terra-cotta water jars and platters of blue-green faïence.

A man in hunting clothes came out of one of the half-timbered houses. He wore a shag of hair that joggled on his eyebrows like the forelock of a pony. Grinning, he touched his fingers to his head in a nonchalant salute.

"Welcome, Your Honors. Are you the diplomat from Ankara?"

Kenan looked the man up and down. His leather boots

were new, and he wore a revolver in a heavy holster that dangled almost to his knee.

"I suppose you don't know Ethem Bey?"

"Don't I?"

"Or this Tewfik Bey? Or any of these so-called roving squadrons?"

The man showed a row of yellow teeth with several vacancies.

"They come and go, Your Honors. It's not like Ankara."

"I want to talk to them."

"Then why are you standing here, Your Honors, out in the rain and cold, when you could be sitting in a cosy restaurant?"

And he led Kenan through dripping alleys, under gloomy eaves, all the while discoursing upon the salubrious climate of Kütahya, the sweetness of its melons and the exquisite flavor of its waters, which were beneficial to hepatic functions, rheumatism, various afflictions of the kidneys, impotence, nocturia and premature ejaculation.

When Yellow Faik came back to the house and said that a stranger was waiting in the Sunshine Restaurant, Abdullah sprang up with a cry of annoyance.

"That's Crimean Yusuf Bey. Why didn't you bring him here?"

For three weeks he had been anticipating the arrival of this mysterious Asiatic ideologist. It was an insult and a waste of time to relegate a man of such importance to the outer circle of one's crude system of personal defense. Feeling for his knife, his pistol and his dwindling money belt, Abdullah hurried across the upper hall, which served as a sort of storehouse, and pawed through shepherds' cloaks and overshoes.

Yellow Faik was standing in a bay that overhung the street.

"It's snowing, sir."

Abdullah went to the window. A few flakes of snow were

falling with the raindrops, melting as they touched the ground. There was a gentle rustle like the folding of a shroud around the town. Winter was closing in at last—the white blessing, isolating and insulating all these fortresses and picket posts along the Western Front, imposing a more pervasive armistice than any peace treaty yet devised.

"I thought it would never begin," Abdullah said. His breath against the pane was like a sudden fog that blotted out the view. "Now we'll have time to find ourselves, God willing."

And he went down the stairs, smiling in anticipation of his first meeting with the Party functionary who had come to help the Green Armies of Kütahya rebuild the ideology that they had lost in a summer of dust and blood. How desperately Abdullah was longing for relief from the conversational companionship of Hairy Murat and Ertoghrul the Ironsmith!

At the corner, he passed several of his men who were opening their mouths and sticking out their tongues to catch the first snowflakes. With their childish faces lifted to taste the virgin snow, they looked vulnerable and sweetly innocent. Contentment glowed like hearth light in their placid eyes, suffused with delicious memories of fire and sword, incandescent churches and polluted wells, sequins bursting out of ruptured mattresses and farm girls trapped like sheep among the tufts of windblown pampas grass.

Perhaps they were no worse than other men: simply more cautious, senile, callow, careless, malodorous and degenerate. But the mere sight of them reminded Abdullah of how far he had drifted from the naïve and beautiful ideals of Shehzade-bashi. What was the point of an intellectual's becoming a man of action if he turned into a creature no better than a hungry animal? It would be preferable to go back to his pharmacy, to live in the shelter of his own vine and fig tree and search for another Eleni Trigonis to fill the emptiness of his heart.

In the weariness, the loneliness, the horror of this pitiless peasant war, Abdullah's only sustenance had been the hope of Asiatic revolution. His heart still quickened to the promise of a continent in turmoil. He could sense the immanence of rebel nations rising in Samarkand and Merv—military allies against the reactionary nations of the West. If only the Bolsheviks of Central Asia could send some money or some ammunition! There were reports of a revolutionary congress in Baku, on the Caspian Sea. Delegates had come from Dagestan and Turkestan, Khiva and Bokhara—Hindus, Persians, Chinese; Tatars from Kazan; Kalmucks from Transoxiana; and Azerbaijanis from the littoral of the enormous inland sea. When Zinoviev, the Russian emissary, spoke against the capitalistic Europeans, he was incessantly interrupted by throaty cries for vengeance, accompanied by the clashing overhead of sabres and revolvers wrought in Afghan silver.

Then word had come that one of these ferocious delegates was on his way to Anatolia, bringing the spark of revolution with him like a fulminating pin in a Gladstone bag. During the dark solstitial lull, this firebrand would keep company with the dreamers of Kütahya, lighting bonfires to herald the early spring of human freedom.

He would beguile Abdullah's mind with definitions of the proletariat, with trenchant criticisms of the Empire and Islam, with theoretical discussions of the uses of atrocity, the *propaganda fide* and the Hegelian dialectic; and on many a blustery, snowbound night, with a fire snapping in the stove and lantern light reflected from the windows like a host of little torches in the sky, they would plan the international regeneration that would follow this winter of despair.

Abdullah was breathless with impatience. He turned a corner. Light from the windows of the restaurant carpeted the slush. The panes were dim with a steamy warmth that hinted at food and companionship inside.

At the door, however, he felt a twinge of foreboding. He tried with the heel of his hand to wipe the moisture from the glass, but he could see only the opalescent outlines of a man at a table. He pushed open the door and caught his breath.

"God is great!" he said, and he spread out his hands, upturned to Heaven. For a moment, neither Abdullah nor Kenan could utter a word.

The restaurant was almost empty. There were three or five vacant tables along the wall, an empty basket on the floor, an empty birdcage on a hook. Behind a whitewashed bulwark, shoulder high, the cook was standing like a sentry. Endless rows of pomegranates and persimmons perched along the wall, like ruddy little heads displayed on the battlements of a captured city.

The cook came out the sally port of his barbican, mumbling some sort of greeting and flicking a rag across the tables. But Abdullah pushed him aside and advanced on Kenan with outstretched arms. Kenan's face was twisted into an involuntary, convulsive rictus that resulted from his injuries. Kissing his cheek, Abdullah began to laugh.

"I was expecting—Why, I had given *you* up to the holy martyrs, and here you pop up like one of the Seven Sleepers from the cave at Ephesus!" He put his arm around his brother's shoulders; but Kenan stiffly drew away. "We'll go to my house," Abdullah went on. "I can't welcome you properly here." And, lowering his voice: "I want to serve you a small glass of that transparent liquid—you know, the stuff the dervishes call *white writing?*"

But as Abdullah turned to lead the way, Kenan said: "Just a minute." He gestured toward the table. "Sit down. I have some questions."

Abdullah was more surprised by the harshness of Kenan's tone than by the rudeness of his words. He put it down to the shock of an unexpected meeting. He, too, was startled by the

200

complex and awesome mechanism of fate that had brought them together, face to face, in this unlikely spot. But Kenan seemed to find it unnerving and distasteful. He looked old and sick. In any case, what was he doing here, immersed again in war? He should have been in some sweet, reposeful place like Yalova or Bursa, with clean air, warm soda springs and leafy trees, where he could recapture a few of the earthly joys of this stolen world.

"All right," Abdullah said, sitting down. "We'll have some supper first. Did you come from Ankara?"

Kenan tipped his head affirmatively to one side.

"And how about yourself?" Abdullah went on. "How are you? Are you well?"

Kenan tipped his head again. Then, thrusting forward his tired, corroded face across the table: "Look—are you familiar with this so-called Green Army? I came here to speak with the so-called leaders—Ethem Bey, Tewfik Bey, Reshid Bey and so on."

"I see," Abdullah said. A ripple of anxiety squeezed through his chest. He examined Kenan more closely—his boots, his plain high-collared tunic, his woolly hat—as if some oddity of appearance might explain this coldness. Kenan's manner was so arrogant, so discourteous that it suggested madness.

"Ethem Bey. The Circassian," Kenan repeated.

"Yes, I know them," Abdullah said. "But let us talk first about yourself. Have you had word from Mother?"

Kenan drummed the table with the tip of one finger. His mouth was fixed in an unyielding line. Although he appeared to be merely asking for information, his questions had the tone of an ultimatum. Abdullah sighed and cleared his throat.

"Well, as for Ethem the Circassian, he seems to be away. They say he is in a hospital in Ankara. And his brother, Re-shid Bey—the one who's deputy from Saruhan—he seems to

201

have vanished. Tewfik Bey you might find in Simav, God willing. If you can find a way of getting to Simav."

"Who is commander here in Kütahya?"

Abdullah smiled.

"I am the man to take you to him. But, unfortunately, this is his dinner hour." And he got up and went into the kitchen, where he raised the lids of the copper casseroles and sniffed extravagantly. There was a dish of dried beans cooked with strips of mutton fat, some shreds of mutton boiled with spinach and a stew of leeks and eggplant. The cook plunged a wooden spoon into the stew and dredged it up enticingly, but Abdullah clicked his tongue.

"Too late in the year for eggplant."

"Sir, this is a special dish. It makes you like a ram."

"Do I need that during a winter bivouac? Give us some of the beans and the other."

The cook turned up his apron to shield his head from the snow and ran out to buy a loaf of bread. Abdullah paced back and forth, his eyes cast down and his thumbs thrust under his sash, from which protruded his dagger and his silver-handled pistol. He knew his disappointment must be showing on his face, but he could not make the effort to conceal it. He had been so elated, so proud to see his brother here. He had expected Kenan to be impressed by his appearance, curious about his accomplishments. Kenan's exaggerated formality was completely baffling. There he sat, drumming his fingers on the table and staring ahead with the haughty expression of a one-eyed falcon. When the cook came back and dropped a warm half loaf on the table, Kenan pushed it aside without even glancing up.

Abdullah snapped his fingers. The cook brought in a platter of beans and a dish of meat with spinach; then he carried in a serving of the eggplant stew.

"Who are those men outside the door?" Kenan said.

"It's too late for eggplant," Abdullah said to the cook. "Take the stew away."

"I thought the other gentleman?" the cook said. He took the dish away.

"Who are those men?" Kenan repeated, standing up.

"Good bread," Abdullah said, tearing apart the warm loaf. "No chestnut hulls in that bread." He raised his eyes. "Sit down, Kenan. They are my own men."

"*Your* men?"

Abdullah bowed his head. Kenan looked around at the cook, then back at Abdullah again.

"Who is the commander of the independents here?"

"I am," Abdullah said.

"You? The Nietzsche of the pharmacy?"

Abdullah put down his fork. His eyes smarted.

"You are as sarcastic as ever," he said. "I had forgotten the impact of your tongue."

He got up and opened the door.

"Hakki? Come in here. Mehmet?" Trembling, he pushed the two rough uncles into the room. "Now, let's end all misunderstanding. I am the commander here. What is *your* business in Kütahya?"

Kenan stared at Hakki and Mehmet, whose faces were unshaven and whose turbans gleamed with stolen metal. He pressed his lips together.

"Put down your weapons," he said. "I am the representative of the Grand National Assembly. I don't speak to the eye of a revolver."

The two men looked at Abdullah.

"Put them down," Abdullah said. And, turning back to Kenan: "How did you come to represent Mustapha Kemal's parliament?"

But Kenan did not answer. He reached under the table and drew out a portfolio.

"The Grand National Assembly has decided that the independent forces operating out of this area should be brought into closer cooperation with the army command in Ankara. The recent failure at Gediz has shown the need of this."

Abdullah reached out for a sheet of paper. It was covered with beautiful lines of hand script, as delicately formed as the calligraphs around the pillars of a mosque. After reading a few lines, Abdullah forced out a strained laugh.

"Well, I see what the Grand National Assembly thinks of us! 'No organization.' 'No budget.' 'No discipline.' "

Hakki, hovering at the doorway, snickered foolishly.

"Yes, that's right," Abdullah said. "The Grand National Assembly thinks we need an *area* commander. We need a *chart* of *organization*. Like they have at the *General Staff!*"

He rolled his eyes at Hakki, who showed his tobacco-colored teeth in appreciation. Mehmet was scratching his backside. Their eyes were fixed on Abdullah's face; their mouths hung open, waiting for his next witticism.

But he turned back to the document and skimmed through it, line by line. It was, indeed, a treaty of capitulation to Mustapha Kemal Pasha, whom all the irregulars despised. Yet its terms were honorable. Abdullah's Army, if they knew the contents of the agreement, would probably approve it, asking only: "Will the Pasha send us money? Will he send us ammunition?"

Rereading the words, Abdullah thought about the Baku Congress, the Green Armies, the Asiatic Revolution and the winter visit of Crimean Yusuf. He felt a sudden weakness. The early snow, the ceaseless pressure from the Greeks, the rivalry of Ankara, the stupidity and rapacity of his own men —all had undermined his confidence in the outcome of this protracted revolution. In theory, Abdullah could accept the necessity for violence in the cause of the proletarian revolution; but in its service, he felt debased and stained with

204

blood. Contemplating the stalemate at Gediz, the winter bivouac in Kütahya, he wondered whether the independent squadrons could survive another winter, even with the additional support of a fierce Crimean ideologist. His spirit was slowly sinking like the body of an exhausted swimmer who feels himself swooning into the cold current of the undertow. Rubbing his chin, he gazed at Kenan. Perhaps a union with Ankara would be the best solution.

Tapping his breast pocket, he drew out a clipping. It was something he had brought along to show Crimean Yusuf—an article written for *Yeni Dünya*, the journal of the Green Armies in Eskishehir, to clarify the aims of the insurgents.

"Pay no attention to the style," he said. "I wrote it so a man who moves his finger and his lips can read it aloud to one who can't even recognize his own name." His face grew warm as he watched Kenan. "Do you see the implications of it? I make the points with great precision, one by one, as lucidly as Trotsky. But the underlying purpose is to direct the reader to the real enemy. When the revolutionary army develops from these small bands, the soldiers and peasants already will understand that the Greeks are not the true enemy. The Greeks are just an extension of the colonial system—part of the general pattern of capitalist exploitation."

Kenan put the article aside and began in a monotone to reiterate the terms offered by the Grand National Assembly: "Amnesty ... Submit to discipline ... Requisitions ... Commissions ..."

"So we are not just bandits, you see. We have aspirations. I have my *own* oath to uphold."

That was an ill-chosen word. Kenan's face quivered. But Abdullah went on recklessly, swept up by the self-destructive impatience that sometimes comes upon a man who has toiled to complete a delicate design and then, making a small mistake, flies into a rage and destroys his handiwork. "I am more concerned with class war than I am with the war against the Greeks."

"Is that the oath you believe in?" Kenan said. His unrelenting, cyclopean eye gleamed with malice. "To me, the Greeks are a cancer of the soul. The only treatment is extermination."

Alarmed by the expression on Kenan's face, Abdullah lifted his hands in a conciliatory gesture.

"I suppose, in military terms—I assume you're talking about tactics?—Whereas I'm speaking of the Greeks as a race."

"So am I," Kenan said.

Abdullah opened his mouth to speak, then closed it again. Finally, he reached out for the warrant from the Grand National Assembly and put it into his pocket.

"I'll have to think. I haven't made up my mind."

"I have," Kenan said.

The citadel of Ankara was floating in a dismal mist that emanated from the Bloody Lake. As the train pulled in, Kenan peered out and saw the lights of the stationmaster's cottage, where Mustapha Kemal was living in a room above the tracks. Through the windows of the cottage, one could often glimpse the Pasha's iron face, hovering near the telegraph. A black Decauville locomotive, facing westward, stood in constant readiness at the door, its furnace stoked with blocks of camel dung that smoldered in the twilight. Kenan thought about the loneliness and courage of the Pasha, isolated in the solitude of leadership, and he tightened his jaw.

He took a springless wagon to the Ministry. It crossed the swamp and climbed the hillside, past the gallows, the empty coffee garden and the mosque. The wagon box was filled with soldiers wearing soggy overcoats. A foreigner in a hunting jacket squatted in one corner, wiping his nose with a brown silk handkerchief.

The wagon climbed through alleys hung with orange sad-
dlebags and harnesses made of turquoise beads. One by one,
the soldiers tumbled out and disappeared among the lighted
stalls. The foreigner said in French: "So this is Ankara!"

Just as the wagon reached the compound of the Sultaniye
School, the call to sunset prayer came faintly through the fog.
Kenan got down and paid the wagoner and hobbled across
the muddy yard. The lycée had been appropriated to the
uses of national defense; it was guarded by a company of
Lazes wearing daggers in their belts and shouldering Martini
rifles from the War of 1897. The door stood open on the
empty vestibule. Notices pinned to the wall were curling up
with dampness. Moisture trickled down the windowpanes.
There was a peculiar stillness about the building, like the
silence of a garrison after a heavy shelling. A major came
down the varnished stairs.

"What's the matter, Nuri?" Kenan said.

But Nuri shrugged his shoulders and walked on.

Kenan put his head inside a doorway. A sergeant was sticking yellow papers on a spindle. He looked up, surprised to see
a civilian.

"They seem to have gone out, Your Honor."

"I'm the M.P. from Alashehir," Kenan said. "To see the
Minister."

Suddenly, he longed to lean against the desk, to lie down
on the floor. If only he were in uniform! Military clothing
holds a man together.

"Ah, yes, Your Honor," the sergeant said. "I'll go see." And
he gestured Kenan to wait in comfort. But there was no place
to sit except on the sergeant's campstool. Kenan stood in the
middle of the room, swaying on his cane. All his pain, his
wounds, his disappointments, his defeats welled up and
choked him. He shuddered with a convulsive chill. Then the

Minister came out, pale with exhaustion, and took hold of his arm.

"You offered the commissions, did you? To the leaders of the gangs?"

"Like an imperial firman," Kenan said. "Wrapped up in green silk with gold tassels. Delivered with a military band and a chamberlain to kiss the script."

"Wonderful, wonderful," said the Minister, and they went into an empty classroom that reeked of cold ashes. On the wall was a map that showed the western sectors of the Front. Red pins represented Turkish posts and blue pins represented Greek advances. Blue pins outnumbered red pins, two to one. Turning back, the Minister squinted at Kenan. "Do sit down," he said. "What are you listening for? You know a Turkish barracks—if it isn't noisy then it's quiet."

"Has something gone wrong?" Kenan asked.

"Everything . . . and nothing," the Minister said. He closed his puffy red-rimmed eyes for an instant. We've been waiting for your report. The Pasha wants to see you."

"I am at his service. And at yours, Sitki Bey."

Sighing, the Minister took his place behind the desk.

"God willing, we'd have hundreds like you. What keeps you going?" And the Minister's own weariness seemed to overpower him, so that his fragile yellowish hands fell open on the desk.

Kenan did not reply. He knew that an honest answer would horrify Sitki Bey, who was goodhearted but utterly stupid. Members of Parliament were presumed to be motivated by noble sentiments of patriotism, personal honor and service to God and country—or at least to profess such sentiments. After a moment, Sitki sighed again and went on: "Well, I pray you have a good report for us. We need it."

"I do not know whether it is a good report or a bad report. I can only say that whoever suggested we might bring these

208

so-called Green Armies into the regular military organization must have eaten his sense with bread and cheese."

Sitki's mouth came open with a soft, popping sound and his throat moved.

"Is the situation that bad? I had no idea it was that bad."

"When these so-called roving squadrons see an officer, they act as if they've been visited by the Angel Gabriel. As for their leaders—" Kenan put out his fist, opened it slowly and blew on the palm of his hand. "Most of them are as worthless as dust. What can you do with men like Lord Wrestler and Lame Ishmael and Cap'n Ahmet and Blond Mehmet? They can't even read their own writing. They're as ignorant as the Forty Thieves. As for Blond Mehmet, he wouldn't recognize his own face if he saw it in the mirror. He talks like a nomad. When I saw him, he had only five men, every one with the Frenchman's Disease, and living in a ruined fortress called the Castle of the Goats—a rock pile on a hilltop. There lay Blond Mehmet, the famous privateer, like a houri in the gardens of Paradise, lolling on a bed of cedar boughs and eating mastic candy! I asked him, 'Why aren't you out fighting the enemy, my friend?' And, do you know, he told me he was waiting for the train? The *supply* train from Afyon! He likes to improvise his own equipment, as the expression goes. Can you imagine asking Blond Mehmet to file written dispatches? And make out requisitions?"

"I had no idea it was that bad," said the Minister, staring at the floor.

"It is worse than that," Kenan said; and he gazed in bitter satisfaction at the disappointment of the poor, unhappy, goodhearted, slow-witted Cabinet Minister.

"Isn't there a single person out there we can count on?" asked Sitki Bey. "What about Ethem the Circassian?"

"A traitor."

"What about Black Abdullah?"

Kenan drew in a long breath. "Who?"

"The one at Kütahya. Don't they call him Black Abdullah?"

"Ah, yes," Kenan said. To gain control of his voice, he took another careful breath. "He's an amateur soldier. A dilettante. A sort of freebooter with intellectual pretensions. Unreliable."

"Is that right?" The Minister raised his eyebrows as though he knew more than he was saying. "I had heard . . . What a shame!"

"Why is it a shame? We're better off without them."

Even as he spoke, Kenan was certain this was true. There was no room for sentimental and romantic ideologists within the sphere of the Pasha's leadership; and without that leadership the entire race of Turks would decay into a breed of spineless dreamers, mooning after Greek women and Marxist utopias. God willing, Mustapha Kemal would hold this nation in the vortex of the hurricane, would save them from the fatal danger of romantic speculation. He would cast out the rebels, cowards and idealists; and the nation would emerge like precious metal from a crucible, with the dross burned away.

"Kenan Bey?" the Cabinet Minister said, squinting intently. "Are you all right? I asked what you would recommend."

"They must be wiped out," Kenan said.

"Is that your official recommendation? The Pasha will be heartbroken."

"Do you think so?" Kenan said. "I think the Pasha has always known the necessity of this. Sending me to the Green Armies was only baiting a trap to catch Ethem the Circassian!" And he let out a gust of choking laughter.

But Sitki Bey closed his reddened eyes.

"I cannot contemplate such a thing with amusement. These men are our brothers."

"You are exactly right," Kenan said.

*T*hat winter Christos took Sophia to Athens for a visit to commemorate the twentieth anniversary of their marriage. The military campaign in Asia Minor had come to a triumphant end: a major step in the restoration of the Hellenic Empire. Thus, as his life was reaching its fulfillment, Christos was privileged to see the Great Idea approaching consummation.

At the same time, however, there were portentous natural phenomena (a bloody sunset with a crescent moon, a royal death, a riot in the streets) that a pessimistic oracle might have interpreted as warnings of a civic tragedy. Exactly one day after the Allies and the Turks finally signed the peace treaty at Sèvres, two assassins—Greeks of the Royalist persuasion—stepped out of ambush at the Gare de Lyon in Paris and fired point-blank at Eleftherios Venizelos.

When the news reached Athens, patriots wept and howled in the public coffeehouses. By noon, a mob with sticks was pushing through the streets surrounding Constitution Square. Along Stadiou Street and past the House of Parliament, they carried a portrait of the irreplaceable Cretan, framed in crêpe and tied with purple garlands. When this distraught cortege came to the office of a Royalist, they would pause, and there would be a crash of glass, a splintering of wood and a reek of burning paper. Smashing the windows of the Dardanelles Café (renamed Dorée, but still the favorite of the Royalists), they overturned the tables, broke the chairs and threw the dishes on the pavement. That night, on the road to Psychico, two or three men in the uniform of government policemen waylaid John Dragoumis, the brightest deputy in the Royalist cause, and left him dying in a ditch.

It turned out that Prime Minister Venizelos had been only wounded in the shoulder and the thigh. After a week or two, he came back to Athens and delivered to Parliament the treaty that confirmed Hellenic rule in Asia Minor. Then, proud and weary, Venizelos dissolved the Parliament and called for elections in November.

The government at once began to marshal its strength in all those newly liberated provinces where Venizelos was regarded as a hero. Demarchs, nomarchs and demogerontes assembled in Athens from every section of New Greece. There were Asiatics who carried wreaths of gilded laurel with a leaf for every city in Ionia; sober little muftis, dressed in crimson robes and dirty white turbans, from the Moslem towns of Drama and Kavalla; Epiriots in sheepskin boots; and island fishermen as black as Arabs. Christos went to Athens as a representative of the Orthodox Community of Ephesus, a totally deserted ruin in the marshes of the River Cayster; and his Ephesian Artemis was none other than his own Sophia, dressed in a traveling suit of woolen jersey, which Christos had ordered made for her in Paris, in the newest fashion, with a belted jacket and a man's cravat. (Too late, he realized that the sharp lapels and padded shoulders made Sophia look acerbic, like an English suffragist, and the brim of her hat completely covered her remarkable burgundy hair; but no minor disfigurement could mar their visit, its vivacity and its excitement.)

The Acropolis was lighted every night with blue and white spotlights from the Zappeion gardens. Partisans tramped up

212

and down Eolou Street, displaying political placards as if they were ikons. Far into the night, one heard them chanting "Long live Venizelos," or sometimes, defiantly, "Long live the Olive," which was the symbol the Royalists had taken in remembrance of the old Constitutional coalition of Theotokis and Tricoupis.

On the very night of their arrival, Christos and Sophia, with the other provincial delegates, attended a performance of Aeschylus's *Persians* in the ruined Odeon, against the flank of the Acropolis. Afterward, there was a feast to celebrate the triumph of the Great Idea. The fish was called *poisson Dardanelles,* mayonnaise; the entrée Adrianople veal, *garni.* Next there was a roast of Smyrna turkey, served with wines of Magna Graecia; a Dodecanese *salade;* an Epirus *glacée;* a Macédoine of fruits; and, finally, *Champagne de la Victoire,* which, it was suggested, Venizelos had carried off from France. Through the open windows, the dinner guests could hear streetcars passing, vendors hawking roasted pumpkin seeds and bouzoukia plinking in the taverns. The breeze from the Saronic Gulf brought in a scent of olive wood and eucalyptus oil from those congested neighborhoods that climb the slopes beyond the Boulevard of Queen Amalia.

Christos felt himself lifted and carried along in the torrent of speeches. He filled his glass again and again, put his elbows on the table and raised his voice. Later, walking Sophia home, he sang like a Cephalonian recruit; and in the morning when the other delegates got up to start a ten-day tour of Thrace, which had been liberated from the Turks in July, Christos and his beloved stayed in Athens to savor the present and the past that were so cosmic and so personal.

For several days, they did little but sit at a sidewalk table at Yannakis, opposite the entrance to the Hotel Grande-Bretagne. Yannakis was exclusively Venizelist, and one of those locations, like the veranda of Shepheard's in Cairo or the Galata Bridge in Constantinople, from which one could see the whole world go past.

Later, Christos inspected the Rizareoin on Kifissia Road in search of pedagogic notions to transmit to the faculty of theology at the new University of Smyrna. He listened to a lecture on the linguistic reforms of Korais at the Parnassos Literary Society; lunched at the Athens Club with a cousin who was in the wool business; and once, for diversion, left Yannakis Coffeehouse and took a seat at Zacharatos, where he talked as extravagantly as a student, pausing occasionally to inhale the fragrance of the bitter oranges on Constitution Square.

Every conversation sparkled with exaggerated aphorisms, epithets, obscenities and paradoxes on the politics of the election; nobody mentioned the war in Asia Minor. But Christos offered his opinion that the Kemalists would sign the Treaty of Sèvres in return for diplomatic recognition. The other strategists agreed that Venizelos would conclude a peace with the Turks before the end of the year.

Each evening, Christos would stop to buy Sophia a box of marzipan or *babas au rhum* at a little French delicacy shop on Mourouzi Street, beside the Royal Gardens. Then, crossing the Kifissia Road and passing between the frowning mansions of the Royalist Pezmazoglous and the Liberal Bennakis, he would come to Kolonaki in the dusk, ready for the comfort and stimulation of the Maison Villaras.

This nightly ritual was a poignant recapitulation of his middle-aged courtship twenty years ago—the zoomorphic statues, the Lenox china, the English ladies—and he found that he loved Sophia more than ever; but it was here that Sophia began to manifest the symptoms of a disturbing nervous complaint. It began the night they heard about the sickness of the King, young Alexandros, the son of Constantine. Alexandros was a pale, romantic man of twenty-seven, with so little appetite for power that the Allies had felt completely safe in giving him the throne when Constantine was sent to exile. He was so negligent it amounted to *lèse majesté*. He willfully had married Miss Aspasia Manos, the daughter of the Royal Master of the Horse, and recently the two of them had contrived to find a love nest somewhere on the Continent.

But, now—what a ridiculous accident! While the King was walking in the park, his little monkey bit him, and the wound developed septicemia. It was just the sort of unbecoming mishap you might have predicted for Alexandros.

To Sophia, the illness of the King was an obsessive horror. Again and again, she spoke about the vagaries of fate, using the Turkish word *"kismet."* Christos had to walk out every few hours to learn the latest medical prognosis from the coffeehouses.

First, the poison settled in the young man's lungs. He was shaken by chills, drenched by sweat, wracked by hideous convulsions. Then he developed purulent pneumonia. His strangulation lasted for more than a week. Finally, the toxins reached his brain. He suffered frightful agonies, which so terrorized Sophia that she could scarcely eat or sleep.

At twilight on October 25, the church bells rang, announcing that Alexandros was dead. It was a squally day, with gusts of rain across the gulf. Branches tapped against the shutters, which had been closed at nightfall while the Vespers bell was tolling for His Majesty. The drawing room was cold. Christos examined a new painting by Gérôme, who was the rage of Constantinople, while Sophia drank cup after cup of tea.

"I suppose we'll have a regency?" she said at last.

"Why not? Prince Paul is young. I favor Admiral Koundouriotes. Although he's not a boy."

But Sophia shuddered, gripping the arms of her chair.

"What a dreadful death! God spare us all from such a painful death!"

Christos, gazing at her stricken face, felt a pang of sorrow —not for the King, a frivolous young man whose loss would not affect the turning of the earth, but for mankind, himself and this inimitable woman, who would die someday and be consumed by the voracious clay. He stretched out his arms to draw her toward him, groping to detach her fingers from her chair. Her cheek was wet against his lips. His hand fell gently on her bosom.

But Sophia pressed her fists against his chest and freed herself.

"I suffer for that poor girl, that poor Miss Manos. *Quelle tristesse!* And the mother . . ."

"Of course, my dear. Your tender heart."

He opened his arms again. His eyes were smarting with emotion. But Sophia twisted from his grasp and went to warm her hands above the brazier. As if to herself, she murmured: "It is absolutely *tragic. . . .*"

"What is?"

"The way our country is divided, half of us believing the other half are traitors. I'm for Venizelos, but I think we need King Constantine."

"Nonsense, my dear." He patted the cushion at his side to hide a slight feeling of annoyance. "I think you know well enough how I feel about Constantine."

"We ought to have them *both,*" Sophia said. "We should emulate the English."

"Impossible. If you knew history, you'd understand. Violence, dissent, ostracism—those are the fibers of our politics. Themistocles was banished. Alcibiades was banished. Even Pericles was made to suffer through the persecution of his friends. We Greeks demand the right to be capricious. To destroy our leaders when they displease us. We couldn't behave another way if we wanted to. Sometimes it seems we're compelled to re-enact our sins, like souls in Hades, endlessly repeating all our errors of the past. . . . Come and sit down."

But Sophia hesitated, frowning at him.

"No, I think it would be better to have Constantine back than some poor regency."

"Now, please."

"No," she repeated stubbornly. "We should have them both."

"In Christ's name!" Christos shouted. "Does it make Constantine a better king because his son is dead?"

Sophia gasped, and her beautiful eyes began to fill with tears. Then, quite without warning, rushing at him in a moist cloud of silk and rose perfume, wet cheeks and sobbing kisses: "Oh, Christo! Take me away from here! I have such a dreadful feeling, such an oppressive sense—I want to go home."

And now it was Christos who detached himself—gently enough, but warm with anger—and clucked his tongue and patted Sophia's velvet wrist and left the room. What an outburst of infantile emotion! Given an hour or two, a day at the most, this fantastic seizure should have sobbed and sighed and ebbed away.

But, from that moment, Sophia did not cease teasing and imploring and harassing him to take her back to Smyrna. Her dreams, her premonitions and the palpitations of her heart foretold disaster. Christos, in an access of stubborn rationality, refused to yield to her hysteria.

He took to his room. The porter, wearing Turkish slippers and an apron of denim ticking, brought the papers twice a day. Christos immersed himself in the progress of political events. Cries of "Olive!" and "Anchor!" woke him in the night, and he lay awake, thrashing and groaning with anxiety about the vagrant disposition of the Greeks and their fatal desire to re-enact their prior tragedies. In the hours before

217

dawn, he sometimes felt himself succumbing, like his wife, to an impalpable dread.

The public rallies were becoming dangerously nostalgic. Forgotten leaders of King Constantine's regime appeared on balconies entwined with sprigs of olive: Gounaris, Mercouris, Rhallys, Stratos, wringing their hands and waving their arms, while dusty tears ran down their faces. They raved about the national humiliation, the tragic degradation of a country with its sons, its husbands lodged in Asia Minor at the whim of England and its rightful King deposed and exiled at the whim of France. Look how Venizelos had debased the honor of the nation! How abjectly he had groveled at the feet of Clemenceau, of Lloyd George—even of the contemptible Italians!

Christos laughed at these extravagances from the lips of men who had been resolute defenders of the German royal house. But there were other listeners who stood with downcast faces, burning with a sense of personal disgrace. They remembered the proud recalcitrance of Constantine—Son of the Eagle, Restorer of Byzantium—who seemed, indeed, to be a better king now that his son was dead.

A week before the voting date, the European Allies sent the government a public warning that its credits would be blocked in London and Paris if Constantine regained the throne. This diplomacy succeeded in convincing many Greeks that they should vote in favor of the Royalists, if only out of obstinacy.

On the day of the election, Christos left his room and walked through Constitution Square. It was a Sunday morning, fresh and quiet. Bells were throbbing. Portrait photographers, dressed in long white smocks, were sitting under the citron bushes, surrounded by buckets, sponges, tripods, tapes and picture galleries of brides and corporals with carmine lips. The voting urns stood in forty-nine locations in the city.

At every polling place there were 107 urns, the number of the candidates. To cast a vote, one passed his hand above the urns and dropped a marble in the vessel of his choice. This was the ancient way, appropriate to Greek democracy.

Outside the Zappeion, some men were drinking coffee in the sunshine while others stood in line in the exhibit hall. Couples were walking slowly up and down the gravel paths. Inexplicably, Christos felt his heart grow lighter. It occurred to him that the political antagonism of the Royalists must have been depressing him. This would explain his flash of anger, his intolerance of Sophia. Isolation had improved his temper. His steps grew quicker; he swung his cane through drifts of yellow leaves and smiled at some children playing with a hoop.

But when he got back to the Maison Villaras, he found that Sophia and her sister had gone to church. Afterward, they would spend the afternoon at Psychico—it was safer than in the city on a day like this; and Christos had to spend another day alone.

At nightfall, he heard the first results of the election. Later came the first official tabulation, which was even worse. Outside the Liberal Club, a derisive mob was chanting, "Olive! Olive!" and hundreds of soldiers tottered up and down Stadiou Street, singing:

> "The Son of the Eagle is marching ahead . . .
> And he leads us to glory with sword unsheathed!
> To take Constantinople and Aya Sophia . . .
> And drive back the Turk to the Red Apple Tree!"

The Royalist coalition had won two seats for every seat retained by the Liberals. On Wednesday, Venizelos and his family left the country.

That day, Christos joined some bankers from Constantinople in forming a Council for the Preservation of Hellenic

Rights in Asia Minor. He anticipated that the King would try to end the war without fulfilling the imperatives of the Great Idea. To forestall that possibility, the Council planned a series of atrocity reports in European languages, public demonstrations and petitions to the President of the United States. Every day they talked from four o'clock to midnight, consuming liters of coffee and okas of pistachio nuts. Then they went to dinner in a group, reluctant to be separated in a city that had suddenly become so lonely.

At the end of the month, the government conducted a plebiscite on the restoration of King Constantine. The vote was "Yes" 999,905, and "No" 10,883. In the middle of December, His Majesty returned from Switzerland.

The Royalists anticipated his arrival with illuminations of the Parthenon and gun salutes from Mount Lykabettos. Houses bloomed with intersecting banners and photographs of Constantine and Sophie.

On Sunday morning there were crowds along the edge of Syngrou Boulevard from the Columns to the Bay of Phaleron, watching the gulf for a sign of the *Averoff*. But the royal family had debarked at Corinth to avoid the nauseating sea around the Peloponnesos. They came to Athens in a private train, which moved so slowly that throngs of men jumped onto the footboards and climbed to the roof, where they lolled on their bellies all the way to Athens.

The train disgorged at a secondary depot in a neighborhood of work sheds. The King was wiping his eyes; Queen Sophie wore a heavy veil; and the Princesses were weeping.

When Christos heard the anthem starting and the roaring as the King came down the platform, he turned his face to the wall. He could hear someone shouting, *"He* is coming! *He* is coming!"

He! As if that pasty Teuton were the Lord of Hosts!

"Olive! Olive! *He* is coming! . . . Christ is risen!"

Men were swarming on the balconies and rooftops, over-turning tubs of jasmine and dislodging tiles, which tumbled on the screaming throng. There were soldiers and sailors, students in uniform, shopkeepers—even a few women, who were tossed from side to side as roughly as the men. One of the women, dressed in a jersey traveling suit, was staring at him wildly. Christos clapped his hand on his forehead.

"What on earth are you doing here?" And they were pushed together, face to face, by a movement of the crowd. "It isn't safe." And he caught his breath, inhaling the deli-cious emanation of her scent.

A company of evzones pressed forward, with their rifles on their shoulders and their pleated white fustanellas swinging like the kilts of mountain shepherds. An iron bell began to toll.

"*He* comes! *He* comes!" the people chanted, while the soldiers beat their palms against the stocks of their rifles. Christos put out his arm to encompass Sophia's waist. Her bosom rose and fell in a frenzied rhythm, and her irregular breath was warm against his throat. It stirred him with a sense of masculine nobility. He braced his back against the raging crowd and drew his wife nearer, under the protection of his shoulder.

"How did you find me? You might have gotten lost. . . ."

But Sophia, passing her hand across her eyes, looked around in confusion and shook her head.

At last the royal coach appeared, through a flurry of con-fetti, down a corridor of olive branches thrashing like a forest in a storm. And there was Constantine!—his pale, accusatory face, his long, pale mustaches, his measured gestures, his shoulders heaving with the catarrhal spasm that perpetually wracked his chest. It was like seeing the ghost of a forgotten monarch, the reincarnation of some remote, medieval Con-stantine whose singularities had suddenly been restored to public knowledge by a cache of artifacts dug from a mound: his German wife, his military training in Berlin, his contract bridge, his yacht at Phaleron, his hunting parties in the fields of Thessaly, his temper tantrums, his incessant smoking, his jigsaw puzzles, his magnetism for disasters.

The carriage flashed along with a metallic glitter—bridles, panels, fenders, medals. Postilions, liveried in blue and silver, were mounted on the running boards, and flowers were entwined among the spokes. Constantine waved his hand; Queen Sophie smiled; and they were gone. The crowd poured in like water closing on the traces of a boat.

Christos looked at Sophia and tried to smile.

"Now I understand what was worrying you."

"Oh, no, Christo! I feel such a pressure, like a black fog lying on my heart. Won't you take me home?"

"How could things get worse?"

But, shortly after Christmas, he agreed to put Sophia on a steamer from Piraeus. A few weeks later, bored with the Council for the Preservation of Hellenic Rights and suffocated by the politics of Athens, he followed her back to Smyrna.

USHAK

DECEMBER, 1920

*T*o Dimitris, the election was a cataclysm. Within a week he had received notice of his transfer to I Corps command at Ushak, an exposed, unpleasant town on the deepest salient of the Army of Anatolia. He greeted this news with an agonistic demonstration: he howled, wept and tore his uniform; then he got drunk on mastic brandy, sang ballads sacred and profane, played the sandouri, cursed his enemies with blinding, fired his rifle at a chimney, fell and slashed his knees on the parade grounds, vomited and finally, very late, found his way to Eleni's house and fell asleep in tears on the shoulder of the cook, Polixeni, the only human being, he avowed, who had ever understood him.

Notwithstanding this performance, he was ordered out. The King's Men, as the expression goes, had served him fucked pilaf. The convoy was filled with Venizelist officers who were being shifted and degraded, and they all conceded that Dimitris had the most repulsive destination. It evidenced the special interest of somebody in the General Staff. But Dimitris, with his forehead on his hand and a handkerchief pressed to his mouth, muttered: "No, no, no, no, no." He had never made an enemy on earth. His politics were private, as those of any loyal officer should be.

Ushak was a railhead, a bazaar, a whorehouse and a few cafés. The wind blew from the north, across the flat gray plain of Banaz, and early snow was lying in the creases of the hills. At dawn the new commander called a muster in a field behind the regimental cottage. The ground was frozen; footsteps rang like hammer strokes; and the weakest orator spoke with the power of Demosthenes.

"Today, my fellow officers, we mark the end of a disastrous period of national disunity. The loyalty of thousands of Greek officers was questioned. They suffered exile and disgrace, demotion and financial ruin. Why?" And the new colonial, a pale, pseudo-Teuton named Ophis, who had recently undergone disgrace, demotion, exile and, presumably, financial ruin, stamped his foot resoundingly on the wooden platform that had been erected between some leafless saplings. "Why? Because they refused to put the political advancement of *one man* and his Party above their patriotic duty to our country, our language and our God!"

On either side of him, the officers of the divisional staff, their faces mottled by the cold, were standing with their shoulders hunched up like the wings of vultures. They wore enormous whiskers, monocles and Prussian scabbards. On their chests were rows of medals from the War of 1897 and the Macedonian campaigns of 1912, and they carried little riding crops to thwack against their scrupulously polished boots.

Colonel Ophis preached forgiveness.

"Henceforth, the rancor of the past is swept away. Hand is clasping hand in amnesty, philanthropy, Hellenic brotherhood. . . . Long live His Majesty! Long live King Constantine!"

He left the platform, and the patriotic martyrs followed, thrusting out their chests and frowning as they tottered down the steps. A regimental captain gave the order to dissolve. Dimitris looked at the whitewashed headquarters shack, the frozen pastures and the naked trees along the ditch. Some patriotic Hellenes on fatigue duty had laid a fine mosaic on a tumulus of earth on the edge of the parade ground: the regimental crest, in painted stones; the Greek cross, in blue on white; the double eagle of Byzantium, in gold on purple; and the Earth, made out of plaster and surmounted by a model of the Parthenon. Over at one side there was a statue done in wire and clay of the Spartan mother, holding out a shield inscribed: "Return with this . . . or on it."

"I'll be out of here in a week," he said to the man on his right.

"I thought you were going to bayonet a Turk."

"Do you think that takes a week? . . . No, this doesn't appeal to me, a place like this."

The other man agreed that it would be a national disaster to waste one's talents in Ushak. Smiling confidently, Dimitris wandered across the regimental yard. Some new recruits from Athens, in preparation for a winter of affliction, were heaping mounds of earth around the edges of their tents.

But at Divisional HQ, Dimitris learned that his appeal for emergency leave to rush to the side of his dying father had been denied for lack of substantiating evidence.

"What am I supposed to do?" he shouted, flinging out his arms. "Produce my poor father's corpse?"

The injustice of the ruling stung the other Venizelist officers like the lash of a whip. The case was celebrated as a modern tragedy until the information got around that Dimitris' father actually had died six years ago; and, after that everyone realized that Lieutenant Kalapothakis was a genius. He became the hero of the camp.

Day after day, he lay on a sheepskin in his tent, regaling visitors with memoirs of his reckless youth, while he delegated corporals and sergeants to impose a course in military science on his men.

The Royalist command had beset him with a company of volunteers from Asia Minor. Like all Ionians, they were cowardly, lascivious and filled with delusions of persecution. The mainland Greeks detested them, as soldiers always hate the people of a land they are defending. Their peculiarities of dialect, their obsessive terror of the Turks, their Corybantic love affairs, their sensitivity, their discontent, their celebrated incapacity in battle—every quality that marked, or was believed to mark, the Asiatics—lowered them in the esteem of the Europeans. It was fair sport to badger them, and in this game Dimitris was the laureate.

He would get up in darkness to tumble shivering Bergamese grocery clerks out of their bedrolls for extraordinary lectures on the Mannlicher rifle, the Tyler motor lorry and the Schneider-Danglis mountain gun. He would drill them in their underwear in stony pastures. He made them dig latrines with kitchen spoons and measure the parade ground with a matchstick. It was Dimitris who originated the midnight Turk-seed call, reverberating through the darkened bivouac: "Turk seed? . . . Turk seed? . . . Turk seed?" until some Asia Minor Greek would wake and cry out in fury; whereupon, the callers would pounce on him: "Ah, yes! You answer the call. You *admit* you're Turk seed, don't you?"

Then they would strip his trousers off, ostensibly to check his circumcision, but, in fact, to plaster him with cowflap.

One night as Dimitris was walking to his tent, someone threw acid on him from the darkness. It was meant to blind him, but it struck his chest and only burned his uniform.

He ordered the company assembled on the parade ground. It was after midnight. Flakes of fine, dry snow were whirling around the master sergeant's lantern. The men filed past in their underwear, keeping their mouths in tight control.

Dimitris held up the ruined uniform on a stick.

"This is a capital offense. One of you is guilty. The rest will suffer until I find him. . . . Now, let him step forward and spare his friends."

But, as Dimitris had expected, the men stared at him mutely. He ordered the sergeant to begin the drill. The company marched until dawn, when he allowed them to rest and talk for five minutes. Then they marched again until noon.

Sometimes, when he felt his anger failing, he went into his tent, threw himself down on his sheepskin and closed his eyes, trying to imagine the eternal burial of blindness, his face disfigured and his sight destroyed. Tears of self-pity burned on his eyelids. He would lose his mind just thinking of the horror of it! He ran to the parade ground and screamed at the silent men.

"Have I treated you so badly? If I was strict with you, it was for your own benefit. You'll be glad of this when you march to Persia! Have you forgotten the *Anabasis?* Don't you Turk seed know the history of our nation?"

The men marched back and forth in silence. Their eyes were glassy and their lips were caked with yellow slime.

"March them! March them!" Dimitris shrieked, shuddering at the sight of his own tunic, which was hanging near the flagpole, pierced with jagged holes.

Late in the afternoon, a half-wit named Johnny Sakoutis stumbled out of line. Falling to his knees, he crossed himself and bowed his head. When Dimitris went to him, he stretched out his arms and whined like a dog.

"I never threw—I swear to God—never threw a thing! " And he pressed his face against the ground and clutched Dimitris' ankles.

He was shivering so violently that they could not make him stand. Dimitris had to kick him to break his grasp. Two of the corporals gripped him under the arms and dragged him behind a tent,where they stretched him on a wooden laundry table.

Dimitris called the guards. There was a little Cypriot named Mimos and some Macedonians with brutal faces. One of the Macedonians sat on Johnny Sakoutis' chest. Mimos sat on his knees. The others held his arms and legs.

"Take off his shoes," Dimitris said.

"Sir, he isn't bright," the corporal said.

"Did I ask about his brain?"

The soles of Sakoutis' feet were dark and thorny, like the heels of a Kurdish stevedore. They looked as tough as leather; but every time the bastinado struck, he gasped and twitched spasmodically. His groans grew louder and louder. At first, he cried out in Greek: "My God! Oh, my God!" Later, he dashed his head from side to side and bellowed: *"Allah! Allah!"*

"Turk seed!" Dimitris shouted. He spat on the ground and took a firm grip on the stick. "Count aloud. Or I will lose my count."

Mimos and the Macedonian guards counted the strokes of the bastinado. But Mimos farted, the guards laughed, Dimitris lost track of the number and they had to start again at "one."

When Dimitris had finished, the guards lifted Johnny Sakoutis and set him on his feet. He screamed and fell down. His shoulders heaved convulsively. A hollow, rattling groan rose from the depths of his chest; his eyes rolled upward; and a froth like thick pink cream appeared at the edges of his mouth.

The guards clicked their tongues disapprovingly. Mimos went to get a piece of leather strap to put in Johnny Sakoutis' mouth.

"When he gets over that, take him down to the guard-house," Dimitris said, looking away. "No, first put on his shoes. His toes look like beetroots."

And Dimitris went back to his tent, exhausted.

On his cot was a letter from Eleni Trigonis, addressed to D. Kalapothakis, I Corps, Anatolia.

"Dear Mr. Kalapothaki: How slowly the days have passed

since last I saw you. I pray your health is good and you are not in danger...." Her mother and father were still in Athens, and she missed them. Her brother George (she missed him, too) was with the Smyrna Division near the Lake of Iznik, where (as Mr. Kalapothakis undoubtedly knew) the Nicene Creed of Our Lord was adopted many centuries ago....

Holy Jesus! Was that supposed to start a fire in your guts? The girl was really a drab mare; and to make matters worse, the old man was still being sticky about the dowry. There must have been forty girls in Smyrna with richer dowries, and all of them better-looking!

On the last page, she had added a note in a different-colored ink: "Am sending this with a friend because I haven't your exact address. Please write soon. *Something has happened.*"

Taking the letter in his hand, Dimitris crossed the yard to talk to Kostas, who was paring his fingernails in the cold red light of the sunset.

"My God, Kosta—I'm dying for a roast." He rubbed the envelope against the fly of his trousers. "When you get used to it, you've got to have it regular. It gets to be like drinking water."

Kostas wiped the blade of his knife on his knee.

"That's all you ever think about."

"That's all I care about. Bring on Miss Insatiable, with a rump like a couple of ripe casabas. I'm wasting, wasting."

"Well, you won't have a chance to ride around this place."

"Don't I know that? I'm dying of deprivation."

"You'll just have to pour by hand."

"What, like *you* do?"

And they began to talk about the belly dancers on the Rue des Grandes-Tavernes, who touched their heads against their heels and snapped their fingers while their spangled breech belts undulated like the surface of the sea. They speculated on the married women, with rouge on their cheeks and jeweled combs in their hair, whom you saw eating baklava at Kosti's, and the blonde Italian girls in the Houses near Caravan Bridge.

"We'll go to the place in Ushak tonight," Dimitris said. "Twelve Ways, they call her." And he tapped Kostas significantly on the wrist.

But when they reached the gate, the sergeant of the guard stepped out and blocked their way. Passes of leave had been rescinded. Dimitris stared at the guard in astonishment.

"What stupidity! Maneuvers in the middle of December?"

"Do you doubt me?" the sergeant said quickly. "Look at this." But Dimitris pushed the paper away, took Kostas' arm and walked toward the officers' mess. Near the ammunition shed, another guard was marching his post in a negligent manner. Dimitris took out a bag of tobacco.

"Well, Mimo? What about this winter maneuvering? Are the Turks going to attack us?"

"No, sir. We're going to attack them."

"At this time of year?"

"Why not?" The soldier watched Dimitris fold a cigarette paper and sprinkle it with tobacco. "The Turks will be caught napping. One big artillery barrage by the Skodas. Then a cavalry attack, like lightning. It will end the war."

"Tomorrow, Mimo?"

Mimos was silent, watching the tobacco.

"Monday, then?" Dimitris said.

"Sir, do you think I'm the general?"

"Every Greek soldier is a general."

Mimos did not laugh. Dimitris lit the cigarette and blew a whiff of smoke in the soldier's face.

"How is Johnny Sakoutis?"

"How should I know, Lieutenant? I hear they took him to the hospital."

"Does that worry you, Mimo?"

"Why should it worry *me?* All I did was hold—"

"Never mind what you did!"

Mimos closed his mouth. Dimitris handed him the lighted cigarette.

"So you think we're going to launch the final attack?"

Mimos tilted his head. Behind him, Kostas laughed.

"Well," Kostas said, "the oracle has spoken." Leaving Dimitris behind, he walked toward the officers' mess. But Dimitris turned back.

"If you ever open your mouth about that again, I'll gig you like a frog."

He thrust the pouch of tobacco at Mimos, who accepted it without raising his eyes.

In the morning, the canvas tents were snapping in the wind and the ground was white. A runner brought around the order to advance.

Dimitris crossed the yard to regimental headquarters, scraped his boots on the step and presented himself to an adjutant who was seated at a wooden table, eating bread and smoking a cigarette.

"The major sent for me."

"He's busy."

"Fine, I'll come back."

"No, you'll wait."

There was only one room in the shack, but someone had hung a lace-trimmed window shade on a wire to screen the major's office from the door. After finishing his bread and crushing out his cigarette, the adjutant went behind the screen. Dimitris could not hear the conversation. At last the adjutant permitted him to step around the curtain. The major looked up, frowning. For several moments, the two men stared at each other. Finally, Dimitris said:

"Congratulations on your promotion."

Mavropetros still wore the pencil-line mustache that accentuated the dark moles along his chin; but he had added that glorious embellishment of the Royalist costume, a monocle.

"Kalapothaki?" he said, putting in his eyeglass and reaching for a folder of papers. "The man has died."

"What man?"

Major Mavropetros turned the pages of the file.

"Sakoutis. Private Ioannis Apostolos Sakoutis, Third Company. At 3:15 A.M. today, Base Hospital, Ushak."

Dimitris looked at the floor. He might have known. The man had bad blood. . . .

"You know, sir, Sakoutis had convulsions yesterday. He should have been disqualified."

Major Mavropetros continued to turn the papers, one by one.

"Kalapothaki," he said, "you have a very bad record."

"May I sit down, sir?"

"No."

"Major, I don't know what you mean about my record."

The major raised his cold, pale face and glared with the malevolence of a Spartan chief. Dimitris stiffened. He had been disarmed by a ridiculous Prussian monocle. He had forgotten that Mavropetros had endured a period of persecution—almost exile—with its supernormal sharpening of memory.

"You know *exactly* what I mean," Mavropetros said.

Permitting his lips to tremble slightly, Dimitris drew a long breath.

"No, sir. As for my military record, sir, my battalion was in Macedonia in 1917. I was in General Anselm's expeditionary force to the Ukraine. I was in the original landing force at Smyrna."

Mavropetros, however, cleared his throat and began to read:

"On May 15, 1919, during the investment of Smyrna by the First Division, Lieutenant D. Kalapothakis deserted his company when it was ambushed by Turkish snipers in the vicinity of the Ottoman Army barracks. He was absent without leave for several hours. No disciplinary action recommended. In August, 1919, he sprained his wrist while riding in the back of a truck en route to the border station at Karemköy, and was returned to Headquarters, Smyrna, for limited duty. In October, 1919, at the Officers' Club, Smyrna—"

"May I ask—"

"One minute, Lieutenant... At the Officers' Club, Smyrna, Lieutenant D. Kalapothakis participated in a brawl in which he and an unidentified civilian viciously and feloniously assaulted Captain—now Major—Loukas Mavropetros, Second Battalion, Fourth Infantry Regiment, with a piece of table silverware; to wit, a *fork*. The file containing Captain Mavropetros' formal charges disappeared from First Division Headquarters, apparently as the result of theft, and the case was never—"

Dimitris smiled. The major glanced up with a flashing of his eyeglass.

"Do you find this amusing, Kalapothaki?"

"Not amusing, Major. Fantastic. May I ask what source—"

"The source doesn't matter."

"Yes, sir. It matters."

They glared at each other. The major closed the folder.

"The report goes on to describe how you told a corporal you'd cut off his buttocks if he didn't vote for Venizelos. It also tells how you got yourself assigned to the civil government in Smyrna. And about the various attempts you made to avoid assignment to the Front. And so on ... Do you know what I'm going to add to it?"

233

"Sir, it's completely false. It's one of those political intelligence reports, so-called, made up in Athens by some dimwit."

"Do you know what I'm going to add to it?"

"Someone maliciously—"

"Don't speak!" the major cried out, slapping the table with his open hand. "Try to think for an instant. You've got no door to your mouth." He waited, puffing through his nostrils. "Now, then . . . Do you know what I am going to write concerning the death of this man Sakoutis?"

Dimitris heard a bugle in the yard. Hostlers were shouting orders to each other as they lifted boxes of ammunition onto the backs of mules. A mechanic was cranking the engine of a truck, and prisoners were rolling drums of kerosene across the field.

It was impossible to find a strategy to deal with such a man as Mavropetros, a fanatic, who refused to let an officer sit down, neglected to serve coffee, even failed to offer cigarettes. Dimitris thought with envy of the piece of bread the adjutant was eating. He wanted to sit down, cross his legs, smoke tobacco. Instead, he was tormented.

A knot of hatred gathered in his throat. Was it for this they sent you to the Military College of the Evelpides, subjected you to years of study, discipline and hardship, just to hand you over to a man like this? A poisonous old cuckold, puking out his meanness and his disappointment on a younger man. Mavropetros was positively snarling with malevolence—and why? Surely not because Dimitris had whipped a maniac for splashing him with vitriol! No! Because of his political beliefs!

It brought to his mind the martyrdom of Captain Dreyfus; and he could see his own court-martial—the perspiring witnesses, the writers making notes, the papers, with little sketches of the judges done in pen-and-ink, and savage effigies of Mavropetros, screwing in his monocle; the members of the

Cabinet, simpering; the King, suppressing a yawn; and Venizelos, standing like Demosthenes before the Areopagos. . . . No, that was impossible. Venizelos had fled to France. The Liberals were now the exiles. A Venizelist army officer could be accused, condemned and executed, and the world would never know.

Stifled by a sense of helpless isolation, Dimitris let his shoulders droop. He examined Mavropetros' features for a sign of that compassion that is supposed to ooze like *myron* from those who have suffered. The major's face was pitiless. Dimitris sighed.

"You know, sir, these Anatolians are very stubborn about their training. It's a prickly situation. Somebody told them they were going to be used as translators, and they had day-dreams of torturing Turkish prisoners. Whenever we put the heat on, they rebel. They wet their beds. They soil their breeches. They sneak away from drills. One of them tried the other day to cut his toe off with a razor."

The major detached his monocle. He breathed on it and rubbed it with a handkerchief. Dimitris tried to swallow, but dryness constricted his throat.

"Then, sir, this Johnny Sakoutis. He could have blinded me."

"Yes," the major said. He held his eyeglass toward the light, squinted, breathed, rubbed, squinted again and rubbed again, replaced the glass, replaced the handkerchief and rested his elbows on the table.

"Sakoutis died of brain congestion."

"Exactly, sir. Brain congestion."

"That is the physician's diagnosis," the major went on. "But what about the whipping? If I add that to the report, I have to recommend a court-martial."

Their eyes met. The major gestured Dimitris toward a stool.

"What year was your class, Kalapothaki?"

"It was '16, sir."

"A hothead group," the major said. He held out a box of cigarettes. "You went up to Salonika, I suppose, before you got your commission? And joined the so-called National Defense?"

"Yes."

"You thought it was dull, being loyal to the King? Fun to be a rebel like Mr. Venizelos?"

"No, Major. I've never been disloyal."

Mavropetros closed his eyes. "You thought the King was holding back the country, right? Always waiting, preserving what we had. With Venizelos, you were on the move—attacking, crusading, demanding, inventing. Correct?"

"Yes."

"I understand these things. Cadets are rash. The College of Evelpides is hard. Up at five-thirty in the morning, working steadily until ten at night. If you don't get t.b., you're lucky. The restrictions almost drive you mad. I understand these things. In my time, we were all for Colonel Smolenski, because he had defied an order to retreat. It was as natural as rain, to side with someone who defied authority."

Dimitris lowered his head. Suddenly, he saw the terms of reconciliation, just as a clever merchant can predict, in the midst of a negotiation, what the customer will ultimately pay. A moment later, Mavropetros spoke about "a pledge of loyalty." Dimitris wagged his head in grave stupidity.

"Do you mean, sir, it's something I have to *sign* with my name?"

"Don't be dense. We ask only cooperation. The final offensive will begin tomorrow morning. We need every officer."

"Yes. But the pledge?"

"Merely your word."

"Ah."

"The war will be over in a matter of days. These Turkish

236

irregulars—Circassian Ethem's men—have broken with Mustapha Kemal. They're coming through our lines and giving up. Kemal will have to quit." The major smiled as if he, personally, had accomplished this miracle. "You wouldn't want to be in prison at the hour of victory?"

"No, sir," Dimitris said, adopting an abject and whining tone. "I promise to cooperate."

But Mavropetros, taking out a sheet of paper, said:

"Assemble your company and read this statement to them."

It was a public disavowal of Venizelos. It criticized the Liberals for poisoning the army with the taint of politics, and urged the men to show their patriotic sentiments by rallying around the King.

"You'll read that?" the major asked. His face turned hard again. Dimitris folded the paper. "Will you?" the major repeated. "In public? Answer!"

"Yes, sir."

"One thing more. Take this piece of paper and write down the name of the civilian who attacked me. The big fellow."

"I've forgotten."

"You said he was your brother-in-law."

Dimitris shrugged. In any case, George was far away. He took the paper and wrote. Mavropetros threw back his head. The monocle gleamed.

"You are even weaker than I expected."

"Only because Sakoutis died," Dimitris said; and he left.

The yard was jammed with donkeys, stretching out their necks and bellowing. Pyramids of cartridge clips and hand grenades were strewn across the frozen mud, and lines of men were waiting at the commissary to receive a dram of dry tobacco and a quarter loaf of Monday's bread.

As Dimitris crossed the yard, there was a sound of lashing

and whinnying at the gate. A squad of horsemen, showing a white flag, rode through the arch, past the newly built mosaic of the crown of Greece. They sat their horses stiffly, clasping enormous carbines to their chests. From time to time, the leader would tilt back his head and give a harsh, falsetto cry.

It was the first of the Turkish guerrilla bands. Later, the bandits came in steadily. After dark, they carried brushwood torches, and one could hear their brainless howling far across the plain.

For almost a week, the guerrillas had been drifting south-ward, hounded by four divisions of the Turkish Army. Now, all the splendid little squadrons of Lord Wrestler, Cap'n Ah-met, Black Abdullah and the rest were caught in the foothills north of Ushak, with the Kemalists behind them in the moun-tain passes and the Greeks below them on the plain; and the question of which way to turn imposed itself with painful urgency.

At dawn Abdullah noticed a glint of brass and turquoise moving in the underbrush below the forward guard post. Several minutes later, a line of men on horseback emerged at the bottom of the hill. The leader raised his hand as the horsemen circled in the frosty twilight. Then, one by one, they wheeled off and galloped toward the plain. One troop, at least, had come to a decision.

Turning around, Abdullah trotted back along the barren ridge, keeping his right shoulder toward the peak of Murat Dagh, the only landmark to guide him to the thicket where his men had tied the horses. The naked hills were flecked with snow, and the morning sky was as white as porcelain. Now and then, imagining that he saw a line of riders on a distant slope, Abdullah dived into the bracken and inched forward, with his heartbeat pounding in his ears; but no fur-ther groups broke loose. The others, like his own, were waiting for advice from some sublime authority.

When he approached the camp, his army was still intact. A few of the men were crouching in the first pale rays of sunshine, quietly mending bridles; the rest were squatting around a copper brazier. Abdullah stopped in a clump of scrub oaks, made a cigarette and smoked it slowly, wondering what to tell them.

Either way, the men were certain to be enraged. They had wanted long ago to stop and join the other independents in a fight against the Pasha. They had talked of making a stand in one of those long defiles below Kütahya; or on the upper plain; or on the gray plateau of Örenjik; or, finally, at Gediz. Outnumbered, outmaneuvered and steadily retreating, they had boasted of lightning tactics that would trap the Pasha's horsemen in the snow.

But the guerrilla bands were always scattered; and the Kemalist cavalry was always fast. Now that it was too late to fight, the Green Armies of Kütahya had no alternative but to surrender to the Pasha or the Greeks.

An impossible choice. The men detested Mustapha Kemal; he was the uncompromising enemy who wanted to curtail their freedom, restrict their plunder and enroll them in the very army that many of them had deserted during the Great War. Yet who among them would willingly capitulate to the contemptible Army of the Hellenes?

Abdullah's own attitude was even more ambivalent. At one time, he had admired the Pasha and had discerned in him the makings of a revolutionist. After all, Mustapha Kemal had quarreled with the Sultan, had criticized the Young Turks and had disagreed with all the other military leaders of the war. He seemed to have the characteristics of an irrepressible radical, like Lenin, in whom rebellion was endemic.

But lately the Pasha had begun to show a dictatorial attachment to his army and religion, a growing animosity to progressive, independent movements of the proletariat. Abdullah called this Menshevism. He foresaw the danger of bourgeois reaction in the Ankara regime. His suspicions of Mustapha Kemal were intensified by his fear of Kenan, whose fanaticism was like a virulent disease. If Kenan's politics should infect the Grand National Assembly, that chamber would become a directory of counterrevolution.

Crushing out his cigarette, Abdullah shrugged his shoulders. In any case, he would have to move today. He walked into the camp and told the men to saddle up. They gathered their weapons, bound their bellies and went out to find the horses. Abdullah stood with bowed head, warming his hands above the copper brazier.

When the coffee boiled for the third time, he poured it into an empty 75-millimeter shell. Inhaling that fragrance, tainted with the stink of brass and sulphur, he remembered lofty conversations in the coffeehouses of Shehzade-bashi: the Islamic proletariat, the Eastern Ideal, the Red Apple of Turkism—all the subject matter of his burning speculations and his fervid dreams. What had become of his revolution? Where were the Party agents from Baku? Where were the textbooks, the ammunition and the money? Sighing, he put down the empty shell. He would have to take the men directly to the gap, before the snow turned soft. It would not be wise to give them time to reconsider.

While picking up his saddle jugs—one coal oil, one fresh water—he was inspired to make a distribution. He lifted his rifle, fired a volley at the sky and gave the word. At once the men began to yammer like a pack of street dogs. Hakki drew out his dagger and slashed it through the air; Daddy Mahmut unsheathed an enormous sword; and Shükrü bit off the head of a bullet to express his joy.

Abdullah leaped onto his horse and galloped around the circle.

"Hakki? Ertoghrul? Why are you stopping, looking at each other's faces? Let's go!"

And the men sprang up, laid on their whips and spurred their horses close to Abdullah's side, until their knees were touching his and their stirrups clanged against his ankles. To drive them off, Abdullah had to lash his leather quirt from side to side.

"Have you lost your minds? You act as if your brains were cooked! I ought to give your mouth its share."

The men retreated. Abdullah checked his trembling horse. He groped under his shirt. The men leaned forward, sucking air. They had not seen the money belt since the bandit Lütfi had exhumed it from a shallow trough beside a spring in Eshme, and they regarded it with apprehension, as though it had infernal powers. Unwinding the rotten fabric from his waist, Abdullah lifted it three times above his head; then he rode around the circle and placed a coin in each man's hand. When he had given to the very last, who was Midhat, the canvas belt that had been the sinew of the Turkish revolution was empty. He dropped it on the ground. The men were quiet, holding the coins in their mouths to taste the gold.

Abdullah lifted his fist.

"Comrades, shall we ask asylum from the Greeks or from the Pasha?"

For several moments, none of the men spoke. Their eyes were riveted to their horses' ears. Finally, Daddy Mahmut raised his head and said in a husky voice:

"God willing, we shall do one or the other, since there is nothing else to do."

"Then follow me where I lead you," Abdullah said. He did not wait for a reply. Spurring his horse, he swung around and galloped into the underbrush.

First, he led his band of shrieking martyrs up the slope in

the direction of Kütahya, toward Mustapha Kemal. Then he reversed his course and took them down a stony glacis, along a dry ravine, through thorny brakes that rose above their shoulders, toward the Greek lines. They plunged through gullies moist with blackened ferns and woodlands quivering with sleeping birds; past fields of dirty snow; up switchbacks and reverses; and down canyons strewn with glittering obsidian. At last he reined his horse and waited while his men came crashing through the brushwood, shouting frantically.

"Black Abdullah! We're cut to ribbons! What's the matter with you?"

Blood was glistening in deep gashes on their cheeks, which had been raked and torn by brambles. Their lips were drawn back from their teeth, and their breath rasped in their throats. Smiling, Abdullah looked around at this ring of callous mercenaries who had so many times deceived and disappointed him. By the whiteness of their nostrils and the darkness of their eyes, he could tell that they were close to hysteria. It struck him as a singular compliment that these brutal, unsentimental men, who now were bound to him by nothing but habit, had pursued him through such hazards toward an unknown destination. He wondered whether any of them felt the faint stirrings of a sense of duty to the revolution, to their leaders or to one another.

But it was, perhaps, too late for such conjectures. As Abdullah's Army sat their winded horses, a party of Turkish cavalry came over the crest of the hill, dragging a field wireless and a small cannon. The leader was mounted on a white stallion. Holding a megaphone to his mouth, he shouted instructions that shattered unintelligibly on the slopes: "Confiscation of arms . . . unconditional surrender . . ."

The second man in the column was a civilian, dressed in a cloak and a kalpak of gray lamb's wool. As Abdullah rode forward, this man detached himself from the line and moved ahead of the officers; and Abdullah's heart oozed from his breast in a dull, subsiding moan.

Kenan was staring at him without recognition. His eye was blue white with the blindness of the totally insane. Abdullah reined in. The breath of his men was on his back. Any moment, as quietly as grains of barley slipping down a funnel, they would be all gone: a last, flickering glint of metal, a final, barbaric cry, and the revolutionary radicals would disappear forever—the Asiatic Congress, the Eastern ideology, the expectations of the future and the restitution of the past.

"Oh, wait!" Abdullah called out, and he goaded his horse again and flailed his arms to beg attention. "Hear me!"

"Stay close together," Kenan called, bringing a megaphone to his lips. "We represent the Grand National Assembly of the Turkish nation."

"No, listen!" Abdullah shouted, facing his men. "This is no amnesty. This is a trap."

The Turkish cavalry suddenly spread outward.

"Turn back!" Abdullah screamed. He tried to block his men with his outstretched arms. "Go to the Greeks!"

One instant more, the Kemalist cavalry hesitated, glancing over at Kenan, whose face was dark and twisted with malevolence. Then Kenan cried out:

"He is a traitor. Kill him!"

But Abdullah pulled his horse around and forced it up a steep embankment. Its hoofs were slipping on gravel, and he could hear the panting of animals behind him. He threw his arms around his horse's neck, kicked its flanks and goaded it toward a patch of naked brambles. Then, crashing though the trees, he darted left and struck out across a field of snow.

As soon as he was in the open, the Kemalists began to fire on him, first with pistols, then with rifles. But the distance opened; the other riders fell behind. Abdullah reached a thicket in a damp ravine, and the firing ceased. He ran the horse until it was half dead. Then he trotted it on relentlessly, casting glances over his shoulder.

He was following a canyon toward a gap that led to Ushak. The horse slowed its pace to the slow *rahat* to which it had been bred and trained, and he could not spur it into moving faster. Little by little, his senses returned. He noticed again the reddish color of the soil, the scent of dead ferns and the sound of water trickling down the hill in rivulets. The sky was growing cloudy; a chill came into the air; and there were flights of somber birds along the reaches of the canyon.

Now and then, Abdullah shuddered violently. He had to grip the saddle to keep his balance, and he saw the face of his brother crying: "Kill him!"

At sundown he thought he must be near the plain. He stopped and let the horse browse quietly among the shrubs while he was making up a torch of juniper branches. When the sky was dark, he soaked the torch in coal oil, set it afire and rode on toward Ushak to conclude a separate peace with the invaders.

*W*hen the last of the Turkish guerrillas had slipped
through the lines, the Greeks began another campaign to end
the war in Asia Minor. The object was as simple as the
strategy: to cut the railway line to Ankara, isolate the Kemalists and negotiate an advantageous peace. Within a week or
two—a month at most—the Anatolian adventure would be
over, to the everlasting glory of King Constantine and the
considerable relief of the Greek treasury.

On the fifth day of the offensive, George Trigonis left a
reserve camp in the vicinity of Bursa with four other members of an artillery replacement unit in the back of a Tyler
motor truck. The men lay together on the bouncing, quivering, creaking baseboards of the lorry, warming each other
with their body heat and talking about the Turks. How could
a race of such inferiority have maintained its power so long?
Aleko Papakostas, who was the granddaddy of the group (he
was thirty-seven and had seven children), suggested it was
because the Turks were such good fighters; but the others
hooted. Didn't everybody know the Turks were always
wounded in the *kolo?* The men made bets among themselves
on who would kill the first Turk, the last Turk, the ugliest
Turk, the largest Turk, the highest-ranking Turk.

George looked from one to another. Although they were all
as inexperienced as he, nobody showed a sign of fear. Every-

one seemed delighted with this thrilling opportunity to be killed or maimed.

George said he'd settle for the *most* Turks, devil take their rank; and the other men agreed that Big George was catching on.

They crossed a muddy plain below the slope of Ulu Dagh, which is the Asiatic Mount Olympus, climbed the ridge above Nicaea and descended into a fallow valley of tobacco fields. It was snowing on the mountaintops and raining in the lowlands. Once there was a loud explosion, and George leaped up with his rifle in his hands; but it was only the backfiring of a motor convoy coming down the hill. The sergeant, who was riding with the driver, looked back and laughed.

When the trucks passed through a Christian village, women came outside and threw rice and bolls of cotton to give the soldiers strength and cushion them against the enemy. Leaning out, the men stretched their arms and tried to touch the women on the rump.

"We'll bring you back a bag of Turkish ears! We'll bring back the Pasha's prick. . . ."

The air turned colder. Aleko tried to tie down the canvas flaps. To keep warm, the men sang a song about King Constantine twisting the Sultan's pudenda. Then, one by one, they fell asleep.

George leaned on his elbow and looked at them. They were the princeliest of men, superior to any others he had ever known. Aleko, the patriarch, was a farmer from a village called The Poplars, where the only vice, the deathless source of humor, scandal, speculation and research, was the venereal association of a human being and an animal; yet Aleko's range of talents was extraordinary. He could shoe a horse, winnow wheat, blend cheese, press wine and cure tobacco, and he was pointer of the Schneider-Danglis mountain gun.

As for the others: Loukas was a country gentleman from Ödemish, a grocer's son, with muscular arms and lively eyes: he was operator of the breech. Goufas was a Smyrniot with a face as calm and Oriental as *rahat loukoum:* first ammunition passer. And Sakellariadis—bombastic, fanciful, the ancient archetype of Pergamos—was the extra passer, pointer, loader and water carrier.

George had described them in a letter to his mother: "As different, one from the other, as flakes of snow, yet more affectionate than brothers." Beyond this, they were exemplars of maturity: shrewd, tough and earthy, with immense experience in carnal matters.

Above all, they were brave—incredibly, touchingly, idiotically brave. Whereas George was haunted by morbid fancies of a cruel, ironic death (on the last day of the war, a stray bullet ricocheting from the rifle of a brother Greek), his companions gave their thoughts to robust pleasures: food and drink and sexual congress. Day after day, they lounged around the barracks, meditating on the whores of Bursa, who wore their hair in saucy ringlets plastered to their cheeks with sugar and albumen, and on the accommodating peasant girls who worked at the spindles of the textile factories, sitting all day with their backs against the steamy water pipes, which kept their bottoms soft and white and made their yielding bodies smell like rotting vegetables. Riding toward the battle zone, these healthy bucks sprawled side by side in tousled, animal sleep, with smiles on their lips and fingers clenched between their thighs.

Late at night, the lorry stopped in Bilejik, at the bottom of a foggy canyon. Bilejik did not resemble Paris, but it was the most important place the infantry had taken. The Turks had tried to hold it for two days. The headlights shone on pyramids of rubble, still smoldering from the bombardment. Creeping up the hill, the truck passed a company of reserves standing with bedrolls in the shelter of the station. George said to himself: "We'll see the Front before those guys get up for breakfast." And, with a shuddering sigh, he fell asleep.

At dawn, when they reached Söghüt, the other men were still asleep, coiled together like the litter of a sow. George lifted the edge of the canvas. He could see some flat stone houses by the road and, farther on, a clump of bare poplar trees and a minaret with a stork's nest on the top. A cold mist hid the mountains. By putting your hand behind your ear, you could hear the hollow thumping of the Skodas, coming from a great distance through the fog and shaking the earth like the footsteps of God. George crossed himself three times and woke Aleko Papakostas.

The lanes were clogged with Italian camionettas, heavy French caissons, oxcarts, ambulances and wooden wagons. Donkeys with boxes of ammunition on their backs were plodding toward the slopes. Horns were blowing. Grooms were howling. The urine of the animals was steaming in the mud.

A sergeant major, dressed in an undershirt and muddy trousers, marched each new gun crew down the road to an old stone building with a red crescent painted on the door, where they drew cotton pluggets for their ears. Then they fell into line again and passed beyond the poplars, which were filled with a motionless black symposium of ravens. The minaret faded into the fog. There was no north or south, no front or rear—only the obscure telegraphy of the moving column. Footsteps clanged; breath roared out in geysers; bootstraps and helmet buckles creaked like the trappings of a caravan; and drops of water, falling from rocks above the pathway, clicked as loudly as a trigger.

Far up the hill, the sergeant major, straddling a spavined mule, broke out of the mist. The air above was clear and honey-colored. They could see a mountain gun, deserted, set in a fragile cup of stones.

A captain came and scrutinized them. He had heavy brows

and narrow bluish eyes, the kind that Polixeni said could dry up a cow or sour a cask of wine. He was wearing a thick khaki overcoat, sheepskin gloves and a gray cap that looked like a Turkish kalpak.

"Only these?" the captain said. "Mother of God. They send them young enough, don't they? Most of these kids are nothing but tears and snot. What about the big one? How old are you?"

George saluted and gave his name and age. The captain raised his heavy eyebrows. His face had been blistered by the cold. He scarcely moved his lips.

"Don't announce your name. This isn't training camp. I'll call you Second Passer." Looking down, the captain muttered, as if to himself: "You're the best they've sent me. I can tell you're not like these snotheads who are scared by the sound of their own poop. How old did you say?"

George told him again. But the captain did not seem to hear; and George said: "Is this the Front, sir? I mean, is that our gun?"

"No," said the captain, staring at him strangely. "I carry all the guns up here." He made a vulgar gesture, and the other men laughed. The captain began to pace to and fro. "We have two kinds of guns. Large bores and small bores. The Whores and the Virgins." The captain smiled as if his face hurt. "They are *all ladies!* We have My Darling Bouboulina. My Lovely Iphigenia. My Gentle Despo—she's a virgin, my Little Despo-Despoula. She's our Itsy-Bitsy Despinoula."

Suddenly, he made a choking noise and walked away. The sergeant major frowned. After a moment, he marched the crew to the vacant gun. Someone had left a map, a broken whistle and a compass in the hole. Aleko spread out the map, and George read the place names aloud. Directly south, as white and powdery as a mound of almond cookies in the window of a sweetshop at Epiphany, was a mountain called Three Martyrs. Over to the left was a hill called Toothy.

Beyond the ridge were the jumbled hills of Porya, ebbing away like frozen waves. A few miles farther on, invisible and out of reach, were the tracks that led to Ankara.

In midafternoon, a corporal whose neck was swathed in dirty flannel brought around some anise-flavored bread and mealy white cheese in a brass washbasin. Aleko, poking holes in the map with a stick, talked about watermelon, shish kebab and coffee.

"I suppose they'll start with an artillery bombardment," George said. The bread and cheese formed a lump high in his throat. "Then, afterward, we'll send the infantry through there." His finger was trembling as he pointed toward the hills of Porya, but no one else seemed to notice. They were looking at one another's faces.

There was not a sound along the line. The mist lay at their feet and swept around them like an ocean lapping at an island.

At last, Goufas said in a quavering voice: "I'd give my pair to know. Let's somebody go and ask what's going on."

They chose George. Grateful for their confidence, George bounded up like a jackrabbit. An instant later, he sprawled on his belly, laughing and trembling. Aleko whistled.

"In Jesus' name, Big George! Don't get yourself killed off before you get the answer!"

George crawled along the slope until he found the sergeant major, who was huddled in a shallow dugout, tearing up pieces of paper.

"I'm Second Passer," George said.

"I'm Mustapha Kemal," said the sergeant major.

George flashed an obliging smile. He squirmed into the dugout.

"We were wondering—are we waiting for orders from the captain?"

"No."

"The captain's funny, isn't he?"

"No."

"He seemed a little . . . funny. What's he called?"

"Mustapha Kemal."

"Oh."

"If you want to know, his name is Captain Triandafilakos. Johnny Triandafilakos. He's the man they had in mind when they made up the saying that it takes forty-five Johnnies to equal the sense of a rooster."

"I see."

"The hell you do."

George turned away, but the sergeant major grabbed his wrist.

"Look, kid—can you sit still for exactly five minutes? If anybody comes along, if the captain comes, you'll let me know?" And, stretching out on the ground, he went instantly to sleep.

When George reckoned that five minutes had passed, he touched the sergeant major's shoulder. The man lay there like a bag of pine cones.

"Hey, Sarge? Please, Sarge . . ." And George began to shake the sergeant major in a sort of frenzy, mumbling and almost sobbing. Suddenly, he realized the man was awake and staring at him.

"Get your Goddamned hands off me," the sergeant major said. His eyes were red and piggish, and he showed his long teeth. George flinched away just as a colonel and a red-faced orderly rushed at them out of nowhere.

"What in God's name are you still doing here? Are you wounded? Why are you lying here?"

George looked at the sergeant major.

"Let's go," the sergeant major said. "Take down that gun. Don't talk."

"We were waiting for the captain," George said.

"Get out of here!" the colonel screamed. "What are you doing here?"

George took off across the frozen slope, back to his comrades, waving his arms, not bothering to duck his head. The men stared at him, wild-eyed. Then they began to dismount the gun, casting glances over their shoulders and groaning. George stood over them, urging along first Goufas, then Loukas, who seemed to have quite forgotten the workings of the gun. As George was taking the barrel into his arms, there was a prolonged, unearthly sound, a sort of panting shriek, above their heads. It seemed to fill the sky and pierce the earth. Aleko dropped the end of the barrel. His face went gray—not pale, but gray and shadowy, like gauze. He knotted his hands across his belly, opened his mouth and vomited.

All at once, the gun crew flew apart like cinders in a breeze. They spun out, rolled, scrambled across the gravel, speechless with terror, while George staggered under the weight of the gun barrel, and the ground rose up and shuddered with a terrible concussion. It broke his ears, pulverized his teeth; and afterward there was a silence like the ringing of a thousand bells.

"Help me," George called out. "Help me take it down. That wasn't very close."

But the other men lay on the ground, tasting the gravel, waiting for another shell to fall.

"Oh, help me! The captain wouldn't want to lose his Despinoula."

At last, stunned and shuddering, the men stood up and fell upon the gun in fury. Hatred deranged their faces. Their tongues unraveled. They sobbed and screamed at Despinoula, cursing, gasping and coughing as they dragged the cannon through the scrub brush. When they felt the ground slope downward, and the cloak of mist surrounded them, they lay down and wept and spat; then they sprang up again,

252

stung with terror, strapped the gun barrel on the mule and plunged down the trail, two by two, carrying the block among them.

After dark, the captain met them in Söghüt, where the line was moving out. He said General Papulas had decided to terminate this "reconnaissance in force," having achieved the objective of exploring Turkish strength along a crucial gap.

"You will be happy to know that our division, according to the dispatches, encountered only sporadic, light resistance."

In the truck, Aleko Papakostas put his hand on George's shoulder.

"You acted like a regular palikar, Big George. Are you trying to get a medal?"

George looked down, sick with shame. In truth, he had been in terror of his life.

*W*hen Christos got back to Smyrna, the balconies along the Quay were decorated with papier-mâché gargoyles, harlequins and dragons. The bay was sparkling in the misty sunlight, and trolley bells were clanging near the passport shed.

Throwing back his head, Christos inhaled the pungent winter scent of cured tobacco, turpentine and mastic. How good it was to feel the ripeness of the Asiatic atmosphere after the stringent dryness and the sterile wind of Athens! The months he had spent in Old Greece had drained his energy; now he felt a quickening of strength. His spirits lifted in anticipation of the Lenten Carnival. True, he was not a sprout who could wander the streets with a reed flute and a triangle, begging for candy under the windows of young girls; but neither was he a shrunken skin! He had known the dark, cathartic witchery of carnivals in Bucharest and Varna and Constantinople, down to the waterfront, out to the citadel, staggering, swollen, ithyphallic, with a mask, a drum and a shoat bladder, linking arms with a disreputable throng of libertines around a barrel organ; and now, God willing, he'd go out with his dear wife and his daughter and his daughter's young lieutenant, all together, pounding pots and shaking rattles, dancing on drifts of paper snow, smiling behind their velvet dominoes, forgetting the quirks of politics and the disappointments of a wayward season.

His carriage jingled past the Splendid Palace, which was laced with colored streamers, the Sporting Club, the Smyrna Theater, the Danish Consulate. A moment later, Christos saw the handsome Britannic façade of his own house; and then, inexplicably, he remembered Sophia's forebodings, and his joy was swallowed in a wave of dread. Perspiration began to tingle on his body.

Climbing the steps two at a time, he struck the front door such a blow with his first that the crystal panels trembled. A dried-up May wreath from the year before fell off the lintel.

Sophia came slowly down, clasping a handkerchief over her mouth. At the bottom of the stairs, she threw her arms around his neck and began to cry. Christos felt his heart fly out of his body.

"George?" he said in a choked voice.

"No."

"Not Dimitris?"

"No, no. They're both all right."

Abruptly, she put her finger to her lips. Looking around furtively, she went and closed the door that led to the kitchen. After standing for a moment more, listening reflectively, she led Christos to the library, leaned against a tier of books and wiped her eyes.

"Oh, Christaki! What a catastrophe! Fire has fallen and burned us."

Sophia's skin was blotched with stains of brown and yellow; her eyes were ringed with shadows. Groping for Christos' hand, she drew him closer. "Your daughter—"

"Then it's Eleni?"

"She has missed twice. Maybe three times—she's very irregular."

And Sophia burst into tears again. She went to the window

and looked out, blowing her nose. Waves were bouncing up and throwing spray across the Quay, which gleamed like an immense, lethargic fish. All the warships in the harbor roads were hoisting strands of blue and yellow lights in celebration of the Carnival, and the evening sky was shot with rivulets of copper. Christos squeezed his head between his hands.

"Slut!" he whispered, under his breath. Then, louder: "Are you sure?"

"Does a girl make up such a thing?"

"Ah! There it is! She told you herself—but has anyone inspected her?"

"Not these old Smyrna wives. That would be like shouting it from Mount Pagus."

"Then you? Or Polixeni?"

"Nobody knows but yourself."

"God in Heaven," Christos said. He sat down on the horsehair sofa, very European and uncomfortable, which Sophia had bought a few years back in one of her seizures of affection for France. "How, in the name of God . . ."

"I just don't understand it," Sophia murmured. "Do you understand it?" After a moment, she went on wearily: "It seems to me people simply aren't as decent as they used to be. When I was a girl, we were so naïve. If some young dandy picked a flower for me, I was dizzy for a week."

Pausing again, she sighed for the bygone days when a girl like Eleni, compliant and unspoiled, would have been married at sixteen (if she had escaped the earlier attentions of a bandit or a pasha) to a Christian gentleman of forty-five, the owner of some ships or vines—a second father, as Christos had been to Sophia; a man who would have treated her like a daughter, at least by day, and would not have gotten her too many children.

"We were so simple. Nobody talked about politics and wars and massacres. We went to our church, the Turks went to their mosque. There wasn't all this filth of politics and wars and massacres and immorality of every sort.... I don't understand it. When I was a girl, we weren't allowed to sit alone in the same room with a young man. Certainly not to touch him, kiss him, play with him, let him *feel* everything as if you were a piece of clay!"

Suddenly, Christos raised his head.

"But who is he?"

"What do you mean?" Sophia said, staring at him in amazement. "Did you think it was the night watchman?" Their eyes met, and she smiled bitterly. "Did you think he was neuter, like Saint Gregory?"

"Oh, Jesus," Christos said. "Does she confess it?"

"She refuses to give his name, but it's obvious. Polixeni says he hung around here like a tomcat while we were gone. Five months is too long to be away. I felt it at the time. You remember what I said?"

Christos waved his hand. To be reminded of what might have been always annoyed him.

"At least we know the man," he said. "We know he's not a savage." Sophia's shoulders quivered. "And it's fortunate we learned about it now, before the start of Lent. I can have him back in Smyrna in a day or two. They can be married immediately."

But Sophia whipped back her head with an outraged gasp.

"What about the banns?"

"My dear, the girl is virtually delivered. Just be thankful she hasn't begun to show yet. Or has she? . . . Look, the announcement can be published in the churchyard and the marriage performed before Clean Monday. Where is the boy now? In Ushak?" Absently, he patted Sophia's shoulder. "Listen, it's not a tragedy. I've always liked him. To me, he seems to represent a certain type of Christian manhood, bold, courageous—"

"Oh, please," Sophia said, hiding her face in her hands.

So Christos left her by the window, her head bowed in a recapitulation of her own desirable, uncomplicated youth, that era of felicity when Greek women were shy and illiterate, wore little velvet caps embellished with gold coins and kept their hands to themselves.

Dimitris arrived at Basmahane Station three days later. A swarm of men rushed down the tracks to grasp the train and drew it in like fishermen landing a net at dusk. By the time the cars had reached the platform, innumerable messengers, peddlers, brakemen and policemen were clinging like a layer of mussels on the captured seine. Porters squirmed through the windows, scooped up boxes and valises and hurled them out the open doors.

At the stationmaster's shack, the captain of the guard exchanged Dimitris for a piece of paper signed by Christos Trigonis, Demogeronte of Smyrna, who stood there, blinking behind his lavender glasses in piscine stupidity.

"You are releasing me without an explanation?" Dimitris said.

"What is there to explain?" the guard said. "You're just another nail to me."

And Christos, without a word of greeting, turned and led Dimitris down the platform. His expression was remarkably severe for a man who was welcoming home a future son. Dimitris had almost to run to keep up with him, jostled by peddlers holding jugs of almond milk and watered yogurt, elbowed by American missionaries and Italian monks.

Outside, they passed a throng of people, cloaked in velvet hoods, carrying a paper lantern on a pole. Christos shouted for a carriage. A fusillade of chick-peas rattled on the curtains as they left the square.

"It's good to be back," Dimitris said.

But the old man, who was usually so gabby, did not answer. They entered one of those attenuated lanes that passed as boulevards between the station and the waterfront. Overhead, the balconies were clogged with women's faces—cataracts of wavy hair and golden crucifixes, creamy bosoms overflowing crimson blouses, elbows on the railings, cannonades of lentils, lamb bones, hare's feet, serpentine and raw potatoes, sesame seeds and macaroni. Dimitris could hear the clash of tambourines and the hiss of rockets from the Quay. Roman candles sputtered in the drains, and maskers circled in the light of Bengal flares.

Old Christos cracked his knuckles and cleared his throat. Then a shudder convulsed his shoulders and he looked away.

"Look," Dimitris said. "Aren't you going to give me any explanation?"

Christos turned back with a look of misery. Suddenly, as if to end a long and bitter argument, he took a large revolver out of his pocket and pointed it at Dimitris' chest.

"All right. Either you marry her immediately—" The weapon trembled with the jolting of the carriage, and the old man, puffing through his nostrils, held it with both hands to steady it. "And treat her honorably—"

"*Marry* her?" Dimitris said. He laid back his head on the cushions and began to laugh.

All the way from Ushak he had been trying to understand the document of transfer. Finally, he had deduced that Mavropetros had deceived him: the monarchists were going to prosecute him after all. His thoughts had leaped forward to the trial: celebrated lawyers pleading in the Areopagos, pamphlets and polemics bursting on a startled and indigant world. He saw himself confronting Mavropetros with a devastating accusation. Mavropetros countered with a lie. They traded cards. They met at dawn. But Mavropetros, yellow as a baby's stool and shivering like rose-water pudding, could

259

barely stand on his two feet. Dimitris shot him neatly through the heart (but was exonerated). He was promoted and was being sent to Athens for assignment.

"Haven't I always planned to marry her?" he said.

"Have you?"

"Do you think I could get married while I was at the Front?"

"You'll marry her tomorrow?"

"Tomorrow?" Dimitris studied the revolver, which was as thick as a rifle. "Why not?"

"Thank God," said Christos. "I knew you'd make the honorable choice." He put the revolver away. Folding his hands, he immediately began talking of other things—the plebiscite in Greece, the military situation, a second-rate performance of Bizet's *Carmen* that he had seen at the Dionysus Theater in Athens. "I just got back, you know. Athens is like a prison. Depressing. The Liberals hardly dare to greet each other on the street. We spent five months. But it's a difficult city—so egocentric! All they think about is Athens, Athens, Athens."

"I suppose so," Dimitris said.

"It's true. Don't be blinded by your loyalties. . . . I stayed to see the opening of that museum of antiquities that His Majesty calls a parliament. Every fossil Venizelos got rid of ten years ago is back again. And do you know the first bills they reported out? Back pensions for His Majesty! Compensations for themselves! And a big increase in the royal civil-service list."

He stopped for comment, but Dimitris said:

"Look—I don't see why there's such a hurry about the wedding."

"According to *her*, there's cause for a hurry."

"What do you mean?" He stared at Christos. Then, suddenly understanding, he laughed tolerantly. "Oh, what nonsense! Does she think you get a bellyful from shaking hands?"

The old man opened and closed his mouth with a clicking sound.

"I never thought I'd hear that sort of talk from you!"

"What in the devil am I supposed to say? She must have let her imagination get the best of her."

"Oh, Dimitri!" the old man said. "I don't want to hear any denials or evasions. She doesn't accuse you. She wants you to acknowledge your responsibility for the sake of your own honor. You've taken something innocent and pure—"

"You don't know what you're talking about," Dimitris said.

As a matter of fact, that innocent, pure little girl harbored a voracious itch between her milky, marble shanks. She was as easy to mount as a gypsy saddle. No wonder he had momentarily forgotten! It was a fragile memory, the carbon tissue of a moment: the taste of mastic brandy in his mouth, his hand between her legs, a penetrating curiosity that tingled in his nostrils; and then the aching, swelling of desire, the maddening abrasion of his trouser buttons, the shoddy army wool, her hand, the moisture, a momentary, twitching probing, a bitten, suffocated cry; and that was all. A dryness in the mouth. The moldering aroma of the fallen leaves behind the summerhouse. By morning, he remembered only the upsurging of desire, not the satisfaction, and the camion was on its way to Ushak. Had he thrown a sleeve?

"Well, what about this dowry?" he said. "We never settled that."

"Dowry! There can't be any dowry in a marriage of this kind. That would be like paying a premium on debauchery."

And Christos went on to explain, smiling calmly, that the dowry, in any case, had always struck him as a deleterious and parasitic institution. Historically, it must have begun with some pagan usage. Or perhaps the Greeks had adopted it from the Moslem system, God forbid. The whole process was an incubus, an example of the Greek's insatiable desire to

261

accumulate instead of investing, and a severe impairment to the national prosperity. One should not have to provide a dowry to get rid of a fine, healthy, strong, well-tempered girl, who did crochet and needlework, spoke French and played the piano.

"I think a girl should have a modest, very modest, gold account in London, for her own protection. That much I intend to provide. But I'd sooner give my daughter to a Turk than to hand her to some boy who thinks about nothing but accumulating property."

Dimitris, grinding his teeth in rage, was moved to tell the old bag of wind that the Trigonis gang was not *giving* their precious daughter to anyone, but forcing her onto the market, like a crippled cow at a tax auction. But Christos nudged him and said: "Anyway, I think you have substantial property, don't you?"

"I am penniless," Dimitris said. To marry a girl without property would ruin his career. He was appalled by the meanness of these Smyrniots, who considered themselves so civilized. "You'd be condemning her to a life of poverty."

"You should have thought of that," Christos said, with a self-righteous smile.

When they came to the house, Eleni was helping an old woman down the steps. She turned and shaded her eyes from the sunset. Dimitris studied her figure.

"How far along is she supposed to be?"

"She's three months gone," Christos said.

Eleni came toward the carriage, smiling timidly.

"Dimitri? Is it really you?"

But Dimitris scowled at her. It was obvious to him that she was faking. He had heard of women doing that. Sometimes in their prurience, their sexual hysteria, unattractive girls would imagine they had been ravished by whole companies of men. Their bodies would balloon like melons with nothing inside but their inflated imaginations.

Father and daughter grinned at him in triumph, licking their jowls. Hyenas! What made them think they could blackmail an Athenian officer into a loveless marriage without even offering a dowry?

Eleni's smile was not triumphant; nor was it, strictly speaking, a smile of happiness. She was too rational, too skeptical, too self-conscious for those spontaneous emotions; and there were too many unsolved questions in her mind.

Her sensation was relief—a great, harmonic chord of consolation after weeks of dissonance. Dimitris had come back: he had decided to acknowledge what was his. That was enough. She did not dare to analyze the circumstances.

That night, she was the first to reach the Club, rushing ahead in a rented carriage to try on a costume that her mother had commissioned at the last moment, in a mood of crisis euphoria. The seamstress was waiting in Box Theta, first tier: a beaky, kinky, hazelnut woman named Mrs. Stratou, who was leaning on the balustrade to survey the new arrivals. Mrs. Stratou considered herself the gadfly of the *haut monde*.

"There's Beatrice Pezmazoglou," Mrs. Stratou said. "She's never gotten back her waist."

And they proceeded at once to the final assembly of Eleni's dress. It was a yellow satin, with a farthingale to lift the panniers of the skirt, which floated on the hips like mounds of foam. With it went a dainty shepherd's crook, trailing a nosegay of pastel ribbons, and a saucy bonnet, trimmed with lace, that perched above the eyebrow. Eleni's thick black hair would be completely covered by a white peruke.

As the dressmaker's long, bony hands moved around her waist, Eleni wondered whether anyone could feel a difference there. Yesterday, that possibility had made her regard

263

the Carnival Ball with apprehensive horror; tonight, it did not matter. What a pitiable irony! The same act, by the same people, with the same result, could be the occasion of pride if you were married and a source of shame if you were not. The difference between delight and sorrow, beatification and damnation, was only the matter of a few words, a few moments of sacramental ritual in front of the bema. That was the sort of man-made morality, stinking of hypocrisy, that she would never understand.

Mrs. Stratou made no comment on the state of Eleni's abdomen. Bouncing up and down, stitching and pinning, the dressmaker was entranced by glimpses of Anatolian society outside the velvet curtains of the stall. An ape and an arab, florid and perspiring, were urging each other along the corridor toward the ballroom. Below the balustrade, in a growing pandemonium of painted masks and ostrich feathers, the waltz orchestra was tuning up.

"I don't like jazz, do you?" said Mrs. Stratou, raising Eleni's shoulder straps. "I like the waltz, the two-step, the mazurka, the polka. Even the tango. I mean, I'm broad-minded about the tango. But this jazz! Where's the music in it?" And, kneeling to baste the hemline: "I like the old ones, too. The Butcher's Dance, the *karagouna,* the *ballo.* But this Shimmy! Mother of mine!"

"I love them all," Eleni said. "I'd dance to anything."

Never had the costumes seemed to her so clever or the decorations so imaginative. The stall had been transmuted into an adorable, peek-in Easter egg, bright with cambric draperies and crêpe-paper flowers, and stocked with buckets of champagne and baskets of Jordan almonds. A baby lamb with lavender fleece was shivering among the gilded chairs. Across the room, the Giorgiadises had contrived a Fiji Island, overgrown with paper palm trees. The DeHochpieds occupied a cardboard fortress with a portcullis that raised and lowered on a chain. There was a Flying Carpet, flanked by a Moorish palace and a gigantic tissue-paper crocus with a shining beetle on its petals. The Tzavellises' Taj Mahal was firing cyclamens and chocolate candies at the Papazoglou Pagoda, while the first dancers, under a barrage of pumpkin seeds and grains of rice, were beginning the movements of the Spanish tango.

"You'd dance to *that?*" Mrs. Stratou stepped back, pins in her mouth, to study Eleni's bosom. "Not if you were *my* age! When you've seen as many Carnivals as I have, you begin to develop a little discretion." And she offered a hand mirror.

Eleni turned from side to side. She wrinkled up her nose and dimpled her cheek. They had dusted the wig with a silicate that glittered in the candlelight, and flecks of the material floated around her head like tiny stars. It was the loveliest costume she had ever seen: a transformation. She went to the balustrade and leaned out, laughing, to wave to the incoming crowd; then back to the mirror to examine her complexion. She had blanched her skin that afternoon with a sublimate of mercury and marked a beauty spot with oak gall on the left cheekbone, near her eye, to draw attention to her most appealing feature; and she was not disappointed.

It was a face that she had never viewed with vanity: too long and angular, too dark and rubicund, like her father's face —the reddish, Cretan genotype. For a man, the ancient mold was virile and aristocratic; for a girl, it was too coarse. Older women, with the honesty of those to whom physical beauty is no longer important, often told Eleni she was a "classic type." Eleni interpreted this to mean "austere."

Yet Dimitris had found her face acceptable—and, God knows, he was handsome himself! It was *he* who had pursued *her*, in a relentless campaign, like one of those lascivious seductions that Polixeni had endured on Naxos; but Eleni, unlike the cook, had been too dazzled to resist.

265

No, that was not true. She had never lost the power to resist. Even at the beginning, swept away by the ecstasy of Dimitris' searching hands, with her nostrils trembling to the scent of his cologne and her lips touching the golden warmth of his skin—even then she had understood the dangers and the probabilities. In her inherent honesty, she had known the risk that she was taking; and when the consequences had become apparent, she had not been dismayed. She knew that this crisis would test the very qualities in him that she had been unable to appraise: his honesty, his loyalty, his courage.

She had written to him. He did not answer. She concluded that the message had been vague. She wrote again. He did not answer. Then, as weeks passed and she saw that she had made an irremediable mistake, she sank into despair, confessed to her mother and numbly waited for the inescapable results: the wrath, the shame, the ostracism. There was one thing that she would never do: that was to name the man who would not name himself.

"Are you pleased with it?" said Mrs. Stratou.

"I'm at the gate of Heaven," Eleni said.

Professor Paleologos, in an orange cutaway, jolly as an English jug, poked through the curtains, shepherding some Turks in sober business suits and dark tarbooshes. They were guests of the Hellenic High Commissioner and had consented to enliven the evening with a public toast to Greek and Moslem friendship. The intelligent young man on the left had only recently decamped, so to speak, from the Turkish insurrection to work for international peace.

Eleni glanced superficially at the three Turks, who clustered together with their hands behind their backs. She was too preoccupied to be polite to Moslem politicians who had been brought in for reasons of strategy.

But something about the youngest man attracted her. He was as sunburned and blistered as a peasant, and his calloused hands were split and stained; yet he had the bearing of a gentleman. His eyes followed her with a devouring urgency. All at once, she recognized him and burst out laughing.

"Why, you're the man who comes to the garden to visit Papa in the middle of the night!"

Abdullah's eyes bulged. He looked so miserable that Eleni regretted teasing him. It could not have been pleasant leaving one's own side in the middle of a war. She supposed he must be some sort of captive.

"Are you glad to back in Smyrna?"

Bowing, Abdullah muttered a feeble gallantry about the beauty of Smyrna women.

"Do you really think the war can be ended?"

"If both sides would only yield a little . . ."

"I'd like it to be over, wouldn't you? My brother and my fiancé are in." Noticing that his eyes had fastened on her fingers, she covered her left hand with her right. "I've never had anything against the Turks."

But the dressmaker jabbed her with a pin, and the Professor led his prisoners out.

"Turks at the Lenten Carnival!" Mrs. Stratou said. "What's happening to society? No, I've had my fill of this sort of vulgar entertainment, frankly. All this heat, this noise, this smoke, this wine. And, later on, this disgusting metamorphosis. Men turn into women. Women turn into cats and snakes. That's when you have these stabbings, these perversions and these blasphemies that would sicken a pagan." She dipped up a fistful of Jordan almonds and went on talking as though she had a mouthful of pebbles. "I've seen hundreds of Carnivals, and there's *always* someone dressed up like a doctor, carrying an enema syringe to squirt water on the ladies' shoulders. There are *always* monkeys, *always* arabs, *always* dervishes. And, forgive me, dear, but *always* Dresden shepherdesses. Like yourself."

And, turning to Sophia, who had come in abruptly and was

looking nervously here and there: "Madame Sophia? Do you remember when we used to go to bed the last night of Carnival with little bits of macaroni in the pillowcase to make you dream about the man you were going to marry?"

"Oh, yes. I *think* I do," Mama said, with a distracted smile. She came and stood next to Eleni, and her knuckles whitened on the railing. Eleni peered at her.

"Is something wrong?"

"Not now," Mama whispered.

"Of course, it didn't work," the dressmaker continued, fussing with Eleni's gown. "One time I dreamed about Caruso. Once about the Sultan. Once about my younger brother—isn't that *awful!*"

Sophia groaned softly. Taking hold of Eleni's wrist, she nodded toward the door.

But the Oriental orchestra was coming from the dressing rooms, and the corridor was jammed with dancers moving toward the floor. The musicians wore baggy cotton pants and woolen vests embroidered with pentagons and crescent moons. Greasy purple handkerchiefs were tied around their heads, and golden crucifixes glittered at their throats. Sauntering across the floor, they picked their teeth with chips of wood, languorously eying the buttocks of the women.

Next it was someone famous at the entrance. The Petrodakis ladies, in the adjoining box, were fumbling for their opera glasses, while the Petrodakis gentlemen, in feathered hats and paper dominoes, were leaning out like gargoyles and complaining that the decorations blocked their view. There was such a crush in the vestibule that nobody was moving in or out, and voices rose in tight anxiety.

"Oh, look!" Eleni said. "There's Papa."

Sophia gave a nervous start. Eleni nudged her and pointed.

"Who's the man in the devil costume. Is that—" She began to laugh. "Not Dimitris?"

But the musicians struck a chord, the lights were dimmed and the first notes of the anthem sounded. Eleni felt her mother moving restlessly. When the orchestra struck the final octave, Sophia turned on the dressmaker.

"Go along, Mrs. Stratou, I beg you. I have to talk to my daughter alone." And, taking hold of Eleni's hands, she said in a strangled tone: "Listen. This is a dreadful situation. The young man refuses to admit his responsibility."

Eleni drew her hands away.

"Do you mean Dimitris?"

"He says there must be a mistake."

"What mistake? No one has accused him of anything." And, feeling suddenly nauseous, almost faint, she sat down and fanned herself, wiped her forehead with her wrist and dried her moist hands on her skirt. Then she snatched up the poor, grotesque little lamb and squeezed it in her arms, murmuring: "Oh, God in Heaven. I can't stand it!"

"It is up to you to name him," Mama said. "Then we can force the issue."

"No, Mama," Eleni said. The muscles of her throat began to tighten strangely, and she could not speak.

Down below, a doctor with an enema syringe was splattering cold water on some girls from Bornova. An orator climbed to the bandstand and began a sermon on the meaning of the Carnival in time of war, a Carnival of spiritual hope. Eleni could see her father moving across the center of the ballroom. Forcing his way, he pushed aside a yellow chimpanzee that whirled around and threw chopped paper in his face. The monkey laughed; Papa hugged him; and they slapped each other on the shoulders. Where had the devil gone?

The speaker's voice rose steadily. Never had the Greeks of Smyrna met the Lenten season with such solemn hopes. The military victory at Inönü was more significant than anyone had dared to dream. The youth of Smyrna had won their crown of laurel in that vast *empyriòs* of flame and ashes!

"Long live the Tenth Division!" someone cried; and the audience cheered.

"If you refuse to speak, there's nothing we can do," Sophia said. "There is nothing except his word."

"Hope of peace!" the speaker shouted. "Three-way talks . . . A clever Greek Prime Minister . . ."

Behind Sophia's back, the curtains parted. A peddler with a tray of paper hats and cascarones shouldered in, followed by Christos, a purple satin Mameluke whose face was crumpled with anxiety.

"You've told her?"

"She refuses to speak!"

But a strange paralysis suffused Eleni's body, like the shock that follows an accident. Her father looked at her in despair. The orator's voice was becoming polemical; and as his rage increased, the audience stiffened in anticipation of the epiphonema.

"How shall we now fulfill this hope that sears our hearts as we begin our Lenten fast? How shall we guarantee the triumph of Hellenic culture in this ancient land? With God's help—"

"I feel sick," Eleni said; and she stood up and clawed the curtains aside. Halfway down the stairs, she heard the audience begin to stamp and clap. As she reached the ballroom door, her father caught up and took her by the arm.

"Don't shame us!" he whispered, and he led her to the bar and ordered two glasses of brandy. But while he was taking out his purse, Eleni slipped away and ran across the foyer.

In the center of the ballroom she hesitated. Flurries of confetti sifted down through rays of colored light. Paper arches trembled like the walls of Jerico. A netful of balloons was swaying like a giant punka, directly overhead. Ah, look!

The devil himself was linking his fingers with a woman dressed in black.

No, there was another devil, frenzied and furtive, quivering among the draperies. And another near the stage. And another in the corner by the door. She trapped one of them by the orchestra, embracing a pretty milkmaid, and snatched off his mask. But the devil was a muscular stevedore, moist-lipped and humid-eyed, who clutched at his partner's waist and grumbled: "What the hell? You've got no right—" And the milkmaid was an androgyne with close-cut, crinkly hair and a bluish chin: an erstwhile man, caught in the mystic ecstasy of metamorphosis.

Eleni turned with a shuddering sob and ran away.

The ballroom overflowed with devils, leaping up like red mullets to snap at the eddying balloons, simpering in the decorated boxes, cowering in the drapes. She bumped into them blindly, paying no attention, retching into her handkerchief.

Only one person spoke to her and looked at her with sympathy. It was that Turk, Abdullah; it was he who took her by the hand and led her toward the door.

Abdullah and Eleni were married at noon the next day in a garden in Göz Tepe. Bees were humming in the lavender wisteria, and the ocean was as white as turpentine. The witnesses were Hadji-zade Nüvit Bey, a cousin of Abdullah's father; an arithmetic instructor from the Sultaniye School; and the imam of the Karatina Mosque, who read the wedding contract in a hesitating, astonished voice, as if he had never heard such ideas expressed before.

Abdullah looked down at Eleni to reassure her, but she was staring straight ahead. After the recitation of the verses from the Holy Book, the women took Eleni to their rooms to offer her cologne and candy, and Cousin Hadji-zade Nüvit Bey,

271

who was stingy and old-fashioned, served each of the men a thimbleful of homemade anisette.

It was Cousin Nüvit who had opted for a swift and inexpensive marriage. He declared that the Lord intended men and women to be mated with as little pageantry as possible. The perfect wedding took place at the zenith of the day, in accordance with the regulations of Islam, and was as simple as the Prophet.

Abdullah would have chosen to display his love with opulence and splendor; but Eleni preferred to bow to his tightfisted relatives. At her suggestion, they discarded all the Turkish wedding customs, as they had the Greek. There were none of the familiar preparations—no exchange of poems and gifts, no Henna Night of bathing and hair dyeing at the women's bathhouse, no bridal throne in clouds of net, no wedding veil of silver threads, no wedding feast, no sesame sprinkled on the nuptial sheets.

When the witnesses were gone, Cousin Nüvit locked the anise cordial in a chest and Abdullah went into the bedroom where Eleni was sitting on a cushion, gazing downward, with a yashmak of rose-colored gauze across her face. He lifted the veil and kissed her on the mouth. Her lips were cold and flaccid, and she looked at him expressionlessly.

"Is it over? It seemed rather short."

"That's the style of a Moslem ceremony," Abdullah said. "It's a contract, not a sacrament."

"There's nothing left to do?"

"Nothing."

Eleni sighed and looked around the room. Abdullah had heard that many brides were melancholy; but Eleni's depression was more profound than the momentary sadness of leaving home. Her unhappiness was obvious, and it puzzled him, not only because it differed conspicuously from his own jubilant mood, but because it was unlike the spirit of the vivacious girl who had teased him from the window of her room.

Yet Abdullah was reluctant to examine the state of her emotions. He sensed that his pride would suffer if he were to know her motives for running away with him. In the spirit of an old-fashioned Moslem, he was willing to accept good fortune with gratitude and without question: kismet. If Eleni did not love him now, she would learn to love him later. He put his masculine faith in the priapic magic of the wedding couch.

The servants brought a wedding soup of tripes and spices. Abdullah put on a dressing gown and moistened his hair with lemon verbena. He led Eleni to a copper tray, sat down beside her, stroked her hands and fed her spoonfuls cooled against his lips. Now and then she would murmur a few words of thanks or ask him for the bread, the salt, the lemon; but she never turned her eyes to look at him. This he attributed to virginal shyness, and his blood began to pulsate in his ears.

He paced around the bedroom, adjusting the curtains and the window blinds. First, it seemed too hot and stuffy, then too cold. He wondered whether she was bothered by the draft. Then he noticed the accumulated Moslem bric-a-brac—olive-wood intaglios, Osmanli yataghans, Kula prayer mats—which a Greek would find exotic; and he quickly gathered them up and put them out of sight.

Eleni was absorbed in thought. Kneeling, Abdullah took her head between his hands and gently drew the long pins out of her dark, fragrant hair, which tumbled down in waves around her shoulders. She looked around frantically as he pressed her down on the cushions.

Neither of them said a word. Abdullah threw off his dressing gown and grasped her hips between his hands. But when he tried to cover her, she twisted away from him, panting through her closed teeth and sobbing, "Oh, I can't." Locking her knees together, she shook her head and braced her hands against his chest.

Abdullah pressed down on her, laughing at first: "All right, little princess. Do you think I'll hurt you?" Then, choked by a surge of anger, he pushed her down roughly while she thrashed her hips from side to side. Her skin was hard and cold to his touch. Blue-white crescents gleamed between her half-closed eyelids, and her lips were rigidly pressed together. Insulted and perplexed, Abdullah whipped up his passion with a flood of self-recrimination: he was a fool; he was being cheated; he was unmanned.

But his desire faded. He got up, smoked a cigarette and wandered silently around the room, which was flooded with topaz sunlight. Perhaps that was the trouble: the afternoon was too warm, too bright. After dark, when the air was cool and azure, Eleni would find the animality of marriage less frightening. That night, however, she pleaded that she was not ready. She was exhausted, nauseated and in a taboo period of the lunar cycle. Overwhelmed by her arguments, Abdullah gave up his priapic magic and went to sleep on a carpet in the corner of the room.

Dreams tormented him. Before daylight, he woke his bride and told her they would have to leave Smyrna before the police came after them.

"So soon?" Eleni said, and she seemed to be making calculations in her head. But she did not protest. As the sky was growing light, they rode up the Quay in an oxcart. Peaks of yellow foam were racing across the surface of the bay. Eleni held the edges of her scarf across her mouth, exactly as a Moslem wife would do. Abdullah wore a skullcap and a shirt without a collar. By the time the sun was up, they had crossed the Bridge of Caravans and left the city.

Inland, there was yellow mustard growing in the fields. Nymph Dagh and Boz Dagh were covered with snow, the streams were flowing to the brim with chalky, reddish water and peasant women knelt among the white gauze shields of the tobacco flats, transplanting seedlings. The countryside looked poorer than Abdullah remembered it. He smiled to reassure Eleni, who was sitting there in silence, with her hands together in her lap and her charshaf billowing around her like a pirate flag.

At dusk they found an inn at Nif, beside a camel wallow. Eleni made some tea with muddy water heated on a charcoal brazier. After drinking half a cup and picking at a piece of bread, she fell asleep on a carpet on the dirt floor; and Abdullah, leaning on his elbow, stared down at her face until the night devoured him in its dark, omphalic fastness, reeking with the urine of a million caravans. In Kassaba and in Salihli it was exactly the same: the damp quilts, the muddy tea, the earth floor that breathed a nitrous residue of centuries, and the sorrowful, elusive girl whose face floated away from him in the darkness like a water lily in a turbid stream.

On the fourth day as the sun was going down, they forded Alashehir Creek through the middle of a herd of blue-gray water buffaloes, and the town appeared above them, plum-colored and apple green on its three golden hills.

"It's not Constantinople," Abdullah said, "but the life is comfortable." And he talked about Laurel Konak, his mother, and his sisters as the cart creaked slowly through the twilight.

It seemed, however, that the Greek Army had taken Laurel Konak for a barracks. Mahmut Zia had been expelled from office. Abdullah's mother, sisters, grandmother, uncle and aunt were living all together, like a flock of chickens with a single rooster, in a three-room shack below a vineyard at the Chakirjali farm. The farm had been a military homestead of his mother's family for two hundred years; but it always had been let to peasant tenants. The walls were infested with chicken lice, the well was brackish and the chimney smoked.

"It's the blessing of God we don't have to live in a pasture," Mahmut Zia said. "It would have been different if your brother Kenan had been here to help us."

"Or even you," Abdullah's mother said.

Abdullah went outside and brought in his wife. Eleni's skin was bluish with fatigue and she was so weak from riding in the swaying wagon that she had to be almost carried inside. The women dropped their sewing on the floor. Awkwardly, they bowed and touched their foreheads to Eleni's hand.

"Welcome to my home," Abdullah's mother said. She led Eleni to the bedroom, which was furnished with a pile of quilted mats, a cherry-wood commode and a magazine illustration of some white horses flaring their nostrils. The other women followed Eleni in, carried out their bedding and slammed the door on their Greek sister.

"What a surprise," Abdullah's mother said, studying her son with the penetrating gaze that Kenan had inherited from her. "When were you married? She's in a tender condition, isn't she?"

"No, she's exhausted from the journey," Abdullah said.

But his mother gave a tight little smile that stung him like a slap. As soon as he could ask permission to withdraw, Abdullah went into the bedroom and stood over his wife with his feet wide apart and his hands clenched together against his heart.

Eleni opened her eyes and blinked as he dropped to his knees beside her, fumbling with the buttons of his clothes. He had been cheated, deceived, unmanned and goaded to frenzy. Moaning, he threw himself onto her like a murderer, stifling her cries with his calloused hands, his bandit hands, catching his thorny fingers at the edges of her soft mouth, sealing her breath with his breath; and the weight of his body forced open the impenetrable, trembling pocket of her thighs. He nudged through to the point of pain, and the salt of her tears was in his mouth: pain to her, pain to him, but bloodless, curtainless, to his ultimate extension and the shuddering satisfaction of his seed.

And then, as he rolled aside, gasping, primitive anger roared in his head. He dug his fingers into the tender socket of her shoulder.

"Where is my wedding flag? Whose window did you hang it from?"

Eleni reared up, shook back her hair and glared at him. Drawing down the edges of her mouth, she said in a grating voice: "Did you expect to steal a virgin at the Carnival Ball?"

"Daughter of a pig!" Abdullah said. "Are you stoked up, too? Did your shoat rut his farrow in your belly?"

But his voice broke. Blindly, he groped for his clothes, put on his boots and went out through the back door.

Under the moist black breast of Boz Dagh, the yard was twitching with the revelry of a dozen cats, and the wind was chortling wickedly among the leafless poplar trees. The earth exhaled a musky, seminal aroma. Abdullah walked to the well and lowered the wooden bucket boom, which creaked like the springs of a bed as the diagonal spar plunged into the murky orifice. He drank from the dipper and washed his hands and face; and then, sensing the residue of an abominable pollution, he let down his trousers and washed his body in accordance with the half-forgotten, atavistic regulations of the Prophet, dipping and pouring with his right hand and wiping away with his left the glutinous traces of his sexual contamination.

His anger ebbed away with the cold water and the pious monotony of the ablution. The pounding of his blood subsided. He looked up without resentment, almost with sympathy, when Eleni's ghostly figure crossed the yard. Stumbling and lurching with every step, she staggered halfway to the well. Then, with a sharp cry, she fell forward.

Abdullah went toward her; but she flailed her arm from side to side.

"I am losing it. Oh, God in Heaven! Oh, help me! My mama! My mama! My mama!"

And Abdullah, grasping her by the shoulders, saw the dark, amniotic stain clouding the cold earth, the moist, seminiferous earth that was strewn with fruit pits, tufts of cat fur and twists of rusty tin.

Sobbing, he buried the evidence of his disgrace among the furrows of the vineyard.

For days, weeks, months, Eleni sat beside the brazier in the kitchen, picking stitches from a quilt around her knees. Her husband's people came and went without a sound, like a colony of coenobites restricted by a rule of silence. If Eleni should look up, they would turn their heads away.

Every afternoon, the mother took down a wicker basket and a pistol from a shelf, veiled herself in black and left the house. The aunt went into hiding, and the uncle languished in a shed behind the house. As for Abdullah, he trudged around the vineyards with his eyes cast down and his hands behind this back. His constant, importunate demands on her had ended. Eleni counted it a blessing to be so isolated and ignored.

The farm itself was like the tomb of a forgotten saint: neglected, useless and silent. There were no dogs, no goats, no geese, no chickens in the yard; no carts, no cars, no caravans went past the gate; no visitors came to the door; no peasants worked in the vineyards, which were damp and ruby-colored with the embryonic leaves of early spring. The companions of her solitude were a younger sister named Gulnar, whose only interest was in mixing facial cataplasms; an older sister named Yildiz, who was mentally incompetent; and an old grandmother, who was petrified.

Watching them from the inert black deeps of her despair, Eleni saw the granny as the emblem of them all, that hideous old woman. Years ago, the desiccation and warping of old age had finished her; now she was like a withered pod that would retain its color and shape, dehydrated, until it suddenly disintegrated into dust. Her place was on the doorstep. Smoking, coughing, slobbering, she sat and watched the empty road.

For more than half a century, she had vegetated in the sacred seclusion of the harem. She had never learned to read or write, to dance, to paint, to draw or do calligraphy, to play an instrument, to sing a song, to cook a meal, to dress a child, to ride a horse, to speak a foreign language, to roll a cigarette, to drive a vehicle, to play a game, to grow a flower, to know by sight a single bird or plant or animal, to count above one hundred. She had never had her picture taken, never been aboard a ship or train, never spoken to a Christian (except a servant girl), never made a trip (except a picnic outing), never seen a puppet show, an opera, a concert, an athletic match, a shadow play, a horse race or a camel fight. She had hidden behind a wooden screen while Sultan Mejit, Sultan Azziz, Sultan Murat, Sultan Hamit and Sultan Mehmet came and went, a ship canal was dug in Egypt, a railway line was aimed at Baghdad, wars were fought and a machine was taught to sew.

But she cared nothing about such things. Her empty mind contained a single memory, the blissful recollection of her wedding. It had lasted for a week and was attended by eight hundred guests. Three thousand bowls of saffron pilaf were distributed in alms. She had been seated on a rose-colored throne, with silver sequins on her cheeks, and spent her wedding night on sheets of spun gold, which had been sprinkled with sesame to guarantee a fertile union. After bearing three children, she had been widowed at age twenty-two.

If she spoke, it was to mention her lovely wedding. While Abdullah was rolling her a cigarette, she would close her eyes or stare distractedly along the road; and she never recognized Eleni, who sat and studied her, the black tulip of Moslem domesticity.

Toward nightfall, the old woman would emit a feeble screech, and Eleni, looking out, would see Abdullah's mother entering the yard with her black veil thrown back and her mouth convulsed.

"What next? They've burnt the furniture for firewood." And then, coming inside: "They're using the kitchen for a stable. I sent a kid around to take a look, and they dumped a night pot on him."

The uncle, who had been confined all day, burst out of his shed, rolling his protrusive eyes and shouting: "These Greeks are all alike! If only Kenan were here!"

Sometimes, the mother would have overheard a rumor that an army requisition squad was coming out the road to Sarigöl. All the women, accordingly, would spend the next few days crouching in a thicket of bamboo beyond the vineyard, shivering and speechless, ringed around by tins of olive oil and sacks of meal that they had carried from the house to thwart the predatory Greeks.

Abdullah, however, refused to hide. He pruned berry bushes, patched fences and carried jugs of water, while his mother called to him from the thicket.

"Don't you know they'll put you in the work brigade?"

No answer.

"I suppose you'd like to spend three to five years building roads?"

No answer.

"You don't expect your *wife* to save you, do you? If they find *her,* they'll say you stole her."

No answer.

Eleni watched him moving back and forth, aloof and self-absorbed. He had the narrow, graceful gait of a city man, and she could remember the immaculate refinement of his ap-

pearance in the days when he had affected a Stamboul cutaway and patent-leather slippers: his small, manicured hands,
his dainty feet, his eager, puffy little face. Something had
hardened his body, saddened his features and bridled his
tongue since those autumn evenings when he would come to
the Villa Trigonis to sell his father's grapes; but Eleni lacked
the energy or interest to imagine what had happened. It was
incredible that he should call himself her husband, this man
about whom she knew so little. He seemed to be a decent,
educated man; yet his own people treated him with contempt. Was that merely because he had married outside his
religion? Or was it because he had returned to Greek territory while the brother, whom they all admired, remained in
Ankara?

At night, Eleni lay awake and listened to Abdullah's
mother, endlessly scolding him about the damages, the unpaid rents, the insolent commanders and other afflictions that
the Greeks had poured upon her.

"Don't think they wouldn't like to seize even this little
shack we're living in. They'd like to put me on the straw.
They've taken all the rest—the wheat, the carts, the cows, the
raisins. They pretend they're paying for the things they steal,
which makes it all the worse. They weigh your calf on their
own scale, and some flunky calls out the weight in Greek, and
they never let you so much as peek at the marks on the
balance arm. God knows, they simply make the figure up. No
payment for the horns, the hoofs or the leather—just five
pounds last week for a heifer that would have brought fifteen
to twenty in any market. I think they're probably the cruelest
race of people in the world."

"Mother, for the love of God," Abdullah said. "Do you
want her to hear you saying that?"

"She's probably heard worse about the Turks at her father's knee."

"Don't you like her, Mother?"

"Why not? I think she's pretty. Don't you think she's pretty, Gulnar?"

"Who?"

"His wife."

Eleni put her ear against the wall, but Gulnar's voice was indistinct. Abdullah was saying:

"It was difficult for her to leave her people."

"It's difficult for every girl to leave her home," the mother said. "If she's lonely, why don't you let her go stay with a Greek family in town?"

"Put her out to board?"

"Why not? She's Greek, isn't she?"

"She is my wife."

"Look," Abdullah's mother said. "It's time to speak frankly. This Greek girl does not care for you. I don't know why she married you, but it is obvious she does not care for you." Abdullah did not answer, and his mother went on: "Look, proving something, escaping from something, punishing someone—that is not the proper basis for a marriage. Why did you marry her?"

But Eleni could not hear Abdullah's reply. She lay on her back and thought about the plaintive song that Greek girls sing at country weddings:

> Farewell, my father dear, farewell
> Farewell, my darling mother;
> I'm going to a stranger's house,
> To serve my husband's mother. . . .

Abdullah came in and lay down in the corner of the room, sighing heavily. Eleni stared up at the darkness.

"I can't go home," she said. "I have no place to go."

"Neither do I," Abdullah said.

INÖNÜ
MARCH, 1921

*F*or two months, George waited with increasing anxiety for the next attempt to cut the Turkish railroad line. He counted the passing days with the sensations of a man condemned to death.

Although he never talked about the shelling at Söghüt, the memory of his panic fear dominated his thoughts. Was that total paralysis of soul a normal response to danger? Or was it the reaction of a coward? Had the single, intense exposure to the germ of terror immunized him like a vaccination? Or was fear like an earthquake, followed by an endless series of successive temblors, each one adding to the damage and horror of the first?

He knew that Aleko Papakostas, who was more than twice his age, had been stricken with nausea. But Aleko later explained that the sickness was caused by some tainted bread and cheese; and several others recalled that they, too, had felt a touch dyspeptic. Nobody ventured to describe the state of his emotions.

George wrote frequent letters to his parents. He tried, for his father's sake, to render every aspect of his life in vehement terms, filling pages with such phrases as, "I felt my blood grow hot," "I swore to have revenge" and "I thrilled with patriotic pride." No matter how extravagantly he boasted, his mother always answered as if he were a little boy at boarding school in Switzerland. One of her letters, which he carried in his pocket, gave off a musky fragrance that reminded him of home:

"I always pretend, *mon p'tit,* that you are wintering in Montreux. What does Second Passer mean? . . ."

His good companions—Aleko and the rest—looked upon him as their natural champion. They admired his size and strength; and this esteem made him even more aware that he would fail again.

On a rainy morning, orders came to march again on Inönü, that crucial village on the route to Ankara. The other members of Despoula's crew were overjoyed. Here was an opportunity to recapitulate their earlier, brave "reconnaissance in force," to shatter the power of Mustapha Kemal and end the war.

They took the very route that they had followed twelve weeks earlier, across the fields of pale tobacco and the ridges striped with snow. The same enthusiastic women greeted them with showers of rice and cotton; the same battalions lost direction in the fog; the same Turks sniped from rocky places; the same piles of rubble fumed in the streets of Bilejik. Then, the 10th Division came against a place called Chepni, which was shrouded like a corpse in winding sheets of icy mist; and nothing was the same.

Never had George known such agonizing cold, such cutting winds, such clammy and unfathomable darkness. Heavy American draft horses froze to death at night; hostlers would find them in the morning, lying on their backs, with their bellies swollen and their nostrils white with rime. Buckets of drinking water turned as hard as stone and broke their bindings with a snap. It was impossible to stay awake, impossible to stay asleep. When the crew moved Despoula up the hill, the earth resounded under foot like a plate of iron. Captain Triandafilakos, wrapped in a sheepskin, lectured them on the gynecology of mountain guns.

At daylight the barrage began. Whores and Virgins alternated, spraying crimson splashes on the slopes. Then the artillery stopped. They waited for the mist to clear on Chepni. George looked at Aleko, wondering whether he, too, was thinking about the infantry below them in the gorge. How would you feel if you were down there, waiting to receive the order to attack? Would you behave with courage? Or would you show yourself to be the coward who had panicked at Söghüt?

Crouching next to a shell box, searching for reassurance in Aleko's patriarchal face, George heard a clamor of voices. It was the ancient battle cry for air—*"Aera!"* He crawled forward on his knees, looked down the scarp and saw Greek soldiers moving up the slope of Chepni in a broken line. They wallowed among the stones like swimmers under water, as leisurely as figures in a dream. Puffs of smoke from the flank artillery were disintegrating softly in the milky air above the ridge.

Halfway up the slope, the slow-moving, broken line of Greeks began to waver. The forward movement stopped; and then, a second later, the line was slipping backward. George heard the voices of the officers and the rattle of machine-gun fire; but the leading column fell to pieces like a heap of ashes scattered by the wind, and you could see the faces of the Turks, as red and puffy as newborn babies, emerging from the yellow boulders on the ridge.

All at once, an enormous horde of Turks was rushing forward—down the hill and up the scarp, up to their own defenseless battery, panting through jagged teeth and screaming *"Allah! Allah!"* with the cold sunlight pricking out the daggers of their awful bayonets, which had long, hollow grooves to drain the blood.

"Oh, Jesus God," Aleko murmured, and Sakellariadis raised

his head to shout a warning to the others: "Too late to dismantle. Run!"

But the captain stood behind them, waving his pistol.

"Load her!"

"We'll hit—" Aleko cried.

"Load her!"

"—our own men!"

And George, staring at the captain in abomination, saw a fiend without a soul, a cannon wad, a heartless mercenary, shouting wicked, sadistic, suicidal orders to enforce his murderous whims. In his hatred of the captain, he turned on his own beloved friends and shouted in their faces, raging at this bloody madness: "You heard him! Load her, for Christ's sake!"

They shrank from him, whining, but George screamed at them until the captain blew the firing whistle. No one had positioned the gun. The shell burst in a snowbank left of Chepni. But the Greek infantry, scattered just below them on the hill, looked up in horror, empty-handed, openmouthed and bleating like forsaken sheep.

"Position downward fifteen degrees," the captain shouted. And George cried out again, mindless with hatred, "You heard, Aleko! Point her, in Jesus' name!"

They fired again, directly at the faces of the Turks. Somewhere on the ravaged slope between the line of cannons and the line of Turkish bayonets, a man was screaming in pain. George turned and lifted; turned and lowered; turned and lifted; and held his ears. The firing whistle blew again.

At last the Turks slipped backward, scurrying toward their hiding places over the Chepni ridge. Below the gun, a Greek rifleman was lying face down among the boulders, kicking like a naughty child. A priest came running down the hillside, carrying the presanctified elements of the Holy Eucharist in a pyx wrapped up in khaki cloth. When he saw the rifleman, the priest began to cross himself.

Some bearers clambered over the escarpment with a stretcher made of poles and blankets. As they passed, the covers fell open on a rigid, cyanotic face, marked with streaks of blackish blood that looked as if they had been wiped from someone's fingers.

"Shrapnel in the guts," said one of the bearers. "How the devil were we supposed to get to him?"

Captain Triandafilakos strode around the gun, pressing his fist against his hip.

"Good work, boys. You'll be decorated. . . . Second Passer?"

George was sitting among the stones. He raised his face indifferently.

"Up to Gentle Bouboulina," the captain said. "The Pointer took a stray bullet in the elbow."

George did not move. He scarcely heard. His hands and arms were isolated from his brain; his body from his legs; his feet, his tongue, his heart, his liver from each other. This internal separation, like a blizzard in a mountain province, permitted him to enjoy an interval of peaceful solitude, since no reports of supplication, protest or alarm moved through the snowbound passes of his soul. With a feeling of oblivion, he was evacuating in his trousers.

*F*or several weeks, neither Christos nor Sophia had stepped outside the Villa Trigonis. The blinds were drawn all day, and unopened mail accumulated in the foyer. Sophia's celebrated Thursday *soirées* were canceled.

Christos spent many hours trying to determine the proper course of behavior for both of them to follow; but he could find no clear precepts, even in the finely detailed calendar of Anatolian social life, which decreed an appropriate date for almost every human activity. It was customary, for example, to eat fish chowder at the seashore on Epiphany, to serve artichokes on Tulip Hill on the first Monday afternoon of Lent and to cool a watermelon in a fountain during the Festival of the Assumption, when the sultana grapes were being harvested. But when and how did one go about expiating a family scandal?

At last he decided that no juncture could be more opportune than the 25th of March, the centennial of the dramatic and passionate birth of modern Greece. This luminous date, which is simultaneously the anniversary of the nation and of Our Lord's Annunciation to the Virgin Mary, was an occasion of military, religious and political display throughout Asia Minor. Evzone guards in winter uniform paraded in the streets; the Holy Synod of the Church announced that sainthood had been accorded to the famous Patriarch Gregory V, whom the Turks had hanged on Easter morning in 1821 as a warning and punishment to rebellious Hellenes; and King Constantine chose a new Prime Minister—a languorous, Achaean lawyer named Dimitris Gounaris, who was *persona non grata* to both France and England.

Christos spent the early morning composing a long letter to his son, commenting on significant developments in the struggle with the Turks. He reassured George that the Gounaris appointment, prickly as it was, would not really alienate England because of the well-known philhellenism of Mr. Lloyd George; and, apropos of the diplomatic talks in London (which seemed to have collapsed), he pointed out that no one but the Turks could have been so stupid as to have thought you could gain anything in diplomatic conversations with the Greeks, the British and French.

"The Allies' purpose in inviting delegates from Ankara and Constantinople obviously was to persuade the Turks to accept the peace terms without further resistance. Of course, we Greeks can *force* the Turks to accept these terms, but the Powers of Europe apparently would like these military skirmishes to stop. . . ."

On the last page, in a visibly trembling hand, he told George about Eleni.

Then, over the objections of the cook, who suggested a year of fasting, seclusion and prayer, he took Sophia out for a public drive. Dressed in black, powdered and perfumed like a pair of Theban soldiers, they drove all the way from Smyrna to Bornova in a handsome new landau, open to the sky. Spring was coming on; the air was mild; and the earth smelled of mint and stagnant water.

Reaching the village before midday, they went to Mass, then circled past the Anglican and Roman chapels, nodding

stiffly to the Pattersons, the Whittalls, the Girauds, the
LaFontaines—all those innumerable, overlapping families of
Anglo-Levantine merchants who had lived so long in Bornova and whose approval was so important to one's position
in society. Afterward, their carriage clattered up and down
the avenue that runs between the station and the market
square, past neoclassic villas of conspicuous extravagence;
and Sophia turned her head from side to side as if she had
a muscle spasm.

On their last trip past the station, they saw Dimitris sitting
at a table in an open-air café; but, as soon as he noticed their
carriage, he turned away with an expression that Christos
assumed was resentment. Christos burned with shame. He
looked at Sophia, whose head was bowed.

"How wrong we were to accuse him!"

And Sophia, with moisture shining in her eyes, suggested
that they go to Dimitris at once, explain the reasons for their
error and ask him to be their son.

"You are perfect!" Christos cried, overwhelmed with admiration. "We'll stop and have a bite to eat with him. We'll
talk as friends."

But when they stopped, Dimitris sprang up and looked
around wildly.

"Don't come near me. I am an innocent man!" He began
to babble incoherently about recriminations, blackmail and
armed threats. Christos advanced through a blur of tears,
murmuring consolingly: "I know . . . I know." When Dimitris
saw at last that Christos was not antagonistic, he sank onto his
chair with a wavering sigh.

"I've been so upset. You can't imagine."

Christos ordered some mastika for their nerves. For several
minutes they did not speak. Then, to cheer the boy up, Christos read aloud a short translation he had made into literary
Greek of a scene from Shelley's "Hellas."

"The world's great age begins again
The golden years return;
The earth doth like a snake renew
Her winter weeds outworn.
Heaven smiles and faiths and empires gleam
Like wrecks of a dissolving dream."

"I had planned to read it today for a program of the Smyrna
Drama Club," Christos said with a feeble smile. "Now such
affairs have no interest for me."

He brought Sophia to the table, but she was too shy to
speak. Christos sat with his head down and his mind flooded
with painful memories. From time to time he would look at
the young lieutenant, smile pitifully and sigh. Finally, he said:
"You know, I always favored her."

"No one could have been more generous," Sophia said.

"I always gave her things to make up for her plainness,"
Christos said. "If only she could have been a little more
patient."

"I don't see whom she takes it from," Sophia cried out,
gulping tears. "Not from the Mavrogordato side. It isn't *my*
blood. My mother was a Koundouriotes."

"And she was not that plain," Christos went on. "Why,
with her property, one could have married off the Medusa."

All at once, he felt an urgent desire to show Dimitris everything the girl had thrown away. Getting into the carriage,
they drove along a lane that ran between walls of lava topped
with bits of broken glass, barbed wire and railway spikes.
Sophia, looking around, gave a low moan; but Christos patted
her hand. At the end of the lane, they stopped outside a
handsome little house that had been rented in recent years
to some Turks from Macedonia.

It was all that a Bornova establishment ought to be, with
its overflowing cistern, its glassed-in porch, its lemon trees
and Basra palms. There were round beds of scarlet sage, like

velvet pillows scattered on the gravel drive; a black-and-white mosaic under the porte-cochere; and, on an artificial knoll, a white gazebo, as pretty as a sugar pastry for a pasha's picnic.

"A dowry house?" Dimitris said. "I thought she had none."

"Oh, I would have given it to her eventually," Christos said. "I would have given her everything, if only she had kept herself morally pure."

It touched his heart to see how downcast Dimitris looked. After all, the boy had loved her, too!

They went back to Smyrna together. No one spoke again about Eleni, but a sense of common understanding linked their hearts, and from time to time they glanced at one another fondly. Eleni had drawn them together, like members of a persecuted cult. The disparity of their ages, interests and experience was nothing to the unanimity of their resentment toward that wanton girl who had disgraced them all.

Christos looked on the young lieutenant with particular concern. Great as was his own sorrow, he knew that it could not be compared to the agony of Dimitris, whose whole life was ruined. What greater insult could a man suffer than to have his fiancée desert him for a Turk? Christos determined he must do more to help Dimitris, to atone for the false accusation, the disappointment and the dishonor.

With his considerable influence in the High Commissioner's office, Christos soon was able to have Lieutenant Kalapothakis appointed liaison officer to a group of civilians who were investigating some alleged atrocities in the occupation zone. Earlier, Christos had thought of asking the assignment for his son; but fortunately, George possessed sufficient nervous stamina to endure the obloquy that weighed so unbearably on poor Dimitris. George would look out for himself.

THE MARMARA
APRIL, 1921

*W*hen the weather turned warm, the Greek government began an educational and administrative program to reduce the number of Turkish Moslems living in the occupied zone of Asia Minor. Naturally, an undertaking of this sort involved certain inconveniences to the civilian population; and these discomforts resulted in complaints to the International Red Cross that the Greeks were committing atrocities. On the very day that Dimitris arrived in Gemlik, on the Sea of Marmara, to investigate these fantastic rumors, a deputation of Turkish villagers had unburdened themselves of ten hours of defamatory testimony before a committee of Belgians, Switzers, Poles and other Europeans of luminous national virtue; and the Greek officers of the district were in a panic.

The commander of the civil government section—an absurdly immature, stammering, potbellied major with the Germanic manners of a Royalist—admitted Dimitris to his inner office after less than an hour's delay. For all the major was a pompous bird, he knew enough to recognize and welcome intelligent assistance. He even offered Dimitris a cigarette.

"It's of the ut-ut-utmost importance," he said, "to ga-ga-gather independent evidence to refute these revolting charges." The nervous blinking of his eyes indicated that an officer's career could wax or wane on the results of the investigation. Dimitris assured him they would obtain irrefutable documentation; and next morning, in high enthusiasm, he went cut to consummate this patriotic duty. He had seldom seen a better opportunity for advancement—or a finer day.

Almonds were in blossom, young olive trees were shimmering like puffs of smoke among the hills and the sea stretched out as pale and mottled as a sheet of marble at the margin of the plain. The villages along the coast looked innocent and peaceful in the silver light.

But Dimitris had learned in Macedonia that the village with the whitest minaret, the neatest row of poplars and the clearest fountain always harbored the meanest, most intransigent inhabitants; and he transmitted this point of wisdom to the noncommissioned officers of his patrol as they breakfasted on bread and olives in an orchard dappled by the early sun. The infantrymen carried their rifles cocked and ready as the column slowly climbed the soggy hillsides; and the artillery pieces, carried on muleback at the rear, were ready to be assembled in five minutes. From time to time, Dimitris stopped the procession on the outskirts of some unmistakably Christian village to gather information. Everywhere people were talking about Thoma, Christos, Michaelis and their gangs, who had been making certain impositions on the district. Dimitris was pleased to learn that the impositions had been visited primarily on Moslems, although he concluded that this information would not be relevant to his report.

High on the ridge, they passed through a woodland of umbrella pines. Foresters had trimmed the lower branches as firewood, goats had chewed the underbrush and country wives had carted off the needles, leaving the woods as tidy as a park; and in this protected eminence, Dimitris ordered the artillery squad to assemble the guns.

He had noticed that on the other side the land sloped down to a village of about two dozen houses, whitewashed, roofed with red tiles, sweet as a cherry pudding. Smack in the middle, there was a single minaret, decorated like a barber's pole with stripes of red and white. Not a soul was moving in the village or the fields around it—no smoke, no barking dogs, no crying children. Dimitris smelled a Turkish plot. The pimps unquestionably were lying in their cellars, rifles loaded, waiting to ambush and murder this unsuspecting, fact-finding patrol. At the very thought of such duplicity, Dimitris' lips tightened in anger; and, for the safety of his men, he ordered a light bombardment.

"Start with the minaret. They'll understand the message."

He glanced at his watch. It was almost five o'clock: the Moslems would be gathering for sunset prayer. An appropriate time to play a trick on them.

The first shell went up and whistled into an orchard just below the town. The second brought up a geyser of plaster from the minaret. While the men were loading the third shell, an old man came out of the village, dressed in woebegone calico and carrying a wisp of white cloth on a crooked stick. As he approached the forest, stumbling over boulders and stopping to catch his breath, Dimitris saw that he had roses stuck into the creases of his turban. His mouth was stained green from chewing grass.

"Ask him the name of the village," Dimitris said.

The translator, prancing up and down in an access of self-importance, shouted manfully: *"Köyünün adi nedir?"*

But the old villager, grinning stupidly, answered: "My village." He appeared to have something wrong with the roof of his mouth.

"Tell him to go warn them," Dimitris interrupted. "Tell them we'll knock down every house unless they send out ten men with all the rifles and cartridges in the place."

Smiling idiotically, the old man listened to the ultimatum.

In Turkish, it sounded unbearably calamitous. His mouth hung open, oozing greenish spittle.

"My honored sirs," he said, "they will not come. The village belongs to Black Petros now."

"Who's this Black Petros?" Dimitris said. "Tell him to come out and talk with me."

"Black Petros is a lion, my honored sirs," the old man said, the emerald saliva trickling down his chin. "He was born with all his teeth, and when the midwife came to draw him out, he bit the cord himself."

"Let him come out!" cried Dimitris, squaring his jaw. But the old man grinned and said: "He will not come, honored sirs."

Dimitris fired the battery again. Immediately afterward, a nauseating stench drifted from the village. The translator stared at the old man and muttered something indistinct; then he turned back to Dimitris and said: "I think he's the only one left, sir."

Turning his back, Dimitris allowed the bombardment to continue. The stench grew intolerable; the men tied handkerchiefs across their faces. Close to sundown, he halted the barrage and ordered the infantry to charge in squads of four, widely deployed, as if they were storming the Dardanelles.

"Fire if you see them armed," Dimitris called after them. "We'll bombard the mosque." And the old man waved his banner and saluted as the men scampered through the orchards. Their lengthening shadows bounded backward across the reddish clods.

When the infantry sergeant signaled that the village was empty, Dimitris and his translator moved forward, discreetly marching the old man in front of them as a hostage. The single street of the village was wide enough to pass a broad wagon. It was paved with lumps of stone, and on either side were substantial houses built of mud and stones and washed with white lime. Shafts of light were slanting between the houses, through motes of dust and chicken feathers raised by the artillery. Halfway down the street, Dimitris spotted a furtive figure by the pond. Flattening himself against a wall, he fired with his revolver; but it turned out to be a piece of cloth that had been spread across a bush to dry.

At the end of the street was a building with the star and crescent painted above the door. A cloud of flies was listlessly revolving in the open doorway, and the yard was littered with mattresses and filthy bedding. Dimitris motioned the translator and the old man inside.

Through the doorway, he could see that a bookcase had been overturned in the waiting room. Village registers were spilled across the floor. There were some manuals of Ottoman procedure, some volumes of statistics and a Civil Code in French. Dimitris went inside far enough to touch the covers with his boot. Some of the pages were stained with rusty liquid. From down the street, he heard some of his men calling in excitement. They had found the bodies of several women, kneeling in a stable, with their pants pulled down around their ankles and their nipples cut off.

The translator called to him in a peculiar voice. But Dimitris went down the hall, revolver in hand, and broke out the parchment windowpanes of the director's office. There were some letters on the desk. One carried a postal cancellation from Constantinople several years before the Great War. Another, written in French, began: "My Dearest Son: Your father is much improved . . ."

The translator called again: "Up here, Lieutenant."

In the upstairs hall, the body of a man was lying face up on a table. He was sinewy and swarthy, like an Arab, and his arms and legs were spread apart. His hands and feet had been nailed to the corners of the table, and his sexual parts had been cut off and put into his mouth. There was dried blood caked in the bristles of his mustache and inside his nostrils. Dimitris heard a choking sound and turned around. The translator stood behind him, quivering.

"There's another in the next room," he said.

Dimitris smiled and handed the man a box of matches.

"That's your opportunity to perform a double service for your country. Bring up some of those books and papers and pile them underneath."

But when they set the pyre aflame, the corpse began to twitch and writhe. The eyelids popped open. Fluid poured from every orifice and sizzled into steam. The belly swelled; the jowls shook; and the contents spewed out of the mouth.

The translator screamed and toppled on the floor. Dimitris had to call two riflemen to carry him. Between this diversion and the problem of igniting the mosque, it took two hours to fire the village. Everyone was tired and hungry by the time the column reassembled in the pine woods.

Then, after a long march back, with only a few hours' rest by the sea and no breakfast to speak of, they were met with an astounding display of ingratitude. The stammering major was as red as a freshly butchered beef, windmilling his hands and howling like a Senussi monk, all because a Red Cross team had gone to a village in the hills that morning and taken eyewitness testimony that a Greek army patrol had destroyed the evidence of a massacre.

"Your stu-stu-stupidity," the major bellowed, "has exactly doubled our difficulties. You ought to be busted to corporal."

"It must have been another unit," Dimitris said. "My men can assure you we didn't go near that sector."

But the major was as close-minded, as vindictive, as any Royalist: a new demonstration that one could never trust the King's Men.

"I can assure you," he said, "your fr-fr-friend Mr. Trigonis won't have any influence where I'm going to send you."

*T*he persecutions in Alashehir coincided with the
month of Ramazan, when the Turks were weakened by the
fast that lasts each day from dawn to sunset. Requisition
squads came past the Chakirjali farm and helped themselves
to jugs of filtered olive oil, bits of scrap metal and bags of
kidney beans. The threat of arrest hung over every Turk who
dared to voice a protest; and there were rumors that some
Moslem peasants in the vicinity of Sarigöl had been kidnaped
and put to work in a slave battalion at the Front.

Now and then, Abdullah risked a trip to town to buy rock
salt, spices, sugar, kerosene and newspapers. Usually, he kept
to Moslem neighborhoods, muffling his face and avoiding
conversation. But on the last Friday of the fast, he neglected
caution, opened his mouth and came back to the farm with
a three-inch gash across his right cheekbone.

Pushing open the kitchen door, he found his uncle
hunched at a table with a cigarette behind his ear, a glass of
water ready at his hand and a basket of bread in front of him,
waiting for the signal to break the fast.

"Gulnar?" Abdullah called. "Yildiz? Go help my wife with
the ox."

No one moved. At last they heard the dim percussion of the
sunset cannon from Top Tepe. Mahmut Zia drained his tumbler, Yildiz brought a glowing stick to light her uncle's ciga-

299

rette and the women, with trembling hands, lifted the napkins that covered the salads, the yogurt and the platters of cold cooked vegetables.

Abdullah accepted a glass of water from his mother. She stared at his face.

"What happened?"

But Abdullah tossed his head and went out to wash at the well. His mother followed him into the yard, calling after him.

"I told you there would be trouble. You don't understand the bitterness people have. You don't know what they've been through." She glared at Eleni, who was still sitting in the oxcart, wrapped in black from head to food, with her small head cloaked, her shoulders draped and her breasts concealed in folds of thick alpaca.

Abdullah bent to the water. Its coolness tightened the cuts in his scalp and pounded into his aching teeth. Filling his mouth, he let the liquid trickle slowly down his throat. Then he worked at the side of his face until the roughness of dried blood had been eased away. The lacerated cheekbone throbbed with a cold arc of fire.

His mother raged at his back, shouting that he had brought the wrath of the authorities upon them: it was the end of everything. Couldn't he have thought, just once, about the safety of his family? All over the zone, the Greeks were arresting and deporting Ottoman officials—judges, muftis, kaimakams deported to a prison island in the Archipelago: twenty-one from Ushak, thirty-two from Nazilli, twenty-five from Salihli, eighty from the Meander Valley. Hadn't he considered the danger to his uncle?

"Nobody asks to be beaten up," Abdullah said.

"But you took her with you! Why did you disobey me?"

"Even Moslem women go out," Abdullah said. "She is not accustomed to this confinement." He thought of adding: "I

300

took her because all of you are slowly killing her." But his mother went on:

"Now you've antagonized the Greeks as well as your own people."

"Probably."

He tried to smile, to mollify her, because she was his mother, she was old and she had suffered; but his face was stiff and swollen. His ribs hurt, his knee was stiffening and he was perishing of hunger. All he could do was to touch his forehead gently to her wrist.

"Believe me, Mama—it had nothing to do with Eleni."

"Where did you go? Straight past the Orthodox church? Or did you stop at the Friday mosque?"

"Mama, let me eat," Abdullah said.

For the first time since his circumcision at age twelve, he was keeping Ramazan by the most stringent rule. He had forsworn even to rinse his mouth with water during the daylight hours; and he spat out his saliva so that nothing would pass his throat.

This outburst of self-abnegation was not motivated by religion: Abdullah remained essentially as skeptical as ever. Nor did it derive from the influence of his uncle, who imposed a stern Islamic puritanism on the women of the family. Rather, it resulted from the failure of Abdullah's secular ideals, the collapse of his revolutionary dogmas and the humiliation of his marriage, all of which had left him with a confused need of positive accomplishment. For the sake of his self-respect, he had to complete some form of personal ordeal, even if it was only the discomfort of a fast.

Thus, although he was contemptuous of his uncle's piety, Abdullah exactly imitated Mahmut Zia's religiosity. The two of them sat together, nose to nose in the brotherhood of Islam, wolfing their supper while the women waited and Abdullah's mother carried on her unremitting monologue.

301

In her consuming love of property, her joy in commerce and her appetite for profit, his mother was more like a Christian than a Moslem; but her resentment of the Greeks had become a passion. The arrival of an unhappy, alien daughter-in-law in her crowded household had done nothing to sweeten her temper. Her indignation settled on her son.

"I should have thought you'd have more sense. A man with so much education . . ."

Abdullah tore apart a piece of bread and stuffed it into his mouth; but he could not swallow. His mother was right: it was his intellectuality that had betrayed him. He had been trying to find a rational cure for a disastrous marriage, and his efforts had put the entire family in danger.

He had begun with the supposition that Eleni needed friends—some women of her own religion, better educated than his sisters or his poor, stunted grandmother. He had gone first to see a Greek exporter named Phessopoulos, who was said to have some daughters schooled in French. Phessopoulos, however, had left for Switzerland after the defeat of Venizelos. His house, like Laurel Konak, had become an army barracks; and Abdullah's visit only resulted in his being questioned for an hour or so by the commanding officer.

Next he had called on Abdurrahman Bey, a kingly old Turk, whose countless female relatives had been educated by a German governess. But it developed that Abdurrahman's son had been killed by the Greeks at Lüleburgaz. Abdullah left the house without mentioning the reason for his call.

Finally, he had gone to see a blacksmith, a man of vulgar tastes, whose only distinction was that he came from Crete, where most of the Turks spoke Greek more fluently than Turkish. The smith, however, was a bachelor.

Somehow these researches had been reported to his mother. She accused him of abandoning his family. If Eleni needed companionship, what was wrong with Gulnar? With

Aunt Emine? With herself? Did he want to infuriate the Greeks by parading his partridge around the town? Even if she were veiled, she would be noticed: Greek women had that peculiar way of walking. And her accent! Had he thought of that?

He had thought of that, and much else; but Eleni's loneliness had weighed on his heart, so that he had taken her to Alashehir that morning. He had helped her to fix her veil, had reminded her to keep her mouth shut and had taken her directly to the grocer's shop, where she could hear her own language spoken and could see and smell the familiar commercial products of the city.

Eleni had hesitated at the doorway, breathing in the scent of soap and kippered fish. Blocks of halvah, slabs of garlic beef and lumps of white cheese in jars of water stood beside the weighing pans. She moved from one product to another, reading labels, touching bluish bottles of denatured alcohol, bending to smell the bins of chick-peas and the strings of yellow onions. Her delight was a reproach to him; and her conduct was flawless until the grocer, who had been whacking slices off the garlic beef, leaned forward and held out a morsel on the point of his knife.

"No, no! Take that away," Abdullah said: even to smell of it was torture.

But Eleni put out her hand; and the grocer, with a conspiratorial and fawning smile, went on: "A piece for you, *hanum efendi?*"

Eleni took the *pasturma* without a word.

"Don't be afraid," the grocer said. "Why should I tell somebody? Can't I keep a secret?"

Then Abdullah, swelling up with that irrepressible urge to instruct and ameliorate the world, had explained proudly:

"My wife and I believe in a society where people of various religions will live as harmoniously as ourselves."

The grocer had stared at Eleni, and his smile hardened.

"Not everyone is so liberal," he said.

At the edge of town, five men with chips of flint in their hands had jumped onto the wagon. Shoving Eleni to one side, they pulled Abdullah backward into the wagon box. They were cutting the drawstring of his trousers when an army police patrol came down the street.

Knowing that he had been a fool made Abdullah helpless against his mother's anger.

"I won't take her again," he promised; and to escape the lecture, he went to bed.

Deep in the night, a drummer passed along the road to wake the countryfolk for their last meal before daybreak.

"O Moslems—rise! Prepare yourselves. Tomorrow you shall fast again. . . ."

Abdullah, who had not been asleep, lay in his corner and listened to Eleni's breathing. It was the most tedious hour of night, the time when doubts rise up in overwhelming strength and insuperable numbers; and Abdullah saw himself, with all his high ideals, his ideologies and his utopias, as a nonentity whose life was as insignificant as a grain of sand dropping between the fingers of God, falling unnoticed into the emptiness of the universal night.

He got up, barefooted and shivering in the white cotton drawers that he wore as underpants, and went to the back door. The drummer had stopped at the gate. In the dark of the waning moon, Abdullah could see only the whiteness of a uniform and a helmet, one of those odd Ottoman adaptations of the German *Pickelhaube* called an enveriyeh.

"Wake up, O Moslems! Honor your faith! Remember God in order that He shall remember you in these days of suffering. . . ."

Suffering, indeed: and to what end? Greek and Turk wrought this suffering on one another, and it neither gained nor taught them anything. Yet those dreamers like himself who tried to turn this meaningless torment into a revolution failed worst of all, because they were unable to transform their thoughts to passions and their ideologies into love. If one could not make sense of his own life, how could he lead an army?

The drummer, trudging on toward the hot springs, shouted back: "When you feel the pangs of hunger, think about your sons, your brothers, fathers, husbands, who are fighting to defend the sacred soil of the Fatherland. . . ."

"Sacred soil!" Abdullah repeated, spitting on the ground. The ancient shibboleths endured while the new inspirations withered and died in this desert of traditions, bigotry and inertia. If only these warring nations could open up their souls, as the fanatic dervishes do, welcoming the wounds of God and saying: "Let there be love!"

Abdullah turned back and saw that Eleni was awake.

"It was my fault," she said. "How can you forgive me?"

Abdullah went and sat down next to her.

"What shall I forgive you of first? For causing the sun to come up in the east? For causing you to be a Greek and me to be a Turk? For starting the war?"

Eleni touched his swollen cheekbone with her fingertips.

"I never thought I could marry a Turk," she said.

"That is because Turks are so cruel and barbaric."

Eleni stared back at him without smiling.

"I suppose I thought God would strike me dead."

"Who knows?" Abdullah said. "He may do it yet."

He took her hand and held it against his throat, just under the curve of his jaw, to feel the pulse of her heartbeat echoing in his blood; and, for the first time since he had discovered her deception, he lay down with her.

305

BURSA
AUGUST, 1921

*I*n early July, the army of King Constantine began the campaign that was to end the war in Asia Minor. The Smyrna Division moved south from Bursa in a diversionary maneuver, while the principal attack swept north from Ushak. Two divisions closed in on the railroad junction at Inönü, which fell without a shot.

The King himself came out from Athens to take command. Royal pamphleteers piled epithets like laurel wreaths upon his head. He was Konstantinos Bulgaroctonos—"Constantine the Bulgar-Killer"—in the ancient manner of the Byzantines; "The Enmarbled King"; "The Commander-in-Chief of the Anglo-Greek Forces in the Near East"; "The Son of the Eagle"; and "The Emperor-Designate of Constantinople."

"I am departing Greece," he wrote in his announcement to the people, "to place myself at the head of my army. There, where Hellenism has battled for centuries, victory, with the help of the Almighty, will crown the combats of our race, which is advancing irresistibly to meet its destiny. . . ."

The Allies publicly declared their neutrality.

From the beginning, the campaign was a brilliant success. By the time George's battery reached Kütahya, the town was surrounded by masses of Greek artillery. The Greeks marched in as briskly as palace guards parading through the streets of Athens. Within two weeks, they were frolicking into Eskishehir, the largest city in Turkish territory. The Kemalist army had been almost annihilated by casualties and desertions. Out of 90,000 Turks who had defended the tracks at Inönü in March, only about 20,000 still clung together. A reconnaissance plane that followed the retreating column reported that the few remaining battalions of Mustapha Kemal's "National Defense" were engaged in digging zigzag trenches on the banks of the Sakarya River, virtually at the western gates of Ankara.

On the last day of July, King Constantine reviewed his army in a thistle patch just east of Eskishehir. Two priests, whose black cassocks were smudged with the inevitable dust of Anatolia, said the Office of the Dead at a field altar. The wind was lifting the edges of the altar cloth and fluttering the pages of the Holy Bible. On either side, the regimental standards, soiled and bullet-torn, dipped and trembled. Six men fainted, standing at attention; but the crew of Gentle Bouboulina, field artillery, 10th Division, stood "with great fortitude" (George wrote his mother), because Private Trigonis was among the heroes to be decorated to commemorate the victory.

The King drove onto the field in a dusty phaeton that bounced among the furrows with springs groaning and toolboxes bursting open on the running boards. He was accompanied by his son Crown Prince George; his Chief of Staff, General Dousmanis; and his brother Prince Andrew, who was reputed (George wrote) to be a strategist of dazzling prognostic wisdom.

George stared with insatiable curiosity at this incomprehensible Nordic king, who had returned from exile with an unimpaired eagerness to rule as well as reign. From the instant he regained his throne, Constantine had interceded minutely in the disposition of companies in battle, the positioning of batteries, the order of promotions. Signing his proclamations with a sweeping Beta, in the fashion of the Byzantine emperors, he summoned reviews, issued citations and delivered eulogies. He toured the Front in an open car, despite the warnings of his staff that he would surely be assassinated by the Venizelists. Out in the burning sunshine, in the choking dust, Constantine stood erect, inflamed with sunburn and excitement, coughing incessantly against his fist as the troops marched past. He was, after all, the King of Greece, First Constantine of the House of Schleswig-Holstein-Sönderborg-Glücksburg, and he would become, God willing, the twelfth Constantine to rule the Empire of Byzantium. In his dedication to the principle of temporal glory, Constantine personified a certain ideal of superhuman heroism that appeared extremely ambiguous to a young man who was stepping smartly forward to be decorated with a piece of cloth and metal for his conspicuous bravery at a moment when he had, in fact, been incontinent with terror.

As a further reward for his heroic service, George was promoted to corporal, put in command of Gentle Bouboulina and dispatched to the coast with Aleko Papakostas to bring back seven breechblocks, three gun barrels, twenty hams and a cask of oil.

A journey to the rear generally was considered the equivalent of a trip to Paradise. Aleko, however, regarded it as an imposition. He feigned a stomach ache. Then he pleaded overwork. Finally, he staged a sort of tantrum in Captain Triandafilakos' tent, shouting that he was being persecuted just because he was an Anatolian. Nothing availed, and Aleko was dispatched with George to Paradise. They left at dawn in a boxcar under the surveillance of a sour old sergeant major named Pileides, who spoke an atrocious Pontic dialect and smelled of raki.

As the car ground slowly through the railway yards, through rows of gutted locomotive sheds built in the heyday of the Berlin-Baghdad Bahn, Aleko held his head between his hands.

"This is a terrible mistake," he said. "I warned them."

The train was jerking nervously, with a crash of metal catches and a creak of wooden frames. George gazed out in loathing at this jumbled earth-brown city, the fraudulent grand prize of their painful march against the Turks. The Porsuk River, narrow as a ditch and thick as clabber, slithered below the trestle, hissing malevolently. It was said to be inhabited by stinging eels and fishes ten feet long, stone-blind and poisonous to eat. On the very day the Greeks had occupied the town (which henceforth would bear its ancient name, Dorylaeum), an evzone corporal, ignoring orders, had gone swimming in the river and was drowned. When others pulled him out and pumped his chest, they noticed that the milky Porsuk waters had not even washed away the crab lice from his groin.

But as soon as the train had left the city, George felt a lightness growing in his chest. The dried-up pastures were the color of dark chocolate that has melted and turned hard again; the sky was like a sheet of polished bronze; and the wheels were saying, "Bursa tonight, Bursa tonight, Bursa tonight..." Pulling out a bottle of raki, Sergeant Major Pileides offered everyone a drink; and George accepted. Aleko slept.

At Karaköy, in the canyon on the other side of Inönü, a line of mules and trucks and oxcarts was waiting by the tracks. Some Turkish prisoners with sweatbands around their heads were lifting ammunition boxes that had come by boat from Smyrna to Mudanya, on the Sea of Marmara; then by narrow-gauge railroad to Bursa; by caravan to Inegöl; by truck up the switchbacks of the Ahi Dagh and down to meet the railway again at Karaköy.

Contemplating this intricate logistic chain, George felt a heavy pressure returning to his heart. Hour after hour, riding down to Bursa in a wheezing, square-wheeled lorry, he watched the endless column coming up, bringing rifle bullets and machine-gun clips, spools of wire and flasks of iodine. Overheated trucks erupted on the road and stood there, steaming, dripping rusty water. Axles bent and bearings melted. Camels puked. Mules collapsed. A thousand oxcarts waited while a peasant flogged a buffalo that would not move.

Finally, George looked over at the sergeant major and said: "Does it mean we're building up for another offensive?"

"Just as sure as I see you and you see me," Sergeant Major Pileides said. "His Majesty came out, took a look at all this desert and said, 'Boys, I want it. Let's go to Ankara.'"

George tried to smile.

"It's pretty far to Ankara."

"It'll bust your ass off," said the sergeant major. "And you know what you'll see? Nothing. Hills that look like ash heaps. Villages that look like rabbit warrens. Salt wells. Brine pools. Lakes of alkali. Your ass will drop right off your back."

Aleko was staring at the sergeant major with a look of anguish. To protect their faces from the dust, they all had made masks of their handkerchiefs and soaked them in water from a can that smelled of gasoline; but Aleko's mask had fallen off while he was asleep, and his lips were crusted with a brownish slime.

"What makes you think the King decided?" Aleko said.

"Did I ever say he *decided?* People are hanging pictures of him in the windows of Constantinople. They are saying, 'He is coming. He's going to be the Emperor of Byzantium.' So he will march to Ankara. He didn't decide. It was *written.*"

And he pulled out of his pocket a clipping from one of those subversive magazines published in Constantinople by Venizelist officers in exile; and he read aloud:

"'Will the King extend the war? The answer is obvious. Constantine suffers from a self-destructive mania. He is like

310

Napoleon advancing into Russia. Each victory takes him deeper into Turkish territory. While the enemy withdraws, shortening his supply lines, Constantine extends himself. The Front grows thinner, harder to defend. The supply lines grow longer. The costs grow heavier every day.

" 'Why, then, does Constantine not turn back? Because he believes it is impossible to do so without jeopardizing his throne. He thinks that turning back would be interpreted as a defeat—and how can an egomaniac endure defeat? He is restless, ambitious, stubborn, undisciplined, insatiable for glory.

" 'So Constantine will go forward to his destruction, to the destruction of us all.' "

Pileides folded up the clipping, made a face and offered the raki bottle. Clearing his throat, George said: "When are we going?"

"Did you ever hear me say *I'm* going?" the sergeant major said. *"I'm* going down to Bursa, boys. I'm going to rent a double bedroom in the best hotel in town, take off my boots and pour myself a glass of raki. I'm going to drink until I'm drunk, and then I'm going to pay a little visit to the noncom's Arsy Palace. After that—well, maybe I'll decide I'd like to throw a second one. Who knows? And, after that, I'll walk around until I find a little place I know, a little charcoal broiler, and I'll have a double helping of döner kebab. Lots of fat and lots of garlic. And I'll eat it slowly, slowly, like a pasha, breaking up my bread and pouring lemon soda. Now, then! I'm satisfied. My toothpick in my mouth. My mustache full of grease. I tip my little hat and stroll around and smell the gardens in the moonlight. Slowly, slowly, like a pasha. Past the Turkish tombs and underneath the arches. Later on, I pay another visit to the Arse House, drink another glass of raki, eat another serving of döner, drink another glass. Until I'm absolutely jaded, like a boiled potato. Then, *kismet!* I have an awful accident. I break my thumb. Maybe I also sprain my ankle. Detached service."

George drew in his breath. The rest of the way to Bursa, no one said a word.

George and Aleko spent four days and five nights in Mudanya, waiting for their requisitions to be filled. There was not a bedroom or a bed for rent; so they slept outside on quilts beside the water, in the fashion of the humble countryfolk who camp along the Quay at Smyrna in the summer when the figs are coming in. It was a noisy dormitory, but carefree and restorative. The discipline, the hierarchies and the arbitrary courtesies of army life were cheerfully ignored. Sailors, porters, cavalry officers and commercial agents stretched out, side by side, around the harbor cornice. A concertina played all night outside the wineshop. Soldiers wandered up and down the railway ties, and a never-ending line of men stood at the doorway of the House of Liaison.

Each morning, George would call on the sergeants of supply, who were the satraps of Mudanya. Sensitive and proud, corrupt, incompetent, forever absent from their posts but always momentarily expected, the 4th Bureau noncoms ruled over a wilderness of hardware strewn along the narrow tracks: drums of wire and sacks of barley, cordwood, canvas, saddle wax and cartridges piled up together, rotting in the sunshine, while the sergeants took their time.

In the immemorial custom of the army, everybody waited while the sergeants waited. Dulcet days and raucous nights slipped past. George and Aleko gorged themselves on cantaloupes and mackerel, strolled along the jetty, wallowed in the sea. When the requisitions were finally honored, George looked at the bill of lading with a feeling of shock.

He had just come back from bathing at a beach they called the Little Boz Burun, a spit of grayish sand that jutted toward the open sea. His hair was stiff with salt; his blistered skin was peeling from his nose. He had been eating melon in the sun, and he could taste its watery sweetness in his breath. Glancing at Aleko, who was chestnut brown and caked with brine, George saw a startled, disbelieving smile. How short a time it had taken them to lose connection with reality!

"The crates are on tonight," a sergeant of supply was saying. "Transship at Bursa via motor transport . . . Then, of course," with a suffocated yawn, "the train at Karaköy, up to your outfit."

"Overnight at Bursa," George said dreamily. "Döner kebab . . . The Arsy Palace . . ." The sergeant, to his delight, looked annoyed.

They took the short line back to Bursa and hired two beds for the night at the best hotel they could find. It was a room for six: the other beds were rented by some dark Armenians from Tarsus, who were sitting in the passage in their underwear, arguing about raw-silk prices while dealing out bezique.

George suggested they begin with some raki. Aleko picked at roasted hazelnuts and salted roe of Missolonghi. Then they walked through the streets until they found the noncommissioned *kolohani*. But at this crucial point, Aleko recalled his age, his farm, his wife, his children and the dangers of venereal disease; and George, too, suffered a diminishment of lust.

So they searched out a small rotisserie and ordered double portions of döner kebab, which they ate as slowly as they could, like pashas, savoring the meat, the fat, the garlic and the spice, as if to satisfy all hungers, past and future, with a single meal. Afterward, they ordered fruit and baklava and sent the counter boy to get some lemon soda. Then, putting their toothpicks in their mouths, they clasped their hands behind their backs and sauntered through the fragrant, shadowy streets of the old Osmanli capital. Summer dust lay sadly on the wilted leaves; the air was sweet with the scent of ripe

313

peaches; and swallows darted to and fro among the minarets.

They passed the citadel, the turqoise tomb of Sultan Mehmet Jelebi and the Emerald Mosque; then they walked out beyond Emin Sultan, which overlooks the misty valley, soft and bluish in the moonlight, and sat and smoked and picked their teeth under the shadows of a cypress tree.

Although they agreed it was too hot a night to eat döner kebab, George allowed that Bursa served the best döner kebab in Anatolia. Aleko bobbed his head morosely.

"Somehow, though, a big feed never makes up for the meals you've missed," he said. "It's like trying to store up for the future. You just can't do it." His voice was heavy. Reading his thoughts, George touched him on the arm.

"Some Greeks are Cassandras, Aleko. Always seeing black in front of them."

"I know," Aleko said.

"That sergeant major was the worst I've ever seen. What a peddler of catastrophes!"

"I know."

"And what he was planning to do—to maim himself!"

Aleko sighed, staring down at the toothpick in his hand.

"I don't know which is worse—to be a coward or a fool. Only a fool would go out and try to catch himself a bullet. But here we are, peaceful and safe, and tomorrow, of our own free will, we'll go back to all that misery."

George did not answer. He wondered whether Aleko suspected the shameful fantasies that filled his mind. How incredibly easy it would be simply to turn away from it all, to *not* go back tomorrow, to opt instead for fish and melon and swimming at the Little Boz Burun. But how could you live thereafter? Where could you raise your head, cut off from Fatherland and father, ostracized from the community of Greeks? And to George, who was unable to conceive of a community outside the limits of his church, his language and

314

his nationality, the rational course appeared to be impossible; the irrational inevitable.

He lay awake most of the night, tempting himself and testing his disheartened spirit, while Aleko and the four Armenians rumbled with uncomplicated sleep.

In the morning, however, Aleko was gone. The night clerk had not seen him leave. The Armenians were still asleep. George went back alone.

At Karaköy, the transfer point, he saw Sergeant Major Pileides, who had broken neither his thumb nor his ankle but was seeing demons.

"A week of ecstasy," he declared, through gray and trembling lips. "Got drunk. Got sober. Rode one. Rode another. Then got drunk again. . . ." His face was twisted, and his reddened eyes were damp with tears. "Oh Jesus, it's a shame! So brief! Some raki and some rides. A plate of greasy meat. And then you're going back again. . . ."

As the sergeant major said, it did not matter what one decided, but what was written.

*T*hen the Hellenes began their march to Ankara, which was to be their final march as surely as God was with the Christian Greeks. The route was eastward through the valley of the Porsuk, a windy wasteland overgrown with spiky plants. Beyond the valley lay the Turkish lines, in hills as sterile as the ash of bones: salt wells, brine pools and lakes of alkali.

At dawn the 10th Division broke its bivouac at Alpi-köy and formed along the railway tracks. The cavalry led out, the horses frisking up the dust in lazy streamers. Half a mile behind: the engineers, with truckloads of pontoons, dynamite and wooden poles for the field telegraph. Next went the creaking water wagons, pulled by buffalo; the Skodas and the smaller field guns; the mountain guns on mules and camels; and finally the infantry, with pup tents, mess kits, kitchen wagons, cartridges.

Ten thousand men made up the 10th Division, and there were seven more divisions of equal size proceeding eastward out of Eskishehir. They raised a boiling cloud of dust that waved across the sky of Asia like the plume of Alexander's army. Some colonels of the General Staff, watching through binoculars from a meerschaum quarry on a hill behind the city, held their breath in wonder.

Within the line, the vast historical perspective was obscured. George could see before his face the lofty, palpitating anus of a dromedary, whose seasick rider angled sideways now and then and vomited. Behind him, the sleepy Asiatic face of Goufas, the patrician face of Loukas and the sweating face of Sakellariadis floated in the amber mist.

No more Aleko, simple as the sun. The captain, snorting angrily, had asked some questions and recorded George's answers in a book: end of the subject. Desertion was a common crime, repulsive but devoid of passion. Like a disease, it was uninteresting to almost everyone except the victim, and frequently contagious—something to avoid, not to discuss.

The march to Ankara should now absorb the minds of all loyal Greeks. What a surprise, to be devouring Anatolia as calmly as a snake digests a frog! Many of the men were singing as the column started out. Sakellariadis shouted, "On to Ankara!" The dust went up their nostrils, and they shut up suddenly; but their remarkable euphoria continued, swelling like a lemon in the gullet, until suddenly a voice would rise and they would start to sing again.

George was perhaps the only member of his battery whose mood was pessimistic, and he had the fewest grounds for complaint. Hadn't he just enjoyed a week of cantaloupe and döner kebab? He did not dare to voice his doubts. But with every mile they marched through heat and dust, he reckoned the distance back to Eskishehir, to Bursa, to Smyrna, and wondered why he had botched his opportunity to withdraw from this idiotic campaign. By now, Aleko would be returning to his children and his chickens in the bottom land of the Meander.

At sundown, everyone fought for bathing places on the Porsuk River, drowner of evzones and spawner of sheatfish, a lukewarm, polluted stream that purled along some dusty clumps of pampas grass. George teetered for a moment, fully dressed, on the embankment and then fell forward with a

317

magnificent, milky splash. Slowly drifting in the current, he stripped off his uniform and threw the wrung-out garments on the shore. The refreshment was not precisely equivalent to a swim at Little Boz Burun.

When it was almost dark, some engineers went fishing with a piece of dynamite. The explosion in the pool brought up a catfish, belly skyward, and almost killed a corporal, who happened to be lolling in the water. The ruptured corporal set off at once for Eski in a wooden oxcart, followed by derisive cries of envy; and the engineers carved up the fish and skewered it above a brushwood fire. It was reported to be flavorless and pithy.

Captain Triandafilakos' battery was served a ration of boiled wheat, delivered by a commissary wagon after George had gone to sleep.

They covered more than twenty miles a day. The valley narrowed. Mottled ridges, streaked with rusty limestone, hemmed them in. Enormous spaces opened in the columns as the weaker men fell back in weariness.

Each day at dawn, an airplane passed above them, flying toward the Turkish lines. The 10th Division always spread a piece of canvas on the ground to mark the course. They would see the pilot leaning out, with the sunlight gleaming on his goggles, as he dropped a can of messages. The Turks were massing 40,000 men along the banks of the Sakarya (to be known to the Greeks hereafter by its classic name, Sangarius), but the Greeks outnumbered them by two to one. West of the river, there was nothing but a token force in the vicinity of Sivrihisar (to be known hereafter by its Byzantine name, Justinianoupolis).

Captain Triandafilakos would read these morning bulletins aloud, with frequent piercing glances sidelong from the page. Soldiers are notoriously inattentive and obsessed with proximate considerations: maggots, weevils, drinking water, bowel movements, body lice and breakfast. Ah, yes, breakfast . . . Regrettably, the commissariat had been delayed again, and, as a consequence, the morning ration would be a nourishing infusion of boiled wheat in water, portioned out as reverently as the Eucharist. Wheat infusion was said to be remedial for duodenal ulcers. All members of the battery cursed the wheat infusion heartily; but this was taken by the captain as an indication of their robust health. To the captain, almost any sign of animation in a soldier, short of enuresis or insubordination, was an evidence of health.

But walking twenty miles a day and drinking wheat infusions gradually began to drain away the buoyancy with which the men had started out from Alpi-köy. Their eagerness to meet the enemy became a hungry and exhausted passion, and still the Turks eluded them. Far ahead, the cavalry would see a band of Turkish horsemen disappearing up a canyon—but the men in the artillery would never even hear the distant rifle fire.

Wrongly, George had imagined ancient armies on their treks through Asia Minor reciting epic poetry and polishing their armor in the glow of blazing campfires. In fact, there was no poetry—and no firewood—on this dry plateau. Captain Triandafilakos ordered a general search for chips of dung to burn. But there was nothing in the fields except red pebbles, gopher holes and rabbit droppings. And thistles. There were five kinds of thistles: a nest of salmon-colored darts; a ringlet formed of cucumber burs; a malevolent tawny blossom with a heart of daggers; a carduaceous bile-green skewer; and a burst of sunny golden spikes.

Cucumber ringlets made the nicest cigarettes, according to Sakellariadis, and were remedial for duodenal ulcers. But no one devised a remedy to palliate the cold of night or the heat of day.

All in all, George might have gone into the ultimate battle

of the war in a depressed and even despairing state of mind had it not been for an inspiriting encounter near Beylik Bridge, where the Porsuk, flowing eastward, meets the Sangarius, flowing northward, to form a letter "T."

An infantry lieutenant from the 1st Division, who had somehow caught a ride in a lorry carrying pontoons, stopped to argue the interpretation of a map with Captain Triandafilakos. Hearing that familiar voice, George rushed over with a cry of joy, not stopping to consider that Dimitris might harbor some bitterness against him.

In fact, Dimitris greeted him politely and asked about his mother and father. Dimitris looked cool and clean. Apparently, he had not been walking twenty miles a day on wheat infusions. You could smell a trace of garlic on his breath.

"Did you ever see such a laughable excuse for a military chart?" Dimitris said, flicking the map with his fingernail. "That's got a scale of two hundred and fifty thousand to one, and you can't even figure out the relief lines."

George looked at the map. Somewhere east of Beylik Bridge, against a range of hills, were the ruins of the ancient town of Gordium, where Alexander of Macedonia had used his sword to cut the famous knot of cornel bark that was too difficult for any human hand to unravel.

"You know, we're really only seventy, seventy-five miles from Eskishehir," Dimitris said. "It always seems farther when the territory's new to you."

"Seventy-five miles," Captain Triandafilakos muttered, turning away. "We'll all be dead of exhaustion before we fire a shot." And he wandered off, leaving George beside the truck.

"It's an interesting geographic problem," Dimitris went on, flicking the map again. "We'll undoubtedly hit them here, and the crossing won't be bad. Although the stream is swift, of course. Then our southern corps will cross down here and turn Mustapha Kemal's left flank. This was the Gordian knot, this range of hills, and Alexander became the master of Anatolia when he cut through the tangle. See how history repeats itself, as your papa would say? Here we are, about to cut the knot again!"

And he looked so well disposed that George felt his own faltering spirits rising. With growing enthusiasm, he studied the outdated, inadequate, inaccurate map and saw the route to Ankara opening like a festive gate.

Unfortunately, the hills behind Gordium, which looked inconsequential on the chart, proved to be steep and heavily defended. After a day and a half of artillery fire across the river, the 10th Division turned south, across the Salt Desert, to join the Greek armies that were advancing by a southern route. The two columns came together on August 24, ten days out of Eskishehir, at Five Bridges, and there the decisive battle of the war began.

Sakarya was the battlefield Mustapha Kemal had chosen.

Without resistance, he had given up the richest town in Anatolia, which he regarded as a burden to defend, and had let his weary soldiers trickle eastward to the river line. Hundreds had been killed and thousands wounded at Kütahya. Thousands more had torn the crescents off their uniforms, thrown away their military boots and disappeared. It was more important to keep the remnants of the army intact, the Pasha assured the Parliament, than to retain a city—even one as valuable as Eskishehir, with its locomotive sheds and ammunition factories.

But, despite this painful sacrifice, the Kemalist army continued to deteriorate. To the conservative and pessimistic members of the Grand National Assembly, it appeared that God was against the Ankara rebellion. They paraded relics of the Prophet, chanted prayers and offered the lives of innumerable propitiatory animals; while the Pasha ordered a national confiscation of supplies.

Cavalry patrols went through every village, collecting blankets, leather, gloves and hawsers, seizing mohair, cambric, calfskin and linen. They conscripted carpenters and joiners, cartwrights and tanners, blacksmiths, sword grinders, tinkers and saddlers; appropriated pocket watches, telephones, electric poles and rice; sequestered shops and storerooms; requisitioned insulators, motor trucks, French glue and tea.

By law, the government had the right to levy only 40 percent of a merchant's stock. But who could judge the extent of a grocer's storeroom in a land where tax evasion is an ancient art? Who could estimate the national supply of auto tires, corn meal, tallow or vaseline? The collectors simply took whatever they could find.

Every house was ordered to prepare a parcel for the national defense: a pair of shoes, a pair of socks, a bolt of cloth; and every man and woman in the country was conscripted to transport soldiers and supplies to the new line of defense in the tangled hills just west of Ankara. Columns of women, dressed in scarlet vests and gingham bloomers, passed artillery projectiles hand to hand on a hundred mile chain from the Black Sea to the center of the Anatolian plateau. Toiling up and down the slopes, they carried missiles on their backs in slings of calico cloth, which sometimes cradled both a baby and a shell. All night, heavy *chagni* wagons rolled through the streets of Ankara with wooden axles screaming. Bands of country dandies, carrying old-fashioned Mausers on their shoulders, left for the Western Front, stripping whole villages as they passed.

Kenan observed the ordeal of his nation with the cold fury of a man who has passed beyond the unreliable, humane impulses of his youth to the relentless, dogmatic convictions of old age. To the more flexible politicians of the Grand National Assembly, he was clearly a fanatic: his vehemence, his narrow-mindedness, his implacable hatred of the Greeks marked him as a dangerous chauvinist; and his growing religious obsession irritated even the orthodox Moslems. His speeches dwelt on retribution, annihilation and blood sacrifice; and they were not well attended.

When news came that the Greeks were moving eastward through the Porsuk Valley, Kenan began an extraordinary fast, which was ordained to him in a vision by the Caliph Ali. The Caliph wore a robe of emerald satin and a white turban, upon which gleamed a carbuncle as large as a pigeon's egg, and he spoke in a voice like the ringing of a thousand and one bells.

In spite of Kenan's physical weakness, this fast did not abate the sudden surges of kinetic energy that frequently swept over him, causing him to limp around the Hay Bazaar, shouting prophecies in a language that no one could understand. He therefore added a regime of ablutions and prayer at the Haji Bayram Mosque; and when he heard that a full division of the Greek Army had crossed the Sakarya near Beylik Bridge, he let it be known among his followers that God, the All-Powerful, the All-Seeing, required a further evidence of piety.

As soon as daylight touched the citadel, sacred pilgrims crowded through the streets. Slowly, they descended Pulley Makers' Hill, the district of Great Souls and the Horse Bazaar, led by the thumping of a leather drum and the ready piping of a *zurna*.

There were dervishes of the profuse and enigmatic Nakshibendi, whose ritual of devotion begins with a thousand and one reiterations of a single prayer, each repetition counted by a pebble; and divine Rufais, miraculous healers, who howl the name of God until their lips are black with suffocation, who swallow fire and lie in embers, slashing their chests with broken glass, piercing their guts with daggers and calling their ghastly wounds "God's roses"; and pallid Mevlevis, known to the world as Whirling Dervishes, who dance until they swoon in transcendental vertigo.

The dancing Mevlevis wore towering hats of felt, shaped like the vase of light that held the Prophet's soul before his mission to the earth; and each one carried three large stones inside his sash in imitation of the Beggars of the Lord, who bind their waists to quell the anguish of starvation. The Kadiris had roses embroidered on their crowns in memory of Hassan and Huseyn, the Prophet's martyred grandsons, who were the roses of his life. And the Bektashis wore twelve-sided caps and cloaks of camel's hair, belted with ropes that were tied in knots symbolic of the dervish vows of candor, honesty and chastity.

Behind these holy brothers came the guilds of tradesmen, carrying the flags of their vocations, which are each protected by a saintly dervish: first, flail and saddle makers; then knife and sickle grinders; next sellers of crude salt, mohair and hardware; rope and pulley makers; coppersmiths and ironsmiths; tanners, potters, butchers, weavers, gardeners, horseshoers, leatherworkers, cobblers, tailors.

High on the citadel arose a pandemonium of flutes and drums. It was the Seymen Company, whose origin was buried with the tribe of cabalistic warriors that had founded a republic in Ankara centuries ago.

Three holy madmen, writhing and spinning in a corybantic frenzy, led the procession down the rocky lanes around the coffeehouse of Yellow Ahmet. These fanatics of the Kizilbashi sect wore long white bloomers and cone-shaped hats. They threw their drums like gleaming goblets, beat them above their heads, crawled with them through the dirt. Casting their eyes to Heaven, they slavered, groaned and tore their tangled hair; spun on one foot, crouched and leaped and dragged themselves along the ground. Their vests, embroidered in gold and silver thread, flew out like wings. Pistols and daggers clattered on their leather belts. On their chests they wore gold coins and amulets of polished jade, like the miraculous and precious *yedé* stone that Gabriel gave to Noah to permit him to control the rain.

Behind them came the hatchet bearers of the Seymen Company: great, brooding men, shouldering pikes with rusty blades the color of blood. In their midst, the leader of the company, wearing a thick black beard and lifting up an ancient yataghan, chanted: *"Doh! Doh! Doh!"* while the men around him, moving slowly forward, echoed in a deep growl: *"Doh! Doh! Doh!"* This imprecation sent a shiver through the crowd of men who watched like sacrificial cattle while the curved blade rose and fell.

Last were the marchers, wearing prayer cloaks on their shoulders and turbans of black and green. They flashed their tambourines above their heads and cried out: "Ah, Compassionate! Ah, Forgiving!" as they descended toward the mosque of Haji Bayram.

Exhausted by a night of prayer and hunger, Kenan waited by a pillar on the porch. The courtyard and the surrounding streets were teeming with hajis and hojas, monks and pilgrims, poets, teachers, judges—whosoever was left in the embattled shrine of the Moslem East. It was impossible to perform the movements of the prayer in such a crowd. Kenan stood helplessly, waiting for a chance to speak. The voice of the imam, reciting the Holy Koran, was drowned in a storm of coughing, whispering and sighing; but the Moslems outside in the courtyard would cry "Amen!" whenever they could hear the murmur of a prayer.

At last, the flag of the sainted dervish, Haji Bayram Veli, unfurled itself above the portal, and the Sacred Scripture

325

moved forward, borne on a bookstand draped in green and carried on the head of a pious deputy from Erzerum. A hair of the Prophet's beard rested beside the Holy Koran in an emerald reliquary.

Kenan raised his arm.

"Brothers!" he called, but his voice was weak with fasting. "This is the time for every man to go out with a gun or a knife and join the army on the hills of the Sakarya. . . ."

But the crowd was pushing toward Karaoglan Street, past the carter's shed and the smithy's furnace, down to the intersection of Stone Khan, past the Teachers' College, the ruined caravanserai and the Meshrutiyet Hotel; down toward the little granite Parliament, where they performed the gesture of *tekbir*, the mark of faith, with palms upturned at shoulder level.

Kenan collapsed three times before he reached his room, but the Caliph Ali guided him. He uniformed himself in a tunic and a pair of jodhpurs, a belly sash and a turban; took a carbine under his arms; and staggered through the empty, sunstruck streets to the station.

In recognition of Kenan's position and his known loyalty to the Pasha, a transportation captain put him aboard a Decauville locomotive that left that afternoon for Polatli. By oxcart, he reached the village that had been chosen as command post for the northern pivot of the line. It was the weakest sector of the Front; Mustapha Kemal had begun to maneuver southward in anticipation of a major Greek attack.

Just outside the village, however, was a peak called Basrikale Tepe, where a few machine guns and a nest of rifles had been planted in a mound of reddish gravel. One could look down on flats of wheat and barley and the river wandering across the plain. Beyond the valley was the citadel of Sivri, which the Greeks now called Justinianoupolis, rising from the haze like an immense, decaying stump; and then the

326

hills along the course of the Porsuk, shimmering and fading toward the setting sun. To stand on Basrikale as night fell upon the Turkish nation was like standing on the final promontory of a deluged land, pounded by rising waves.

It was here that a patrol discovered the deputy from Alashehir, performing the movements of the prayer in a violent, mindless paroxysm of devotion, several hours after sundown, and carried him to the first-aid station at Karapinar.

*C*hristos was among the first in Smyrna to hear of the great battle. He had primed a petty editor to send a messenger if there was military news. At daybreak, a boy was pounding on the door, calling: "Sakarya! . . ."

"Sangarius, for God's sake," Christos said. "Haven't you read Antipater?"

He threw off the bellyband that he wore at night to prevent a liver chill and dressed to go to Bornova. Sophia was living in the village to escape the summer heat.

"No tip for me?" the boy cried, trotting along beside the carriage. Christos threw down a Turkish pound, a magnificent gesture. He felt the day had started well. The driver cracked his whip above the horse's back; the trappings made a sprightly, jingling sound. On the Rue des Roses, they passed a sweeper who was dragging her twig broom through the gutter. Christos leaned out.

"We're attacking on the Sangarius!"

The woman looked up stupidly and pulled her scarf across her mouth.

"That's bright news," said the driver. "Ain't it?"

"Any fool would know it means the war is over," Christos said.

He told the bright news to some camel drivers squatting in the dust, to a woman sloshing water on her doorstep and to a boy raking gravel in the garden of a coffeehouse. Passing Basmahane Station, he heard newsboys mispronouncing it around the portico; and he ordered the driver to stop while he gave a brief lesson in Anatolian geography, as recorded by the Regent of Macedonia in the 4th century B.C. Grocers and butchers in wooden clogs stopped to listen, then rushed away to decorate their shops with bunting.

"Can we beat the train to Bornova?" Christos asked the driver. "I want to be the first to tell my wife. Our son is in the Tenth Division."

"What a shame," the driver said.

They settled on a price—exorbitant, but Christos was impatient. As they came into Bornova, the sound of bells surprised him: he had forgotten the Festival of the Dormition. A Luna Park was open in the meadow, and railway cars filled with dried sultanas for the bulking sheds were decked with boughs of laurel. All the way from the station to the square, it was pressed cherry juice, roast pumpkin seeds and colored ribbons, balloons and parasols, Sakarya and Sangarius. Excited girls were promenading up and down in velvet bodices and tiny caps with silken tassels; and the young men who walked in pairs a few steps behind them had cigarettes behind their ears and sprigs of laurel in their buttonholes.

It seemed impossible that anyone could still be sleeping, with barrel organs skirling in the streets; but Polixeni came out to meet the carriage, holding her finger to her lips.

"Don't try to shush me up!" Christos said indignantly. "Haven't you any sense of history?" He could see Sophia, half asleep and ghostly in a silk kimono, lurking in the vestibule. "I have some news," he called, climbing the steps. "The final attack has started in the Valley of the Sangarius."

"That's good, isn't it?" Sophia said.

"Of course it's good. It means the end."

But Sophia grasped his hands.

"Oh, Christo! What a blow! A letter from Eleni—"
And she began to cry, rubbing her forehead with her wrist.
"She's in Alashehir. She's well. But, oh, Christo! She says
she was never pregnant. She made it up because she couldn't
stand the idea of marrying Dimitris. Does that make sense?"

"Nothing makes sense," Christos said. "Is she married to
this Turk?"

Sophia smiled tearfully.

"She says she is blissfully happy. . . . Won't you go get her
and bring her home?"

But Christos felt a stifling pressure in his throat.

"Happy is she? With all the lives she has ruined? As far as
I'm concerned, she can stay forever with her Turk. As far as
I'm concerned, we have no daughter."

He took the letter from Sophia's hand and tore it into tiny
pieces.

Sophia watched him. At last, wiping her eyes, she said:
"That's wonderful about the war. The end of it, I mean." She
blew her nose. "That's really wonderful. It means George can
come back, doesn't it?"

"Yes. I suppose so. Did she ask about her brother?"

"Christo, she mentioned everyone in the family."

Sophia drew a heavy, rasping breath. Then, standing up,
she asked if he would like a *café au lait*.

Christos remembered the carriage driver and went to pay
him. Outside the iron fence, which resembled a row of upturned spears, peddlers were spreading heaps of melons from
Kassaba. Gypsy girls were fanning trays of pomegranates.
Small boys in white aprons were grilling lambs' kidneys on
charcoal braziers, slowly rotating the greasy skewers, waving
off yellow wasps and peering restlessly up and down the
street. At the corner, some soldiers were tacking sprays of
wilted white oleander to an arch of triumph. That *did* seem
to be pretentious foolishness, when nobody knew for certain

whether the attack would mean a victory or a defeat.

The carriage driver was eating a piece of watermelon. "How did the family like the news?" he said.

"They took it very well," Christos said.

SANGARIUS
AUGUST, 1921

*T*he key to the battle was a mountain at the center of the line—Chal Dagh: bilious, jaundiced, torpid, insurmountable. At daybreak, Dimitris watched it crystallizing from the darkness like an arid yellow wall that reached to Heaven. Lying in his tent, he could hear Major Mavropetros vilifying the accursed mountain at the morning muster:

"This stony monster in our path . . . this fearful barricade . . ." Dimitris raised his head and studied the slopes of sallow gravel, paling in the sunrise. "This final stumbling block on the road to Ankara . . ."

There was a responsive rumbling sound from the men. They were a new and confident regiment. Like the rest of the army, they had marched across the Salt Desert. Then, at Melon Seller's Bridge, they had been held in waiting. Other heroic Greeks had enjoyed the honor of making the first deceptive sally across the river at Beylik Bridge, under the very noses of the Turks who held the knotted hills of Gordium. Other Greeks had been privileged to shell Tambouroglou, to capture Kartal Tepe, Besh Tepe and Kara Tepe. Devoured by envy, these hot young recruits longed to hurl themselves against the saffron slopes of Chal Dagh and gnaw it up like cheese.

"My soldiers!" Mavropetros screeched. "This will be our greatest day! The Turks are in despair. Listen—here is their order of the day, which our spies have intercepted: 'God commands you to defend this peak against the Unbelievers. Remember, O Turks—the Greeks are terrified each time they hear your mighty battle cry!'"

Derisive laughter. Mavropetros was, if nothing else, a master of meaningless forensics. He stung the men with insults, taunted them, inflamed their pride. It filled Dimitris with disgust to see how easily most men could be persuaded to give up their lives to gain a certain mountainside, a little hillock or a field of boulders strewn with rabbit turds.

"Hear what the Turks are saying: 'Soon the Greeks will limp away, licking their wounds. Then we shall follow them with mighty blows. . . .' "

The regiment spontaneously shouted: "No!"

Dimitris closed his eyes. His hands were damp and cold. "If I should die . . ." His eyes popped open wildly, and he stared in horror at the yellow mountain. He had a terrifying premonition about the danger of that peak: it was so bleak, so dry, so sterile! All the mountains east of the Sangarius were yellow, black or red; and the Turkish Army clung to each of them as if it were the very citadel of Ankara. But this Chal Dagh had a particularly minatory aspect, perhaps because it was the only mountain Dimitris had ever contemplated climbing.

"My soldiers, listen!" cried Mavropetros. "Long did our people suffer, groaning and perspiring, under the Turkish yoke—" His voice was lost in the beginning of the dawn barrage, a terrible kerrrrrrr-UMP, kerrrrrrr-UMP, kerrrrrrr-UMP. The Turkish guns began to answer. Drowned in thunder, Mavropetros went on shouting exhortations to his soldiers to destroy themselves: "Our sacred land . . . our holy cause . . ."

Dimitris, kneeling in his tent, took out his service pistol, spun the barrel, put the muzzle into his mouth and closed his eyes. An ecstatic chill shot up from his legs into his bowels. For an aeon—the passing of a shell—he knelt there, quivering, with icy rivulets of perspiration running down his ribs and the cold taste of metal on his tongue. Then he took the weapon out of his mouth and put it back into its holster.

"The will to greatness!" cried Mavropetros, snorting like a bull. "A nation at the threshold of its destiny . . ."

Reaching out, Dimitris touched a canvas sack. It held some little parcels that the major, in his never-failing generosity, had passed along without instructions.

One envelope contained the worldly goods of one Panos Paxinos, a corporal: six drachmas (paper), blotched with a disgusting brownish stain; a Turkish medal, taken from the body of a prisoner; a poem called "The March of Hellas," written by a lawyer educated at the university of the Sorbonne. In the other packet—a knotted handkerchief—was the legacy of Vassilis Dimaras, a sergeant: seven letters from a girl named Athina, who seemed to be the housemaid of a family at Nea Phaleron; and a half-completed letter of reply, beginning: "My beloved Athina, When you receive these lines, our greatest battle will be over. . . ."

Both men had died of dysentery.

"Uplifted generations . . . freedom . . . Greece . . ."

The speech was ended, and the footsteps of the men went past. Dimitris heard his sergeant saying in a waxy tone: "No, sir. He isn't here. He'd answer us."

But somebody smacked the canvas with a stick, and Mavropetros said at the flap of the tent:

"He's there. Reach in and grab his foot."

Dimitris called out: "What is it? I'm coming right along."

"Kalapothaki?" said Mavropetros irritably. "What the devil are you doing?"

He put his face inside the flap. His skin was as pale as usual, despite the awful heat. Dimitris glared at him in hatred: a man without a shred of talent. Even his so-called courage was only an illustration of the bliss of ignorance. He was too stupid to imagine death. This morning, having puked his daily belly-ful of rhetoric, he was prepared to aim his nose in the direction of the Turks, cross himself three times and gallop up the mountain, crying, "Aera! Aera!" the battle call of the Hellenic klephts, his pistol raised, his ridiculous monocle flashing fiery signals from the sun. Dimitris called him "Zeus," because he owned an absurd nanny goat named Amalthea, and it was commonly supposed that he not only suckled her but climbed her.

"Don't you know the Turks are waiting?" said Zeus. "What are you doing?"

"Getting my pistol," said Dimitris, looking at the pitiful remains of Paxinos and Dimaras.

"Bubbles!" said Mavropetros and he whacked his swagger stick against the tent again. "You're pissing in your pants!"

And, hitching up his belt, the major bent over and went scurrying along the trench, calling to the officers: "Assemble, men. Move forward under cover. . . . Jesus and Mary, what's holding *this* platoon?"

Dimitris pressed his face against the earth. He imagined himself disintegrated by a fleck of searing metal, smaller than a raisin, faster-moving than a shout. He could feel a rush of blood, a sudden blackness, a roaring like the coming of a train; and then the endless, endless, endless.

He loosened a peg at the corner of the tent and peeked through the slit between the canvas and the dirt. The men were sneaking up the hillside, one by one, to take their places in the rocky crevices in which they were foredoomed to die. Twenty men and twenty mules had dragged a Skoda up the slope and set it in a crude revetment. The crew was squatting over grindstones, milling grains of wheat.

God, how he hated all of them! How they had persecuted him, degraded him, misunderstood him, lied about him! They had slandered him in Smyrna, blackmailed him in Ushak, assaulted him with acid, driven him from place to place. A determination to outwit them made him tremble with excitement. He took his pistol out again and pressed its muzzle to his chest, his throat, his forehead. Finally, with his belly churning and his throat constricted, he clasped both hands around the pistol, put it out of sight between his legs and brought his knees together.

The detonation was tremendous. He thought the pistol must have burst like a grenade. His legs were numb, and there was moisture on his hands. Then somebody pulled him roughly by the ankles, and he screamed.

The bearers came and raised him to a stretcher. An agonizing pain began. His knees were locked together in a spasm. His leg seemed to catch fire. Somebody gave him morphine and a sip of brackish water.

Field surgery was in a whitewashed shed. An orderly was saying in a Spartan accent:

"That's right, pal. One drachma for a drag."

"And twenty drachmas for the shitting cigarette?"

"That's right."

"I'd rather drink dust."

"That's what you'll drink, my friend. This is the only pack of Karavassilis from here to Ankara."

"But they only cost you twenty drachmas for the pack in Eski."

"Eski? Where's that?"

Then Dimitris heard the surgeon say:

"Here's another one who shot himself."

They were in a grove of yellow poplar trees. Somebody said Chal Dagh had fallen, and the Turks were in retreat. The Greeks had won the Battle of Sangarius.

Three days later, however, the Turkish field command was still in operation at the village of Karapinar. The telegrapher in the headquarters shack was slumped across his key; the Honorable Deputy from Alashehir lay sleeping, fogged with morphine; but a private stood sentry at the door, listening with astonishment to the chirping of birds—hoopoes, they appeared to be—in the parched defile of Jem-Jem Pass.

Kenan raised his head. Parchment hung in tattered shreds across the windows. The lumpy pods of a honey locust were scraping the sill. Yellow leaves had fallen onto the floor inside.

What had become of the huffing, crashing engine that was taking out the wounded? Why had the walls of the command post ceased to tremble to the constant hammering of mortar shells? He pulled himself up and hobbled to the doorway, where he leaned out and gazed across the village.

The dust was deeper than your knee. An old man in cotton slippers was shuffling along the alley, carrying a basket of roots, as he had been carrying jugs of water to the gunners on the Basrikale ridge. Where was the ammunition for the Bergmann automatics?

Kenan turned back, squinting his eye. The telegrapher was sitting up. His black hair was flecked with chips of whitewash from the walls. He eyed Kenan distrustfully.

"Doctor's coming back in a minute, sir. You'd better lie down, sir."

Without a word, Kenan went back and sat down on the canvas cot. He remembered the crash of couplings on the tracks behind the village after the great artillery barrage; and looking down with field glasses at the Greek soldiers, digging field latrines and bathing in the river; and he remembered General Fevzi Pasha, carrying a beautiful, handwritten copy of the Scriptures in a silver box; and the Pasha's orders to move the generator back to Alagösh.

The telegrapher was standing at the doorstep, yawning and cracking his joints.

"Rain's coming," he said.

Kenan did not answer.

"God willing, it'll stick their trucks."

"Ah, yes," Kenan said. He rubbed his knee with his hand as he groped among the recollections, the hallucinations, that lay in his mind like disconnected bones, half buried in the dust of sleep. At last, warily, he said: "Which way are they moving?"

The telegrapher turned around, tipping his head in curious sympathy.

"They're going back, Your Honor." And then, realizing that Kenan wanted to know more and was ashamed to ask, he went on: "They took Chal Dagh three days ago, but they couldn't seem to use it. We waited for the blow to fall, and they never struck. They just wore out."

Kenan sank back, remembering now the Pasha's final orders: let every soldier stand in the defense of every hummock, every field and every stone.

So the Greeks had expended all their strength in the penultimate assault against the yellow mountain at the center of the line! Now they had fallen back, exhausted, while this drowsiness descended on Sakarya.

Soon the autumn rains would start. The dust would turn to mud, and cataracts of yellow water would come tumbling down the desert canyons. The Greeks would draw back, contracting their extended lines, while Mustapha Kemal pursued them westward.

The Turks had passed the crisis of their struggle. Years from now, this would be reckoned the turning point, the moment when they began to look ahead again. After another winter and another spring, the country would be free; the vast regeneration would begin; and it would be time to think of settling up accounts.

With sudden clarity, Kenan perceived the course of punishment and restitution that lay ahead: the courts and tribunals, the exiles and executions; and his cold, haggard body glowed with warmth.

The telegrapher continued to gaze at him, with that peculiar, distrustful sympathy.

"The Pasha was worried about you, sir. Said you needed plenty of rest."

Kenan turned away to hide the spasm that constricted his mouth.

"The war is not over," he said. "Not over."

SEYIT GAZI

DECEMBER, 1921

*W*inter brought a recess in the war. The Greeks retreated from Sangarius to the positions they had held in early summer. Their expeditionary force was spread along a line that reached from the Meander Valley to the Sea of Marmara. The Prime Minister went to Paris to ask for help; but the Great Powers of Europe had lost interest in financing the revival of the Golden Age, and the Greek treasury was empty.

All along the thin frontier of the Hellenic Empire, strands of barbed wire twanged and twisted in the wind. Jackals whimpered in the fields. There were weevils in the barley, when there was barley, and excisions in the mail, when there was mail. In Seyit Gazi, a captain named Karanoglou sat down in the dining hall after the outdoor Mass on St. Barbara's Day, put a Colt pistol inside his mouth and squeezed the trigger just as his fellow officers were coming in to eat a dinner of boiled beans and moldy bread.

Seyit Gazi (anciently Prymnessus, or perhaps Nacoleia—its history was murky) was the Paris of the Front. It had a splendid setting, on a hillside girt with forests of Saint-Étienne machine guns, and high repute as an eastern outpost of Hellenic culture.

The Officers' Chamber Orchestra played Tchaikovsky's "Serenade for Strings"; the Soldiers' Theater played Molière

340

and *Loukas Laskaris;* the petty officers played tricktrack at the Athens Coffeehouse; and an ill-favored Moslem girl from Serres played saddle to an endless cavalcade of riders in the stoke room of a Turkish bath. It was in Seyit Gazi that a pamphleteer commissioned by a Panhellenic club in Manchester found the perfect image of Greek rule in Asia Minor: a company of modern hoplites, throwing snowballs near a monastery where the earthly remains of a Byzantine princess named Irenoussa lay commingled with the humus of a Moslem prince.

In Seyit Gazi there were fewer body lice and milder cases of malaria, insanity, amoebic dysentery, impetigo, typhus, scarlet fever, enteritis, syphilis and gonorrhea than in such uninviting posts as Alpi-köy. The chief malady in Seyit Gazi was political discontent; and that complaint was tempered by the realization that if one manifested his disaffection for the King, he might wind up in some place even worse. Few men cut off their toes, set fires, spread Venizelist tracts or falsified their musters; and only once did someone make obscene use of the King's photograph, scattering the evidence in front of the latrine.

For George, who had been promoted to sergeant and was now master of My Darling Bouboulina, the winter at Seyit Gazi was an agony of pretense. He had entered the army reluctantly, suspicious and afraid. Nothing had transpired to change his attitude. Yet the good companions of his gun battery, whose affection he valued more than comfort or security, marveled at his courage, his endurance, his resourcefulness. They solicited his opinions and awaited his decisions with a sort of humble faith that inflated his self-importance and filled him with guilt. He carried the burden of all their fears. On those rare occasions when the Turks would drag a Skoda forward and drop a few projectiles into a pasture, or when the clang of cattle bells and kettle lids

341

would warn that Turkish cavalry was nipping at the barbed wire, Bouboulina would perform heroically, coughing out her ration of two or three shells; and the men would shower George with praise. Obviously, all of them depended on him to save their skins.

The greatest hardship for everyone was Captain Triandafilakos, who had returned from the Sangarius with a terrible affliction: the captain could not sleep. He paced around his room incessantly, slapping his forehead with his hand. For a while, he had been billeted with several other officers in a shanty near the monastery; but the others found his company intolerable, and now he lived alone and burned his lamp all night.

In the early evening he would write to his mother, drink a flask of wine with water, say his prayers, look at a book of trigonometry and trim his fingernails. Then he would start to pace. Long after midnight he would stumble down the hill to the encampment: "Wake the sergeants!"

And the sergeants of the battery would get up, shivering and groggy, put on their coats and stagger to the mess hall for a lecture on morale.

The captain's skin was scaly and shrunken on his face. His strange blue eyes were flaming. He could talk for hours without becoming tired.

"What is morale? It's discipline. Dis-ci-pline! The only thing that's going to save us. We *must* have better discipline. . . . If you sergeants can't maintain good discipline, don't blame it on the weather, the food, the enemy. Blame yourselves! It means you've been too weak, too soft."

The sergeants hid their anguished yawns and rubbed their burning eyes.

"It's not enough to take muster twice a day and keep the grease from freezing on the guns. You've got to stop these little meetings, these political debates. Suppress complaints. Prevent conspiracies."

Then, as it was turning light, he would command the non-commissioned officers to turn out the battery. Marching the exhausted men to the parade ground, he would criticize their slovenly appearance, their lackadaisical behavior, their meddling in affairs of state.

"You talk as if you thought you were in Parliament! Blaming the King for this, Theotokis for that and General Papulas for something else. If you know so much about the conduct of the war, why didn't they make you commander-in-chief?" And he would shift his penetrating glance from one face to another, letting each man feel the onus of his accusations. "You gobble up these articles that Colonel Kondylis writes in the Constantinople magazines. You gobble up these leaflets that the Turks stick on the barbed wire. Why don't you pay attention to the ordnance lectures, delouse your uniforms and leave it to the politicians to run the government?"

An hour or more before the morning bugle sounded, he would run the battery up the hill, unfed, unwashed and groaning with exhaustion, and put them through a drill.

After the third or fourth of these polemics, a man named Kyriakis, second passer on Iphigenia, went over to the Divisional Headquarters and signed a statement formally complaining that Captain Triandafilakos was unsound of mind. Nothing came of it, except to Kyriakis. The captain had him watched perpetually, woke him several times a night to ask him questions and accused him of incredible conspiracies. The poor man developed hallucinations and was cashiered out.

George, as the youngest of the noncommissioned officers, was chosen for the captain's personal attention. He was called out with the others for the predawn lectures on morale; and he was also invited to the captain's cottage in the evening.

They discussed morale.

"You understand me, don't you, Sergeant? Don't hesitate

to disagree. You may speak your mind to me as if the two of us were fellow officers. . . . Some raki?" He uncorked a bottle. "I could drink this stuff all night. It's all a matter of conditioning. Like Mithridates, taking larger and larger doses of poison until he could take a dose ten times enough to kill an ordinary man. . . . You'll change your mind?"

George accepted half a glass of raki, to conclude the dissertation.

"Now, these men of ours," the captain went on, striding back and forth, "they think I'm a fanatic. They don't seem to care if they get beaten by the Turks. They just don't want to have to *think* about the Turks. Know what they think about? They think about their mamas' nipples and their sweethearts' bottoms. Playing with themselves all night." He peered at George malignly, under those forbidding eyebrows, with that hostile and accusing gaze. "Cream puffs!" he said. "As mawkish as a bunch of girls. Well, I don't have to make them into *men*. I only have to make them fire the guns. . . . Have some more?"

Pausing a moment in his pacing, the captain raised his glass.

"I don't sleep much, you know."

George lowered his eyes. He felt a twinge of pity for the captain. He remembered saying once: "The captain's funny, isn't he?" Even in his loneliness and torment, Triandafilakos did not win one's sympathy, but only the reluctant pity that one sometimes feels for a disgusting animal like a hyena, which plays a repulsive role in the economy of nature.

"You know what's wrong?" the captain said, resuming his didactic tone. "It's politics. Venizelos. Constantine. The Liberals. The Royalists. Old Greece. New Greece. Politics has no place in army life. Why, just a month ago, a corporal killed a young lieutenant down in Dumlupinar—*stabbed* him to death!—because the lieutenant put him on report. But this lieutenant was a Venizelist. So when this crazy corporal came up for trial, he suddenly revealed himself to be a monarchist, and the court-martial gave him twenty-one days' confinement on a plea of self-defense." The captain's voice was growing thick. "What can you do? I've heard of batteries so corrupted they sent threatening letters to their *own* commanding officer—'Dear Captain,' with the writing slanted this and that way to disguise it, 'You'll be killed. We'll put your eyes out.' Threats like that. Did you ever hear of that?"

"No, sir."

Filling his glass again, the captain riveted his eyes on George.

"You never hear them talking about me?"

George hesitated, and the captain said:

"Don't be afraid to answer, Sergeant. They think I'm a fanatic, don't they?"

"Yes, sir."

"Of course. I speak the truth to you. You speak the truth to me. What else are they saying about me?"

"They think you're very strict, sir."

"Do they think they're picnicking at the Columns?"

"No, sir," George said, looking at his hands. "You interrupt their sleep."

"*I* interrupt *their* sleep! Oh, God!" And the captain laughed, with his gray lips drawn tight against his teeth. "Have they ever considered what it's like to carry the whole thing on your shoulders? Do they think I get any pleasure out of making them do things they hate?"

He paused for a moment, not to invite a reply but to emphasize his words.

"They figure I'm some kind of freak, don't they? Triandafilakos never gets lonely. He never gets discouraged. He doesn't need any friendship or understanding. . . . Well,

George, that just isn't true. I'm no different from anybody else."

George noticed with uncomfortable surprise that the captain had addressed him by his first name. This intimacy was harder to endure than the anonymity of being called Second Passer: it seemed to draw him into a privileged relationship with the captain, from which the other men of the battery were excluded. George deliberately answered in a formal tone.

"Sir, we sergeants try to help as much as we can."

"George, you're the only one in the entire bunch who's worth water. Don't you recognize the difference? It's not just because you're a big, well-setup fellow. You've got a *brain*, George. You've got some sensitivity. How can you waste your time with those roughnecks?"

The captain was silent, breathing deeply through his nostrils. Suddenly, he sat down on his cot and looked up at George with an odd, childish smile.

"George? Why do you keep holding back on me? You know how I feel about you. Help me go to sleep...." Swaying a little in his drunkenness, he held up his arms. Then he stretched out, and tears ran down his wind-burned cheeks. "I feel as if I'm going to sleep," he said. He pressed the tips of his fingers to his eyes. "George? Go look at the guns. Take someone with you.... Isn't safe ... "

George turned and ran. As he was going out, the wind caught the door and closed it with a bang. A few dry flakes of snow were blowing down. Shuddering, George turned his collar up and took the path that led around the mountain to the gun emplacements.

Only a madman would have manned these guns at night. But early in December, the captain had decided to assign a third of every crew to duty at all times. He inspected the positions several times a night. He had never sent around a substitute before. There was nobody he could trust.

George went to Despo first. To reach her, you walked past a pinnacle and up a slope, five minutes' climb.

The barbette was empty. The gun was pointing upward, frozen in position by a sleeve of ice, and the shelter was dark. George threw a pebble on the roof. He called Tall Johnny. No one answered.

Visions of disaster flashed in his mind. Holding his breath, he listened for the Turks. He could hear the sheep bells on the barbed-wire fences, jingling softly like a herd of grazing animals. When the pounding of his heart subsided, he struck a blow against the canvas door. But the shelter was empty and the little stove was cold.

He took the lower trail to Sakellariadis' gun: it, too, was deserted.

The third gun was his own, My Darling Bouboulina, which was beyond the others on a jagged spur of rock. Running down the ridge, he bumped into something and fell back with a cry.

Immediately, someone called: "Who goes there?"

George sat in the middle of the trail.

"Who goes?" the picket called again. "Is that you, Captain?"

George put out his hands. He was face to face with an enormous effigy of stone and snow, which stood with outstretched arms, like a Crucifixion, in the middle of the path.

"Give the password or I'll fire," the picket called.

"Aya Sophia," George said.

"That was last week."

"Is that you, Taki?" George said. "Wait. I know the pass. . . . It's Parthenon."

"Advance."

The flap was open, and a fire of twigs and dung was burning on the dirt floor of the hut. Goufas looked out and raised his eyebrows.

"Why, it's Sergeant George! Come in, come in."

All of them were lying there—his own men, Sakellariadis' men, Tall Johnny's men—leaning on their elbows in the firelight, handing around a bottle in a pitiful approximation of a party.

"He'll whack off your butts," George said.

"Don't you know what night it is?" said Goufas. "It's Christmas."

"The guns are frozen."

"Why, Sergeant George—you sound just like the captain!"

"To hell with the captain," George said. "I'm thinking about the Turks. What if the Turks came through the wire?"

Folding his arms, he scowled from one man to another. If they should detect the uncertainty in his voice, his tentative, untested influence would be broken. They would begin to scoff his orders, laugh at him, defy his arbitrary power. The captain had warned him about the problems of maintaining discipline.

But Sakellariadis, bleary and grinning, was holding out the bottle of raki.

"Screw the Turks. Merry Christmas, George."

George looked around at his good companions, who had been with him at Manisa, Inönü and the Sangarius, who had comforted, admired and sustained him when he had deserved to be despised. Another Christmas: all alive. And would they be together for another year? Who dared to look ahead? Tears swam into his eyes. His good companions drew him toward the fire. Goufas took hold of George's hands and splashed them with cologne; Sakellariadis handed him the flask of raki. George stretched out his legs, and his boots steamed against the fire.

"Is it really Christmas? How can the days be so alike?"

Loukas was adding twigs to the fire. The flames sprang up, but no one mentioned the danger of the enemy. Sakellariadis tore apart an empty ammunition box and fed it to the blaze. Goufas stood up, fitted his lighted cigarette behind his ear and dreamily began to dance. He arched his body, spread out his arms and slowly dipped and twisted, teetering above the fire. Bluish smoke curled around him like a cloak. The raki bottle passed from hand to hand. One by one, the men got up, lifted their arms and wheeled around the narrow circle while the others snapped their fingers lazily. The stone walls glittered with the condensation of their breath. George, lying on his belly, creased a slip of paper and tapped in a mixture of tobacco, bran and shredded leaves. Tall Johnny held out the lighted end of a cigarette.

"Hey, George? Did you hear what the captain said to me?"

"Let's not talk about that shithead," George said. In truth, it almost overwhelmed him with nausea to think about the captain, reaching out his trembling arms with a look of desperate longing. "I can't believe it's Christmas," he said. "A few more months and it's spring."

And, to drive the imprint of the captain's pleading face from his mind, he thought of tulips on a windowsill; a young girl's hair, touched by the sunshine; a country road; a warm and brightly lighted barbershop, with vagrant footfalls of the city going past the door, a row of vials along the shelf, a linnet in a cage, an aloe in a pot, a picture of the Matterhorn above the mirror and the gossip of the barber as he stropped the blade. The fragrance of tobacco and cologne rose in his head; and his heart sobbed with misery.

Then he heard the sentry calling out the challenge. Sakellariadis raised his hand for silence.

"That's him," he said.

"Him?" said George.

Nobody moved. The men were looking at each other. Again they heard the sentry calling:

"Halt! The password."

"Is it really the captain?" George said. "Look, I'll go and talk to him. He'll understand, it being Christmas."

He stood up, suddenly moved by the captain's loneliness. A moment afterward they heard a rifle shot.

The sentry came inside. He was a handsome boy named Takis, with a seedling mustache and damp eyes. The captain had once called him an immoral influence. He was holding his rifle tight against his chest.

"There's been an accident," Takis said, looking at Sakellariadis, who was his sergeant. "I shot someone. He wouldn't answer."

Sakellariadis turned to George.

"Sergeant? Did you hear the sentry give the challenge?"

"It must be the captain," George said, starting toward the door; but Sakellariadis held him by the arm.

"Did everybody hear the sentry?"

The men said yes.

"And you, George? You heard the challenge?"

Looking at Sakellariadis, George felt again the challenge to his tenuous command. If he were to support the men, he would be joining their conspiracy against an officer, and he would relinquish the moral superiority that had enabled him to influence them in the past. Yet if he set himself against them, he would lose their friendship forever.

"I heard it," George said.

Next day, the battery was placed at the command of an overaged lieutenant who was neither sensible nor just. Morale and discipline deteriorated; and, before long, a few of the men confessed they missed Triandafilakos. But even the worst conditions can be endured when one is surrounded by his beloved friends.

350

MUDANYA

FEBRUARY, 1922

*T*he King's Men sent Dimitris to a purgatory called Mudanya, on the Sea of Marmara. It was a murky afternoon in February, and the empty harbor was as melancholy as a grave. The sea was dark; the sky was somber. Foam lay on the water like a greenish mold. Dimitris walked along the jetty, leaning on his cane, and stared at the deserted ammunition sheds and the barracks sealed with rusty padlocks. Weeds were growing in the storage yards.

In the autumn this had been the port of entry for the grand and misbegotten march on Ankara. Later, while Dimitris had been lying in a hospital bed, it had reverted to a fluke-hold on an unimportant inland sea, transshipping hides and gallnuts to Constantinople.

Nothing of importance could come in, since there was nothing left in Greece to send, and nothing of importance could go out. Mudanya had become a catch bowl for the broken and the unreliable—three hundred men and twenty officers, who were entitled by their injuries to be returned to Greece but were condemned by their political opinions to remain in Asia Minor.

Discontented soldiers frequented the coffeehouses, throwing down backgammon chips with gestures of exasperation. Cripples scraped along the jetty, up and down, as awkwardly as turtles, never speaking, eying one another's mutilations with contempt. The senior officers, mustached and blubbery, like walruses on boulders by the sea, would slowly turn the pages of a newspaper called *Rombia,* which was published at the Naval Station once a week and carried news reports from Tokyo and Hyperborea, facetious items noting the discovery of North America and letters posted just before the Battle of Thermopylae.

Nobody laughed at *Rombia:* it was reality. The exiles of Mudanya were like the seven derelicts in the cave at Ephesus, who had slept for centuries and woke to find their language dead, their wealth declined, their government supplanted and their religion overthrown. No flags, no signs, no posters beautified the windows of Mudanya; no photographs of Venizelos or the King. All that ancient world of spicy Hellenic rivalry and joyful controversy had disappeared. Greece was disintegrating. It was not a world to which Dimitris wished to waken.

He had enjoyed for a while the comforts of a hospital in Bursa, lying on his pillow, waiting for a visit from "Mother Anna," in a pleated uniform and veil, carrying a box of chocolate candy, or from a brace of giggling "Soldiers' Sisters," bearing hand-knit socks, outdated copies of *Ethnos Kyrix* and colored lithos of the saints. How tenderly they had regaled him with pistachios in strips of caramel, with jars of candied orange peels, postcards from Luxor and the Taunus, pamphlets dealing with atrocities in Macedonia!

The ward was a pleasant, clubby sort of place, confined to minor injuries—the little toe, the right forefinger and the rump. They burned the lights all night to discourage buggery; and most of the officers just lay there, sleepless, dreaming of some simple but authoritative post behind the lines. In the middle of the night, some amiable fool would usually get up, pull out his mandolin and start to sing. Or they would sit up, playing dominoes, until daylight crept across the gray impending slopes of Ulu Dagh.

Later, one could go on leave in Bursa. The army ran a club for officers, a whorehouse in a Turkish bath and a Soldiers' Center, where men who couldn't read or write dictated letters to a battery of girls from the Greek lycée. One could sit in a pastry shop and eat *tel kadife* with buffalo cream and watch the rain. In Bursa there were always interruptions, entertainments and recalls to glory—one never had to be alone. Lord Jesus, how he hated solitude! When he was by himself, he always thought about his injury, saw himself at Chal Dagh, kneeling in his tent, the muzzle of his pistol on his temple, on his chest and in his mouth.

To think—he might have killed himself! He sometimes had a frightful vision of a cenotaph, one of those ugly little souvenirs of war that can be seen in every neighborhood of Greece. This dirty yellowish marble stele stood in the center of Khalandri, where his mother lived, and Lieutenant D. Kalapothakis was buried under it—an unknown soldier, peed on every night by some disreputable drunkard coming from the wineshop. Decaying in the earth, Dimitris heard the happy youngsters singing as they crossed the square above his grave —"My Salonika Girl" and "Madelon" and "Tipperary"—and as they staggered home at midnight, stopping there beside the little cenotaph to pee on him.

How close he had come! He must have been delirious! It struck him as a tragic irony that on the very day that he had taken such a painful and dangerous step to escape, the General Staff had halted its incessant orders to attack, and the Battle of Sakarya had quietly ended. And now (a greater irony!) the Royalists were punishing him, who had been so harshly punished by fate.

In Mudanya he was always lonely. He tottered morosely through the wet and windswept streets, which smelled of kerosene and cabbage, the gamy breath of winter. Nobody wrote to him; and if anybody did, the bandits in the censor's office burned the letters. He was crippled, cut off, forgotten:

the unknown soldier. On many a bleak midwinter night, he got into his cold bed, shivering in all his clothes, with nothing to console his spirit but a few grams of olives and a small flask of medical alcohol.

One morning, Grace of God, an artillery captain came limping toward him on the jetty, saying with the passion of a curse:

"He's taking the waters at Salsomaggiore."

"Salsomaggiore?"

The captain, resting on his crutches, smiled eagerly, examining Dimitris' face.

"I said. 'He's taking the waters—' "

"I heard you, Captain," said Dimitris, feeling stupid and annoyed. The captain's smile evaporated.

"Mistake," he said, and he swung away.

Within an hour, Dimitris saw the captain on the mole again, conversing with a young lieutenant with a reddish face, who had been peering up and down as if expecting someone. When the captain left, Dimitris followed the lieutenant to a waterside café. Smiling fraternally, he chose a chair at the adjoining table, tapped on the lieutenant's back and whispered: "He's taking the waters at Salsomaggiore."

"Let him drink deep," the lieutenant answered. "Where are you from? Bursa? Good God, they just let you out, didn't they? Your face is the color of goat cheese."

"I'm never ruddy," said Dimitris, staring at the lieutenant's bulging cheeks, which looked like apples, mottled with a fiery color that suggested a naïve and apoplectic temperament. "What's new?"

"First Division?" the lieutenant said. "I thought you were a captain."

"I should have been."

"Ah. So should I." The lieutenant laughed humorlessly. "When I think of the things they've done to us ... It nauseates

354

me to realize the German swine is still alive."

And he showed Dimitris to an empty warehouse in a salt marsh, where a dozen officers were sitting at a table, muttering lugubriously. The crippled artillery captain looked up and gave a nervous start, but Dimitris went to him and whispered: "One can't be too careful!"

The meeting started. A lieutenant colonel, who appeared to be in charge, led off with a long critique of the infantry. Gripping the handle of his cane, Dimitris bounded up.

"Look at me! One leg two inches shorter than the other!" He fixed his gaze on the most badly injured officer among them, a cavalry lieutenant whose right forearm had been taken to the elbow. "Each of us picked his little *rosebud* on the slopes of Chal Dagh. In those days, we all were interested in victory. And I, for one, am *still* interested in victory. I will not give up *anything* that we have won. I will not leave Asia Minor except with four bearers!"

The others cheered hysterically. Huge tears ran down their leathery faces. Their bearded jowls quivered as they thumped their casts, their canes, their crutches on the floor. Then they began to argue furiously. Each of them had a more or less detailed proposal for remodeling the world.

Lieutenant Golos, for example, was a true conservative. He thought the King should abdicate in favor of one of his brothers, who would ask the English to negotiate a settlement in Asia Minor. Captain Klainos, on the other hand, favored retreating to a smaller zone surrounding Smyrna. Captain Papagrigorios argued for a military junta followed by dictatorship; Lieutenant Mavrocordatos wanted Greece to threaten to give Asia Minor back to the Turks—a form of diplomatic blackmail that would force the European Allies to intervene; and Major Skinos, who once had ridden in a Blériot from Lemnos to the coast, proposed an air raid on Constantinople.

As for the apple-cheeked lieutenant, whose name was Michael Pappas, he was bewitched by what he called an "exemplary solution."

"I'd do it myself," he said, growing redder by the moment. "But look at my thumb. I'd never trust my aim. It *nauseates* me, thinking of the opportunities we've lost! At Lavrion Station, for example, when they brought him back from Switzerland. The idiots bombarded him with flowers and confetti! I'd have sprinkled him with something else—steel tangerines! Iron grapes! Of course, *I* wasn't there."

Barrels of claret (which was scarce), jugs of raki (which was scarcer), bushels of tobacco (which was scarcer still, like cantaloupes in February) were consumed at this and subsequent debates; and Dimitris no longer suffered from loneliness.

He was entrusted with the work of liaison. Mastering the cipher, he developed an elaborate correspondence with mischievous officers all over Anatolia. There were Asia Minor Defense Committees in every army camp. At Afyon, two thousand men had signed a petition to the High Commissioner, asking him to take command of military operations in an Independent Anatolia. God alone knew whether the High Commissioner had any sense, but at least he was a Venizelist. General Papulas was reported to be "sympathetic"; so was the Patriarch; and every Venizelist could be counted on.

Still, the various Committees never quite agreed on what they wanted, or on what to do about it. In Greek politics, there were advantages in being vague. As Dimitris told Lieutenant Pappas, the first objective was to establish empathy.

"You know how we Greeks are. We've got to know what the rest of the community is doing. Remember when those naval officers shot Venizelos? Men all over Greece felt pains go shooting through their bodies. That's what I mean by empathy—like the Corsican Brothers, multiplied into a nation."

Before long, the Royalist government in Athens began to

feel empathetic pangs from the Venizelist cabal at Mudanya, and an order came to break up the concentration camp, which had become a forum of dissent. Some of the officers were sent to Bursa, others to Piraeus or Salonika. Dimitris, proclaiming that he was the victim of relentless persecution, was returned to Smyrna in the company of Lieutenant Pappas. He renewed his oath of loyalty to the Asia Minor Defense Committee, sealing it with many whiskery, tobacco-smelling kisses on the cheek; he had never felt more empathy.

Lieutenant Pappas pranced around the deck, raving about the splendid opportunities ahead.

"He's bound to come through Smyrna, and we can close his pages. Good God, a single bomb would do it, tossed into a passing car or planted in a tent. Remember when he passed through Ushak on his way up front? One grenade would have done it."

His face was as red as a pomegranate, and his fingers twitched as he tugged at imaginary fulminating pins. But Dimitris, breathing the fine spring air, wore a calm and saintly smile.

"I see it as a great occasion for self-renewal," he said. "A man who has been wounded for his country deserves an opportunity for reorientation." And he commenced a long and inspiring rumination on the waterfront cafés of Smyrna and the sprightly little Houses under Caravan Bridge.

*W*hen the first grass appeared in Anatolia, in the historic season of young love and military offensives, a new supreme commander took over the Army of the Hellenes. For fifteen days, this diligent, hyperactive soldier traveled up and down the Front, inspecting fingernails, boot polish, haircuts and insignia. He looked inside the mouths of horses; and at Afyon, he put some officers in jail for wearing uniforms with tarnished buttons.

Lieutenant General George Hadjianestis had been living in Lucerne as an exile for half a dozen years, but he did not intend to run the army as a vacation resort. He hoped to provide a personal example of those fundamental military virtues—stringent discipline, rigidity of character and cleanliness of body—which would equip his men to endure the worst tests that the Turks could impose upon them.

God only knew how deep the Hellenes had fallen into slothful habits in these recent years of politicking and rebellion! The general was disgusted to discover officers with lice and scabies, men with ulcers on their tongues and others so demoralized that they dealt promiscuously with the Turks, exchanging cigarettes for food, and cartridges for bits of cloth. Although many thousands of courts-martial were pending, few had been convened; and it was said that fourteen thousand soldiers, mostly Greeks of Asia Minor, had deserted

—had simply drifted home to tend their vineyards and enjoy their wives.

The men who remained in service indulged their thoughts with every sort of futile, rainbow-colored omen of hope. Whenever the Foreign Ministers of France and England met to consider the crisis in Anatolia—first in London, then in Paris, then again in London—the Greek soldiers dreamed that somehow the Powers of Europe would save them from the inevitable onslaught of the Turks. In Afyon and Alpi-köy and Seyit Gazi, homesick men laid wagers on the date of the evacuation. When the diplomatic conferences crumbled and the Powers of Europe turned away, the foolish hopes persisted in the ghostly fashion of illusions, which endure as prejudices long after they have been dispelled as rational ideas.

As General Hadjianestis made his way along the line, ordering punishment of frightened, hungry men as if they had been unruly cadets at a French military school, the army, incredibly, took courage. Even those unhappy soldiers who had passed the winter in the undernourished camps on the inland plateau were only mildly shocked to hear the general promising to win the war.

After all, the general's back was straight; his beard was neatly trimmed; his eyes were glittering. How could the Venizelists continue to say that he should be committed to a mental hospital? He seemed to brush away the threat of Mustapha Kemal as smoothly as a flatiron pressing nits from an infested uniform.

"Of course we'll take Constantinople!" he would say. "And when we get there, I'm going to yank the beard of that so-called Patriarch for the things he's said against our King!"

No one's spirits were more uplifted than those of Christos Trigonis. On the very day of the general's triumphant return to Smyrna, Christos made a gesture of faith so noble and magnanimous that he could scarcely contain his elation—in fact, could not contain it when he happened onto Professor Paleologos at the corner near the Hunters' Club. The Professor, dressed in a topcoat and a homburg, was giving his most baleful and pessimistic attention to some naval vessels in the harbor roads; but Christos rushed at him like a wrestler.

"Do you know what I've just done?"

"I suppose you went to welcome General Hadji-what'sit, the new old general. The old new general."

"I saw him, yes," Christos said. "Afterward—"

"What is this excitement about a general?" the professor said. "Alexander the Great had a tent spun of gold thread, with fifty golden pillars. But his bedclothes got pediculous, and off he went to the Elysian fields."

"Well, I admit Hadjianestis isn't Alexander—"

"He's a cock-a-doodle with a Saint-Cyr education," said the professor, whose opinions on all subjects had been strengthened by the recent publication of his monograph, *The Aberrations of Hellenic Thought,* which detailed the corruption of Greek humanism as a result of its syncretistic fusion with the Semitic concept of a father-god. "We've hired the town fool to pipe us on our march to doom."

"Ah?" Christos bit his lower lip. "You are more than normally elegiac."

"Yes. I confess to being deeply depressed each time I think about a Front four hundred and fifty miles long, defended by a few hungry boys and sheep dogs, with Mustapha Kemal on the other side."

"It's easy to stand back and criticize," Christos said. "I happen to have pledged five thousand drachmas today to a special fund the Metropolitan is raising for the defense of Asia Minor."

"Five thousand drachmas? How many millions are needed?"

"Oh, we shall have the money," Christos said, putting down his irritation. "A new war tax on goods and property. Great fortunes shall be taxed up to a fifth of their total value. Don't smile! I'm willing. What's money at a time like this?"

He paused, breathless with triumph. But the professor flapped his hand.

"If *I* had five thousand drachmas," he said, "I should use it to buy passage to Brazil."

With that insulting pessimism gnawing at his mind, Christos walked toward the Quay in such annoyance that he bumped into Dimitris Kalapothakis without recognizing him. Turning away, too cross to speak, he saw the lieutenant's face, and his spirits immediately bounded up again.

"This *is* a good omen!" he said. "The day's complete."

And he led Dimitris to a sidewalk restaurant. A soft wind that smelled of kelp and pine resin was blowing from the sea, and the awning cast a shadow on their heads.

"We've just greeted the new supreme commander," Christos said. "Isn't it a splendid day?" He smiled to indicate that in the fourteen months since they had seen each other, he had forgiven whatever needed forgiving in an exuberant young man. He could not forget the vulgarity with which Dimitris had greeted Eleni's accusation. But who could blame a boy for reacting crudely to an unfair charge? In any case, Dimitris obviously had suffered enough. He looked considerably older than he had a year before: his eyebrows came together in a scowl, and he was carrying a cane.

"I've been here for a week," he said. "Too busy to call."

"It doesn't matter," Christos said, feeling for the first time that it *did* matter. "What do you think of our General Hadjianestis?"

"That old scarecrow? He hasn't commanded a Boy Scout troop since 1913. He's fifty-eight years old."

"Does that strike you as archaic?"

"Also he's a hyena. Of the King."

Christos smiled.

"I'm no Royalist, as you know. But I admire him. There's nothing very warm about him. But he's firm. Precise. Objective."

Dimitris stuck his lips out disagreeably, but Christos went on:

"You and I may not agree with his politics, but it was a daring step, appointing him supreme commander. That's the sort of measure we need. He's a little strange, relatively unknown, but brilliant. A student of Pétain, Foch, Ney. A disciplinarian . . . Coffee for you, my boy?"

"Bring me a double raki."

"A double raki for the lieutenant," Christos said, hoping that his voice did not betray his disapproval. It was nine in the morning. "And one coffee, medium . . . We can't pretend we're not in danger. Fortunately, we're a people with ideas, imagination, infinite talent."

Dimitris stared glumly at the Quay, which had been decorated with flags and fronds to welcome the general.

"Wounded at Sangarius," he muttered, "and what did they do? Put me in a concentration camp."

"I'm absolutely sure we'll get a new loan from the English," Christos went on, searching his mind for cheerful news. "And the priests have been superb."

He felt that he must impress Dimitris with the daring measures of diplomacy and statesmanship that even now would save the Great Idea if only the Greeks could keep their faith. The High Commissioner of Smyrna had proclaimed an Independent Nation of Ionia. The Foreign Minister had announced a plan to seize the city of Constantinople as a hostage. Even the resuscitation of General Hadjianestis was an extreme expedient, like resurrecting a dead saint as an act of policy.

As for the cost of waging the war, that, too, required imagination and a sanguine soul. So it was that the Minister of Finance had risen in the Parliament, taken out a pair of shears and cut in half a hundred-drachma bill. In this simple, dramatic fashion, he would force a public loan of a million and a half drachmas: the portion of the bill that showed a portrait of George Stavros would remain in circulation, value fifty drachmas, while the other half would represent a loan to the government at 6 percent.

"But in my opinion the civilian population is not doing enough," Christos said. "We need *total* conscription. Even women. What do you say to that?"

Dimitris barely flicked his eyelids.

"You think it's too extreme?"

Christos knew there were certain functionaries in the High Commissioner's office who considered him fanatical. They called him, behind his back, Christos Bulgaroctonos, the Emperor of Byzantium, and they ridiculed his projects: his proposed balloon attack on Ankara, his youth brigade, his women's infantry, his Anti-Bolshevik Crusade of Christian Nations. As the leader of a delegation of demogerontes, he had called on the former commander, General Papulas, to demand more soldiers; and General Papulas, pulling out a desk drawer, had said sarcastically: "Where shall I find them? In here?"

"Because I'm really not extreme," Christos went on. "The Metropolitan has been asking for total conscription. All males from seventeen to fifty. There is no limit to our patriotism."

"Listen," Dimitris said, "if you really want to help, you'll stop quoting newspaper propaganda and give me some money for the defense of Asia Minor."

Christos sighed happily.

"You'll be pleased to know I pledged five thousand drachmas today to the Metropolitan Chrysostomos—"

"Bugger the Metropolitan," Dimitris said. "What about that house of yours in Bornova that's standing vacant? Can you give that to the Committee?"

Christos stared at Dimitris in bewilderment. The young man's tone was so hostile that he seemed more of an enemy than a compatriot. How could one reach him, through that thick tissue of battle scars, to convince him that his sacrifices had been worth while, that the fight would continue?

"Is it money for weapons?" Christos asked.

"Everything we do is confidential."

"Yes, I understand," Christos said, lowering his voice. "I mean, generally speaking?"

But Dimitris stood up.

"There's no point in arguing. Either you want to help us or you don't."

"But I *do*," Christos cried. "It's only my Greek curiosity." His mind raced through the ledgers of his fortune: his creditors, his cash, his properties, his crops. He thought of his old age, his duties to Sophia and George's patrimony; but none of them seemed to warrant such an extraordinary obligation as did this crisis of his nation. Dimitris was right: five thousand to the Metropolitan was a bubble.

"I'll give the house," he said. "Eleni's dowry house." And he saw an ironic smile twitch in the corner of Dimitris' mouth. "The staff, of course. A thousand a week for your expenses. What do you need? My bond for your debts? If we lose the war, there will be nothing left, in any case."

"I can assure you of this," Dimitris said. "We will never abandon Anatolia."

"Thank God," Christos said, almost in tears. Overwhelmed with emotion, he rushed off to the editorial office of *Amalthea* to write a prayerful editorial, thanking God for General Hadjianestis, the Metropolitan Chrysostomos and the Asia Minor Defense.

364

His monomania was like the ego of a young recruit who always thinks that God is on his side: Even when his fallacy has been disproved by ample evidence, he gulls himself with the illusion that the callous God, so arbitary and aloof, the God of stars and fire and endless space, will not subject him to a painful or ignoble death.

*F*or two months, the Greek people waited in growing anxiety for the beginning of the Turkish offensive. There could be no doubt that the attack was imminent. Every effort to forestall the showdown through diplomacy had failed, and the rival nations drifted toward their ultimate encounter, propelled along by the sort of blind complusion that drives a herd of migratory animals to its preordained place of death.

Every day or two, a squadron of Turkish cavalry would raid some crucial gap along the Front; and on each of these occasions, the agitated Greeks concluded that the campaign had started. But, in fact, the Turkish strategy was to allow the Front to stagnate during the heat of summer, while the Kemalists perfected their logistics, practiced their marksmanship and enjoyed the first fruits of their rebellion.

Mustapha Kemal's dusty little capital, deep in Anatolia, had become a symbol of the hopes of Asia. It was Holy Ankara, shrine of the fanatics, ideologists and opportunists of the Moslem East; and Unholy Ankara, bane of the imperialists, missionaries and concession seekers of the Christian West. Pilgrims and explorers crowded in until the old half-timbered houses on the slopes of the citadel almost bulged. The drinking water dwindled; the sewers overflowed; and still the votaries converged in homage to the Turkish miracle.

There were copper-colored disciples of Iqbal and Jinnah, from Lahore and Hyderabad; Egyptian princesses in exile, writing memoirs in French with dainty silver fountain pens; Parisian *journalistes,* eager to dedicate themselves, politically and physically, to Mustapha Kemal; bearded chauvinists from dying nations on the Asiatic marches of the Russian Soviet; Balkan terrorists; British agents; refugees from Shiva, Daghestan, Abkasia, Bokhara; pretenders to the leadership of Central Asiatic khanates, South American dictatorships and African sheikhdoms; Tatar revivalists and Mongol separatists; Ishmaelis, Druzes, Pontic Lazes; New England spinsters, doling out macaroni, wool socks and Sunshine Takhoma Soda Biscuits; Leninists and Marxists; Galato-Phrygian archaeologists; retired American admirals in search of mineral concessions; Jewish converts to Islam from the Masonic ledges of Salonika; devil worshipers of the Yezidi persuasion; Whirling Dervishes; Kalmuks, Khirghizes and Kuban Kossacks; false Popes, false Patriarchs, false Imams, false Mahdis, false Messiahs.

After the stalemate at Sakarya, the wayward, changeful, mercenary world perceived that fortune favored Mustapha Kemal. Its emissaries waited patiently for the end; while out on the line Greek and Turkish soldiers traded cigarettes for honeycombs, fresh eggs and briskets of wild boar, and swam fraternally in the Meander River, shouting back and forth as they were wringing out their uniforms.

The Pasha's master strategy was now complete. There would be two diversionary thrusts—one on the south, along the Meander Valley, the other on the north at Karaköy, the staging place for Greek supplies—and then the main assault, on the weakest, deepest outpost at the center of the line. The moment was chosen: a lucky Saturday, an early hour.

General Hadjianestis, at the same time, had prepared for the inevitable attack by shifting several of the strongest units

of his army out of Asia Minor to ward off the presumed men-
ace of Bulgaria, to which the general was inordinately sensitive, having served his active duty in a short campaign
against the Bulgars a decade earlier.

At dawn on August 25, the Turks in the vicinity of Seyit
Gazi showed a disturbing wakefulness. They set fires, beat
drums and scattered torches across the plain; and their cavalry galloped incessantly to and fro, stirring up clouds of dust
that masked the positions of the infantry encampments and
the field artillery.

The Greek artillery commander, a gaunt gray stork named
Farros, was standing in his dugout, looking through binoculars, when George came in. His sword was lying on a cot,
unsheathed; his freshly polished boots stood on the table. His
assistant, Major Varnoff, sweating in a helmet, regimentals
and shoulder boards, was holding up a map.

"Simple-minded Turkish trick," Colonel Farros said, with
his long white beak between the barrels of his field glass.
"Noises. Torches. Dust. Who the devil do they think they're
fooling?"

"Not you, sir," the major said. "It's just silly-smartness."

"What do you expect from the Turks?" Colonel Farros said.
"You don't get calligraphy from the ass end of the miller's
wife."

George came to a salute, standing in the doorway; but the
old colonel ignored him.

"Why, they haven't got more than one regiment across
there. It's just a diversion. They're really planning to attack
us farther north. Or south, for that matter. If I were old-
fashioned, Varnoff, I'd look through the shoulder bone of a
lamb, pretend to see the future and predict that the attack
wasn't coming here *at all.* Everyone would think I was a
soothsayer."

And he called a runner and dictated a dispatch, reporting

that the heavily armored Turkish 1st and 41st Divisions were massed against him, threatening an immediate attack.

George saluted and gave his name again.

"Where have you been?" Colonel Farros said, picking up his binoculars. "Will you accept a field commission? ... Great God, what a lot of dust they're making!"

"Right now, sir?"

"Don't you hear well, Trigonis?" cried the major, turning scarlet. "The colonel wants you to say yes or no."

"We're short of junior officers," the colonel said, almost apologetically. "We've had to transfer Belkis and promote Lamparis. Standards have evaporated." The colonel's breath was sour with age and indigestion, like the reek of a military cardroom. He was notoriously gloomy; and the only event that had heartened him all year was the visit of General Hadjianestis, a man of his own generation, who had won his respect by refusing to wear colored glasses in the sunshine because the younger men had none. "When I was your age," he told George, "I was studying log tables sixteen hours a day at the Military Academy, hoping I might be commissioned in time for the Battle of Armageddon. Now we take them right out of the cradle."

"That's right, that's right!" the major shouted. "And they show it, too."

George looked at the ground.

"I have to tell you something, sir. About my battery. Most of the men in my battery are committed to the idea of withdrawal."

"Withdrawal?" the colonel said.

"An orderly retreat, sir."

"In the name of Jesus," Colonel Farros said. "Don't you realize I have enough on my mind?"

"Retreat!" shouted Major Varnoff, panting with rage. "Is that all you young fellows have to think about?"

369

George did not answer. As a matter of fact, the tantalizing, seductive hope of abandoning Seyit Gazi without a fight had sustained his own sanity for several months. With nothing to eat but barley flour, nothing to do but talk and nothing to think about but home, the crew of Gentle Bouboulina had become preoccupied with retreat to the exclusion of all other subjects, even sex. Some of the men were in favor of withdrawing only as far as the former borders of Smyrna Province. Others were all for sailing to Greece and abandoning the accursed country to the Turks. Everyone was enchanted by a rumor that the General Staff had prepared a forty-day evacuation plan: five days to notify all units at the Front; eighteen days to move men and equipment to the coast; twelve days to evacuate a million Greek civilians to the Motherland; and five days to destroy all railways, bridges, roads and houses before waving goodbye to Mustapha Kemal. In six weeks, the modern myriad would be home; the Great Idea would be forgotten; and dreams of empire could be left for the millennium.

"Ah, these perpetual complaints," the colonel said, putting down his binoculars. "What if I ran over to Eskishehir every time I had a problem? 'Oh, General Soumilas! The men were disappointed with the wine we served them on His Majesty's name day. They call the cigarettes *suicide sticks*. My orderly has psoriasis. Major Varnoff's orderly has worms. One of the sergeants says his gunner wants to go home to Mommy.'" Suddenly, he bent and hissed in George's face. "Do you know what General Soumilas would say to me? He'd say, 'Don't you realize we have a Front that stretches all the way from Bursa to the Big Meander? Don't you know the Turks have one hundred and thirty thousand men? And five thousand cavalry? And four hundred planes on order? And you bring me the information that the men of your battery would like to go home!'"

The colonel appealed to Major Varnoff with a grimace. But George said:

"The men keep hoping, sir. I'm not sure what they'll do."

"You'll just have to learn the language of command. How old are you?"

George answered; and the colonel closed his eyes.

As George was leaving the dugout, the sun came up, and the morning barrage began. It continued longer than usual. George was halfway to the battery when a corporal ran down the hillside, shrieking: "It's started!"

On either side, men threw themselves onto the ground and lay like corpses, pale as cement. Others ran around in circles, picking up objects and putting them down again, or dashed behind the cottages to void their bowels. Shells were falling in the center of the town.

George crossed himself and ran toward Despinoula, thinking: Where the devil can I go and sew my patches on?

He bumped into Loukas. They looked at each other blankly. Loukas said:

"I'll go move my gun behind the hill."

"No, wait," George said. "They've just put me in charge. You have to wait for my orders."

Loukas stared at him, blinking in astonishment.

"That's fine," he said. "Did they commission you?" He raised an equivocal salute. "I'll go move my gun, Lieutenant."

"You haven't heard my orders."

"Give them, in the name of God!"

George thought for a moment.

"Go man your gun," he said. "Stand by for word from the colonel."

"That's idiotic," Loukas said. George watched him turn away.

"Oh, Louka?" he said; and his friend, the country gentleman, came back and waited like a servant. "Pass the order to the others."

"Yes, sir," said Loukas. A peculiar smile creased his cheek.

The mountain trembled underfoot with the concussion of the barrage.

*W*ithout explanation or apology, the Greek command returned Laurel Konak to its Turkish owners.

Eleni, who had never lived there, was pleased to move to town. Through the lattice she could see across the tops of fig trees to a little graveyard where an old man sat cross-legged on a tombstone, reading the Koran.

She felt as if she had been rescued from imprisonment, like the Prisoner of Chillon. Her life was suddenly bewildering and rich. Household goods that had been hidden, God knows where, began to reappear: Bohemian sherbet glasses, wine-colored Ladiks, Bokharas, Kayseris. There were enormous wooden chests that smelled of rose oil, bolts of damask, gold brocade and satin jackets trimmed with silver beads.

Even Abdullah's mother began to radiate a meager warmth, now that her property had been restored. On the morning of Kurban Bayram, the Festival of Sacrifice, she took some folded garments from the chiffonier and smelled them, one by one.

"Now, this, your husband wore. . . . This, my other son, Kenan, wore at his circumcision. . . . This cloak belongs to Granny—Grace of God, these things were hidden from the Greeks! Look at this—it was my mother's dress, the loveliest I ever saw. It cost a hundred francs. She wore it when she visited the leading wife of Sultan Abdul Hamit." Then, impulsively: "Why don't you try it on?"

Eleni held the faded ecru silk against her breast.

"I think, for me, the waist is small."

"Her waist was like your thumb. But try it on, my love. I want to see you."

The gown was cut in the high-necked style of Paris in the 1880s—years of her father's boyhood, a hazy, golden time. Gulnar, Yildiz and Emine came over with gleaming eyes to touch the garment that had visited the Sultan's palace.

Eleni had never felt them drawn to her before. She was strongly moved. It was as if she had been looking through a stranger's family album and had found there, on the final page, a picture of herself. Her husband's mother, who always had been so disapproving and aloof, murmured: "Lovely, lovely. . . . How well I can remember how we watched Mama climbing into that black Victoria to go to Yildiz Kiosk! Of course, she wore a charshaf and a *very* heavy veil. No one would walk to the end of her garden in those days without veiling. But when they got to the palace, the ladies took off their cloaks, and all of them were dressed in dancing slippers, evening wraps—the latest Paris gowns! And what a place it was—fountains everywhere and crystal chandeliers ten feet across. In every sitting room there was a magnificent porcelain stove as high as the ceiling, with the Sultan's seal and his initials, *gallicé,* across the panels. And the ladies were exquisite—delicate, pale, charming. Most of them had been purchased from Caucasia as young girls, like Granny was. They had to be taught how to sit in a chair. . . . Oh, what *is* it?" With a gesture of annoyance, she stopped to listen to a servant who was hissing at her ear. "In the reception room downstairs," she said at last. "Make tea. First, apricot preserves. Then tea with lemon." She smiled around. "Well! They are beginning to notice us again!"

And she got up and went to the wardrobe.

"Get dressed, Gulnar. Yildiz? We'll see them *à la Franque* in the reception room. Eleni? That's how you entertain your callers in the city, isn't it?"

Sounds of agitated preparations rose from the salon: the snap of bolts, the creak of hinges and the sigh of draperies. Maids ran barefoot up and down the corridors. Peering down the stairway, Eleni saw two women who were standing close together, fingering the throats of their black dresses.

"Why, they're Greek!"

"Of course," her mother-in-law said, eyes flashing. "It's the candymaker's widow and her kin. Imagine seeing *them.*"

She picked out a robe of azure velvet, badly stained, perfumed herself and put on earrings, pendants, brooches, buckles and a double strand of artificial diamonds. "I've always loved these diamonds," she went on, taking a pot of kohl and an eyebrush from the servant. "My husband said gold was all right for the Arabs, pearls for Greeks—but diamonds were for us."

Gulnar was putting on a green Shiraz brocade. Aunt Emine got out a shroud of purple lace, and Yildiz wrapped herself in a kimono and a Spanish shawl. Going down, they could see the two Greek women sitting side by side, their hands clasped on their bellies and their dark eyes flickering to and fro. One of them was small and tawny, like the berry of a terebinth; and the other fat and watery, the center of a pastry. They bumped each other in their eagerness to take their hostess by the hand, to press her fingertips against their foreheads, to tell her that they "found a welcome."

No one, it seemed, remembered anybody's name. Everyone called each other "Madam" and liberally applied those innocent and otiose diminutives that sound elaborate or intimate in other tongues—my soul, my life, my sugar—but are used in Turkish conversation with a grand impartiality, to soothe a lover or to summon a delivery boy. The can-

375

dymaker's widow, pressing one hand apologetically against her heart, conversed with great fluidity and frightful grammar, gazing at her hostess with a timid smile.

"*Hanum efendi?*" she said at last. "Forgive me, please. . . . Do you by any chance speak French?"

"Of course, my sweet," Abdullah's mother said. "But Turkish is our language, my loukoum."

"Of course, *hanum efendi.* Only my sister—she is actually my sister-in-law, you see—was born in Janina, and she speaks only French. And Greek, of course."

"My daughter is Orthodox," the mother said. "But her Turkish is improving. Isn't it, my love?" Frowning, she leaned toward the Greek woman from Janina and said slowly: "*Écoutez, chérie! Il faut que vous apprendriez la langue turque, n'est-ce pas?*"

"How interesting," said the candymaker's widow, darting a glance at Eleni. "Your daughter is Orthodox?" She turned and murmured something, and her sister looked up quickly.

The small, dark sister, whose forehead wrinkled into pleasant little lines, reminded Eleni of Mrs. Vitalis, who used to call on Tuesday afternoons and stay until she heard the Vespers bell. As for the candymaker's widow, she resembled Mrs. Lascaris, the doctor's wife, who weighed a hundred and fifty pounds, yet was as graceful as a cypress tree. Mrs. Lascaris often brought her daughters to the house, and they would roll the carpets back, turn on the gramophone and dance the tango. Mama always served a famous conserve, made with kumquats, and a marmalade of figs and raisins; then, later, with their tea, they had a box of English toffee and a tray of Danish cookies from the Luna Bakery—almond macaroons and crisp white finger wafers, filled with jam and dipped in bitter chocolate.

"You know, my dear," Abdullah's mother said, "this is a feast day for us Moslems. Our greatest holiday. It commemorates the sacrifice of the scapegoat in place of Father Abraham's beloved son Ishmael."

"*Is'mael?*"

"As recounted in the Holy Book."

"Ah, yes" the Greek woman said. "That's why we called, *hanum efendi*. To say, 'May your holiday be joyful.' "

"After fourth prayer, my son will slaughter two lambs and a goat. We give most of the meat in alms, and the skins this year—"

"It's like the paschal lamb," Eleni interrupted, speaking Greek. She could see before her eyes the springtime lambs of Smyrna, which are tinted rose and indigo in Passion Week, glutted on salted currants and paraded through the fields on Holy Saturday. Her father used to cut the neck veins of the lambs; and Mama would squat beside him like a peasant woman, dipping her fingers in the blood and marking crosses on the children's foreheads and the lintels of the doors. Four years ago, they had sacrificed ten lambs, and Papa sold the wool to benefit St. Charalampos Hospital. "Exactly like the paschal lamb."

"What's that?" her husband's mother said in Turkish. "Please speak the language of the house my love."

Eleni's face turned hot. The candymaker's widow answered hastily:

"Why, *hanum efendi*, your daughter was explaining, it's like our Easter lamb. There's a lot in common, isn't there?"

Abdullah's mother closed her eyes and smiled.

"Very little," she said.

The Greek woman, blotting her forehead with a handkerchief, looked up in relief as the servant brought a tray of preserves and goblets of chilled water. Her eyes kept turning to Eleni's face, as if to ask a question. After tea, when they were going up the stairs, she softly pressed Eleni's arm.

"My dear *madama?* Let me have a word with you."

But they must cross the upper hall where Granny waited with a bony claw uplifted for the kiss of reverence. Then Eleni had to find the key to open the knickknack case. Her husband's mother decreed that everyone must inspect a string of amber beads that had belonged to Granny's husband and a silver box that held her uncle's Holy Book when he was fighting under Osman Pasha at the siege of Plevna. They admired a cup, inscribed with sacred writings, which had been carved from black obsidian found only on the mountaintop where Moses died, and a strip of black silk damask, cut from the covering of the sacred Kaaba at Mecca.

As Eleni bent to close the case, the Greek widow met her face to face and whispered passionately:

"You have no idea how desperate we are! It is the beginning of the end."

Raising her eyes, Eleni found Abdullah's mother staring at them.

"Eleni?" she said. "Shall we show the clothes now?"

Still the Greek woman clutched Eleni's wrist.

"A single word from you, *madama*. It could help us so much. . . . "

Eleni hesitated. Then she drew her arm away and turned in the direction of the wardrobe trunks. The candymaker's widow cleared her throat and said that she reluctantly must ask permission to go home.

"It is a holy day for us, too," she said, looking steadily at Eleni. "Saint Mary Magdalene, the *myrophoros*." And with her lips she formed a silent word.

Before the door was fully closed, old Granny cried out vindictively:

"The milk of their suck is coming back in their nostrils!"

Gulnar was smiling as she put away a box of beads. Abdullah's mother, flushed with vivid color, cast her eyes around the room and sighed in pleasure. Passing the mirror in the hall, Eleni stopped and scrutinized herself. Was it she, parading ancient Paris fashion in a harem? She was so unmistakably a Greek. Her nose and forehead formed a single line. Her nostrils, wide and highly arched, her lips protruding in a stubborn little pout, her father's Cretan coloring—everything proclaimed her origin: the widow and her sister must have known the instant they saw her.

She studied the dress that had been well received at Yildiz Palace. It swayed limply, giving off a little dust. The fumes of its decay assailed her nostrils. The lace was peeling off it like the tissue of a desquamating reptile. The fabric moldered like a mummy's cloth.

"Help me out of this!" she cried. "Where is the maid?"

Her husband's mother crossed the hall.

"I thought you'd want to wear it longer," she said in an injured tone. "But, I suppose, to you a Paris dress is like sending cumin to Kerman."

"Why did those women come today?" Eleni said angrily. "Don't they have any manners?"

And she ran to find her husband, who was making preparations for the sacrifice. He was sitting in the arbor with an imam they had hired to recite the epic of the Prophet's life, in memory of Abdullah's father, the heroic Hilmi Pasha. The old man had taken off his turban and his crimson robe and was leaning back among the dusty leaves. He turned away in horror when he saw Eleni with an unveiled face.

Abdullah came out to meet her on the path. His round, reflective face was strangely vacant. Eleni grasped his hands impatiently.

"What is happening?"

"You mean the war? God knows. It seems to be the end for the Greek expedition. The situation may open some revolutionary opportunities. Who knows?"

"What are we going to do?"

379

"What do you mean?"

"We can't live under Mustapha Kemal."

"We've lived under General Papulas."

"Papulas! How can you compare them?"

"I have never been fond of either of them."

"Where can we go? The Turks will call you a traitor."

"And the Greeks consider me a spy."

Laughing, he gently urged her down the path in the direction of the house. But Eleni drew her arm away.

"What will they say about a Turk who has a Greek wife? They'll persecute you."

"They will be consumed with envy."

"I'll never fit in here, in this house. I'll always be a stranger."

Abdullah looked at her in astonishment. Just then, the muezzin began the call to evening prayer. The imam beckoned from the summerhouse, and the family came across the garden, led by Mahmut Zia, who was carrying a tiny vial of water that his brother-in-law, the heroic Hilmi, had brought back from a sacred well in Mecca.

Eleni waited in the garden while the others prayed. They sacrificed a single lamb, no larger than a dog. It bleated as Abdullah cut off its head; and then the mouth continued bleating and the legs continued kicking as the old imam carried the decapitated carcass to the kitchen to be drawn. At twilight the servants laid the dust with water, hung lanterns in the trees and unlocked the gates. The Turkish neighbors came to hear the celebrated imam chanting the *Mevlut*.

KÜTAHYA
AUGUST, 1922

*A*t dusk on the third day of the retreat from Seyit Gazi, George's battery reached the railway tracks at a place called Alayunt. A runner brought a message from the colonel. George read the order three times.

"With the *rear* guard?" he said at last. "He must be crazy." And he walked back toward staff company, rolling the moist ball of paper between his numb hands.

It had been raining during the afternoon, but at sundown the clouds began to break apart. The night air smelled of smoke and soggy ashes. There were pools of muddy water in the fields, and the tracks were glittering with wetness in the fading silver light. The men of George's battery were lying barefoot in the shelter of the commissary wagons. As George went past, they raised their heads and scowled at him, the symbol of the Greek collapse: an officer who was too young to be respected, too artless to conceal his own uncertainty. Only in desperation would an army have bestowed a position of leadership on a naïve, self-doubting kid who hated the system of ritual bloodletting he was trusted to sustain. Fortunately, George had not yet been compelled to exert authority. There was no word of command that needed to be spoken, nothing to explain except the inexplicable—the westward march, the hunger and the Turks pursuing the retreating Greeks with artillery at dawn and cavalry at dusk.

381

Even before the battery had left the slopes of Seyit Gazi, the last vestiges of Captain Triandafilakos' discipline had begun to fall apart. In the confusion of the first attack, it would have been impossible for anyone to maintain authority. Stunned by the thunder of the Turkish guns, the men hid like rabbits in their holes. Nothing could make them move, not even the horrible threat of a bayonet attack. Only the guardhouse erupted with a burst of energy: a colonel named Nicholas Tsipouras, who had been locked up for speaking insolently to General Hadjianestis, pounded his fists against the bars while the other prisoners screamed for attention. Finally, a squad of riflemen burst in and opened all the cells, crying: "Get back to your regiments! The Turks have broken the line at Afyon. We're finished!" Running out, the prisoners stepped on the sergeant of the guard, who was lying on his belly, kissing an ikon of the Holy Virgin.

It was noon before George received instructions from the commander of the 10th Division to dismount artillery, pick up equipment and rendezvous below. By the time he reached the crest, Tall Johnny's men already had taken down their gun. Streaks of dirt and sweat were running down their naked shoulders as they strapped the barrel onto a mule. George climbed up on the revetment and repeated the commander's order to dismount the gun.

Tall Johnny raised his head and blinked in astonishment. He was as large as George and blacker than an Arab, with a face like a newly burnished sword; and he was not tolerant of supererogatory orders.

"Lieutenant, we're halfway home," he said; and his men rushed down the hill without waiting for further instructions. Their faces were rigid with the shock of the barrage.

Mindless, wordless, the men melted into a growing line of trucks and animals and men. Quilts and mattresses were flying out of windows. A purple cloud of gun smoke trembled in the air. The Turks began to shell again, farther south, and there was an incessant screaming from the mosque, where some cooks were slaughtering pigs to desecrate the ground.

For several hours, the column waited to draw bread—four days' supply—while orders and rumors quivered like electric shocks along the line. First, the 10th was moving north toward Eski; then they were moving south toward Afyon; finally, they were moving west across the valley of the Charkilar. In the end, they only queued up to fill their water bottles at a well. George ordered two of his men to go and find a bucket, and, to his surprise, they went. The gunners stood in line, waiting their turn to drink the flat, brown water. As each man took the earthen jug, he lifted his perspiring face like a communicant receiving the Holy Eucharist.

During that first afternoon, the wireless carried pitiful appeals for help, for leadership, for information. Nobody knew where the Turks were concentrated. At nightfall, from headquarters 350 miles to the rear, General Hadjianestis ordered a "mild attack" in every sector. Colonel Farros groaned; Major Varnoff cursed; and the retreat proceeded without interruption.

A man named Skouras disappeared at Ak-oluk; a gunpointer drifted away as the column was passing through a gorge; and the remaining men would pay attention only to the comfort of their bellies and their feet. Receiving their tiny rations of hardtack bread, they would snarl at George: "Take it back. I'd rather starve fast than slow."

And George, lying shamelessly in defense of the army he detested, would reassure them that there was food and water just ahead. His self-esteem had never been so low. Had he been capable of showing any courage, he would never have reached this point of degradation. He would have counseled mutiny and capitulation. Kneading the wad of paper that carried the colonel's ridiculous orders, he felt a wave of rebellion rising in his throat.

Staff company was a mile back, behind the medium guns, encircled by a suite of guards, stenographers, supply clerks, runners, radio operators and irritable pastry cooks, who rode like pashas in the empty commissary wagons. Five hundred yards farther back was the rear guard of rifles and machine guns, a soft, deteriorating tail in which the colonel now proposed to station George's battery of mountain guns.

Approaching staff company through the soggy pastures, George could hear the wireless sputtering with frantic calls from other Greek divisions: "Where are you? . . . Heavy cavalry attack here. . . . Our left flank threatened. . . . Give position." Somehow, the radio transmitters that belonged to General Tricoupis' group on the Southern Front had arrived in Eskishehir, on the Northern Front. From this vantage point, the operators were disseminating an announcement that the objectives of the army had not yet been clarified.

Generators banged and sneezed and farted clouds of carbon fumes. Sentries and messengers bumped together in the dark. Officers were craning their necks and shouting: "Give position!"

Colonel Farros' tent was the center of a nervous crowd. A pair of sentries held a puffy, weeping man, completely naked and brick red with mud, with his arms bent up behind his back and pinioned like the wings of poultry.

"He's got a funny accent," somebody said.

"Kill him first, identify him later."

And the prisoner, blubbering incomprehensibly, writhed in terror.

"What was he doing? Sneaking around the horses?"

With an appalling effort, the man succeeded in gesturing that he was starving. The guards gave him some crackers and permitted him to stuff his mouth. Huge tears ran down his cheeks. A Greek? Of course he was a Greek! Thirty-second Regiment, Kütahya. The Turks had rushed them like fiends out of Hell: artillery, then cavalry, then bayonets. . . .

He shuddered convulsively. The sentries let him fill his mouth again. Colonel Farros gripped his riding crop, gnawed at his mustache and blinked his eyes.

"How many, in Jesus' name? How many cavalry?"

"Forty thousand. They rode straight through our lines and circled back and circled back again, and every time they passed, they swung their swords. A single blow could take your arm off or split your skull open like a melon. And then their infantry came rushing at us, bellowing and snarling, *'Allah! Allah!'* And they could disembowel you with a single thrust."

His tears were flowing steadily. The sentries let go of his arms, and he plunged his hands among the crackers.

"Where . . . where are they now?" the colonel asked.

But the fugitive, who had bolted several pounds of crackers, turned gray and leaned forward. The colonel went on:

"We'll send you to Division for interrogation. . . . Say, what's the matter there?"

The man doubled up with cramp. The guards laid him on a blanket, covered him with quilts and chafed his hands. Somebody gave him water, but it made him vomit more. The colonel turned away. His glassy eyes passed over George's face.

"Some camomile," the colonel muttered. "A little broth." He pressed his palms against his ears to shut out the sound of retching. George smoothed out the crumpled message and showed it to him.

"Mistake?" the colonel said. "Why, no. There's no mistake. We need you at the rear."

"What am I supposed to tell my men?" George said, and his rebellious anger seethed up and overwhelmed him. "I can't order a battery of field artillery to take the rear. They're already out of hand."

"God in Heaven!" the colonel shouted. "What sort of officer are you? Don't you see the situation?"

And, waving his arms in a wild, hopeless gesture that embraced the telegraph, the convulsive fugitive, the whole hungry, sodden, frightened myriad of the retreat, he plunged into his tent and closed the flap.

In fifteen minutes, the fugitive was dead. His arms were clamped around his knees. A chaplain, passing in a wooden cart, hopped down, anointed the corpse, whispered a prayer, climbed back into the cart and drove on without glancing back. Later there were other stragglers from the 32nd Regiment. They crept along the edges of the meadow, waving handkerchiefs or underpants, which fluttered in the dark like large white doves, Now and then, a frightened sentry, hearing movement in the underbrush, would fire blindly; and the response would be a weak, and despairing sob.

Never had the enemy pressed so close before. Turkish campfires glimmered in the mountains to the north and east; Turkish blinkers signaled to the citadel above Kütahya. The night orders of the 10th Division reflected acute alarm. No campfires. Soldiers forbidden to undress. Division to form a circle, like a troop of pilgrims in the wilderness, with pickets posted on the slopes above. Password: Paschalis-Dardanelles.

But the men fell asleep in the postures of the dead: knees upraised, arms outflung, heads thrown back as if to gasp for breath. George lay on his side with his eyes open. He saw himself addressing them:

"We shall succeed." (More likely, they would fail.) "Everything will be all right." (God willing, half of them would pass Kütahya.) "Remember, you are Greeks. Be brave! Be proud!" (But why?)

Falling asleep, he thought he heard them whispering: Too

young ... Too weak! ... A stronger officer would have refused to take the rear.

Toward dawn a muffled scraping woke him.

"Who's there?" he said in a loud, steady voice. "Step up and show your face."

There was no answer, and he called again. The men began to stir. George held his breath. At the dawn muster, two more crewmen from Despo were missing.

A commissary wagon brought the morning ration—hardtack bread, a handful of crude sugar for each man, and some canned sardines.

"They'll move us north," said Goufas. "It's collapsed on the south."

"It's collapsed on the north," said someone else; and everyone began to argue about the direction of the sea.

Steam was rising from the withered grass. The forward companies moved toward a gorge that led directly to Kütahya; but George restrained his battery. He let the stretcher bearers pass. The engineers came from behind and brushed around them, hauling fulminates and spools of cable in donkey carts that were disintegrating from abuse.

George's men began to look at him in alarm. They could hear the rumble of Turkish artillery. Staff company slipped past, entering the canyon. A row of empty cooking carts went by; and still the battery waited.

Suddenly, George was confronted by the face of Loukas, pale with terror.

"Why don't we move?"

George told him.

"That's ridiculous!" Loukas said, almost weeping. "Who ever heard of putting field artillery in the rear guard? Does he want the Turks to capture us?"

"Of course not."

"Then why does he put us at the tail?"

"It's none of your business where we march."

Loukas stared at him. A moment later, the machine-gun company was passing, and George shouted to the men. They rushed toward the defile. For three hours, the Turks pursued them, lobbing shells on them from above. Two men were killed.

At dark, the division stopped in a place called Genik-deren, where there were some wells of sweet water. Loukas, Goufas, Sakellariadis and five others disappeared during the night, taking with them several sacks of flour. No one could determine whether they had headed north toward Tavshanli and Bursa, west along the gorge of the Simav or south in the direction of Gediz and Ushak.

In precaution, the colonel scattered the remaining members of the battery to other units. The guns were handed over to a sergeant major; and George was ordered to march among the stragglers at the rear. Speechless with the enormity of his failure, George stood waiting to hear the colonel's reprimand. But the colonel was preoccupied. He looked at George blankly and said: "Go! Go!"

The division gave up their effort to find the way to Ushak in order to contact the southern portion of the army. Setting fire to the mean little houses of Genik-deren, they threw a dead donkey into the well and marched in the direction of the sea.

An airplane from Alashehir flew over, dropping a message in an iron box. Ushak had been evacuated and was burning, raising a gray umbrella cloud a thousand yards high. A vestige of the southern army, in a column thirty miles long, was fleeing toward Smyrna after a disaster at a railroad village called Dumlupinar.

*L*ittle by little the people of Smyrna learned about the crisis.

At first, there were terrifying rumors that the army had disintegrated and Mustapha Kemal was sweeping forward with a horde of cavalry. Next came military bulletins from General Hadjianestis, reporting laconically that the army was intact and was regrouping on a new defensive line. Finally, the city was swept by strange reports from Rome and London, fantasies concocted in the coffeehouses and exaggerated stories told by fugitives.

A ceaseless caravan of wooden carts began to enter Smyrna. Men with sweatbands tied around their heads were perched above the swaying oxen, and the women rode in back, half buried in faded quilts and scraps of furniture, and holding on to children. Country priests arrived with wagonloads of satin altar cloths and gilded candelabra, wedding crowns and holy ikons that were dark with wax and crusted with embroidery and silver leaf.

The Metropolitan Chrysostomos ordered dispensations to the refugees. Every day, he walked along the alleys of the Frankish quarter, wearing a heavy golden crown and a brocaded pallium, and distributed a dole of rice and olive oil to women who were nursing babies in the shade of the wagons. The bells of the cathedral rang for special prayers, and the Metropolitan began a fast of expiation.

In the restaurants on the Quay, merchants who had never eaten in a public place were seen devouring plates of greens in oil and reaching for macaroni, watermelons and spinach pies. In the midst of rapid conversation, they would stop and cock their heads as if to listen for a distant sound; then, bursting out with nervous laughter, they would draw their breath again, snatch up their forks and gobble as voraciously as starving cats.

The streets, the churches and the waterside cafés were crowded night and day. There were bearded Greek deserters, dressed as village deacons; yellowish Syrians, who smuggled tubes of opium secreted in their rectums; cold-eyed Maltese, who would exchange a British passport for a diamond ring; and irritable European manufacturers, who carried wallets full of unpaid invoices for merchandise delivered to the Army of the Hellenes. Smugglers from Samos peddled rifles by the case, and boatmen from Crete were offering their tubs for hire at crushing prices.

The harbor filled and emptied every day; yet growing pyramids of goods consigned to Europe accumulated on the verges of the Quay. The commercial districts smelled of rotting fruit. Clever merchants sold their stocks for gold and closed their doors. The rich, the hunted and the perfidious began to leave the city.

When Christos walked along the esplanade at sunset, he would encounter heavily laden carriages rattling down the Quay in the direction of the port. At Pasaport, he saw a Dutchman and his wife, with blond children on their laps and steamer trunks against their shins; next, a Greek tobacco grower; and, a hundred yards behind, a family of Turks, whose look of sleek prosperity identified them as opponents of the Ankara rebellion. The men were wearing Stamboul cutaways and patent-leather shoes, and the women, veiled

390

with filmy tarlatan, carried parasols of watered silk to shield themselves against the luster of the sea.

Faithless! Did they suppose that Smyrna was about to evaporate? A city founded by the Amazons? A city destined by the Lord to wear a crown of life?

Smyrna had never been, like Rome, a seat of power; or like New York, a gate of hope; or like Paris, a progenitor of fashionable manners; or like Manchester, a fabricator of supplies; or like Constantinople, a cynosure of emperors; or like Jerusalem, a shrine of creeds. It had always been a trading city, practical and predatory, strangling its competitors, subjugating its provisioners, fawning on its customers. When Alexander ruled the world, when the Venetians spread their factories around the sea, when Yankee clippers carried Turkey carpets, scammony and tragacanth to Boston Town, Smyrna was the indispensable negotiant between the East and West: heartless, rich and useful.

Because of this, Smyrna would not perish. The world would not give up its railway, its chromium mines, its licorice roots, its dried fruits, its aromatic tobacco, its Quay, its gasworks, its missionary schools. Even if the Greek Army failed, the navies of Europe would move in to protect the city. Christos could picture them, steaming up the gulf at daybreak: a fleet of dreadnoughts, bringing peace and harmony to Anatolia.

But when Christos stared across the harbor, he saw only a solitary steamer riding out to sea, beyond the melancholy shadow of the cape; and when he came to his house, there was a carriage standing at the gate. The marble steps were strewn with packing boxes; the shutters were closed; the door was chained. Through the glass panels, he could see Polixeni, dressed in winter clothing and a heavy scarf, crouching on a carton in the foyer, pressing her hands on her ears and shuddering convulsively. Christos raised his cane and hammered on the grille.

391

Polixeni jumped up and bleated. When she drew the bolt, her hands were trembling like the pinions of a moth.

The corridor was filled with carpetbags and wicker hampers capped with muslin. There were metal-plated chests with blue-green paper pasted on the ends, wooden boxes tied with ropes and Gladstone bags defaced with peeling stickers from resorts in Switzerland. On the stairway was a cataract of dried-up ferns and brownish perfume bottles, empty bonbon tins and broken figurines.

Closing his eyes and swallowing to calm his anger, Christos climbed the stairs and gently called his wife. Down the hall, he saw the burgundy glitter of her hair.

"I can't believe it," he said, following her to the bedroom. It was suffocating with the windows barred, but Sophia was wearing the heavy woolen travel dress that he had bought for her to wear to Athens. As he watched, she slipped a bracelet into her bosom and pulled on gloves to hide her rings.

"Listen to those dreadful bells!" she said. "It's like a wake. Like Holy Friday."

"Sophia, don't you have any faith?"

Sophia responded with a choking noise: she was swallowing her earrings. Pulling out drawers, she covered the top of the dresser with cakes of rouge and jars of ointment. With a sob, she swept them to the floor, opened her arms and came to him.

"Oh, Christo! I haven't slept for weeks. I think continually of fire. Last night a boy started screaming in the street, 'They're coming!' and I was *sure* I heard their horses galloping along the Quay."

"Nonsense. You need a sleeping pill."

"The town is full of refugees. There'll be a plague of cholera."

"Don't be silly. I saw the Metropolitan again today, and he is making a personal visit to all the foreign consulates, asking them to send a fleet of warships."

He pulled at the tips of Sophia's gloves; but she drew her hand away.

"Foreign battleships won't save us from cholera."

"What a lot of fears you have." He stroked her head as if she were a frightened child. "Don't you trust me, Sophia?"

At last she raised her mouth for him to kiss. Her dark eyes overflowed with tears. He led her to the window and opened the shutters onto the garden, which exhaled a scent of jasmine and wet gravel. On the hills above the bay, a scattering of humble lanterns glittered like declining stars.

"Don't you know the Angel promised Smyrna suffering and tribulation, and a crown of life?"

"I know."

"And Smyrna has survived."

"I know."

She raised her mouth again. But Christos gestured toward the lights, as if they proved his thesis. There it was—the deathless city! Lydians and Persians had assailed it; kings of Pergamos had humbled it; Seljuk princes, Ottoman corsairs and knights of the Crusades had conquered it; Tamerlane had filled its port with stones and built a tower of a thousand human heads to commemorate his visit; and the footsteps of Arabs, Genovese, Huns and Venetians had echoed on its shores. Its ordeals were numbered like the stars; yet Smyrna had endured.

Sophia was leaning on his shoulder, breathing quietly, her face relaxing in a placid smile. Then the cook began to scream. It seemed that she had felt a draft of air and thought the Turks were climbing in the windows.

"What a donkey!" Christos said.

But Sophia ran out and leaned over the balustrade.

"Oh, dear God," she murmured, and her breath grew quicker. "Dear God and Holy Virgin. What was I thinking?" She crossed herself and closed her eyes. "It goes at midnight. An Egyptian ship, I think. . . I'll put on my negligee, then my

393

coats over that. Or should I wrap my necklaces around my waist?"

And she rushed to the dresser again and resumed her frantic looting. Christos watched in silence. Finally, he said:

"Sophia, I forbid you to leave the house."

But his wife did not respond. Christos went downstairs to take charge of the cook, who was trying to push a wicker basket out the door.

"Unpack these things at once," he said.

Polixeni cast up her eyes and continued to shove the hamper toward the marble steps. A cart had joined the carriage at the door. The two drivers were flinging boxes on the van and shouting at the cook to hurry up. Christos began to carry the baggage back into the house.

The cook came after him. Her lips were pressed together in a thin line. Taking hold of another basket, she began to drag it toward the door. Christos seized it from the other side. Their faces came together, blank and quivering with effort.

"Idiot!" he gasped. "Let go!"

Polixeni's nostrils widened. She groaned like a woman in labor and tightened her grip. Above them, Sophia was calling: "Has the *araba* come? Oh, thank God!"

"Let go!" said Christos. "I command you!"

But the woman was sturdy, like all islanders, and, like all islanders, insane. Little by little, she drew the basket down the steps. At the bottom Christos lost hold of it completely. Panting, he ran out to stop the drivers. First, he tried to block their way; then, when they simply moved around him, he threw himself on top of crates that they were lifting onto the wagon.

The two gigantic teamsters looked at him in irritation.

"Hey, Grandpa? You've got to stop that."

And they brushed him away like a fly.

Again, he climbed the stairs. Sophia was putting on her

coats and wrappers, one after another. Christos pounded his fist on the dresser.

"I have forbidden this! It's a disgrace to leave. No one is leaving but cowards and profiteers."

"I'm not going to stay and be murdered in my bed."

"Haven't I promised to protect you?"

He tried again to kiss her, but she twisted free. Padded like an Eskimo, she clattered down the stairway, clutching at the banister and calling to the cook. Christos watched her in a wild confusion of despair and rage. At the door she hesitated, drew a veil around her head, then rushed toward the carriage.

Christos followed with a cry.

Polixeni was climbing into the covered landau. The baggage truck was lumbering ahead. Christos waved his arms; but the driver cracked his whip, and Christos had to run along behind the carriage like an urchin.

At the corner he hopped up onto the running board and leaned across Polixeni's lap.

"Does nothing I've said make any impression?"

Sophia did not answer. The wind was hissing through the leather hood.

"Aren't you ashamed to run away? Think of the women of Souli." He waited a moment, then added: "Think of the women of Missolonghi."

"Your mind is always on the past," Sophia said in a muffled voice. Christos grabbed her hand impatiently.

"*Those* women would have stayed for Greece."

"For *Greece*. That's all you think about."

"Is that such a trivial consideration? I love Greece."

"You *worship* it."

"Is that contemptible?"

"It's not the same as love. When you love something, you *need* it. Not for its sake. For your own." She peeked at him tearfully. "Have you ever said you needed *me?*"

Stung with shame, Christos answered: "I will divorce you if you run away from me."

Near the passport dock, they slowed to pass some wagons standing empty in the darkness. The carriage was immediately surrounded by a crowd of country folk who smelled of cattle. A husky farm boy, dressed in a shirt without sleeves, put his hands on the fender and peered inside.

"Give me help, *efendi.*"

He spoke in Turkish with a Greek inflection, and his hand was like a shovel.

"Get your hands off," Christos said. "What are you doing here? You ought to be carrying a rifle."

The boy showed his teeth in an arrogant grin. Thrusting in his sunburned arm, he tugged at Polixeni's skirt.

"Baksheesh, *efendi.* Alms are blessed."

"I wouldn't give you water," Christos said. "You're worse than a gypsy. You ought to be in the army."

"There is no army, *efendi.*"

The crowd behind him growled derisively: "Army? The army is running away."

Christos called to the driver to lash the horse; but the crowd engulfed them, muttering: "There is no army. What are we supposed to do?" The farm boy waved his dirty hand under Christos' nose. "*Efendi?* Do you call yourself a Christian? Give me some money!" And the crowd repeated: "Money! Money!" They stretched out their arms. Their mouths hung open, and their cheeks were smeared with dust. The rims of their eyes were blazing red. "You rich people—saving your own sweet skins."

"In the name of God, get going!" Christos cried.

But the carriage moved by inches, as if the crowd had thrown a net around its wheels. Sophia was leaning back, as stiff as a corpse. Her eyes were closed and her face was rigid.

Terrified, Christos searched his pockets, found a coin and threw it out. The crowd surged forward, and the cab horse tossed its head in panic.

The cook was rearing up as if to jump. She had a flatiron in her hand.

"Throw out some money," Christos said. He dropped a purse. The people swarmed around it with a growl. The carriage drew ahead.

But the farm boy clutched the fender. Christos tried to bend his fingers, but he clung to the carriage like a drowning swimmer on the gunwales of a boat. The heat of his fury filled the carriage as he thrust his head inside, panting in their faces. But Polixeni lurched up with a terrified shriek and crushed his knuckles with the flatiron. The boy fell backward, screaming, and the carriage slipped through the gates of the passport dock.

Sophia was gasping. Christos peeled away the layers of clothing around her throat and breathed on her eyelids, which were as dark as bruises. In a moment she straightened up and said: "How could you subject me to such things?"

They were hemmed in by a throng more numerous than the peasants on the Quay. Porters were staggering barefoot toward the jetty, carrying piano crates. Baggage trucks and carriages were packed around the gangway, and the drivers were beating their horses and screaming at one another. Overhead, the ship was pulsing with a steady rhythm, while the cargo winches made a ceaseless, high-pitched roar.

Christos stared up at the perspiring faces of the passengers who were standing shoulder to shoulder at every railing.

"Profiteers and cowards."

Sophia sat on a steamer trunk and wiped her nose. Whenever she looked at Christos, he would turn away, pretending to be busy with the baggage. At last, she gathered up her things and went in the direction of the ship. At the gang-plank, she turned and waited.

"Christo? You are not a soldier. Come with us."

"I repeat my warning," he said. "I will divorce . . . "

But Sophia covered her mouth with her handkerchief and took Polixeni's arm. Later, Christos could see her leaning from the covered gallery that ran around the boat deck. She was squeezed between a huge Armenian woman in heavy mourning and a decrepit hag whose chin was resting on the rail. Her lovely face was exactly as he first had known it—sensuous, refined and delicately poised between compunction and abandon. Her hand was resting on the rail. Christos gazed at it with unexpected longing.

It struck him that his Motherland was like a human mother, jealous of his mistresses, and they of her, as if his love for Greece precluded rivals. Time and again, the obligations of his race and faith had destroyed his loves.

The whistle blasted and the women at the railing screamed.

Sophia began to wave, as if to beckon him. Through the wailing of the other women, he could hear her calling:

"Christo! Come with me!"

Then he was seized with panic. He ran along the jetty, but the plank was rising. The hawsers fell; the whistle echoed on the sheds along the waterfront; and the ship began to leave the pier.

As the gap of water widened, he saw Sophia clasp both hands against her mouth.

He ran to the end of the pier and waved his arms. The ship became a goblet on the water, then a clasp of jewels, then, finally, a fallen star. In his private grief, he had not noticed that the pier was filled with other men whose heads were bent, whose eyes were streaming, whose shoulders heaved with uncontrollable despair.

Twice a day, Dimitris crossed the Square to a latrine behind the Konak Building, reached into a crevice below the windowsill and took out an envelope. At dawn it had held a stolen copy of the air reconnaissance report, that night a résumé of meetings with the Minister of Navy and the Minister of War.

Carrying the papers to the light, he frowned over the transcript of the meetings. Twice he reread the concluding line: "They shouted, *'We will die before we leave Asia Minor!'* " Finally, he penciled out the word "they," printed in, "Lieutenant D. Kalapothakis, 1st Division," initialed each page, wrote at the bottom "Keep for tribunal" and replaced the packet. After standing a moment, chewing his lips, he added a note on the back of an old requisition form: "Galen: The Doctor is ready to perform the operation. K."

A courier who darted through the city like an insect pollinating buds would gather up the papers in an hour or two. He was said to be a messenger at one of the hotels, a shabby little Communist from Alexandria, as furtive as a gnat. As for "Galen"—who could say? An officer—perhaps a major or a colonel—with a Slavic talent for conspiracy. "Galen" was diligent in spreading carbon copies of the secret correspondence of the General Staff. In the past few days, he had also become presumptuous: he had begun assigning duties, canceling arrangements and withholding information. Actually, it was by no means settled who should lead the Movement. Dimitris himself, returning to the barracks in the twilight, felt an upsurge of ambition that made his nostrils stiffen like a cobra's hood.

The stairs were empty and the nervous pecking of a typewriter was echoing along the corridor. An orderly was kneeling in a labyrinth of half-filled boxes.

"Sir, do you want the folders from the High Commissioner? The convoy goes at ten o'clock."

"Screw the convoy. Did Pappas come? Lord Jesus, can't he be depended on for *anything?*"

He slammed the door and went to look for Michael Pappas, who was sitting at a desk in a deserted office, staring into space as if the roof had fallen on his head. Beads of moisture glistened on his apple cheeks.

"I went!" he cried, the moment he saw Dimitris. "But it was over."

"What did they talk about?"

"Keeping in touch. Maintaining calm. They can't decide."

"They can't decide! To hell with them. Why don't you wipe your face?"

"I walked. It's hot as Hades." Michael Pappas poured himself a glass of water from a cloudy pitcher, drank it noisily and wiped the edges of his mouth with his thumb. "The news is terrible."

"Did you expect it to improve?"

"I thought we'd make a stand at Ushak. But the southern bloc has broken up completely. Worse than the north. No organization left. Even the regiments are barely holding together. But Hadji-Clausewitz, our great general—*he* thinks we can stand around Alashehir! Somebody told him it's Greek."

And he took another swig of water, sluiced it through his mouth and spat it on the floor to show the depth of his contempt. Although Michael Pappas was a decade older than Dimitris, he had not advanced above the basic rank, and he attributed this failure to his unflagging loyalty to Venizelos. What other explanation could there be? He worked assiduously, yet he never advanced. If only he could have another opportunity to rub out Constantine! But they had put him in this clerical detail, under the pointed nose of Hadjianestis, where they could keep an eye on him; and his obsessive hatred of the Royalists had settled on the general.

Dimitris raised the window shade. Out on the drill field, in the dusk, a crew was taking down some bell tents. The peaks collapsed like melting cones of Arab sugar. The soldiers pounded with their fists, beating the canvas into lumpy bundles.

"Hadji-Clausewitz is coming unknotted," Michael Pappas went on. "Brought in a folding cot, but never sleeps. Paces up and down the room, tugs at his beard, twists the points of his mustache. Says he came too late: 'No one could handle this, not even Napoleon.' All of a sudden, he decides to have a train prepared. A *train!* Where does he think he is? Verdun? Then he mumbles to himself: 'Oh, no. I *can't* prepare a train and leave. If I did that, who would command the army?' Tonight he's out again with one of his ladies, eating fillet of sole and drinking French wine. A public appearance to keep up civilian morale, he says."

Dimitris scrutinized Pappas thoughtfully.

"Have you kept a record of the things he says?"

"Record! We're drowning in paper. You should have heard him today about the penmanship on the air reconnaissance report: 'Whose hand is this? Speak up! Where did you go to school? In Ethiopia?' Later on, some priests came in, along with some Elders of the church: 'Please, General. Can the army hold for ten more days?' He was furious. 'Ten *days,* sir? Why not ten *months,* sir?' And he says the Turks are not the problem. Why, the Turks are all of a hundred and twenty-five miles away! The real problem is these refugee civilians— *escapees,* he calls them—drifting into Smyrna. They've got to be turned back. Sent someplace else. 'We can't have refugees,' he says. 'Impossible to handle them!' To prove his point, he takes out his pen and paper and shows the priests it would take twenty days for all the refugees to get to Smyrna. 'Then to get the refugees to Greece'—and he does some fast arithmetic—'would take fifty thousand tons of ship-

401

ping for ten days. That is to say, twenty-five thousand tons a day for twenty days. Or, to put it another way, five hundred thousand tons for one day, if you see what I mean? And we have less than a thousand tons available. Now do you see why I'm concerned about the *escapees*?' And the church people looked at him with tears in their eyes."

"You ought to note it down," Dimitris said. "The date, the time. Evidences of his condition."

Michael Pappas smiled wistfully. He was sufficiently off balance himself to have an acute perception of the general's insanity.

"I could do it sleeping. On the very day of the attack, the twenty-fifth of August, he was saying, 'It might come from the north, it might come from the south. The line is *ridiculously* overextended.' Meanwhile, he was cleaning up his desk and getting ready to go back to Athens for a conference. In came an orderly, quivering like a plate of sago pudding: 'Sir, the attack has started!' The general didn't say a word. He walked across the room and faced the mirror, studying his nose. His nose is very long, you know. And pointed. But what an egopath! I've seen him standing at the mirror, smiling like a whore! 'Gentlemen,' he says, 'these soldiers called me Hadji-terror when I came here. Then I began to shake some smartness into them. Do you know what they call me now? Not *Hadji*anestis, but *Christos*anestis.' *Christ is risen!* "

"Write it all down," Dimitris said. "Eyewitness affidavit."

"It's pitiful, you know? He feels he's been selected as the sacrificial lamb. He talks about the fools in the High Commissioner's office interfering with his work. He talks about the officers who flaunt his orders. He says Smyrna is the Sodom and Gomorrah of the modern world. If he's right, then all the rest of us—"

"Look, Michael. Would you do it on your own?"

"Do what?"

"Get rid of him."

Michael Pappas licked his lips.

"Assassinate him?"

"No, no. *Relieve* him."

"Just the two of us?"

"Don't be an idiot. A group. A small, close-ordered junta. *Tomorrow.*"

Michael Pappas, lower lip quivering, put out his hand in agreement. He was distressed material, but time was running out. Dimitris hugged him absently, wondering whether this was, indeed, the proper moment.

"I'll write some memoranda. You can take them around."

Dimitris could imagine himself confronting General Hadjianestis with a pistol. Stepping forward, he stripped the medals off the terrified commander. Behind him, a telegrapher was spreading the announcement: "All divisions: Hadjianestis has been removed from command. Evacuation halted. National unity and full support of European Allies now assured. Take and hold defensive points at Manisa and the Meander River. Long live Greece! Signed: Kalapothakis."

But next morning, when Dimitris stopped at the latrine to read the messages, a note fell into his hand.

"All Doctors: Serious condition of the patient now precludes all hope of minor surgery. Amputation will take place at the appointed hour. Galen."

He threw the paper down and ran across the Konak Square. An infantry patrol was already walking down the corridor. They came to attention at the general's door. A sentry with his rifle at port arms stopped Dimitris at the stairs, twenty yards behind.

He could hear the general complaining in a piercing voice.

"I was sent too late. What can they expect of a general who's so badly cornered, so badly driven to the wall?"

Then Dimitris saw Lieutenant Michael Pappas standing on

the stairway, wiping his humid red face. The poor fool spread his hands and shrugged his shoulders, saying with his lips: "Don't blame me."

"Who's done it?" called Dimitris. "Is it Galen?"

Michael Pappas shrugged again. Someone was questioning the general.

"If it isn't true you plan to abandon Asia Minor, why did you evacuate the office of the General Staff? Why did you order the construction of the debarkment pier?"

And the general, almost screaming:

"What right have you to question me? I ordered my army to withdraw to a prepared defense line."

"No one here has heard of any prepared defense line. Where is the First Corps?"

"How should I know? They don't keep in touch with me. I know they've been *seen* around Dumlupinar. But I know it only from my own reconnaissance. It's as if my own field commanders were the enemy. They won't even answer my dispatches. What help is that to a general? That implies a decomposition of the forces!"

Again, the level voice of the interrogator:

"My dear Lieutenant General Hadjianesti—how do you *lose* an army corps?"

At last, Dimitris glimpsed the general's pointed nose and his meticulous goatee, surrounded by the sunburned faces of the officers.

"Do you want to know the fatal blunder?" Hadjianestis was saying, pale with indignation. "It was when Tricoupis reported that Afyon was being attacked by eight Turkish divisions. Eight! And there were really only *six!* It's a nightmare. What can I do? What could Napoleon have done? I've never met inertia before. It's a shock to meet her at this age. Can I be everywhere myself? Am I supposed to ride around and *hunt* for Tricoupis?"

Throwing back his shoulders, he advanced along the corridor. He was frowning, and there was a look of confusion in his deep-set eyes. The general's staff came after him, their faces downcast. Just as Hadjianestis reached the stairs, Michael Pappas darted out at him and shouted:

"Lunatic!"

The general shied away as if he had been slapped.

"Look how he walks!" cried Michael Pappas. "Look how stiff and careful. You know why? He's mad! He thinks his legs are made of glass, and they might break."

Hadjianestis looked around as if to make a record of his torturers.

"You'll regret this disrespect," he said.

"All right, Glass Legs," said Michael Pappas. "Easy on the stairs."

The general continued his inspection. In a rather high, thin voice he said: "I go as an accuser. Not as the accused."

With caution, he descended to the Square.

It was a bright and dusty morning, and the surface of the bay was stippled by a rollicking north wind. As General Hadjianestis was crossing to the car, a whirling cloud of powdered dung rose up and struck him in the face and blew his hat away.

"It was incredibly mishandled," said Dimitris afterward. "Now we have nothing but a general in the field. There's a great need for leadership, a great opportunity."

That night, reconnaissance planes reported that the mass of the retreating army had moved fifteen miles closer to Smyrna.

ALASHEHIR
SEPTEMBER, 1922

$\mathcal{A}$t Laurel Konak the traffic of visitors began at dawn.

First was the hoja, a cantankerous, toothless old martinet who struck the knocker a terrific blow and then stood waiting on the doorstep with his arms folded on his chest, wearing his bigotry as plainly as his huge white turban.

The hoja belonged to a dervish order founded by a Persian aesthete in the 7th century of the Islamic Era; and his head-dress, a masterpiece of religious millinery with eleven folds, seven knots and forty turns, symbolized the principles of an elaborate cosmology. It was this esoteric system that the hoja purposed to impart to Abdullah in a series of daily lectures, which presumably would save the misguided young man from the malign spiritual influences of a European education and a Christian wife. Squatting on a leather cushion, inhaling sweet coffee through his mustache and belching comfortably, the hoja passed a pleasant hour discoursing on the blessings of religion; while outside the rosy light of day crept slowly down the three small hills that lay above the town like sleeping yellow cats, and the streets resounded to a steady clattering of wagon wheels, a distant howling like the cry of horsemen in a canyon and, from time to time, the crash of railway couplings, the bellow of cattle and the frantic cries of frightened women milling around the station house.

406

The Greek Army was pulling out. With every hour, the threat of arson, looting and political reprisals grew. It was not an appropriate occasion to search for spiritual enlightenment, but to take one's women into hiding and pray for survival.

"Teacher, are you aware of the time?" Abdullah asked.

But the gossipy old fellow rambled on as if he had not heard a thing. Abdullah had to interrupt again: "Hoja? Don't you notice all that noise?" And, finally: "My dear sir, you must forgive me, but I cannot be your pupil. I am thoroughly committed to the principles of religious disestablishment, state socialism and dictatorship of the proletariat."

"Communism?" the hoja cried. "Oh, I wouldn't *consider* that! To me, it indicates a lack of moral certitude."

"That's right," Abdullah said, bounding up with unpardonable rudeness and almost lifting the hoja to his feet. "That's exactly the trouble with it. . . . And now, sir—another time?"

In fact, Abdullah felt an absolute certainty, moral or not, that he must get his family out of town without delay. The instant the Greek Army left Alashehir, the streets would be overrun with bandits, deserters and irregular cavalry, Greek and Turkish. One must take precautions; and a week or two of armed seclusion on the slopes of Boz Dagh would be exactly the sort of simple, precautionary measure that dervish folklore recommends: Trust God, but tie your camel.

Foreseeing the Greek collapse, Abdullah and his uncle had stocked a deep, volcanic crevice with fresh water, clean grain and several wheels of dry cheese. Even in such fragile company as Granny and Yildiz, they could hold out there until it was possible to assess the mood of the new regime. In any case, the period of acute peril would be short. As soon as parliamentary rule had been re-established, there would be little to fear, unless it be his own brother's deranged wrath;

and that, too, might diminish when the irritating presence of the Greeks had been removed.

For the first time in several years, Abdullah's hopes were rising with their usual ebullience. He foresaw himself returned to honor and influence. (After all, he had served the Turkish people bravely in espionage and later in guerrilla warfare; and when he had been forced to flee into occupied territory, he had ceased his political activities and had avoided contact with the Greek authorities.) In the tolerant atmosphere of the new Turkish society, his marriage would be freed of the political tensions that now afflicted his mother's household. He would be able to take Eleni to Constantinople, to escape from this provincial backwater. He would resume his studies, his teaching, his service to the new order; and his own marriage would serve as an example and a laboratory of the supranational, secular society.

He had learned from the collapse of his intrigues in Constantinople and the failure of his mercenary army in Kütahya that timing is more important than doctrine in reaching a political ideal. For several years past, the Turks had been too much absorbed in the problems of national survival to respond to revolutionary dogma. Potential revolutionaries had submerged themselves in Mustapha Kemal's military organization, while the guerrilla war, which had seemed at first to be an ideal vehicle to propagate the seeds of Asiatic socialism, had deteriorated into an atrocious orgy of banditry and tribal vengeance.

In the immediate future, however, when the Greeks had withdrawn from Anatolia, the time would be ripe for revolution. There would be an inevitable conflict between the reactionary religious fanatics and the bourgeois reformers in the Ankara assembly. Military victory would be followed by political anarchy, and the door would open for Marxist solutions. One could look forward to a period of excitement and opportunity.

But the benighted hoja, with the pessimism of his breed, saw nothing but the Final Judgment in immediate prospect. As Abdullah edged him toward the door, he cried out:

"Take my word, sir—there will be no sympathy for you when the Turkish Army comes back! Don't you realize what Mustapha Kemal Pasha will think of you?"

Smiling, Abdullah opened the door.

"I don't believe he will think of me at all."

"Sir, he will consider you a traitor. You became a willing subject of the Greeks. You married a Christian woman—"

Abdullah made an effort to maintain his smile, but his voice thickened with annoyance.

"You may be right, hoja. But I shall wait until I reach that river before I try to swim. Neither Mustapha Kemal Pasha nor any other Turk has any cause to question my patriotism."

"It is the Greek wife who will cause the questions."

"That is my problem, sir. Not yours. Good day."

But the hoja clung to the handle of the door, fencing with his right forefinger.

"Don't resent what I am telling you. It's for your own benefit. You've forgotten the sacred laws of Islam. You're filled with *self-love* as a result of all this so-called education they've given you. Don't you realize the human soul is like a pitcher? When it is filled with the stagnant water of *self-love,* there is no room in it for even one drop of the Wine of Divine Love!"

"Now you are trying to instruct me in dervish proverbs!"

"Take my word. I am wiser than you think." Lowering his voice, he growled: "Divorce her! The people of this town know what you have done. They want revenge. Divorce her!"

With his turban swaying like a haystack on a mule, the hoja

tottered down the garden path, oblivious to the pathetic outcries of the town, toward which the Turkish Army was advancing with the fury of a thunderstorm. Turning, Abdullah saw a dark figure slip from the stairway to the kitchen door.

"Eleni? Is it you?"

Whenever the hoja came around, Eleni veiled her face and walked as softly as a cat to avoid displeasing the old man, whose wrathful glances terrified her. Abdullah went to the kitchen door and called again; but there was no answer. Perhaps it had been Yildiz. . . .

He went upstairs to the harem and wandered from room to room. The women had completed their packing. The great chiffoniers were empty, and the lattices were tightly closed. Stifled by the dusty air, the heavy scent of camphor wood and oil of roses, Abdullah climbed to the attic balcony that overlooked the town.

Clouds of smoke were drifting overhead. In the direction of the vineyards, one could see the Greeks retreating through the valley, ebbing down from Sarigöl, Eshme and Kula in a vagrant column that was almost hidden by a shroud of dust. Out in the steppes of Anatolia, they had lost all the trappings of their insolence: their guns, their flags, their swords, their brazen music. Alashehir was glutted with the refuse of their broken wagons and the putrefying carcasses of their slaughtered animals. The wounded lay all together on the ground around the railway station; and the clash of freightcars on the siding was answered by the frantic cries of people who were being left behind.

While Abdullah stood in this disconnected lookout post, stirred by a strange compassion for this enemy that had been so inextricably embedded in the Turkish nation through all its centuries of bloody history, some officers rode by on horseback, shouting through cardboard megaphones:

"Stand! Stand for the honor of Greece. . . . Curs of cowardice! Stand for the honor of Greece, or you will be no better
than common criminals!"

But the soldiers trudged ceaselessly along the road. Their
eyeballs darted furtively from side to side. Their uniforms
had fallen into filthy tatters; their feet were wrapped in rags;
and their lips were white with slime. They cared nothing for
the honor of Greece. Less than half of them had saved their
rifles, which they cradled loosely at their sides, as if too weak
to raise their arms.

Three men as dark and gaunt as wolves were hesitating by
the gate. One of them let down his pants and squatted, staring blindly at the latticed windows, while the others, leaning
feebly on the fence, watered the garden with their steaming
urine. Their dullness, their incompetence, their terror and
despair moved Abdullah to pity.

But as he raised his arm to wave directions to the well, a
dull explosion shook the town. Windows rattled, and a frightened chattering rose from lower floors of the house. Abdullah
called to his wife again; but there was no answer. It was not
Eleni but Yildiz who ran from the kitchen and met him on the
stairs.

His mother had installed the women in the cellar. Bolstered
up with coverlets and quilts, they crouched behind a barricade of sandbags and entertained themselves by spreading
out their jewelry on a velvet scarf.

"Look, son!" his mother called. "This brooch belonged to
Belkis Hanum. I'm going to let Gulnar wear it for the celebration!"

Abdullah looked around.

"Where is Eleni?"

"We're going to have a celebration every year to mark the
date of liberation. We'll have a banquet for our friends. Cinnamon soup, omelets with pistachio nuts, *pasturma*, sau-

sages, pigeons stewed with olives, woodcocks wrapped in leaves, stuffed eggplant—"

"You didn't let Eleni go outside?"

"—and sweets! Rose syrups, violet syrups, melons, Jordan almonds, pastries, candied walnuts. Oh, look at Granny's face! You'd like that, wouldn't you, darling?"

"Where?" Abdullah shouted. His voice grated with anxiety.

"Sit down, son. She seems to have gone."

"What do you mean?"

"Some Greeks came past, and suddenly, there she was, dressed up in trousers and a cap, looking like a stableboy, saying 'Keep smiling.'" The mother stopped to wipe her eyelids with the tip of her little finger. "I called her back, but she didn't answer, and when I went to look for her, she *wasn't.*"

"What in God's name are you saying?"

"Don't raise your voice, son! Be calm. I looked and looked. I would have sent Hassan around the neighborhood, but he was afraid to go outside. So I called from the window. Surely you must have heard me calling her?" Sighing, she took up a garnet earring and held it to the light. "It isn't exactly a surprise, is it?"

"Didn't it occur to you that they might have stolen her? Why didn't you call *me?*"

"Who could tell where you were and where you weren't? It seems she just went back to her own people." A small twist of satisfaction puckered the corner of his mother's mouth.

"You drove her out!"

His mother clicked her tongue. Her hands were folded in her lap.

"She thought it would help us if she left. She was sure they'd persecute you."

"She overheard that bird-brained hoja!"

412

His mother reached for his hand.

"Drink a little coffee, love. A cup of tea. Some little thing..."

But Abdullah stood up and bowed to Granny and his sisters.

"It's time you went to the cave with uncle. Hassan will take you. I'll go and bring Eleni back."

Nodding her head, his mother snickered gently through her nostrils.

"My son, my son! When will you learn to understand your people? It's our *own* men who are coming back. The war is over."

"The house is not safe," Abdullah said. "Do as I tell you and go to the cave."

As he went up the cellar steps, there was another deep explosion, like thunder rolling over the prostrate city. A column of black smoke, shot through with streaks of writhing orange flame, rose from the bottom of the valley.

"They have blown up the station," he said.

"Infidels!" his mother cried. "Why don't they leave us alone?"

"Don't delay," Abdullah said. "Let Hassan lead you. I'll bring Eleni back."

The smoke of the burning station began to spread across the sky.

The ashes were still warm when Kenan rode in next afternoon. Greek demolition squads had done their work with care: they always did, unless the Turkish cavalry was ragging them.

Of all the towns the Greeks had occupied, only Afyon had fallen to the Turks intact, unspoiled. The rest were devastated. Ushak was set afire with cans of benzine scattered through the houses at the edge of town; Banaz was crudely fired with brushwood torches; Kula was blown up with dyna-

413

mite. In the countryside, the blackened stumps of vines and fig trees smoldered in the salted fields, the hides of cattle festered in the fountains and the carcasses of donkeys rotted in the wells. The valleys Kenan had crossed were white with ashes. The spider wove its fragile fabric in the ruined walls; the predatory night owl sang forlornly in the empty corridors; and the wrathful hand of God lay heavily upon the land.

As he rode in from Sarigöl, Kenan could see a cloud that rose like an enormous, putty-colored turban above the ruins of Alashehir.

"How long ago did they leave?" he asked the officer who was escorting him.

But the lieutenant, who was young and timid, looked at Kenan's face and was afraid to speak. Silently, they passed the wreckage of a truck in which the blackened body of a soldier was clutching the melted steering wheel. Ragged figures darted through the charred-out buildings, and a nauseating odor of putrescence drifted from the walls. The streets were vacant, littered with the flecks of straw and broken boxes that an army leaves behind: a chicken feather here, a scrap of paper there. Someone had painted a hammer and sickle in blue calcimine on a garden wall and written under it in Greek: "Go home."

The Turkish cavalry had occupied the Hotel City Palace, where they had found an Orthodox Greek calendar on which the days had been checked off with a red pencil up to August 12. The ashtrays overflowed with the remains of Greek cigarettes. A cavalry captain met the delegation in the hall and urged them toward the parlor; but Kenan stood aloof.

"Where is the hospital?" he asked.

"Your Honor, there is no hospital," the captain said, bowing and gesturing instead toward the open door of the reception room, which exhaled a scent of coffee and tobacco.

"Where do they take the wounded and the dead?"

The captain said the Greeks had allowed some Moslem families to shelter in the Forbes House; but the only clinic left was Naby Bey's, with twenty beds.

"Take me there," Kenan said, leaning against the wall to steady himself. "To the mortuary and the ward."

The captain led him toward the hills. Roofless shells surrounded them like craters of the moon. The center of the town was smoldering. The captain, speaking in a whisper, asked if Kenan had known this place. Kenan did not answer.

How could anyone have known this town? This stinking kiln was not Alashehir. Where were the poplar trees? Where was the church? The Mosque of Yildirim? The springs? The vines? The children?

The silence was unbearable.

"Where are all the dogs?" Kenan asked suddenly. The cavalry captain looked at him in bewilderment.

There was no one at the clinic whom Kenan knew; and when they came to Laurel Konak, they found only smoking timbers. Kenan stood at the gate and said in a low voice:

"My mother. My sisters. My uncle. My grandmother . . . "

Hassan, the hunchbacked stableboy, was picking through the refuse with a long stick. To every question, he shrugged a shoulder. Then he brightened.

"One escaped! It was Abdullah Bey, along with his Greek wife. They went to Smyrna."

With a shuddering moan, Kenan bowed his head. His face was wet with tears that trickled from the sightless socket of his eye. Staggering across the blackened garden, he made an ablution with the putrid water of the well and fell to his knees to pray. His head reeled, and the movements of devotion left him dangerously weak; but he exercised with growing ardor, panting and groaning in the painful genuflections. It was only the five daily prayers in their inexorable sequence that now linked him to the human scheme of time and place. With his

415

forehead touching the cinders, he could comprehend that he was alive, that he was locked in a destiny of death and vengeance.

Sometimes, the Caliph Ali spoke to him in a wild, incomprehensible tongue. Sometimes, he did not speak at all, but gestured westward, turning his bronzed, prophetic face to the sunset. It was clear that he was commanding the punishment of blasphemers and heretics. His law of war was irrefrangible. It was the ordinance of God, the axiom of history: Faith and Fatherland must be defended with the sword. Who dared to stand against this first and last commandment of God, the All-Powerful? A man who had abandoned his Faith and Fatherland was like a hollow gourd: he should be cast out. He who preached reunion should be separated; he who prayed for reconciliation should be alienated; and he who fled to save his life should die beneath the heel of an avenging warrior.

It was his duty to God to kill Abdullah, his sacred duty to Islam. He struggled to his feet and asked the captain to collect his escort. They left Alashehir within the hour.

Later in the day, some soldiers found an aged woman lying in the garden of Laurel Konak, near the ashes of a summerhouse. She had been raped and beaten and was mewing like a kitten. When they tried to move her to the women's camp, she died.

SMYRNA
SEPTEMBER, 1922

*T*o protect the Villa Trigonis from vandalism, Christos boarded up the windows, appropriated the rifle of his Cretan doorman, who had disappeared, and posted himself as a permanent guard. Early Friday morning, while he was sitting alone in the drawing room, there was a rattling at the glass door.

Christos tiptoed into the vestibule, his Mauser clasped under his arm. Through the grating he could see a fez, a neckerchief, a suit of homespun wool. Then the figure seemed to spread across the doorway, clutching at the filigree.

"Jesus and Mary," Christos said. He put down the rifle and unlocked the door.

Eleni pressed her face against his chest. Her tears soaked through his shirt, wetting him to the skin. Christos stood in silence, casting up his eyes and crossing himself.

"So he sent you back," he said at last. "Does he think we can swallow what the Turk has puked?"

"I ran away."

"Oh, you ran away. Does that mend your hymen?"

He pulled off her ridiculous fez. Her thick dark hair sprang out in dusty ringlets, filling his nostrils with the stink of smoke. He pointed to her hand.

"What's that?"

"A wedding ring."

"Do they fornicate and call it marriage? And what's this abomination on your skin?"

Eleni touched her fingers to her cheek.

"It's an insect bite."

"An insect bite! Have you been whoring in the fields?"

He turned away, but Eleni cried out and threw her arms around him. Christos tried to draw away.

"It's not up to me to take you back," he said. "You also dishonored your mother, your brother, your fiancé." He groped for his cane. "I'll send you to Chios. Someone will take charge of you there."

Eleni began to writhe and moan. Her knees collapsed. She grasped her father by the ankles. Christos, frantic to escape, kicked her away like a dog.

For an instant, they stared at each other in anguished surprise. Then Eleni relaxed her grip. Christos slipped away from her. At the door he turned back. She was kneeling by the stairway, fingering the polished chestnut railing.

"Holy mother!" he said to himself. "What poison we have drunk!" He slammed the door behind him.

Not a breath of wind was stirring, and the only living creature in the morning sunshine was a small black rooster, bowing to a mound of dung. All the carts and carriages had vanished. The shutters were tightly sealed. Bindweeds and campanulas were wilting on the windowsills.

First, Christos called on Zeki Bey, an Albanian Moslem who was celebrated for his charming manners. The house was in a Christian quarter at the end of a narrow street called Petrokokkino, which was paved with reddish stones. Zeki Bey was in his bathhouse, but he came to the selamlik within an hour, still wearing a terry-cloth burnoose and pressing his hand against his breast. His skin was glittering with perfumed oil; his eyes disappeared into coffee-colored pouches.

Zeki Bey was not the sort of man who lets a military crisis

derange his manners. First, he served some sugared apricots on silver spoons; next, they drank a bottle of German mineral water, which had been kept in the cellar to mellow like a wine; and, finally, they moved on to coffee, cigarettes, rahat loukoum and hazelnuts.

For the first half hour, they talked about the prospects of establishing an autonomous Commonwealth of Smyrna, a secular, multilingual city-state, self-governing and independent, in the manner of the ancient cities of Ionia. Christos ventured to suggest that they should use the Turkish name, Izmir, to disassociate the independent city from the conflicts of the past. The Moslem, gravely tilting his head, made a charming acceptance speech.

At last, Christos cleared his throat and said:

"Zeki Bey, my honored friend—I have a little girl . . . "

Zeki's eyes glinted open, floating in their deep half moons of coffee-colored flesh.

"Ah, my dear friend, this is really too bad. All my sons are married. As for myself—" He smiled and closed his eyes again.

"Oh, no," said Christos. "You misunderstood. I only want the favor of your help." Suddenly overcome by the humiliation of his errand, Christos began to speak more rapidly, to raise his voice and make mistakes in Turkish. Zeki Bey blinked and licked his mustache.

"But aren't there any boatmen, my good friend? Why, I myself know of some Cretan Turks. They speak your language perfectly. Wouldn't they row you down to Chios for a few liras? That's nothing to a man of your wealth."

"But, Zeki Bey, my dear—this is a shy, young girl. A *virgin*. She needs protection. Someone who speaks Turkish. A carte blanche."

"Why, of course. You must go with her."

"But I have to stay here."

"Very well, then—you must keep her here with you!" Zeki Bey spread out his hands. "Don't I give you good advice?" He stretched himself on the cushions. "You never have anything to fear from Turks like me. If only the politicians in Athens understood this. Isn't it so?"

Christos asked permission to leave.

The sun was at the zenith. The cobbles burned beneath his feet. Wiping his head, he made his way past St. Dimitris' and the Armenian music halls in the vicinity of Basmahane Station. Just at noon, while the Moslem call to prayer was sounding, he arrived, exhausted, at the home of a turpentine exporter named Kastritsis on an avenue that ran between the station and the Church of the Annunciation; but the house was filled with frightened nieces, aunts and cousins who had fled from Manisa and Urla, bringing their belongings in enormous wooden dowry chests that were heaped along the corridors. As for the turpentine dealer, he had taken his wife and daughters to Chios the week before.

Plodding back to Basmahane Station, Christos could scarcely draw his breath. His heart was pounding, and his ears were ringing with the unfamiliar silence of the streets. Surely, that ungrateful girl, that harlot of a Turk, did not deserve such painful effort! She could find her way to Chios by herself, dressed as she was, with her hair in a fez and her legs in a pair of trousers. He would go back and send her on her way. . . .

No, that would not do. For the sake of the Trigonis name, Eleni must be saved from further degradation. The reputation of the family had been blackened; but dignity of manners and severity of discipline could restore the honor of their women.

So Christos trudged along, through gloomy alleys overhung by window bays and plaster arches, stopping here and there to climb a stairway, ring a bell and wait, his hand behind his

420

ear. He called in Trassa Street and Bella Vista; he searched the Point as far as Alliotti Boulevard, where the smell of brine rose from the marshes. But there was no one left: only invalids and refugees and fools remained in Smyrna, hiding in the tobacco sheds. Fruitlessly, Christos prowled around Mortakia, through Pissing Alley, Shitty Street and Pigsty Court, behind the hospital. He drifted east as far as Holy Shepherds', near the ancient aqueduct, and finally turned again, so weary he could scarcely stand, to Basmahane.

When he was almost fainting with exhaustion, he stopped beside a mossy well. Visions of Eleni in her filth, her ludicrous disguise, assailed his throbbing eyelids. He felt a terrible compulsion to be rid of her. Her very presence in the city seemed to threaten him, as if he bore the guilt of her disgrace. Why should he feel responsible for her? She had scorned his paternal love. She had rejected the fine young officer that he had found for her.

Suddenly, he slapped his forehead with his open palm and said aloud: "Oh, what stupidity!" And he started off again across the empty Fruit Bazaar in the direction of the army barracks.

On reaching Konak Square, he gasped and shrank against a wall. There was an endless column coming down the Quay. Officers and soldiers, nomads and deserters jostled each other past the barracks in a haze of dust. Teams of water buffalo were pulling broken trucks. Oxen and camels were hauling rusted guns. At the edges of the column, ambulances marked with the blue Hellenic cross were pushing forward, honking ceaselessly and giving off a smell of chloroform.

Gypsy women wearing skirts of crimson velvet trudged along in the midst of the artillery. Convicts from the dungeons of the Rue Maltese clung to the commissary wagons, surrounded by stragglers dragging rifles on the cobblestones and sniveling as shamelessly as girls.

421

A few of the soldiers, who apparently had come by train from Manisa or Aydin, were wearing helmets and puttees, and the commanders of these smart troops rode on horseback, posting as if they were on parade. But the others hobbled along in woven sandals bound with rags. Their uniforms were torn and gray with dust. Some were wearing Turkish kalpaks of black lamb's wool; others had on fezzes or turbans; and many had wrapped their heads in strips of dirty lint that looked as if it had been used for wadding guns. The officers had thrown away their Sam Browne belts; the commanders huddled in their open cars; the stragglers rattled dry canteens against their teeth and licked their lips with shriveled tongues.

Elusive figures, bearded, red-eyed and black with smoke, were lurking on the fringes of the line. The boldest wore outlandish costumes—old-fashioned yellow boots, embroidered corsets snatched from dowry trunks, baggy Turkish bloomers and the woolen cloaks of dervishes. A toothless man was waving a long stick strung with bracelets; and his companions carried heavy strings of gold Napoleons and little silver mejidyes, golden mahmudiyes and huge five-lira pieces known as *beshibiryerde*—"five-in-one-place." When they saw an officer, these looters showed their teeth like the fangs of wolves; but the officers ignored them out of weariness, complicity or disgust.

Not a soldier out of five was carrying a rifle.

"Traitors!" Christos whispered through his teeth. "You are abandoning your country!"

He was blinded by a rush of tears.

Dimitris and Lieutenant Michael Pappas stood by a second-story window. As the column passed the Smyrna barracks, many soldiers raised their bloodshot eyes and shook their fists.

"Traitors! Bring us water. Traitors! Where are you hiding?"

Dimitris moved back from the window to conceal his face. It would ruin a man's career to be associated in the public mind with the incompetent officers who had lost the war. Michael Pappas, puffing with impatience, nudged him.

"He's waiting for your answer."

But Dimitris was staring at a wagonload of dying men. The feverish were twitching in their sleep, like dogs disturbed by nightmares; the mutilated showed their wounds with the audacity of gypsy beggars, lifting purple stumps, exposing blackened limbs and crusted sores, while clouds of flies devoured the empty sockets of their eyes.

"What is his name, again?"

"Plastiras," said Michael Pappas. "Nicholas Plastiras. The Five Forty-second Evzones."

"Who the devil is Colonel Plastiras of the evzones? What does he offer?"

"Well, he's a great root-buster."

"So am I. So's Botsaris, Phesopoulos, Rhigopoulos. Every one of them has his little group."

"Haven't you heard them talk about 'the Black Horseman'?"

"What do I care about those silly epithets?" Dimitris said. "Those are gumdrops cooked up by the sluts of the press." He wiped his forehead with the back of his hand. "Why should I commit myself to some adventurer that nobody ever heard of ?"

His brain was aching from the pressure of decisions. If he waited too long, the inner council of the military junta would be formed without him; if he moved too soon, he might align himself with the wrong clique. One mistake could destroy his political prospects and even put his life in jeopardy. Yet hesitation could be just as dangerous. Should he mollify this Colonel Plastiras with a promise? He had given pledges to the

423

others. He could promise almost anything—a naval vessel, infantry, a telegraph transmitter.

"Look, I'll offer him some cannon."

Michael Pappas clicked his tongue.

"Plastiras doesn't want a promise. He wants a regiment of volunteers to hold the line at Nif and Manisa."

"He's raving. Doesn't he know you can't make soldiers out of corpses?"

An orderly was peeping through the doorway.

"Lieutenant, there's a man."

Michael Pappas went into the corridor, looked over the railing and made a face.

"It's your friend," he said. "The Emperor of Byzantium."

"Tell him to go to hell," Dimitris said. He went back to the window and watched the wagonloads of dying soldiers, glassy-eyed and drenched with sweat, who were staring at the beautiful plum-colored sea. "Tell him I've been evacuated."

But Christos had already climbed the stairs. He stood outside the doorway, florid, weeping, with his arms outstretched.

"It's a disgrace!" he cried out, sobbing like a Roman tenor. "Bad generalship. Nothing else."

"Come in, come in," Dimitris said impatiently. He turned to Michael Pappas. "Why Nif? Why Manisa?"

"He knows that sector," Michael Pappas said. "He thinks the situation isn't half so hopeless as it looks."

"Of course it isn't hopeless!" Christos shouted from the doorway. "With a few fresh troops from Thrace, a sound commander—"

"Doesn't he know how few dependable regiments are left?"

"Poor devils," Michael Pappas murmured. "The minute they see blue water, they want to go straight to Athens."

"To Athens?" Christos echoed. "Then they're *cowards!*" Setting his jaw, he marched into the room, which had been stripped of every piece of furniture.

Michael Pappas reddened suddenly and closed his mouth.

"Cowards!" Christos repeated, thumping his cane on the floor. "Why, I've even seen some of them throw down their guns! Would you believe it? Wouldn't you call that cowardice?"

"Have you ever been shelled?" said Michael Pappas.

But Dimitris took the old man by the wrist and turned him toward the door.

"Now, sir. What can I do for you? We're very busy."

"Ah?" said Christos, drawing his arm away. He looked around the empty room. "Well, if you'll ask someone to bring me a chair . . . "

"No, no. I'm at your service."

"I'll wait."

"Now," said Dimitris.

The old man ran a trembling hand across his forehead. He used his handkerchief to wipe the corners of his mouth. Finally, he looked Dimitris in the eye and gave a sickly smile.

"Very well, then. I won't make it long. I wanted you to know, my wife has gone to Athens. Or perhaps only as far as Chios. She'll stay until the end of the disturbance. So that *nearly* everyone is safe."

"That's fine," Dimitris said, suddenly wondering whether he, too, should go to Chios. The answer would depend on where they planned to organize the coup d'état. It could be anywhere in Greece. To be isolated from the cabal would be as fatal as to choose the wrong associates. He pressed his knuckles into his burning eyes. Why not send a coded letter to this Plastiras, urging that they meet on Lesbos? Or, some other large Greek island off the coast of Asia Minor? Or in

425

Macedonia? Or Thrace? You shouldn't have to lead a suicide brigade to save the country.

"Why in God's name *Nif?*" he said aloud.

"No, no—not Nif," the old man said. "She's *here*. In Smyrna."

"Who is?"

"Eleni." And he added: "The girl you wanted to marry."

"Oh, the devil," Dimitris said. His mind was so enmeshed 'in the complexities of his position, the exigencies of the military crisis, the contingencies of his career, that he might have been anesthetized. First, it was imperative to choose the proper staging platform for the insurrection. In mainland Greece, the army would disintegrate. But on the smaller islands, there would be a dearth of food and water. Therefore, the organization would have to start from one of the large islands—Chios, Lesbos or Samos.

He edged away from Christos, who was slobbering; but the old man clutched at him.

"You know, my boy, how much we count on you. Find her a boat. An escort. Someone we can trust."

"What? You must have lost your mind. You know I wouldn't help her cross the street."

Christos ignored this. Lowering his voice, he went on: "I am thinking of the honor of the family. If my son were here, I shouldn't have to trouble you. Now you have to stand in the role of a brother."

"After she's been lying with that Turk?"

Dimitris turned away as if he were dismissing an impudent caller. Christos stood there, blinking through his tinted glasses. Finally, Dimitris had to push him toward the door.

"Look, Grandpa—take a boat yourself. Don't wait. It isn't safe."

"I'll never leave!" The old man's eyes were brimming. "Venizelos himself sent me back to Turkey, after I had wasted two-thirds of my life as an exile. I shall never forget what he said to me. He said the Greeks of Turkey are like soldiers. We will build the platform of our temple with our martyred souls."

"All right, my friend. If that's what you want to do . . . "

The instant they were rid of him, Dimitris went in search of code books, pencils, writing paper and a box to sit on. In his letter to Plastiras, he promised full cooperation in the coming struggle for the preservation and the resurrection of the Motherland. He would be pleased to join the army of reform on Lesbos.

Then it struck him that if Plastiras was the idol of the cavalry, Colonel Gonatas of the 2nd Division was the darling of the infantry. Should he be disregarded? And what of Karidakis and Daoulis? The 62nd Infantry? The 19th Officers' Group?

He decided he should give the same assurances to each of them. His pen flew over the pages.

"Michael?" he said without looking up. "Get your stuff. I know a boat."

Michael Pappas, standing near the window, looking around at him in silence. Then he said: "You won't go out to Nif?"

"Do you think I've lost my mind?"

Michael Pappas did not answer. He leaned against the wall and covered his face with his hands.

"Oh, God. It's so hopeless! *A temple built of martyred souls!* The hypocritical old pimp! It was pompous, hypocritical old pimps like that who got us into this. *They* betrayed us."

"Who?"

"The Emperor of Byzantium."

"Oh, him," Dimitris said.

He scribbled swiftly, taking out his watch from time to time and groaning in his haste.

427

At exactly four-thirty that afternoon, just as Christos left the army barracks, they were lowering the Greek flag for the last time on Konak Square.

Orange sunlight was gleaming on the columns of the governmental palace, and the balcony overlooking the sea was filled with men in dingy jackets, wearing bands of mourning on their sleeves. At the center was a bald, rather portly man and, next to him, an army officer who seemed to be in tears. A gun salute resounded across the harbor, a cloud of doves erupted from the sycamore trees and the flag slid down the pole and disappeared.

In the column of retreat, some soldiers were singing "Dark Is the Night on the Mountain." Few of them paid attention to the hasty ceremony that officially concluded the Greek regime in Asia Minor.

The Quay was now impassable. The horse trams had stopped running, the restaurants were boarded up and the boats along the steps were swamped. Bands of deserters stopped the wagons of refugees and tried to peddle empty rifle cases, rotten fruit and dying mules. A thick reddish slime lay on the cobblestones, glittering like the effluence of a fatal wound: it was the blood of slaughtered animals, the pulp of raisins and the hulls of watermelons that famished men had stolen at the edge of town.

The refugees were agonized by rumors. They believed that Turkish cavalry was at their heels, that Turkish shells were falling on the city. As Christos forced his way across the Square, he heard a woman crying: "They're in Bornova!" And, with despairing shrieks, the people pushed each other southward in a wild stampede toward Cheshme, where the army was debarking in a state of panic.

The sun lay sobbing on the headlands, bleeding into the purple sea. In the glory of its expiring light, a fleet of acorn barges clustered at the water gate, loading a heavy cargo of clerks and tax collectors, who were carrying their ledgers back to Greece. The *Iron Duke* was waiting for them in the roads. Some of them waved and called goodbye; others wept. The High Commissioner slipped out of the Konak, surrounded by his cohort. A silent crowd was standing on the shore. As the High Commissioner's launch left the Quay, a man cried out: "It was a black night when you came, and it is a black night when you leave!"

Christos left the waterfront and wandered through the twilight of the great bazaar. The shops were barred, and the passages were given over to looters and rats. Solitary figures cowered in the alleys, lashing out with knives if anyone came near them.

At twilight, Christos found an empty landau. He threw himself onto the seat and closed his eyes. But the driver, who was squatting in the shadow of an archway, called out:

"The carriage is sold."

"I will improve the price."

"What's money, Monsieur? Tomorrow, your Greek drachmas won't be worth the seeds of a fig."

"Then I'll give you English shillings. Do I look like a beggar?"

At last the driver stood and scratched his backside and cocked his greasy fez above his eyebrow.

"Five shillings."

"You're insane."

The driver put out his hand. Christos scrutinized his face.

"Why are you trying to stick me up? You're not a Turk."

"Not quite, thank God. They haven't circumcised *me* yet." He took four shillings, bit the coins and put them in his pocket. "I'm a Catholic."

"Then why do you speak Turkish?"

"Why should I speak Greek? Tomorrow your language will

be nothing but bile, like your money. Come to the funeral, Monsieur."

Flicking the horse, he drove the carriage with his head tipped at a jaunty angle. Whenever he saw a figure in the darkness, he would cry out like a porter: "Yay! Look out! Greasy paint!"

They traveled roundabout. Halfway down Reshidiye Street, outside the wall of the Armenian cathedral, the driver slowed the carriage.

"Don't stop," said Christos, who had no fondness for Armenians.

But the street was blocked. There were several hundred men around the entrance to the compound, where a demon in a scarlet hood was crouching on a table, stabbing out his crooked finger: "Listen, brothers—do you think the Greeks will protect you? No! The entire Greek Army is running away!"

The man's eyes were blazing madly. He clawed the edges of his beard, which was as black and matted as the shag of a bear. Each time he paused, the men around him answered with a strangled roar.

"The Greeks *always* run away, my brothers, as their history has proved. No one will protect you but yourselves!"

"Move on," said Christos. "Don't stop."

Every terrified Armenian in Turkey, every revolutionary Hunchagist and Tashnagist of that afflicted and tenacious race, had found his way to Smyrna, carrying an acid bottle and a hand grenade. Their pockets bulged with cartridges and pistols. Their women, dressed in black, were lifting crates of dynamite; and boys were stacking tins of kerosene against the walls. The bandit in the scarlet hood harangued them in a rasping voice.

"This is our fortress. The sword of Jesus will defend us. If they try to drive us out, we'll burn them with us!"

And the crowd repeated: "Burn them! Burn!"

The carriage driver crossed himself.

"That's General Torkum," he whispered. "The Knight of Murmansk."

"Why did you bring me here?" said Christos feebly.

"To save your life," the driver said. He rolled his eyes. "The Turks are everywhere. They've already taken Bella Vista."

"That isn't true."

The men began to turn around with piercing glances.

"Who's that?" called General Torkum. "Come forward, friend."

"Move on," said Christos, shivering convulsively. His mouth went dry, and he could feel his heartbeats pounding in his throat.

"Who is it?" said General Torkum. "If you be friend, come forward."

But Christos scrambled sideways on the seat and dropped between the carriage and the wall. Choking in the dust, his glasses lost, his hat and cane behind him, he turned the corner into Kaymak Pasha Street and began to run.

"There goes a noble Greek!" somebody shouted.

And the fanatic crowd repeated hoarsely: "Noble Greek!"

It was after midnight when Christos reached his house. Half blind, hatless, stifled by an excruciating band of pressure around his chest, he sat at the bottom of the stairs, too weak to cry out. At last he pulled himself up the banister and found Eleni, kneeling in an upper room, surrounded by the contents of her dowry chest. He sent her to barricade the doors and windows.

Eleni obeyed so willingly, so humbly, that his heart was moved. He remembered the lively, practical girl who had scoffed at fortune-telling and parlor games and wanted to be a teacher and cut up frogs: the daughter of his old age, from whom he had demanded and expected so little. Gazing at her

431

face, he could see Sophia in her eyes, and something of himself, too, in her strong coloring. For the first time since she
had humiliated him, he felt a wave of tenderness, or reconciliation. Dimitris was wrong to stand so adamantly on his
honor: Eleni was not beyond redemption. After all, she had
come back to Greece!

He called out to her, then forgot what he had meant to say.

"Don't worry," he said at last. "I'll protect you."

A few minutes before noon the next day, Turkish cavalry
rode past the house. They trotted in a double file, well
mounted, fresh and calm, with an arrogance of bearing that
implied that God himself had brought them back to Smyrna
to reclaim authority. Most of the houses on the Quay were
shuttered as tightly as Villa Trigonis, but a few Greeks in
fezzes showed their loyalty to the Turkish government by
waving crimson flags.

Through a slit in the iron shutters, Christos watched a
Greek platoon come to attention as the Turks appeared. A
Turkish officer called down an order. The Greek commander
translated it for his men.

"Throw your rifles in the sea!"

And the Greeks threw their rifles into the sea.

At eight o'clock that night, a Turkish lieutenant and two
soldiers carrying bayonets came to the Cathedral of St.
Photini. They crossed the courtyard on foot and entered the
crowded basilica.

It was the hour of Evensong and the beginning of the
Lord's Day, Kyriaki. The Metropolitan Chrysostomos was
praying in the sanctuary, hidden by the sculptured wooden
panels of the altar screen, which glittered with fantastic animals and angels painted scarlet, gold and green. When he
heard the frightened chattering of the women in the gallery,
the Metropolitan came out of the holy bema and lifted his

hands in benediction; and the crowd was quieted at once.

Chrysostomos' face was gaunt from fasting. His beard was quivering against the silver fabric of his pallium. Kneeling, he kissed the sacred picture of the Virgin Mother. Then, without looking in the direction of the door, he began to walk among the congregation, giving them his blessing and disbursing bread and olive oil among the refugees. They noticed that he moved his hands with haste.

At last the Metropolitan ascended to the pulpit to begin his sermon. Flames were gleaming in the *polykandilon;* pellets of myrrh and olibanum were smoldering in golden thuribles; and burning wicks were floating in cups of scented oil below the ikons. At the back of the church there were some raisin growers who were not of the community of Smyrna Greeks but had fled to the city from the countryside; and they were wringing their hands and crying loudly: "It's all over. Everything is lost."

Chrysostomos looked directly at them as he gave his sermon, saying: "Holy Providence tries our faith as well as our courage, but God does not forsake good Christians."

A moment afterward, the soldiers came and took him out, along with two of the demogerontes of the Orthodox community—Alderman Klimanoglou and Alderman Tsourouktsioglou, both of whom had been officials of the Greek regime in Smyrna.

The people bowed their heads but did not move, because they understood that this was happening the way it must among the Orthodox.

Three times, Chrysostomos had refused an opportunity to leave the city. First, the bishop of the Roman Catholics had come and begged him to accept a ticket on a foreign steamer. But Chrysostomos rebuffed him, saying: "The tradition of the Greek clergyman and the role of the good shepherd is to stay with his flock." Then the leaders of the army and the civil

433

government had invited him to go with them aboard the cruiser *Limnos;* but Chrysostomos would not consent. Finally, when the Turkish cavalry was entering the city, Father Scagliarino of the Italian Capuchins came to Chrysostomos with twenty sailors from the Consulate of France and offered to conduct him safely to the sanctuary of the Church of Sacré-Coeur. And, once again, Chrysostomos refused to go.

So no one cried or struggled when the soldiers took him. But a woman at the doorway stretched out her hand to touch his stole, and it seemed to burn her fingers with its heat.

As the soldiers led him across the court, Chrysostomos turned and raised his eyes to the marble frieze depicting Jesus and St. Photini at Jacob's Well. Moving his lips, he read the words: "Whosoever drinketh of the water that I shall give him shall never thirst."

This story of the Metropolitan's arrest in the cathedral spread around the city. But there also were witnesses who said Chrysostomos was apprehended in the sacristy. A deacon saw him taken from his palace; and still others said he went that night by carriage with Alderman Tsourouktsioglou and offered himself to General Nureddin Pasha, the military commandant, as a scapegoat for the Greeks.

In any case, that night Chrysostomos made a proclamation from the Turkish garrison, ordering the Greeks to give their weapons to the Turkish soldiers. The Greeks discerned that this communication had been drawn from him by force; and they ignored it. Later, the Metropolitan sent a letter to his brother Evghenio Kalaphatis, saying: "Do not worry."

He passed the night in solitude as a prisoner of General Nureddin Pasha. Like St. Polycarp before his martyrdom, he suffered fearful dreams. He felt a rain of stones against his head, a scorching fire against his face, the talons of a predatory animal against his breast. He saw himself beheaded like St. George, beaten like St. Stephen, devoured by wild beasts like St. Ignatius of Antioch, burned at the stake like St. Polycarp, goaded to exhaustion like his patron, St. John Chrysostom, the liturgist, the golden-mouthed archbishop of Constantinople. At dawn, when he rose from these prophetic visions, he heard the Turkish muezzin at Konak Mosque, a hundred yards away, singing like the Memnon of Thebes at the first light of day.

Nureddin Pasha sent for him.

It has been said that when they met, the two men stared at each other in bitter silence. Nureddin Pasha was a proud and patriotic man. He had been the governor of Smyrna Province before it was assigned to Greece, and the Metropolitan, to weaken Turkish opposition, had induced the Allied High Commissioners to put him out of office.

Finally, Nureddin Pasha spoke. His voice was dark and slowly measured, like the pounding of a deep, threnodic drum. He accused the Metropolitan of treason. He read aloud some written accusations and delations. Then he threw the documents aside and gazed at Chrysostomos with an expression of contempt.

"For five hundred years the Sultan has given his protection to his loyal Greek community, but you have repaid him with sedition. When our country was at war with France and England, you encouraged the Greeks on the coastline to spy for the enemy. You urged the Kingdom of Greece to go to war against us. You sent petitions to the Allied governments, begging them to enslave us and dismember our country. When the Greeks came to Smyrna, you welcomed them as liberators."

Chrysostomos answered:

"I have no regrets. I have been faithful to my ministry. Is it wrong for me to serve my nation and my people?"

"Even if you have wronged *my* nation and *my* people?"

A mob was gathering outside the barracks. Nureddin Pasha

went and looked out the window. Then he told his guards to take the Metropolitan downstairs.

Seeing Chrysostomos at the threshold of the barracks, with his white hair reaching to his shoulders and his splendid episcopal robes spread around him like a cataract of gold and silver, the crowd drew back. Nureddin Pasha leaned from the balcony to address them.

"If this man has done good to you, do good to him. If he has done you harm, do harm to him." Turning away, he closed the window to the balcony.

The Metropolitan Chrysostomos stood blinking in the morning sunlight.

For several moments, no one touched him. The men at the back of the crowd were pressing forward, craning their necks to get a glimpse of this fanatic whose encouragement had led the Infidels to commit such hideous atrocities. When they saw him standing there, impervious, with his sacerdotal vestments spotless and his pious face immaculate, they began to growl like street dogs. Clenching their fists, they thought about the Christian soldiers who had tortured and murdered and driven Moslems from the villages, the Christian bandits who had burned the crops and defecated in the mosques.

Chrysostomos looked from face to face. His forehead gleamed with sweat. A pulse was throbbing in his temple. Suddenly, the foremost of the men surrounded him and pulled him down the steps. He stumbled to his knees. A grinning boy seized hold of his chasuble, trying to tear the fabric; but others, whose hatred had been banked up like a deep, slow-burning fire, pushed the boy aside. Lifting Chrysostomos by the arms, they walked him forward almost gently between two lines of men who murmured curses as he passed. When they reached the shop of Barber Ishmael in the street between the Konak and the Kemer Alti Mosque, they ordered out a stool, a razor and a wrapping sheet and draped the Metropolitan Chrysostomos in the sheet to tonsure him. Among the men around him was a Kurdish stevedore, sweating and naked to his breeches; and this man gripped Chrysostomos by the hair while another stretched out his beard until his face was raised to Heaven. Then they drew the razor swiftly through his hair. The crowd broke into laughter.

But the men at the back were pushing forward restlessly. The stool overturned. The Metropolitan fell to the ground. The crowd trampled him and kicked him. Then, the Kurdish porter straddled him and tore out handfuls of his hair; and the other man lashed out with the razor, cutting off his ear.

At the sight of the blood spurting onto his garments, the crowd began to pant with frenzy. Sticks and clubs appeared. Pieces of chain and metal pipes and cargo hooks as sharp as daggers glittered in the shadows. Covering his head with his hands, the Metropolitan began to run, and the men raised their arms to beat him as he passed. Laughing and howling, they drove him through the fetid alleys, past the Algerian Khan, the Copper Market and the Maidens' Khan, where some shoemakers rushed out of their musty little cells and rubbed his face with feculence scooped from the gutters.

Blood was running through his fingers. His embroidered stole was torn away. He was drawing his breath in rasping sobs. At the gate of the Hisar Jami, the greatest mosque of Smyrna, he fell to his knees with a wavering cry. But when they raised him to his feet again, he shambled forward drunkenly, scarcely flinching from their blows.

He passed the Chestnut Bazaar and the Little Iron Khan, the Fountain Mosque, the Chick-Pea Vendors' Baths, the Cherry Khan, the Pasha's Khan. Everywhere, they spat on him, chanting: "Pig! . . . Son of pigs! . . . Pederast of pigs!" His hair was gone, his eyes were glazed with a yellowish film and a strip of bleeding flesh was hanging from his forehead.

On the Street-That-Tops-the-Cemeteries, which was in the Jewish Quarter near the Madmen's Baths, he fell down again and would not get up. They lifted him and dragged him forward. But his lips were moving awkwardly. Suddenly, he groaned, his eyes rolled upward and he whispered:

"Lord Jesus, receive my spirit."

They saw that he was dead. In their fury, they immediately cut off his nose and his remaining ear. Then they stripped his body of its rags and left it naked in an alley. A pack of dogs as gray as wolves rushed out and buried their ravenous muzzles in his wounds.

Early Monday morning Kenan came into Smyrna with the Pasha and his staff. They had spent the night in Cordelio, across the water from the city. Mustapha Kemal slept in a red-brick house that had been used the year before as a headquarters for King Constantine. Somebody spread a Greek flag like a doormat on the threshold; but the Pasha picked it up and handed it to his orderly.

A parade of automobiles followed the northern margins of the gulf, past the salt marshes and the tannery, and entered the city at the Point of Alsanjak. The tobacco sheds were filled with refugees who peeked out with glittering eyes; but all the splendid villas on the upper Quay were draped with scarlet bunting. As the Pasha came along, men on either side were singing his favorite marching song:

> "Where shall we find the skies and seas?
> And where the stony mountaintops?
> Where are the lovely birds and trees?
> Comrades, march along with me!"

Partway down the Quay the column stopped. Kenan looked over at a pretentious mansion with a picture of Mustapha Kemal, twice as large as life, hanging from the balcony. Behind the shutters moved a pale flicker of faces: treacherous

Infidels who had betrayed their country to the enemy and who now prayed for mercy!

"Who lives there?" Kenan asked, trying to sound indifferent. "It wouldn't be a Greek merchant named Trigonis?"

None of the other passengers knew; but Kenan studied the house with growing excitement. Surely that was the place! He began to breathe so rapidly and deeply that the driver turned around.

"It's the dust," Kenan said. "It always causes asthma."

To calm himself, he rubbed his knee and looked toward the gulf. He did not want anyone, especially the Pasha, to suspect the reason for his interest in Smyrna. His visit was purportedly a "parliamentary inspection," arranged by the army as a gesture of conciliation to the neglected members of the Grand National Assembly. If a member of the G.N.A. should happen to travel with the army under the divine guidance of the Caliph Ali, that was so much the worse for heretics, Infidels and traitors. But the Pasha did not understand the nature of the holy fire that was consuming Kenan: he thought it was an illness, and he always counseled food and rest and good Yalova mineral waters. Yah, God! The agony of bottling up an inspiration!

The cars began to move again. They passed the clubs, the theaters, the foreign consulates, with pyracantha berries flaming against the walls and flags of European states displayed in stiff bravado.

At Pasaport, the Pasha stopped and gave a speech, reminding all the Turks that their national reputation would suffer if there were atrocities in Smyrna. Kenan rubbed his cheek to hide a smile. Armenian and Greek civilians would relinquish arms by seven o'clock tonight, and thereafter any Greek soldier who had not surrendered would be shot on sight. Pacification would be swift and thorough, a source of pride for the Turkish people.

That afternoon, Kenan drove up the Quay to look for the

Trigonis house. He took along four soldiers and a sergeant major, enough army to storm a Russian fortress, witness to his pacific inclinations. The soldiers gazed admiringly at the white plaster furbelows and iron sconces. Then they raised their rifle butts and broke the door.

An old man ran into the vestibule with his arms outstretched. Kenan examined him without sympathy: a stout, florid, perfumed hog with lavender glasses, who held his head up regally. Obviously, he thought himself of great importance. Assuming that the men had come to arrest him, he stood with his wrists thrust out as if bound together with rope.

"I am ready," he said in Greek.

"Stand out of the way," Kenan said. "Do you understand Turkish?"

The old man did not answer. Kenan said:

"Where is the woman?"

But the old man looked at him in a haughty manner and answered in Greek:

"There are no women here."

"Where is the woman who is married to a Turk named Abdullah of Alashehir?"

The old man gave a start. Then he said in a dull voice:

"She is not here."

"Are you Christos Trigonis?"

"No."

"This is the house of Christos Trigonis, isn't it?"

"No."

Kenan turned around.

"Search the house," he said to the sergeant major. He glanced at the proud old man. Then he went into the drawing room, drew back the curtains and pushed open the shutters.

"Field Marshal Mustapha Kemal has ordered harmony and good order in this city," he said. "If I were commander, I would not be so lenient."

He glanced again at the old man, who did not lift his eyes. To show contempt, Kenan sat down in front of him, crossed his legs and lit a cigarette. His foot was throbbing with pain, and his nostrils were polluted with the stink of ashes.

"There were six thousand houses in Kassaba before your army came," he said. "Now there are two hundred. There were fourteen thousand houses in Manisa; now there are one thousand. The mosques are gutted. The vineyards and fields are sown with salt. In Alashehir—" He clamped his teeth and closed his eyes. Then he went on: "In Alashehir there were forty-five hundred houses. One of them belonged to my father, God rest him. Now there are less than a hundred, and my father's house is not among them."

The old man lifted his eyes and stared at Kenan with an expression of recognition. He seemed to be about to speak; but the sergeant major came back and whispered to Kenan:

"Come, Your Honor."

They went to a chamber off the vestibule. Layers of Persian rugs were piled up on the floor. There were tables of vermiculated olive wood, silver zarfs for serving bitter coffee, animal horns on walnut plaques, portraits of young women in brocaded bodices and men in hunting caps, musical instruments, mohair bolsters.

"Look," said the sergeant in an awful voice. "All these things belong to us."

"No, nothing," Kenan said angrily. "Didn't you hear what the Pasha said?" He went back to the drawing room and said to the old man:

"Where are they?"

The old man did not answer. Kenan snapped his fingers.

"Are you dumb? Speak up!"

And he slapped the old man's face. The old man looked at him silently. A little blood from a scratch on his cheek began to trickle down his face.

Kenan went out and told his men to search again. Then he

paced around the carpet, tapping his eye patch with his hand.

"If I were commander, I would blind you and drive you out of the country. Look what you Greeks have done to us! Am I supposed to forgive this? I swear by God the All-Seeing, I will *not* forgive!"

He sent the soldiers to explore the garden, to inspect the cupboards and the bath, to search the cellar. At last, trembling with shame, the Greek said in Turkish:

"Your Honor? Please? Is it possible you are a son of Hilmi Pasha of Alashehir?"

Kenan drew a sharp breath. It seemed a desecration of his father's name to hear it from Greek lips.

"I am the only son of Hilmi Pasha!" he shouted. "The only son who honors that heroic Moslem!"

"Your Honor? Please?" the Greek repeated. "There isn't any woman here." He came to Kenan and put something into his hand.

"What's this?" Kenan said, throwing down a little purse that jingled as it struck the floor. "Is this a war debt?"

"There isn't any woman," the old man said again. "I beg Your Honors to take their soldiers and leave us alone."

Kenan began to laugh.

"Do you think I am interested in that foul whore? I am searching for *him*. There is something to be settled between us, as the sainted Caliph is my witness."

And he summoned the patrol and left the house.

It was the hottest hour of afternoon. The streets were quiet. All the shutters were drawn in this Greek neighborhood; and from a distance, now and then, Kenan could hear a pistol shot. A ship moaned at the Quay. The last foreign residents were putting out to sea. Smyrna seemed to hold its breath.

DIKILI

SEPTEMBER 11, 1922

*O*n the fifteenth day of their retreat, the Greek column from Seyit Gazi reached the sea.

One of the company commanders halted his men in a thicket of oaks above the shore. There, remembering the history of Xenophon and the descent from Persia, he ordered the haggard soldiers to call out in the ancient language: *"Thalata! Thalata!"* Then, like the myriad of old, they staggered downward, barefoot, ragged and starving, dragging cartloads of wounded and dying, and surrounded by a multitude of refugees.

Just as the sun was going down, the leading regiment came into Dikili, a dusty little harbor on the strait that separates the mainland from the island of Lesbos, which is a part of Greece. The earth was copper-colored in the light reflected from the sea; the olive trees along the shore were stirring in the gentle breeze. With pitiful cries of joy, the soldiers plunged into the water, and the sound of their laughter drifted back to George's ears.

He was trailing in the final rank, among the cream puffs and the cripples, with his eyes cast down and his mind adrift. The dust came up at every step and burned his blistered lips. Nobody spoke to him: all the stragglers and cowards were absorbed in their own painful reveries. Yet George often felt accusing glances, which seemed to pierce his chest like swords.

He had learned at Kirkaghatch that Smyrna had been taken by the Turks. For several hours, his mother and his father had absorbed his thoughts; but he found it difficult to concentrate his mind on something far away. His fears, his weariness and his humiliation crowded out all other feelings. His failure weighed on his heart; and his melancholy thoughts showed on his face. At the edge of town, an infantry captain stopped and peered at him.

"Lieutenant? Where are your men?"

"Dead. Nobody left."

He pretended to be deranged by shock, like some of the other stragglers, who soiled their pants and cried continually. But the captain eyed him coldly.

"It was quitters like you that made us lose the war. Get down to the shore and help control those refugees."

To escape the captain's scrutiny, George stumbled down the road and turned along an alley. Control eight thousand refugees? He who could not discipline a platoon of artillery? He would rather have gone back to face the Turkish cavalry.

The refugees engulfed the meadows at the edges of the town, tormenting the army with a constant reminder of its dereliction. There were old women, dressed in black alpaca, who tottered along with a dazed expression on their faces; young girls with golden earrings, who stared at the officers in fear and tenderness; and village priests, who cowered in the backs of wagons, their cassocks streaked with dust, their black cylindrical *kalimavkia* trembling on their knotted hair. Night after night, these people had accumulated on the flanks of the division like a retinue of concubines: Christian weavers from Gelenbe, who spoke only Turkish and crossed themselves fervently at the sound of Allah's name; vintners from Kirkaghatch, who carried wooden flails; and farmers

444

from Kinik, who wailed and shook their heads and shouted curses at the soldiers. Some of the men were wearing fezzes, out of terror of the Turks; others sang hymns, like pilgrims to Jerusalem; and some, especially those who had been prosperous grocers and *kaymak*-makers in Pergamos, gazed back in tears at the fertile valley of the Caicus.

George stood watching in a weary stupor, pitying and hating all that aggregated suffering. Animals were bellowing and stirring up the dust; women were shoving toward the well; children were searching the pastures for catmint, crocus bulbs, wild grains and lupine seeds to fill the supper pots.

Stubborn, tenacious peasants of Ionia and Aeolis—they would endure. Their resourcefulness was touching and disgusting. A girl with heavy braids was smiling at him, lifting the hem of her calico dress. She spread apart her legs, which were crusted with scabies, stuck out her tongue and wiggled it to and fro.

"Both ways, soldier. Nice and slow. Just give me a good loaf of bread. . . . "

Then others saw him—women with babies at their breasts, boys with clay amphoras on their heads—and they all began to crowd him.

"You brought us here, didn't you? You let the Turks run over you. Now you're stuffing your bellies while we starve!"

A squad of military policemen rushed up with bayonets to force the people back. They were pushing too close to the army's supplies, which were secluded in the market place, guarded by a ring of riflemen. The market stalls were filled with sheep and cattle confiscated from Turkish towns along the march. Heaped against the walls were old Ladik and Kula carpets, taken from the mosques, and gunny sacks of bread and barley, levied from the elders of Pergamos that very morning, while the soldiers rested in the ruins of the Baths of Attalus: good barley, winnowed clean, and round wheat loaves, stamped with the Cross, like Lenten bread, to show they had been baked by Christians.

A sergeant of supply was cutting up the bread and doling it out with a carefree hand, as if a bite of food were ample consolation for a national catastrophe. All around him, men were waiting, slouched against the walls, teasing one another with a sort of rough affection. They called each other names, complained about the stink, speculated on the hour of embarkation, passed around a pulpy cigarette.

Gazing at them, George was afflicted by a sense of isolation. He was without a friend, a counselor or a lover. From the beginning of the war, there had been no one, nothing to sustain him. Haunted by the certainty of failure, he had been surrounded by men like his father who had professed to see in him the ingredients of a hero, whereas in reality there was only bewilderment and doubt.

Drawn along by the elusive anodyne of companionship and laughter, George approached the line of men. The sergeant, nodding like a merchant in a market stall, rapped his knife against the table.

"At your service, Lieutenant. I suppose you've got the requisitions for your battery?"

"Well, no." George glanced around. "I . . . *lost* them."

Just behind him, someone snickered.

"Well, sir, that's very serious," said the sergeant, shaking his head with false gravity. "Did you lose the requisitions— or did you lose the battery?"

"The requisitions," George cried, with a rush of hot blood to his cheeks.

"What a shame, my boy. I mean, *Lieutenant.*" The laughter spread. "I can't give no bread without those requisitions."

George swallowed, staring straight ahead.

"I'll take my portion now," he said. His eyelids burned with humiliation. Raising his voice, he went on: "You'd better be careful how you speak to me, Sergeant. I'll put you on report."

"Report!" the man echoed, snarling in contempt. "Where does he think he is? In Athens?"

George snatched up a piece of bread and turned away, almost crying. He stifled the convulsive movements of his throat with a huge unchewed mouthful, which lodged in his chest in a suffocating lump.

At the edge of the harbor he found an empty shed and hid among some moldering paillasses stuffed with husks of maize. All night, refugees argued around the public fountain and street dogs barked. Just at dawn some women in the meadow screeched in terror, and a battery began to fire in the direction of the coastal hills, where someone thought that he had seen a Turkish cavalry patrol.

There was no sign of transport ships until after three o'clock that afternoon. Then whistles blew, church bells rang and pistols cracked across the water. As the vessels neared the shore, George recognized the little ferryboats *Ionia* and *Aetolia,* which for many years had run between the Quay of Smyrna and the suburb of Cordelio. He could remember crossing the misty water on a summer morning with his mother and sister, carrying a picnic basket (pickled eggplants, garlic beef and Russian salad) to a little open-air pavilion under the pines in the Forest of the Yamanlar. But the ferryboats were smaller than he had recalled.

Looking at the fragile hulls, the divisional commander breathed a desperate curse on the cuckolded pigs who had sent them. He ordered the supply corps to begin the slaughter of the animals. In those two archaic cockleshells, it would take forty hours to move the beasts; and in far less time than that the Turks would own the town.

In the market place an enormous, one-eyed hostler stripped off his tunic, exposing a black bosom with breasts like a woman's and the scars of a lash across his back. Flexing

447

his arms, he raised a blacksmith's mallet as the herdsmen drove the oxen forward. There was a man on either side to grip the horns, a boy behind to twist the tail and a butcher standing by to cut the carotid artery. The thud of the mallet could be heard above the screaming of the animals, and blood splashed as high as the roof of the sheds.

The camels, a remnant of eighty that had started from the camp at Seyit Gazi, expired in the streets with a bubbling roar, like the strange and horrifying sound they make in rut; the water buffaloes trumpeted in anguish; and the horses shrieked like human beings.

As for the smaller animals—the sheep, the donkeys, the angora goats and kids, the nurseling camels and the piebald dogs that had trotted for hundreds of miles between the axles of the wagons—they were herded to the courtyard of a caravanserai and shot between the eyes.

A soldier fainted grinding butcher knives. Another fell into convulsions. An orderly, who was bringing towels soaked in seawater, vomited when a steaming jet of blood erupted on his chest. But whenever the butchers would stop to wipe their knives, a cavalry major would lean from a window, his face like chalk, and beg them in a faltering voice: "Don't stop! The Turks have taken Pergamos. They'll be shelling us any minute!"

In the haste and turmoil of the slaughter, many of the wounded animals survived. Bleeding from shattered skulls, they staggered through the alleys, blindly crashing into walls, trampling on sacks of barley, slipping and falling in their own gore, their mouths wide open, uttering mornful cries.

Even creatures that were spared went berserk with anxiety, strangled themselves with their tethers or kicked until they broke their legs. Others were lost in embarkation, for the harbor had no crane, no dock and no jetty, only a fragile wooden pier from which the horses flung themselves in panic and were drowned.

The final massacre, so logical in its military necessity, so stupid in its cruelty and waste, tormented George almost to madness. He wandered through the streets, weeping openly, trying to hide small animals in empty cellars and dark sheds. Finally, he threw his arms around the neck of a mangled horse that was dragging its intestines on the ground. As he stood at the water's edge, embracing the horse and moaning in grief and incomprehension, a supply captain, whose mouth was frozen in a spasm of revulsion, rushed up, drew out a pistol and shot the animal through the head.

"Now you've ended it!" George cried out, blinded with grief. "You've ended it the only way you understand." And he stretched out on the warm, shuddering body of the dying horse, which rolled back its immense brown eyes and coughed up a clot of bloody foam.

The loading of the *Aetolia* began at five o'clock.

First went the telegraph, the sanitation squads and the stretcher bearers, carrying a captain with a septic knee, a corporal whose feet were black and several men with dysentery, dying for lack of calomel and emetine and agonized by every motion. Bending over the pallets, the doctors murmured "Tenesmus" and waved them by. Next went staff company, trailed by a crate of documents; and then Tsipouras, colonel of the 53rd, with a selected infantry to serve as military police. The doctors were inspecting lines of men for bluish lips and vomiting: there had been rumors of a case of cholera at Pergamos.

The refugees, sensing that they were to be abandoned, came running to the harbor, screaming for protection. A regimental major shouted at them through a megaphone. His voice echoed up and down the waterfront, orchestrated by the ghastly moaning of the slaughtered animals. "Keep back! Everyone will be saved." But the refugees knew that he was lying.

At seven o'clock, the whistle blew as merrily as if the soldiers were embarking on a visit to the gardens and casinos of the Cordelia shore. The *Aetolia* slipped westward on the oily sea; and the *Ionia* came in and nosed against the pier.

Through the night, the little ferryboats were loaded and reloaded and dispatched across the straits. A fleet of smaller craft appeared—caïques and rowboats, fishing smacks and barges; and the voices of the boatmen, nervous and rapacious as the cries of sea gulls, rang across the water, calling out their extortionate fees.

The refugees were wailing in their clutter of possessions, weeping for their copper tubs, their metaled chests, their herds of cows. A few would not be parted from their chattels, but sat dumbly in overloaded wagons, clutching samovars and perfume sprinklers, unable to decide between abandoning their property and forfeiting their lives.

Now and then, some senior officer would turn on George and say: "Assemble your platoon and get aboard at once."

But George slipped around the block and hid himself again. He wanted to remain on shore until the very end.

The fear and pride that once had motivated him had suddenly disappeared. With terrible clarity, he saw that what had happened to the Greeks had been of their own design, involuntarily conceived. *It was written,* as the sergeant major had said on the road to Bursa. This intuition of fatality, although it filled George with despair, released him from the bondage of his ego. The narrow circle burst; and he strived no longer.

Toward the last, he joined a sort of cleanup crew of reckless, smoky men with pursed mouths. They pushed the 7,000-meter Skodas to the shore—those priceless cannon the division had dragged so painfully through the gorge of the Simav; loaded, locked and fired two shells in the direction of the Turks; and sank the Skodas in the sea.

Next, they soaked the market place with kerosene and laid

450

a tinder pile of pitch-pine sticks under a mound of broken wagons. This was the funerary pyre of all their dreams: their Anatolia, their Great Idea, their Byzantium, surmounted by a wooden reading stand that held a beautiful Koran, illuminated, bound in cordovan and gold, embellished with an arabesque of yarrow and acanthus leaves and blackened with the ordure of their bowels.

The whistle of the ferry screeched. A vulture rose and wheeled across the ashen sky. They set the town of Dikili afire, and thus relinquished Asia Minor.

*I*t was midday, a dangerous hour, when Abdullah came to the Buja Road and looked down on the rooftops of Smyrna. For several minutes he stood there, breathless with exertion, gazing at the minarets and steeples of the beautiful, unfaithful city, which seemed to be floating like a tangled mat of orange flotsam in a sea of mist. Then, hearing the sound of voices coming down the hill, he scurried across the road and clambered up a stairway to the terrace of a coffee-house.

An excited crowd was pouring down the Buja Road, raising a cloud of dust and shattering the air with piercing cries. Zeybek mountaineers in crimson vests were lashing their crippled ponies; Circassians with sabres in their belts were balancing nonchalantly on narrow wooden saddles; and, on the flanks of the procession, farmers in dusty boots and ragged shirts were carrying antique rifles, shovels, sticks and flails.

Concealing himself behind a wall of stones, Abdullah drew his dagger and tucked it out of sight between his left arm and his body. The frenzied chanting of the looters resounded from the narrow gorges of the mountain; and Abdullah shuddered, more in revulsion than in fear.

"*Gavur Izmir!* Infidel Smyrna! Here we come!"

There were troops of Kurdish nomads, wearing hoods as

452

black as charcoal, and Yürüks of Nazilli, whose women went unveiled, in baggy scarlet bloomers, their cheeks tatooed with purple talismans and their fingertips stained brick red with henna. The women were laughing as they goaded their mangy camels down the slope; but the men, stately and reflective, strode along like hunters, with Mausers cradled in their sunburned arms. As they passed below the stairway to the coffeehouse, a few of the riders raised their heads and stared at Abdullah's hiding place with cold eyes. But the procession did not stop. Entertainment was waiting just ahead. Under an aqueduct named for the Angel Hazir, whom the Hebrews call Elijah, someone had flushed a Christian from a shack. The Mausers coughed; and when the crowd had passed, a man lay naked in the road, with a little heap of rubbish burning like votive incense on his upturned chest.

Abdullah looked around. The arbor was deserted. Stools and tables, whitened by the sun, were piled against a shed. Yellow locust leaves were curling on the ground. As he raised his hand to tap the knocker at the door, Abdullah suddenly drew his breath.

He knew this place! It was the Little Belvedere— a famous coffeehouse where Greeks and Moslems used to meet to barter calves and horses, argue stud fees and complain about the price of raisins. The vista of the cemeteries—Greek and Turk and Hebrew, side by side in the canyon of the Meles River —was a reminder of the brotherhood of death, which would soon enough unite the nations of mankind.

Abdullah pressed his face against the shutters of the coffeehouse. Reflected in the windowpane, his pupils, discolored by the dirty glass, stared back at him with a forbidding concentration. He moved his head from side to side, holding his hand beside his ear to darken the reflection; but spots of oxidation in the glass shone on his cheeks like phosphorescent cancers. His hair was gray with dust; his features had collapsed. It was the face of an old man, driven by mania.

Groaning, he moved to another window. Through the chinks he could see a pile of coffee cups, a silver-plated samovar, a blackboard painted with the bill of fare. His mouth turned moist for lemonade and baklava and heavy cream. He could remember riding out here with his father and Nüvit Bey and Kenan to stop for cherry juice and mountain snow. Kenan had on his circumcision crown, and Abdullah had to ride the pony with a milky eye; but the man at Buja gave each of them a disk of almond nougat.

Someone growled at him: "Get out!"

Abdullah raised his head. A pigeon fluttered in the pergola. There was the soft click of a cartridge bolt, and the voice repeated, in a tone so guttural, liturgical and dark that the coffee garden seemed to suffocate beneath its weight: "Get out!"

Abdullah looked from side to side. The garden was empty, deeply drifted with the golden showerings of the honey-locust trees.

"Remzi Bey?" Abdullah said. "Is it you?"

There was no answer.

"Give me something to eat, for God's sake. Isn't this the Little Belvedere? Where is Remzi Bey?"

Another long silence. Then, quietly, the hidden voice: "Who are you? Christian or Turk?"

"I am Abdullah, the son of Hilmi Pasha."

"Hilmi of Alashehir? God rest him! Lift your face, and let me see you."

Raising his eyes, Abdullah saw the barrel of a rifle pointing at him from a huge nest of twigs and thatch, built like a messy stork's nest on the roof of the coffeehouse. The muzzle seemed to study him. The heavy voice said:

"I have never seen you before. Never."

"I was only a boy, eight or nine years old. With my brother

—he was wearing a circumcision crown—and my father and his cousin, Nüvit Bey, from Göz Tepe."

"Never."

"Come down and fix me something. My soul is going out of my mouth."

"Why are you carrying a stick?"

"I walked here, most of the way from Alashehir. Do you think that's a picnic?"

"Are you a Christian or a Turk?"

"What difference does it make?"

"Where are you going?"

"To Smyrna."

"Why?"

"Because it is my destination."

The tip of the rifle darted outward like the eye of a snail and waggled slowly to and fro.

"You're too late," the voice said. "The Turkish Army came four days ago. The war is over."

"I don't care," Abdullah murmured. Swaying with weakness, he pressed his hand against his heart. "Your Honor? Remzi Bey? For my father's sake, give me one piece of bread and let me go on my way."

The eye of the rifle perused him from the branches.

"Are you a Christian or a Turk?"

"Who are *you*?" Abdullah cried. "Give me some bread!"

"I am the new Diogenes. Open your eyes. You are too late."

And as Abdullah turned, with his head bowed in exhaustion, he saw beyond the belvedere, beyond the canyon that the Christians call the Valley of St. Anne, three lofty pinnacles of smoke rising from the center of the city. With a cry, he ran across the yard.

The three pillars, boiling up in blackness, flecked with bursts of orange flame, tilted slowly northward, melting and distending into the limpid sky above the Christian quarter of the town, until they faded yellow-gray and disappeared among the clouds beyond the marshes of Halkipinar.

"Eleni, Eleni!" Abdullah cried. "Where did you go?"

Nobody knew exactly how or where the first spark had fallen. Apparently, a house had taken fire that morning in Chikir Sokak, a sunken alley in the neighborhood of Basmahane Station, where some Turkish soldiers had gone to confiscate the weapons of Armenian civilians. Someone had fired a shot at the patrol; someone had thrown a homemade bomb; and, shortly afterward, fires broke out in shops and houses from St. Stephen's to the Fruit Bazaar.

Not even the Insurance Fire Brigade, which the European underwriting companies had established to combat commercial arson, could suppress the flames. Water pumps broke down. Hoses caught fire. Bucket squads disintegrated and the men fled.

The firemen blamed their failure on the wind. No one had ever heard of a south wind in September. It carried burning embers toward the Greek cathedral, down the Street of Bath-Towel Sellers, directly through the Christian quarters of the city. Soon the Armenian cathedral was glowing like a crucible. Blazing cinders showered down on Basmahane. The people of the district, terrified of looters, hid inside their houses and shot at the firemen. Within an hour or two, St. Stephen's district was abandoned.

Army sappers went in to dynamite a block of buildings and create a barrier of rubble on the northern edges of the fire. But the explosives only punctured holes and left the walls standing. The fire leaped its boundaries into St. Dimitris' quarter and swept northeastward, toward the cobbled esplanade along the sea.

By midafternoon, the flames were out of control in more than twenty places. Driving up from Göz Tepe, Kenan found the Quay teeming like the throne of Heaven at the final trumpet. The horde of refugees who had pursued the Army of the Hellenes had been augmented by a throng of Smyrniots, driven out by the fire. They were carrying all manner of trifles in their arms—plush pillows, lithographs and tarnished wedding crowns—and each time they heard a siren or a burst of dynamite, they would push each other closer to the water, casting panicky glances inland, as if they felt themselves pursued by demons. Catching sight of the motorcar with its Turkish flag and military chauffeur, the men stretched out their arms and yowled.

"Help us, Your Honor! We need some boats, some rafts. The fire is driving us into the bay!"

But Kenan stared straight ahead, touching a finger to his eye patch, and told his driver to sound the klaxon. It had taken more than two hours to drive from the suburbs, and Mustapha Kemal would be waiting. Meanwhile, of course, the fire had been spreading admirably, and that afforded Kenan some morbid satisfaction.

Although he knew that Mustapha Kemal was shocked by the damage to the commercial sections of the city, Kenan could only look upon the fire with favor. He was impressed by the voracious hunger of the flames, their meteoric speed. These were God's weapons, sent to punish Smyrna for its treachery. They fell with terrible, swift justice on this parasitic Christian colony. If the hands of man had struck the flame, they had moved within the awesome pattern of God's design. Better that this malignant growth, this cancerous community of unbelievers, be cauterized with fire than that it fester in the pure body of the Turkish nation!

On the Quay outside the Pasha's office, some Greeks were crowding around a wooden barge. An old woman as toothless as a hen had seized command. Squatting on the seat board with her black skirts billowing around her, she shouted instructions to the shore.

"The bread! The bread comes next!" and then: "The priest!
The priest comes next!" And the men on shore obediently
handed down a dozen loaves of bread, followed by a florid
old *papaz*, a bearded bullock of a man who held his eyes
closed and an ikon pressed against his heart.

The boatmen, grumbling impatiently, dipped their oars
toward the water; but the old woman continued gesturing,
shouting, receiving bundles and accepting passengers. She
took aboard another priest, a limp child wrapped in blankets
and a young woman with a baby tugging at her breast. The
water lapped a few inches below the gunwales.

Some men with rags around their heads began to clutch at
the hawsers, offering the coxswain purses of coins. The old
woman shrieked and flapped her arms. At last the boat
moved off, deep-rolling like a dolphin in the greasy slick. A
few yards out, it shipped a wave and went down instantly.
The bundles floated outward. The old woman and her priests
were dragged ashore and laid out, side by side, gasping, in
their dripping shrouds. Kenan went inside.

The corporal who brought the latest report was black with
soot. Kenan stood up, gripping the head of his cane, while he
listened to the details.

"How many houses?" he said.

"God knows, Your Honor." The corporal wiped his inflamed eyelids on his sleeve. "Who can say at a time like this?
It moves too fast."

"Which districts? The Pasha will want to know."

"God knows," the man mumbled. Then he toppled over.
Fire had scorched his lips and nostrils, and his pale skin was
streaked with rivulets of sweat that trickled down like drops
of ink.

Kenan banged his cane against the wall.

"Inhalation case, Sergeant," he said to the man who entered. "Don't you have any doctors on call?" As he went up to give the report, he called back: "Get the trucks ready. We'll leave in five minutes."

The building was three stories high, a monument to European capital in the Levant. From the cornice one could see the city spread along the water like a faded shawl. At the center was the blazing orbit of the fire, heaving up globes of flame that billowed, burst apart and faded into whirling smoke.

The Pasha was crouching on the roof with a cigarette between his thin lips and a pair of binoculars to his eyes.

"It makes you sick," he said.

"Yes, sir," Kenan said, letting a metallic coldness sharpen the edges of his voice. He had never been so disappointed in Mustapha Kemal. The man was actually frowning with anxiety! Kenan told him the staff cars were ready to leave for Göz Tepe, where a merchant named Muammer Bey had offered the use of his house. "One of the trucks will lead the way. The Quay is almost impassable."

Sighing, the Pasha stretched his legs.

"Few people are as reliable as you, my friend. Most of your fellow deputies would rather lie at home in their pajamas than follow their leader into this burning Hell."

"To serve Their Honors, Our Pasha, is the only pleasure of my life," Kenan said. He bowed the Pasha toward the stairs.

As they were leaving the building, somebody plucked at Kenan's empty sleeve.

"I have more information, Your Honor."

Kenan shook loose, shuddering. The man was an informer —a Maltese or Rumanian, perhaps—who had pandered to the Greeks, the French, the English. They called him Pefko. His furtive, obsequious, slippery face reminded Kenan of all the vile corruption he despised in this accursed city.

459

"Give it to the sergeant."

"Too important. Too personal." He urged Kenan into the office. "These documents—look! A secret letter from the Greek commander to the Mavri Mira, setting the hour to ignite the fires. I need a safe conduct to Kokarli Yali, a Turkish passport, that's all."

"A forgery," Kenan said, sitting down. "What do I want with forgeries?"

"Without this proof, Your Honor, the world will say the Turkish Army set these fires."

"What do I care about the world?"

"A ride to the suburbs. A temporary pass." Pefko fidgeted from foot to foot, ratty fingers tangled in his hair. "I have more information. Guess what? I saw your brother here in Smyrna!"

Kenan clenched his jaw.

"I have no brother."

"Ah?" said Pefko. "Then it could not have been your brother I saw on the terrace of a coffeehouse above the aqueduct. I thought you were related to Abdullah of Alashekir, who used to keep a chemist's shop in Constantinople, just across from the Valide Mosque."

"No," Kenan said, struggling to stand up. "Don't help me. Just hand me that."

"The holster?"

"Help me put it on."

As Pefko bent his head, puffing with effort over the buckle of the holster belt, Kenan reached out and sank his thumb like a hook into the soft hollow of the spy's shoulder.

Pefko gasped and tried to squirm away.

"Where did you see this impostor?" Kenan whispered. "Lead me!"

They went out. The smoke had overspread the swamps and

cast a fan-shaped stain across the sky. As they were passing
the Italian Theater, where the fire was only two blocks from
the Quay, the sun went down, throbbing like a poisoned
heart.

After dark, Christos went upstairs and opened a pair of
shutters on the garden side. The fire was less than a mile
away. Beyond the drooping shadows of the deodars, the
night sky was as bright as a copper casserole, burnished here
and there by clots of flame.

Christos rested the barrel of his old hunting rifle on the
windowsill. He drew back the bolt and fed a pellet into the
chamber. The gardener's shack was in his sights. Its shadow
wavered in the dancing orange twilight.

Downstairs, somebody dropped a piece of glass.

"Eleni?"

Why did she never answer? He could hear her in the foyer,
taking down the portraits. Her mouth was sealed up tighter
than her brain. Just like Sophia—speechless and paralyzed,
with no thought except to run away!

"Leave those things alone," he called. "No one is going to
get in."

Her silence tormented him. He went to the top of the stairs
and peered down. Feeling his gaze, Eleni raised her head.

"I was only thinking about the fire."

"It'll never get this far," Christos said. Then, angered and
embarrassed by her unbelieving stare: "Isn't there anything
to eat?"

Eleni brought a plate of olives from the kitchen. They were
as bland as chick-peas. Holding the seeds in his fist, Christos
gestured with his forefinger at the rubbish his daughter had
gathered.

"Look at this! Perfume sprinklers! Stags' heads! Dolls!

461

Who's going to put this mess away? This house is not in danger, I tell you. What's this? Your mother's shawl? Why can't you leave these things alone?"

But Eleni took Sophia's paisley shawl and folded it and laid it carefully among the other bits of clothing. Christos, chewing an olive, stared at the back of her neck, which looked thin and tender as she bent to smooth the garments.

"I'll never understand it," he said. "How could you have hurt us so much?"

Eleni looked up, rubbing her forehead wearily with the back of her wrist. It was as if this question had been asked of her a thousand and one times before. Christos moved closer, lowering his voice.

"Now can't you see what savages they are? Now can't you understand our feelings? They're crueler than beasts! Beasts kill out of hunger, but *they* kill simply for pleasure!"

Glaring, he waited a moment for her answer. Then he burst out impatiently: "Mother of God! How could you do it? How could you lie down with him?"

Eleni wiped her eyes. Christos shouted into her ear:

"Wasn't he cruel to you? Abnormal passions? Ah, no— don't tell me! I know their habits. Curse of the world. Rapine. Depraved."

"Our men kill, too," Eleni said.

"Never mind! Don't tell me their excuses. Some of their filth was bound to rub off on you. But they've gone too far this time. You'll see. The world loves Smyrna. Smyrna's not like Afyon or Ankara, some unknown town out in the desert. It's not some isolated village where the Turks can rape and massacre without a Christian finger being raised against them. This is *Smyrna*. You'll see. The Allied fleet is waiting in the harbor."

Eleni glanced toward the shuttered windows, then quickly

462

lowered her head; but Christos, quivering with agitation, took hold of her shoulder and tried to force her toward a shutter.

"Take a look. The ships are standing by. If things get out of hand . . . "

But all that could be seen through the narrow crack between the shutters was a muffled mass of figures crowding toward the water, which was blacker than a grave. Beyond the embankment, people were wading in the shallows, holding babies overhead and screaming incoherently. From time to time, a deep explosion rumbled over this continuous, imploring cry. Sirens rose and fell across the water, and the ships blew their signal horns to warn small boats away— evidence of the world's concern.

"No, wait. It's going to be all right."

And he recklessly threw back the shutters on the Quay, which was glowing under an infernal light. Eleni gave a low moan and gripped his arm.

As far as one could see, there was a writhing multitude of heads, of arms, of bodies huddled on the stones or wallowing in the sea. Cinders and ashes sifted down on them like the ejecta of a ravaging volcano. Black figures, carrying fuel cans, darted through the smoke; and the fierce heat pounded down like the blows of a brazen hammer.

Christos slammed the shutters and bolted them. He turned on Eleni, who was staring at him wildly.

"It's a test of faith," he said. "Don't waver." Suddenly, he cried out: "God in Heaven, why don't they land? Do they want the wind to drive the fire from here to Manisa?"

And he scrambled, crablike, up the stairway, stumbling over Eleni's treasures and shrieking when he felt the shawl entangled around his leg. "Torches! Cans of oil! Where will they stop?"

463

Snatching up the rifle, he rushed to the bedroom window and fired into the murky garden, sobbing in despair and calling:

"Help us! Has everyone deserted us?"

But the Allied warships did not land; and their crews of young American and European seamen, who were not familiar with the Oriental usages of arson, stood on the decks and stared in disgust at the abominable city, seething in its ring of fire.

To these innocent and tenderhearted Western mariners, it seemed incredible that human beings could torment each other so remorselessly. What virus had contaminated them? What curse had afflicted them with this appetite for blood? Sailors on shore patrol saw looters splashing pails of coal oil to spread the flames. Bloated corpses floated in the harbor— tongueless, earless, fingerless, split up the boss like fish. Navigators thumbing the pages of Bowditch on the bridge could hear fearful screaming from the Quay. Thousands of human faces, pale as flowers, crowded the narrow stage along the shore, while out in the gulf the stars were shining and the south wind blew along the sweetly scented coast of Clazomenae.

"Turkish delight," the sailors said, lowering their boats to pluck exhausted swimmers from the bay.

The flames had nearly reached the Quay when Abdullah came to the fire lines. At Konak Square, some sentries had delayed him for an hour or more. Then he came against a second barrier at Kemer Alti Street and stopped to wipe his face.

The dampness of his skin and the giddiness of his head had begun to alarm him. What if he should begin to have hallucinations? He had heard of people who walked into flames, imagining themselves invulnerable, like salamanders. To cool his brain, he leaned against a wall and plotted his route again, mumbling softly as he traced a map with his finger on the palm of his hand.

It had not occurred to him that Eleni might have gone to Bornova, to Cheshme, to any other place except her father's house. Nor had he decided what to do when he should find her. For nine days he had pursued her through the ruined valleys, hiding from both Greek and Turk, with little rest or nourishment and with no clear intention. He knew he could not protect her, and he did not want to punish her. He only wanted to reclaim what she had taken from him—that part of himself, impalpable, invisible and tender, that existed only in her presence.

If he had married Eleni out of conceit, as his mother had assumed, then it was conceit that drove him now, for it was the same irrational compulsion. Abdullah called it love.

Beyond the barricade, a chain of volunteers was passing buckets of water from the bay. It was an absurd performance: puppies barking at the surf. The flames surged up and tossed the water back like drops rebounding from a stove lid. But there was no other way to dampen the fire: the hose that coiled across the cobblestones had melted from the heat.

Abdullah slipped past the line, turned to the right and felt his way along the stone wall of a packing shed. The masonry was almost too hot to touch. People bumped into him, gasped in surprise and then disappeared in the darkness. It struck him that he was the only person in the city who was walking *toward* the fire, and this ridiculous distinction carried him past the searing ashes of the Fruit Bazaar.

A black shape reared up, and the voice of a woman, harsh with fear, cried out:

"Petro? Is it you?"

"Don't be afraid," Abdullah said. But his words, although

he spoke in Greek, terrified her. She sprang up, breathing noisily, and struck at him with her fists.

"Don't be afraid of me," Abdullah repeated. "Give me your hand."

The woman shrieked for help. To escape from her, Abdullah began to run. Tripping and stumbling over crates and cart wheels, he fell down several times before he stopped again to catch his breath. His knees were bleeding and the palms of his hands were torn.

"Idiot," he said aloud. "You always make the same mistake."

Smiling a little, he laid his lacerated hand against his heart, which was leaping in his chest. He had passed through a gap between the walls and entered a little pasture hemmed with apple trees. In every direction the sky was red. He had lost his bearings. The fire had spread from pole to pole. Circling the meadow, searching for a landmark, he sensed that someone was watching him.

"Soldier?" he called. "Who's there?"

No one answered.

He crossed the broken wall again and walked along an alley that he thought must lead him north. After a hundred yards, the lane twisted left and led him toward some burning sheds. The windows glowed like furnaces. He turned back, bumped into an iron door, felt a draft of cool air, changed course three times.

Again, the sense that he was being followed.

"Are firemen there? Who is it?"

His brain was pulsating. He held his head between his hands. Chips of blazing straw where whirling down, spun by the wind, and the hot breath of the fire fell on his face. Listen! Who's there? But the roaring of the flames, the falling timbers filled his ears. He drew his breath with a sob.

"Who are you? Speak out?" And he began to run: sweet air,

night coolness on his cheeks, and Eleni waiting, the tender affirmation.

He ran past the villa in the dark, turned back and stumbled to the garden side. The gate was locked, and the wall was topped with broken glass. Moaning, he searched for the bell: cold mortar, hot mortar, white mortar, but no bell. Clenching his fists, he kicked feebly at the bars.

The light from the window struck his upturned face. Eleni's father, pale with terror, was cowering in the casement, one hand grasping a rifle, the other flailing to and fro as if to brush away a web of vines. Abdullah raised his arms.

"Trigoni? See me here? I want your daughter!"

But Christos reared up with a startled cry, looking indignant and contemptuous, as if to say: What? Marry her?

Raising the rifle, he sighted carefully and shot Abdullah through the head.

*O*ut at sea a passing ship could chart its bearings
by the glow on the horizon. Even on Lesbos, seventy miles
away, some volunteers from Asia Minor, who had gathered in
a grove of pines above the bay, imagined they could see a
ruddy light against the sky, far to the south, beyond the tidal
flats of Phocaea.

"Is it the city?"

"What else could it be?"

"Then the Turk has lost his prize."

A holy monk was serving Mass to the heartbroken Anatolians. The bell rang; the soldiers crossed themselves and swallowed salty tears.

As news of the disaster spread around the island, fishermen
clustered on the roofs of Mytilene. The rifle fire subsided, and
hundreds of rebellious soldiers, who had been chanting and
marching through the streets, put down their knives and sat
in silence in the coffeehouses.

At midnight George was walking near the shore. He
watched the dying light of Smyrna until his eyes began to
throb. Then he sat down and took off his uniform. Naked, he
waded outward, shattering the black-and-silver simulacrum
of the sky. When the water came to his face, he drew a breath.

His lungs constricted in an agonizing spasm. Water exploded from his mouth, and he staggered back to shore. For

a long time he lay there, dripping liquid like a jellyfish. With every gasp of air, he coughed explosively. At last he felt the pebbles under him and heard the rattle of breath in his scalded throat. Opening his eyes, he saw the smoky mirror of the sea, the grove of pines, the little town above the water and the ruby light across the straits; and he knew that he had failed again.

In the woodland a bugle was blowing taps, a senseless residue of military custom. The army had disintegrated. Looters and deserters tramped boldly around the harbor, firing rifles in the air and singing patriotic songs as they broke the shutters of the shops. Under the noses of their officers, they tore the emblems off their uniforms, threw their hats away, sat down and gambled in the coffeehouses, laying loaded pistols on the tables.

One of the commanders sent a team of men to take the rebels one by one; but these bailiffs were more vicious than their prey. They would pounce on a man and drag him to an alley, beat him senseless, strip him to his underdrawers and leave him on the stones. At dawn you saw the stiffened body, darkening and flyblown, in a blackish mire of blood.

These were the last achievements of the expedition to reconquer Asia Minor from the Turks: a coffeehouse rebellion and a Mass in memory of Smyrna.

Some men were coming down the path. George listened to their voices. He wondered whether his lungs would countervail a second time against the sea. Finally, he crawled behind a wooden fishing hull and put on his pants. The men were trailing down the beach.

"Division . . . Protosyngellos . . . Plastiras . . . contacts with the Navy . . . "

"Colonel Gonatas . . . "

"Lower your voice!"

"Plastiras . . . "

469

There were four or five of them—a little clique of minor officers, apparently, with one man plainly in command. George could see the leader gesturing toward the reddish vestiges of Smyrna.

"Rectification . . . crew of the *Averoff* . . . officers of the *Limnos* . . . "

"Lower your voice, in the name of Jesus!"

George raised his head and whispered.

"Dimitri? Is it you?"

The officers froze.

"Who's that?"

"Dimitri?" George repeated.

"Show yourself!"

The harshness of the tone surprised him.

"It's George," he said. And then, before Dimitris could respond, he ran out with his arms apart.

"Well, look at this!" Dimitris said. Like a butcher holding up a piece of meat, he lifted George's arm and twisted him from side to side. "My cousin, gentlemen. Or, rather, my *former brother,* so to speak."

The officers bowed somberly.

"Captain Frangos. Lieutenant Skouras. And so on. Lieutenant Trigonis. You've been promoted, George! You'll be a general before you learn to wipe yourself. Your mother got out safe, did you know? They all went out to Chios, wasn't it?"

And the cabal resumed its pacing up and down the beach, enclosing George within its ranks.

"You understand the situation, George? We want you with us, my boy. The Sixth Division—ready to strike the blow. *The* blow. Colonel Stylien Gonatas will arrive here any time. He'll take command, which seems acceptable. Of course, we'll also keep in touch with Colonel Plastiras. . . . "

The names were meaningless to George. As usual, he felt that he had somehow missed the realities of the political and

470

military situation. Leaning against Dimitris as they walked along, he heard the words, ignored the meaning. So his parents were alive! They must have discerned the danger to the city before the high command acknowledged it. But how could anyone induce Christos Trigonis to leave Anatolia?

"Who? Christos?" Dimitris said. "Oh, certainly. I saw him several days ago in Smyrna."

And he went on about the hour of action, designated by the code H-2. The military password of the day, which everyone approved, would be Greece-Salvation. Turning suddenly, Dimitris said:

"Your people? Are they with us?"

"My people?" George said.

"Your battery. Are they with the Liberation Movement?"

"Well, yes, I think so."

"I don't suppose you saved your gun?"

George did not answer. He could not remember precisely what had become of My Darling Bouboulina.

"Surely you didn't leave it for the Turks?"

"We scuttled all the guns," George said.

Dimitris shrugged. In any case, artillery was not the major problem. The main concern was strategy. Propaganda. Speed. A plane would fly to Athens and Salonika and drop the declaration of demands. Later, the Movement would force the King to abdicate. Then military government and moral reformation, new elections and treason trials.

"Ah, yes, treason trials!" the other officers repeated, growling like fanatics.

At the landing dock the group separated, and Dimitris led George up the hill. Stars were wheeling overhead; the troubled little town was quiet. George felt an almost overpowering desire to tell Dimitris what had happened.

"The last few days," he whispered. "God only knows how we made it. . . . "

471

"What could we soldiers do?" Dimitris said, his voice rough with indignation. "Look what the traitors did! They debased the money. Wrecked the credit of the country. Threw away the friendship of Europe. What could you or I do? Imagine, turning the army over to that pack of useless, inexperienced old men!"

"And young ones."

"We'll see them all shot," Dimitris went on, rasping through his teeth. "Gounaris, Stratos, Protopapadakis. All the traitors. Listen—when the danger was the greatest, these men recalled our strongest troops from Asia Minor to station them in *Thrace!* Theotokis. Baltazzi. Above all, that maniac General Hadjianestis. There is only one appropriate punishment: the firing squad!"

George stared at Dimitris in horror. This was like the raving of a prophet, calling down the vengeance of the Lord on an accursed tribe. But it was not the enemy whom Dimitris proposed to punish: it was the Greeks themselves.

"How can you single out certain men?" George said. "Weren't we all to blame—you and I and my father, all of us? Weren't the Turks to blame?"

"Did something chew up your brains?" Dimitris said. "Am *I* to blame for digging Hadji-Clausewitz out of the necropolis?"

George was silent, shaking his head, while Dimitris eyed him critically.

"Look, pal. You're still puffed up with your papa's romantic notions. Haven't you realized that this war was a mistake? Pointless and stupid?"

Swallowing, George sighed in agreement.

"I never really was as keen about it as I let on," he said.

"Well, then—how do you feel about these politicians who prolonged this idiotic war when all of us wanted to go home? They were reaching for glory, and they led all of us straight to Hell. How can you say they're not to blame?"

Confused by this compelling argument, George glanced around at the unhappy island. He knew he had not willed this disaster; yet the guilt of it somehow weighed upon him. He had participated in the war; he had, in effect, endorsed it; and he gladly would have shared in the glory of victory. Did he not also share the dishonor of defeat?

But Dimitris jabbed at his arm.

"Listen, kid—think about the future. Show some courage. Join the Liberation Movement!"

They came to the cottage where Dimitris had a billet. George felt a caustic, briny liquid thickening in his throat, and his eyes brimmed with tears.

"Dimitri?" he said. "I don't have any men to give you for the Liberation Movement."

"They're not here?"

"No," George said painfully. "I don't know where they are."

Dimitris smiled and slapped George on the back.

"Then tell me their names."

"Their names?"

"Don't you remember them?"

"I remember all of them."

"All right, then."

"That's right," George said. "They're traitors, too, aren't they? Mutineers."

"Who was the leader?" Dimitris said.

"Of what?"

"Of the mutiny, for Christ's sake."

"Will he be court-martialed?"

"Well, I'm not going to recommend him for a medal!"

"Court-martialed," George repeated. "They deserve it, don't they?"

And he began to name the men of his platoon, beginning

with Tall Johnny, whose proper name was Kolinos. Dimitris wrote them in a column, bearing down on his pencil and clamping the tip of his tongue between his teeth. His coolness seemed to be a perfect miracle, his sense of purpose in the midst of this disaster. George felt as if a crushing burden had been lifted from his shoulders. His vision blurred. Thank God for men like this! Such men as Dimitris, with courage, energy and inspiration, would restore the Greeks, revive their nation and reclaim their destiny.

Wiping his eyes, George turned and looked again at Asia, where the sky was growing pale and smoke was rising from the dying fires.

*A*fter a day or two the smoke blew away. Along the Quay the buildings offered an appearance of integrity. The Splendid Palace, Photi's Candy Shop, the clubs and the consulates were standing as before. Drawing near, however, one could see that these façades were only hollow palings like the drop-scenes of a theater. Their empty windows opened onto fields of ashes stretching all the way to Basmahane. Old men crept around with gunny sacks, picking scraps of metal from the rubble.

As for the houses that had escaped the fire, they were converted into Turkish barracks. Eleni rented a springless wagon to move a few possessions to a churchyard in St. Rocque's, a Frankish neighborhood beyond the limits of the fire. Christos hailed the wagon cheerfully, climbed up and squeezed himself among the bundles. He thought the air would do him good.

"You know, I'm going to have to ask those Turks to leave our house at the end of the week," he told Eleni in a confidential whisper. "Army people always overstay their welcome. . . . What a day! Just feel that freshness in the air!"

A cool north wind was blowing—friendly Father Borealis, a blessing to the raisin growers. Christos inhaled deeply and smiled. With any luck, the first sultanas would be coming in this week from Manisa and Kirkaghatch. The seaside vineyard down at Vourla should have been harvested by now. Later in the month there would be a splendid crop from Nif, the best in years, with ample rain before St. Basil's Day and a good north wind to dry the crop. The best sultanas ought to bring twenty-five piastres an oka at the packing houses: big, light-colored berries, clear as honey. The gold of Smyrna . . .

The old man waved his arms around and chattered amiably while Eleni struggled with the reins. He nudged her playfully. How could anyone be so solemn, surrounded by the bounty of the earth? What a joy it was to hear the freight cars being shunted in at harvesttime: the creaking of the wheels, the crashing of the couplings in the gray light of dawn! What balm to smell the Quay in autumn, heaped with bursting sacks of hemp and flax seeds, millet and sesame! Valonia pods as large as pine cones lay scattered on the cobblestones, surrounded by bales of Akhisar tobacco, tubs of linseed oil and licorice paste and terebinth. Women worked from dawn to twilight, drying squares of macaroni in the sunshine, putting down summer fruits in syrup, storing away fat bags of figs and walnuts from the farms at Aydin and Alashehir. . . .

He raised his eyebrows at Eleni. She was crying.

"Now, what on earth? You need some rest. Let the driver take me to the Club for lunch. Then you go home and get some sleep."

"There *isn't* any Club," Eleni cried. "There isn't any harvest!"

Her father rubbed his eyebrows with his thumb and middle finger.

"That's right," he said. "They burned the Club, didn't they." Thoughtfully, he pinched his nose. "I suppose the Hunt Club, too?"

"Yes."

"And the Italian Theater?"

"Everything, Papa."

For a moment, he was lucid. He turned his head slowly from side to side as if to search for that which had existed and was gone forever: St. Constantine's, the Sponti Passage, the Rue des Roses, the Friars' School. A tremor moved his shoulders. He raised his fingers in a feeble gesture, like a salutation to the past, to the Pirocacos, the Baltazzis, the DeHochpieds, the Whittalls and the LaFontaines; to the Prokopious and the Pestimazioglous; to the Persians at the Ajem Khan, the Hebrews at the Noseless Khan and the English Levantines at Paradise; to the Greek Club, the New Club and the Hunt Club, with their billiard rooms, their *thé dansants,* their costume balls and their wrought-iron balconies above the English *scala;* to the tennis tournaments, the games of baccarat, the Splendid Palace, the Cathedral of St. Photini.

His eyes were wet. He bowed his head, overwhelmed by memories. Eleni left him in the garden of the chapel while she went around to ask at the foreign consulates for help.

But all the diplomats had left the city. Throngs of Greeks with European passports were weeping in the courtyards. Who was to help them? There were only ten or twenty vessels in the harbor—some island steamers from Piraeus, a few cargo tramps from France and half a dozen warships from America. An enormous crowd was waiting for the chance to get aboard; and even after you had obtained a ticket, the Turks might stop you at the pier.

Eleni drove up to Alsanjak in the heat of midday. The ticket clerk was an Italian Levantine who was preoccupied with opening a pomegranate.

"No tickets left."

"Then give me space on the deck."

"I'm speaking of the deck."

"Then on a later boat."

"No tickets on the later boats until tomorrow."

477

"Here—to compensate you for the inconvenience."
The ticket seller rolled his eyes.

"What good is paper at a time like this?"

"Here's a coin to give it weight."

"No, give me this." He touched her wedding ring. "And don't go waving these billets around," he added, writing out the tickets. "They'll cut your throat and throw you in the bay."

In the crowd, an ugly man reached out to feel her buttocks. A country priest with widened nostrils and wetness on his open lips came up and rubbed himself against her hip. Eleni shook them off and drew the corners of her scarf across her mouth. She knew that she was beginning to look old, exercising that morbid art of sudden aging that all Greek women understand. In a year or two, desiccated and devoured by boredom and black sorrow, she would have slipped beyond chronology into the ageless, sexless, solemn ripeness of Greek womanhood.

For an instant, regret withered her spirit. She remembered the strange turns her life had taken, its falsehoods and vanities. If only she had been able to love Abdullah as she had loved Dimitris, she might have made an honorable marriage out of that selfish escapade. If only she had been able to respect herself . . .

Then the Oriental aspect of her nature unfolded, and her regrets dissolved in a soft wave of futility. It comforted her soul to know that she had spared Abdullah and his family from persecution on her account.

Driving back, she stopped again outside the Villa Trigonis and stared up at the window of her room. The Turks who had taken command permitted her to take away another bag of table linens and a little box of silver teaspoons. But a harsh, ruinous man with a patch over one eye came out and stopped her when she tried to roll up one of the small carpets in the hall.

"These furnishings belong to me," Eleni said, making her voice sound old and weary.

"Oh? Are you Miss Trigonis? I have something to give you."

He proposed to take her into the captain's office, which had been her father's reception room. But Eleni, frightened by his hideous scars and his burning glances, dropped the carpet on the floor and slipped away.

She picked up her father immediately and drove without stopping to the Point of Alsanjak, looking back from time to time to see whether anyone was following. The pier was separated from the Quay by two high fences forming an enclosure several hundred feet across. Refugees were pressed around the outer gate, which was as narrow as the eyelet of a gypsy's tent. As each person passed examination, he would slip past the guardhouse, dragging his belongings toward the inner fence. There he would join another, larger crowd hurling themselves against another, smaller gate.

In spite of these impediments, a tragic creature in black weeds had tried to bluff the sentries, and they were stripping him while a gang of Turks stood by, howling and poking at the evidences of his masculinity. As the guards were marching him toward the warehouse in his flagrant nakedness, the people at the gate could hear him sobbing, and they turned away in shame and pity. All Christian men of military age were being taken inland to repair the ruined bridges.

Eleni clutched her father's hand, but he was smiling vacantly. He might have been asleep. To him, the city was at peace. The vanished and the dead were resting in their beds. The gentle current of their breathing undulated placidly behind the window screens. Later, when the evening wind was freshening across the harbor, they would wake up like children, heavy-lidded and a little cranky, stretch their arms and splash their eyes with water and go out and drink a cup of coffee at a table by the waterside.

Christos could see them all, his friends and his competitors, strolling in the splendor of the sunset—bankers, poets, patriots—and he smiled. Waiting at the gate, he held Eleni's hand.

"Daughter, I want your pledge. I'm getting old. You'll bury me in Greece? I want a Christian monument, inscribed to a patriot of Hellenism. You'll do it?"

Eleni promised, and Christos kissed her on the forehead. He had forgotten all his bitter curses.

"Sometimes I've disapproved of you," he said mildly. "You're a stubborn girl, and you had bluestocking ideas of education. But I've always treated you well, haven't I?"

"Yes, Papa."

"Don't worry," he said. "I'll take care of you."

But when the guard at the gangplank read Eleni's name, he ordered her into a shed at the end of the wharf. The man who had questioned her at the villa was waiting there, surrounded by soldiers. His solitary eye glittered maliciously; but he laid his hand on his breast in a conciliatory gesture.

"I don't wish to delay you," he said, holding out a small parcel. "These are the possessions of your husband." As Eleni reached out, he added: "His body was found in the street, stripped of everything but these few garments. I made the identification. He was my brother."

Eleni held the little package in her hands.

"He was here?" she said at last. "In Smyrna?"

Staring down through a blur of tears, she knew that Abdullah had followed her; and she understood. She went back and told her father that the guards had mistaken her for someone else.

But the crowd was beating on her shoulders. The odor of

their poverty, their filth, their hungry yellow lips began to stifle her.

"Why can't we go? Why don't they start the ship?"

"Don't worry," Christos said. "I'll take care of you. Our country has a splendid future. Nothing diminishes our grandeur. We have the eternal glory of the Great Idea. . . . "

Eleni gripped the bundle that held her husband's tattered shoes, his fez. She murmured to herself: "Go now."

Having experienced the glory of the past, she knew that she could endure the grandeur of the future.